SAVED
BY
CHRISTMAS

Saved
By
Christmas

By
B. Tybor Leski

Edited by:
Madison Drent
Sydney Leski

Contributors:
Lance Leski
Weston Tybor
Jaden Tybor
Sadie Wilkinson

Dedication

To my six brothers and sisters whom I battled with to get my place under the dazzling lit Douglas Fir Tree on that one special morn. There wasn't much space and the whole room would be filled with nothing but wrapping paper, boxes, and lost bodies underneath playing with toys. To my brothers and sister who taught me to sing harmonies to all the Christmas carols that I still know by heart. To my sisters who curled my hair and dressed me festively for midnight mass to celebrate the birth of Jesus. We were truly blessed as a family at Christmas and in life. As mom and dad would say, the only gifts they desired at Christmas were peace for the world and for all to love one another. Amazingly, those are now my Christmas wishes.

Chapter 1 The Great Idea

He couldn't wait. Pacing back and forth waiting for his teacher to arrive, he was beyond excited. In the 12 years of his life, he hadn't been further than the nearby streets in Harlem, New York. His mother had a panic disorder that heightened in unfamiliar situations, so she hadn't left the house in over a decade. As a result, she didn't like her son out of reach. He didn't know his father and his only saving grace was his grandmother that lived with them but worked two jobs and was rarely home.

He had a fire in his belly to one day help his mother and relieve the burden on his overworked grandmother who never took a day off from work. He loved being at school, hanging out with his friends, and getting involved with the school band. Playing the tenor saxophone took him to a place in his mind where he could be a superhero and solve problems with a single song. He practiced for hours each day at home until his skills transformed a bleating instrument to sound smooth and comforting. On the night of his school band concert, in the sixth grade, he gave the performance of a lifetime. His saxophone harmonized with the other instruments and then he had a solo that would make any mother proud...if she were there. Because of his talent, his music teacher offered to take him and a few others to the Lincoln Center of Performing Arts on Saturday.

On the day of the field trip, he woke up extra early and paced back and forth in the entryway of the rundown condominium until he couldn't take it anymore. He did not want his teacher to miss him. He darted down the stairs of the porch to the main road where he patrolled and kept an eye out for his teacher, who picked him up two hours later.

The young man's senses were overloaded on the tour of the Lincoln Center. He met other saxophonists rehearsing that day. They gave him tips and encouraged the boy to keep at it. He hung on to every word, remembered every recommendation, and asked several questions while on the tour. He felt exhausted after the long day, but kept thinking

1

about his teacher's kindness, the amazing concert hall, and the opportunity to explore the greater beyond of his all too familiar neighborhood.

That was the podcast on the morning show about revitalizing New York City youth in a positive direction. Cyril Haugen took his earbuds out after hearing the 12-year-old's story and he was inspired to do something about it. The brisk November Monday morning had Mr. Haugen walking hurriedly down 50th Street. He stopped at Rockefeller Center to check out the plaza and the area where the impressive 80-foot Christmas tree would soon be placed. He knew from years past that it was a beautiful sight to see with the grand tree lit hovering above the skating rink below with everyone either gliding on skates or bundled up on benches sipping on hot cocoas. He thought that the excitement of the city at Christmas made it the best place to be in the world.

It was a lot of work, but the results made it more than worth it. Every year the expectations seemed to climb higher and higher, which meant every year Mr. Haugen and his staff had to work harder and harder. He loved his job - the coordination of it all, the look on the faces of his staff when they knew they picked the right tree, and the look on the faces of the onlookers when it lit up, that one magical night.

They returned from their first scouting trip in mid-September. They went to their usual places in upstate New York, New Jersey, Connecticut, and New Hampshire. Many families also wrote in and sent pictures of their best spruce trees in their backyards. The staff narrowed it down to a few tree farms in upstate New York. There were some 80-footers there and, of course, they were all Norway Spruces. They needed to narrow down their options more and would have to make one more trip to pick out the most perfect tree for this year.

Reflecting on the podcast stories from the past week and this morning, he wanted to be like that teacher that gave a kid a different perspective. He thought it was astounding how this young man, who got such a small opportunity, was so appreciative. The story needed to mean something, for heaven's sake, it was almost Christmas. He stared at the area where the tree would go this year and wondered how this could impact the New York youth.

Mr. Haugen, the head gardener for the Rockefeller Center in New York City, was a 60-year-old perfectionist with a loving wife, three grown daughters and so far, two grandchildren. Everything for Mr. Haugen was always in its place. A very structured man, he didn't favor change much and had high-performance standards from his work staff. They knew if he asked for something to get done, it was a priority to do it right away and correctly. Now he was going to throw that all in the trash and do something spontaneous. As he left the plaza and walked to his workplace, he did a little kick in the air.

He had a modest office on the third floor at the corner of 49th and 5th Street. It was a shared workspace for his team of five expert gardeners, which were either arborists or horticulturists, as their degrees stated. They were always in the office on Mondays and then hurried around the city, completing their projects to the highest standards during the rest of the week.

Mr. Haugen walked through the door, peeling off his scarf, and stopped at the first desk that appeared.

"Get the team together for an impromptu meeting, will you Jessica?" he addressed the young lady sitting at the desk.

He headed to his office at the back of the room and put his work backpack away. While his computer was booting up, he looked through his Rolodex, which held the phone numbers of everyone he knew in the last 25 years. He found the number under the J files and dialed it.

"Hey Mitch, this is Cyril Haugen, how have you and Glenna been?" he kept the dialogue back and forth scratching the gray whiskers on his face. "Yes, we're doing fine as well. Say listen, I have a favor to ask and it's quite urgent that we put our heads together and formulate a plan."

They talked for another 10 minutes working out the details and logistics of the plan.

Meanwhile, his staff rolled in one after another. When Mr. Haugen walked out of his office, all five employees were in the conference room at the ready with either a laptop or a notepad waiting for instruction. Mr. Haugen walked in with a smile that was totally out of his character, but contagious. Everyone started looking happy for some unknown reason. Everyone was on the edge of their seats anticipating the news that he was holding back.

"Ladies and gentlemen, I have some good news and bad news," Mr. Haugen got right to it. "Actually, it's the same news, but some might see it as good and some might view it as not good. Anyway, for the final decision about which spruce will be picked from upstate New York, it will not be ours to decide."

There were moans and groans and disappointed faces all through the room. This was their baby, their pride and joy of the year. It was like being a superstar for a month or so. This was their bragging rights to their friends who worked on Wall Street, the tech world, or went into film/television. They felt betrayed and that there would never be a good excuse for assigning their job to another team.

"Don't worry. I will give us all full credit for the idea so that we don't lose our shining moments. We have to move fast and I will still need all of you to make the drive out and coach on how we make an educated selection," he said, addressing the noticeable air of discontent.

"Sir, what idea do you mean?" Joshua, the youngest in the group, a recent graduate from Penn State asked.

"Oh yeah, the idea," Mr. Haugen laughed like everyone already read his mind. "I am working with Mitchell Jekel, the Chancellor for the New York City Schools. He and his staff cover all five boroughs. We will draw 10 student names from schools all over the city to pick our final spruce for the plaza this year."

"Mr. Haugen were you listening to the morning podcasts again?" asked Shauna, Mr. Haugen's right hand in the office. She thought she should explain it to the group. "Last week and this week, the public radio station featured stories of kids who got the chance to live outside their world and do something bigger than the daily shuffle around their neighborhood."

"I don't see the big deal," remarked Danny, one of the veteran arborists. "This isn't space camp."

4

"Well Danny, all of their stories so far have been kids just visiting museums or attending an art fair or being taken to a Nets game. Just one new experience impacted them in some magical way that inspired them to dream of doing something bigger," Mr. Haugen continued. "I was inspired. I know none of you take for granted this special assignment, but can you imagine what it might mean to a kid?"

"So, like, these students would all be from the projects?" asked Paul, who was raised in the projects himself. "I am totally on board with it."

"That's the idea, Paul," Mr. Haugen nodded.

The room was quiet as different staff members absorbed the news.

"So, if we are going to do this, what's the plan?" Shauna broke the silence.

"Mr. Jekel will draw names from the underfunded high schools on Wednesday. There will be an announcement and then we will head out on Saturday to Minnechanka. We will take the Northern Loop; it will be breathtaking for the students if there are any leaves still on the trees. When I called the field agent out there to tell her of the idea, she had one herself. She set us all up, complimentary, at the Friend's Inn Resort. They have 20 cabins, all stocked and waiting for our arrival. They will provide dinner at night and breakfast before we head back on Sunday." Mr. Haugen smiled and reflected for a moment. "I can't believe that, in 20 minutes, this all came together."

"Well, you sure don't need me on this trip," said Danny, an older employee, who stood up to leave. "I don't want to be hanging around brats who need some inspiration. I don't have kids and never wanted any, so if I can opt out, I am."

"Danny, I am going to let you, but I hope you regret this," said Mr. Haugen as his smile disappeared and he got serious. "I do need some of you to go and explain the requirements of an ideal tree. While I want this to be fun, I do want us to have a proper tree standing in the Rockefeller Plaza."

In the end, Shauna, Paul, Jessica, and Joshua all volunteered to go on the trip. Mr. Haugen went back to work to ensure that the Brooklyn Bay Construction Company could transport the tree and use one of their cranes to put it in place at the plaza. Everything was falling into place like it generally did for Mr. Haugen. His life either held no trouble or perhaps he handled misfortune better than others. This theory would soon be tested.

Chapter 2 The Teenage Lottery

Wednesday rolled around and news spread to all the New York high schools about the lottery. The press got hold of this story and news cameras and reporters were swarming around Mitch Jekel's office building, awaiting the lucky winning students. At one in the afternoon, the drawing was held. The database held the names of every high school teen and a randomizer tool was used to pull names from the list. Mr. Jekel herded the press into a conference room where a computer was sitting on the table front and center.

He had a reporter from each of the news stations press the button to start the randomizer and then stop it to select the 10 names. First up was Channel 5, and as the newscaster pressed the randomizer, you could see the names flashing quickly throughout the database. At some point, she pressed another button which stopped on a name.

"Vaughn Vetter!" announced the newscaster. "He is from Shelton Brake High School in the Bronx."

Channel 7 pulled Adam Brayer's name. Channel 9 pulled Darcy Venhill. Channel 11 pulled Sergei Vladimir López. Channel 13 pulled Lauren Fairview. After the news stations each had a pick, Mr. Jekel requested his staff to pull the rest of the names. It was fun to stop the randomizer. Wanda Womack, Ryan White, Arcado Michaels, Shannon Dartmouth, and Brianna Germaine were the rest of the winners. A full list of the names and schools they attended were in the hands of the press and Mr. Jekel's.

There was a lot of work to be done. Permission slips had to be signed immediately. Mr. Jekel reached out to the parent or guardian's name on file for each of these kids. It took all afternoon, but he confirmed that they all were able to attend. Each parent or guardian was required to sign the permission slip he emailed them and then they would accompany each student to the drop-off on Saturday.

The next call Mitch Jekel made was to his friend, Cyril Haugen, updating him that the Christmas Tree project was a go. Arrangements were made for a bus to transport the students and Haugen's staff to the destination in upstate New York. The rally point for this departure would be at the plaza on Saturday at nine o'clock in the morning. This was fitting as it was the spot where the tree would be stationed and decorated after they made their choice.

The story went viral on social media. Mr. Haugen thought to himself that this was the best idea he ever had. He just hoped that the children coming from less fortunate homes would behave and not make the wrong impression for this event. He prayed at least one of the students on the trip would be impacted positively. What a surprise they all would have the morning of that Saturday.

Chapter 3 Meet the Students

There were balloons and a small high school band in Rockefeller Plaza that morning. A few major network morning shows aired from the plaza every morning and today they would introduce the high schoolers that were picked to go find the famous tree that would soon stand in the square. Cameras towered everywhere. Famous news anchors reported the news in their warm, stylish coats. The weatherman stood out in front of his green screen and pointed to the edge of Maine and then into New Brunswick, Nova Scotia, and Newfoundland, Canada. There would be a Northeastern blizzard, otherwise known as a Nor'easter, circling up through the Atlantic Ocean that had a good chance of clipping those areas.

As for New York, this would cause the temperature to drop and have slightly elevated winds. You could almost feel Christmas in the air with the anticipation of snowfall.

All networks panned over to center stage where the students, their family members, Mitch Jekel, the Chancellor of New York Schools along with Cyril Haugen and his garden staff were standing. A news assistant would point to each student and then they would go up to an assortment of microphones and introduce themselves. The first student to step on stage was Darcy Venhill. She was a thin, tall, ghostly-looking girl who seemed less than thrilled to be there. She kept her earbuds in and constantly looked at her phone while she spoke her name in the mic and then walked back to her parents. Darcy's mother showed up in a dark brown fur coat and was dressed fancy for what should be a simple drop off. Her father wore a suit and had a warm overcoat. Mr. Haugen looked at the girl and then questioned Mr. Jekel about her appearance.

"Are you quite sure that these students come from underfunded schools?" he asked skeptically.

"Well, you see, that was the original plan," said Mitch Jekel clearing his throat to prepare for what he needed to say next. "With the short time limit, it was hard to pull the underperforming schools into a separate database for the name draw. We did try, and then my assistant came up with a more brilliant plan. We don't discuss status. We mix them all into one bus and have a bunch of kids from different walks of life begin a dialogue."

"Yes, but there's only one problem," Cyril Haugen pointed out. "The randomizer could have picked all above-average schools. This young lady will most likely be uninterested throughout the trip. It won't impact her at all."

"I'm sorry Cyril," apologized Mitch, hoping the rest would all be the kids that Cyril had envisioned, but knew there was a chance that he would have some explaining to do. "Still, this will be a trip of a lifetime. Besides, I also didn't want to be called out on narrowing down our population to just the inner-city kids."

"Really?" replied Mr. Haugen, not believing a word of it. "Well, what will be, shall be then. My staff is ready to go and get this experience moving."

The next to arrive on the plaza stage were two identical twin Latino boys who were accompanied by their mother. They waved to everyone anxiously.

"López's aquí estamos!" shouted their mother as they stopped in the middle of the stage.

"Which one of you is Sergei Vladimir López?" asked Mr. Jekel.

"I am Sergei," said one of the brothers smiling, adjusting rather well to all of the eyes on him.

"I am Vladimir," the other brother admitted. "Thank you, for this opportunity."

"I am their mother," a small, curvy-framed, young, Latina lady with an even bigger smile said to Mr. Jekel. She hugged him. "This is wonderful, thank you."

"Umm.... you're welcome," Mitch said helplessly.

Mitch smiled nervously at Cyril.

"One full name, two students, I did not see that coming," Mitch said. "But what are you going to do? It's a fluke in the system."

"I don't mind it at all," said Cyril, scratching his whiskers. "Having only 10 wasn't well thought out. Sometimes you need a tie-breaking vote picking out the tree."

Next across the plaza stage was a mother, father, and a timid, brown-haired girl with a dash of freckles on each side of her face. They prompted their daughter to introduce herself and she kept shaking her head no.

"Lauren Fairview is here," announced Mrs. Fairview, gesturing to her daughter like a prize.

Lauren was mortified. This was way out of her comfort zone, she desperately wanted to go back home and bury her head in a pillow. There was some clapping from all around and then she scurried off the stage with her mom close behind. Next, two big women walked across the stage. One was the daughter and the other, the mother.

"My name is Wanda Womack," said Wanda loud and proud. Her skin was dark and she wore her hair in a short stylish bob cut with a barrette on the side. Her mother was loud and proud too.

"I am Juanita Womack," she said. "Could you use another chaperone? I could use a vacation." Part of the crowd chuckled at that.

She looked around and Mr. Jekel shook his head no.

"Only students, I'm afraid," he replied but almost seemed flirtatious with Juanita as he said it.

The next student introduced himself by beatboxing onto the stage.

"Vaughn Vetter," he said. The ebony-skinned boy with deep chestnut eyes rapped a few funny and creative lines about going to look for a Christmas tree and tried to look mean, but the crowd just thought he looked adorable, and clapped.

He was accompanied by his dad who rolled his eyes but gave him a fist pump when he finished his introduction. He looked for his mother, who promised to be there, but did not show. Vaughn spent time between parents who lived within a mile of each other. His dad owned a small, worn-down music store where he taught music on almost any instrument. They lived upstairs in a cramped two-bedroom apartment.

11

The next was a six-foot tall, blonde boy who kept pulling his short straight hair to the side, so it would half fall into his blue eyes. He was accompanied by his older brother who stood at six foot six.

"I am Ryan," he said soft-spoken, but you could tell he had a macho ego to keep up. "Yeah, that's all I got."

He and his brother walked away as an attractive, young, trim, dark skinned girl walked right up to the stage. She was accompanied by her mom and aunt.

"Brianna Germaine!" she shouted strongly. She was a girl of well-thought-out words. It was noticeable that she kept her dark long, weaved hair neat with two strands in the front, colored royal blue. She raised her fist in the air. "Power to the women making this trip!"

Her comment rang into the square, empowered by the buildings that towered over everyone. Brianna's mother and aunt started clapping from the side stage and a few more clapped along.

Next, a young red-haired girl waited her turn. She rolled her eyes at Brianna's comment. She walked out on stage and stood almost dead center. Her posture was near perfect and when she talked, she looked charming.

"Hello, my name is Shannon Dartmouth from the upper west side," she commented. Her milky skin seemed to glisten in the sun. "I would like to take this opportunity to thank Chancellor Jekel for this most valuable experience."

As she left the stage, Mitch raised his eyebrows at Cyril. They both didn't get that Shannon always said the right things but didn't mean any of it. Next, a young man who looked like he stepped out of the 1970s stood front and center. His afro was large and purposefully styled. His flared blue jeans had a peace patch sewn on and he wore his dad's old Army jacket with his last name on the upper right side of the pocket. His light black complexion complemented his light brown eyes but looking at him you saw that he had an agenda.

"People of New York, I am Arcado Michaels," bellowed Arcado, who spoke like a preacher. "I am in protest of cutting down one of God's precious trees for your pleasure. Can't we save the trees and put up something artificial instead?"

The echoes from his voice bounced from the plaza's concrete and fell flat.

He got some boos and thumbs down. Nobody seemed to be agreeing with him except for his little sister on the side with his parents. She was clapping and whistling to support him. Some onlookers from the street managed to glance over to see what was so controversial.

"Dang. You're all cold-hearted," Arcado said as he stepped back into the crowd.

Lastly, a husky boy walked across the stage almost tripping and having the yarmulke fall off of his head. He had brown hair and eyes and dressed nicely in slacks and a sweater. His parents walked right behind him smiling.

"Hello," he forgot his name with a crowd of eyes staring at him. "Uh, my name is uh...."

"Adam, tell the people your name," his mother nagged him.

"Quiet Alisa. Let him do it," his dad nagged his mother.

"Yeah, my name is Adam Brayer," said Adam finally and then pointed to his mom.

"And these are my parents."

Everyone in the crowd started laughing. Mr. Jekel motioned for all students to form a line facing the audience on the stage. The high schoolers came out of the cracks to be front and center, leaving family behind. Even timid Lauren took short steps and stood side by side with her peers. She looked down at the ground while everyone else looked straight at the cameras that shot from every angle. Most kids stood there and smiled except for Arcado who had an intense, rebellious look. The cameras all panned around in different directions to capture the students within the grandeur of Rockefeller's gold, red, and silver decor. Then the news anchors instinctively took over to wrap up their coverage. Mr. Jekel and Mr. Haugen had the parents and students form a tighter circle so everyone could hear.

"We will depart now. It's almost nine-thirty so we're right on schedule," said Mr. Jekel in his mature tone.

"This is my colleague, Cyril Haugen, the head gardener of Rockefeller Center. He also has with him his staff of gardeners

13

to help supervise and educate the children on the trees they will be looking at."

Cyril's staff waved as they stood nearby waiting to depart.

"Ladies and gentlemen," vocalized Cyril, now in command. "I want to thank you for letting this adventure happen. I want to give you my cell phone number in case there are any concerns on the trip. We should arrive in Minnechanka by noon. We will stop for lunch, which is provided, and then proceed to the area of the first desirable tree. We will spend about an hour there and then head to the next site where we will evaluate the next spruce. We do have a third contender but it's a little ways out, so we will have to evaluate time from there. Lastly, we will stay at the Friend's Inn Resort cabins for the night. We will vote on the best tree after dinner, which is also provided. We will know the winner by the time everyone is tucked in for the night. In the morning, we will need to be at breakfast by eight o'clock and leave by nine. We should be back at the plaza by noon tomorrow. Any questions?"

As Cyril was answering questions and giving his cell phone number, the kids retrieved their backpacks for the night and waited for the conversations to end. They left the plaza and saw two different buses. They were both short yellow buses - not enough for the students, staff, and equipment to share. Cyril and Mitch were trying to figure out what happened to the large, yellow school bus they ordered.

"Mr. Jekel!" shouted an older, heavy-set Asian-American woman bus driver as she motioned for him to come over to the bus. He and Cyril walked over to the bus driver and she took her gloves off to shake his hand.

"Yeah, I'm Jyung Kim, ya' bus driver," she said in a thick New York accent. "Dat' over der' is Rootah' the udder bus driver, but he don't hear all dat' good, if ya know what I mean? Anyway, I was on my way drivin' da' big yella' one, but I got halfway down the street and the tranny went. Those were da' only keys I got on Friday, but da' short buses have da' keys already in them for sporting events on da' weekends, so we took two. Oh yeah, Rootah' is da' mechanic, but he also has his commercial license, so don't ya' worry."

Rooter was taking a drag of his cigarette near his bus's folding doors and gave the men a wave, acknowledging them when they looked his way. Rooter was almost 70 years old, and he looked every bit of it. His gray thinning short hair and his weathered face that sagged matched his slim, sagging body. He always contemplated when his next cigarette would be and decided to smoke another one to tide him over for a few hours.

"Thank you, Ms. Kim," Mr. Jekel said as he pulled Cyril aside. "How do you want to play this out as far as who rides in which bus?"

"Hmmm. I am inclined to mix the kids in different buses to have a chaperoned trip, but my other instinct says screw it," Cyril never spoke so recklessly. "I think the purpose of this trip is to let the students have a full experience and they can't do that with us breathing down their necks. I doubt they want to talk about botany and the softwood perennial species."

"Good point," said Mitch, concurring. "Besides, you will be right alongside in the next bus if there are any issues. But might I suggest that Ms. Kim take the children and your staff takes Rooter?"

"Not ideal, but I get it," Cyril compromised. "I just pray they both are safe drivers around those mountains."

Mr. Jekel went to gather the students while Mr. Haugen called both bus drivers over to advise them of the plan. He reminded them to drive modestly, especially around the steep mountain curves. As he was doing so, light flurries scattered around the city. This was predicted. But everyone knew that it was only one to two inches of snow, which in New York, was a dusting.

Saturday, November 28th
Chapter 4 The Meet and Greet Bus Ride

The kids gave quick hugs to the relatives that saw them off and boarded the bus. Arcado and Vaughn were quick to grab the back rows, and everyone took their own row with the exception of the López twins who sat together. Wanda sat across from the boys, giving them flirty smiles.

Wanda turned in her seat to Darcy and commented.

"Look at those twins across the aisle. You could get one and I could get the other," she said, adding a wink. Darcy rolled her eyes, put her earbuds in, and looked out the window. "Well, OK then, more for me."

"Hey boys, how you doin'?" Wanda smiled at the López's and gave an excited nod.

"Fine," said the boys, each with the same puzzled look on their faces. After a minor pause, they returned to their conversation in Spanish.

Ryan took the first row so he would get the most room for his knees. Everyone settled in and put their backpacks on the other side of the seat. They eyed up each other with caution and fear that someone might start a conversation. It wasn't the students that started talking, it was their fearless bus driver. The sturdy, old bag stood up to face the kids.

"Now let's get a few t'ings straight. I am Ms. Kim. I have a tricky drive troo' da' mountains with the light snowfall and tight turns around corners and such, so I don't want any distractions. It looks like you're a lively bunch, but I know you kids can get rowdy. Don't even t'ink about it or I will stop dis' bus and let you off. I recognize one of yous' in here, so she can tell ya, I'm not afraid to boot you off," said Ms. Kim and then gave the students a snarl. "OK, now let's have a fun bus ride. Oh, one more t'ing, no loud music. I don't wanna hear whateva' garbage ya' listen to out loud. Put your headphones in and have da' music not drum out of dem' or I will stop da' bus and you can imagine the rest."

The bus pulled off into traffic silently as the kids watched out the window. It was quiet all through the city. Then as they

16

got onto the highway, the twins spoke out loud comfortably in Spanish ignoring the unspoken rule of not speaking.

"I'm bored," Darcy said out loud as she took her earbuds from her ear. "How long is the trip again?"

"Of course, you're bored," Vaughn replied sarcastically. "Are you missing your little dog with a sweater and your bougie friends?"

Darcy gave him a cruel stare and hated that she did have a Pomeranian, who occasionally needed a sweater when he got his monthly shaving.

"Dude, why don't you leave the girl alone?" scolded Ryan, from the front.

Before anyone else could comment, Vaughn walked from the back seat to the front of the bus and eyed Ryan up and down. Ryan thought that this fool was going to start something he couldn't finish. Ryan on the defense stood up and faced Vaughn with a tough look. Ryan came from the mean streets of the Bronx and knew how to stand up for himself, especially to a kid that stood five inches below him.

"Oh my God, it's you," stated Vaughn who started laughing and put his hand out for a cool handshake or fist pump action. "You're 'Hoop de Blanc'. You are known throughout our hood and school as the one that will put the Bronx on the map for basketball."

"Yeah, that's me," Ryan responded roughly, and gave him half of a fist pump. "I've been known to score a few points."

"Sit down now or bot' of you will walk home!" commanded Ms. Kim who changed their cozy bonding moment into a harsh reality.

Ryan sat back in his seat and Vaughn sat opposite him in Lauren's first-row seat. She moved her backpack so he wouldn't crush her stuff.

"I watched you play in the Malloy Courts this summer," said Vaughn, star-struck. "Well not all summer, that's a dangerous place to hoop. A lot of brothers have been robbed or shot for no reason there. Man, how did you survive? You stick out like a sore thumb."

"That's all I look forward to…it's like breathing," Ryan said looking straight.

He remembered playing against the kids in the neighborhood when a cream-colored, Crown Victorian rolled up on the courts and someone started shooting. A bullet nicked his arm, and his best friend LeRoy took two to the leg. LeRoy had to learn to walk again during therapy. His dad sent him to North Carolina to live with his grandmother and grow up in a safer community. That was last year. He hadn't found another best friend since then. Ryan's brother, who was a senior in high school, watched over him while his dad worked at the electric plant nearby. His mother ran off with the dentist to Oregon when he was five. The dentist had his own children and didn't want hers too. In the Bronx, they lived in a predominantly black and Latino community. Ryan knew he stood out, but it was never really an issue among the people who knew he and his brother.

"Yeah, you have a dope three-point shot," Vaughn went on. "I remember you playing against those Brooklyn kids, and you destroyed them."

"That's what I am known for...my three-point shot," Ryan chuckled. "According to my six-foot-seven dad, I may grow a few more inches and I should be able to do a little dunking action, like my brother, Shawn. He just signed on to play at Syracuse next year. All the hope I have in this world is to play for some college team that will give me a full ride so I can get out of this place."

"New York isn't so bad," the comment came from Wanda who was seated behind Lauren and Vaughn. "I live in Queens, and I think there is a lot of great food, culture, and history there. New York is a great place to live."

"Yeah, but I betchya there aren't drive-bys in your neighborhood," Vaughn remarked. "Where we live, you could get cut just looking at somebody."

"No way," retorted Wanda, loudly. "I have four aunties, five uncles, my nana and pops, and fourteen cousins that live on my street. There's nothing going on that we all don't know about. Seriously, it sounds like a good thing, but even the smallest things that go on, you cannot get away with."

The snow continued to fall on the road and surroundings, making everything look like a winter wonderland. Everyone seemed relaxed except for timid Lauren.

"I thought we were only supposed to get a dusting?" Lauren asked sheepishly. "This is going to take forever in the snow. Oh my gosh, we might get into an accident."

"At the rate that Ms. Kim is driving and the stop that is required for vehicles in front of her, she is doing a rather wonderful job. With my calculations if there were an accident it wouldn't be her fault," remarked Shannon a few rows behind, adding her two cents. "According to the GPS on my iPad, if there aren't a lot of obstacles, we should arrive before noon."

"Your parents bought you that nice iPad?" Brianna inquired in a jealous fit. She pulled out her obsolete Apple iPhone which was slow and had a cracked screen.

"At least you have an iPhone," Adam chimed in. "There's no way I am getting a cell phone until I can pay for it myself."

"How do your parents know if you have an emergency?" questioned Brianna.

"They said they'll probably hear me yelling," Adam laughed. "But I do have my handheld gaming system and with Wi-Fi, it does everything a phone can do. I can't live without it. My Aunt Gina gave it to me for Hanukkah last year."

"I don't know how anyone can live without an iPad," Darcy chimed in. "All of my music and movies are on it."

"Of course, you would have one," said Brianna in a snippy tone.

The twins shook their heads innocently, which could be interpreted as either they didn't have one, or they didn't agree with her point of view.

"I have a cell phone, but I got the Samsung," Wanda clarified. "I can watch movies and store music on it. I don't see the big deal with having an iPad."

"I bet you guys have fancy iPads too up in the first row," Brianna asked Lauren and Ryan.

Lauren's eyes opened very wide. She wasn't used to someone talking to her let alone singling her out for having anything of envy. She shook her head no and stared straight out of the window, not speaking a word.

Ryan heard that and turned around to look at her wondering if she really asked that out loud.

"Are you kidding me?" Ryan said irritated.

Apart from his shoes, jacket, and basketball uniform everything Ryan wore was a hand-me-down from his older brother. The phone in his pocket was third generation and refurbished from the community center nearby. Because of the confident way he carried himself, no one was the wiser of his dire straits.

Arcado moved out of the last row and sat next to Brianna, exacerbating the situation.

"Did I invite you to sit here?" she said rudely. "What is your problem?"

"Well, I think you are targeting people unfairly," Arcado whispered as he took out the latest, most expensive, and compact item on the market. "I'm 15 years old and I own the deluxe ultra-iPad. And before you start on about something else, you can't just go around accusing people of whatever goes on in that wackadoodle head of yours. People might think you're crazy."

"Well, nobody asked you," Brianna said angrily with her deep, honest, brown eyes blazing into his. "I can handle my business just fine. If people don't like my questions or my statements, I don't care. I am a STRONG woman."

"You are a LITTLE girl and the only thing strong about you is your smell," Arcado remarked and was no longer whispering as he made sniffing noises. He got up from her row and went back to his seat holding his nose. Then he shouted, "I am going to buy you some deodorant for Christmas...although, I don't know if I can wait that long."

A few kids giggled, the rest saw through her toughness and felt sorry for her. Brianna's tough exterior came from her mother and aunt. They always pointed out the social injustices in the world, which did enrage her but also exhausted her. While most kids had a social life, she was obligated to attend rallies and meetings with adults. Try as she may, the other kids in the neighborhood weren't interested in helping her with most causes, so she had always been on her own.

They were well into the first hour of their trip when they started their ascent into the mountains. The buses went slower than usual because the light snow that started in New York had increased in intensity. Nobody thought to listen to the weather updates on the radio. Data service on their phones was now getting shoddy, which was normal in the mountains.

Ms. Kim didn't like inclement weather, but she was an experienced bus driver so she didn't care if they were hours late; she wouldn't rush through mountains with snow accumulating on her windshield and outside mirrors. She was as tough as they come, but never wanted to be called out for sloppy bus driving. Her pride was bigger than her bus.

Rooter followed Ms. Kim and if it weren't for her steady driving, he would've passed her and kept going. He had no time for mountains and snow. He wanted his next smoke and driving slowly was an inconvenience. As they made their way up the mountain, there was a point where it went from one lane in their direction to two to allow cars to pass slower vehicles. That's when Rooter took his opportunity and passed Ms. Kim. As he did so, it made Haugen and his team a little nervous.

"Don't worry Mr. Haugen, I'll make sure she's behind me at all times," Rooter said as he was beginning to shake a little from his nicotine habit.

Mr. Haugen looked at his team and they went back to reading their books and magazines or typing on their laptops. All was well as each bus climbed to the top and rounded corners doing so. Luckily, there weren't that many cars coming and going around the bends, so it lessened Mr. Haugen's stress level.

Back in New York City, Mr. Jekel was at home reading the newspaper in his comfy chair with the local news on the TV in the background. He always had some type of news station turned on whether at home or work. His wife came into the room with her apron on and offered Mitch a freshly baked peanut butter blossom cookie from the batch she made. This would be one of many kinds of Christmas cookies she would bake.

"Wow, look at that snow and wind blowing," she remarked to her husband. "That Nor'easter took a turn! It's going to hit upstate now and possibly here in the city. I wonder how your project is working out with those kids."

Mr. Jekel was half listening while trying to finish reading the high school sports page that compared the hockey teams, one from his alma mater and the other from the arch-rival school. As he looked up and grabbed a cookie graciously, his jaw dropped when he saw what his wife referred to on the TV. The weatherman pointed out the Nor'easter, which was defined as a heavy blizzard in the Northeastern quadrant of North America. In the days leading up, the Northeast quadrant affected Maine and eastern Canada. Now New Jersey, Pennsylvania, New York, and up to Canada was highlighted with massive snow and winds predicted.

"What on Earth?!" Mitch Jekel said as he reached for his cell phone. He dialed Haugen's number and was relieved when he answered his phone.

"Hey Cyril, it's Mitch," he talked into the phone, hearing more static than his friend's reply.

"Hello, Mitch. Everything is going as planned," Cyril said. But what Mitch heard was a faint response that he couldn't make out.

"Cyril, listen to me. I need you to turn the buses around and come back to New York City," Mitch spoke calmly and clearly.

"I can't hear you that well," Cyril spoke like he was in a tin can from space.

"I said...." Mitch began to speak but there was a dial tone.

He dialed back right away and heard a busy signal. He tried every few minutes to call and he got now a fast, busy signal. Cyril knew the mountains cut the service out but wondered what Mitch was trying to say. He hoped it wasn't important. They would reach the top soon and then it would plateau for a while. He would call back then. His attention was diverted by the snowfall that picked up quickly. The buses crawled uphill slower and slower. There had been a flurry of snow in the mountain pass for over a few hours, but until they reached that bend around one of the corners, they were oblivious to it.

The buses were battling not just the snow, but also the wind, which had picked up to 30-40 mph. It was snowing sideways, up and down, and across. The kids were alarmed by the sudden change in weather and were feeling tense.

"Oh my gosh, we're going to crash!" Lauren said almost in tears.

Ms. Kim was driving her best and slowed down. She knew that after she got over the pass, things would get better. She turned on all her exterior lights and followed Rooter. Rooter was getting reckless; he wanted to get over that pass quickly so he could reduce the tenseness that made him crave his bad habit. The roads were completely snow-covered and the only thing you could see were other headlights on cars. The vehicles themselves seemed to disappear in the blizzard.

Rooter took the bus around the bend swiftly. Sliding downhill in the oncoming lane was a semi-truck transporting logs. They both swerved a little and missed each other, but in doing so, the log truck lost control due to the heavy load and was directed head-on for Ms. Kim's bus. He needed to turn more to avoid hitting her. This forced Ms. Kim to make an impulse swerve, and as she did so, she hit the outside guardrail. The guardrail looked like it was secured down, but in reality, the bolts had become rusty over the years and were pliable when the bus hit it. The guardrail swung wide open, and the yellow short bus went down the mountain. Then the guardrail swung right back into position as if it were a door to the devil's dungeon.

Because of the heavy snowfall and the panic to regain control of the truck, the semi-driver lost sight of the yellow bus. Rooter was already in the next banked turn up the hill after passing the semi and never saw the incident either.

It was like it was almost in slow motion. Ms. Kim tried to control the bus down the ravine with both feet on the brake. Luckily, the one foot of fresh snowfall cushioned the bus as it ricocheted from one boulder to a bush to the next patch of land all the way down the hill. Students were thrown out of their seats and their bags spilled everywhere. Ms. Kim was the only one with a seat belt, so she avoided all of the concussion-type blows from the ceiling.

Everyone was screaming and crying out loud, especially the boys. The López's held on to each other's shoulders as best they could to be more stable, but it only helped slightly. The bus picked up momentum and was almost at the bottom as it broke through the bushes, flew through the air, and onto a fast-moving river. Ms. Kim's head smashed against the steering wheel, breaking her nose and spraying blood everywhere. It also knocked her out cold. The kids either hit their heads on the top of the bus or a nearby seat and they fell limply to the floor, passed out like Ms. Kim.

The kids suffered bloody noses, bumps, and scrapes from the impact of the crash.

The quiet bus was now floating on water. The bus moved fast with the rapids and traveled down the narrow river, turning and dipping here and there. They were unconscious for what seemed like an eternity. Water started to fill up the bottom of the bus which woke the students from their lifeless state. There was a foggy panic when the kids were trying to make out what happened and what to do next. Ms. Kim was still not moving. The kids wondered if she even was alive.

The river was moving rapidly. Outside the bus, you could barely see the river through the snow blowing sideways. The bus would have sunk instantly, but luckily it was a logging river. The bus was floating on five logs that constantly rolled underneath. The lumberjacks upstream cut down trees and hauled them to the river where they would float until they hit the sawmill.

"What should we do!" squeaked Lauren, in a nervous panic, with blood dripping from a gouge across her cheek. "I don't want to drown or freeze to death!"

All of the students started moving toward each other, but the shift in weight caused a log to move out from underneath the bus and the water started seeping in quicker. They stopped immediately, noticing the consequences of their actions.

"Everyone, stay still!" Arcado commanded with a bloody nose. "Ms. Kim's bus doesn't like movement, so let's not give it any."

"That doesn't solve the problem of how we're getting off this bus," Brianna chimed in as her long locks of hair were bloody and mussed. Her pants ripped after the hard landing revealing a sizable gash across her leg.

They all looked outside, seeking a solution. There was a light beacon in the distance downriver that Adam noticed.

"Hey, did you guys see that?" Adam asked.

He had a knot on the front of his head that would grow bigger over time. They all looked and saw a flash of light way up ahead. They couldn't tell how far away it was or if it meant anything at all.

"Yeah, I see it," Vaughn said with blood dripping from his nose and lip. "I think we should try and open the door when we get in range."

"I agree," Ryan said with his left elbow out of joint. "There could be people that live or work there that can help us."

Everyone agreed. They patiently waited as the light grew nearer and nearer. They were moving so fast and began to question the plan.

"I don't know if this strategy was fully thought out," remarked Shannon. Her tousled, red hair was bleeding from somewhere on top and dripping down her forehead. "I think the velocity is too fast to consider a jump. And if my calculations are correct the pressure on the bus door, either back or front would be too great to open. I wonder if we could slip through the windows?"

"You're right. I don't think the doors will open," said Vaughn looking hopeless, and then pointed to Arcado. "There is no way I can fit through any window. And neither can that kid's hair."

Everyone nervously laughed as they saw the water rising. They all were either kneeling on their seats or standing on them to avoid the frigid water pouring into the bus.

"Man, leave my hair out of it," Arcado smirked.

Suddenly, the bus started spinning around. They were coming into an open area where the banks widened, and the logs were separating. They lost more logs and now were floating backward. They started to scream again.

"Lord, Jesus, I don't wanna die, please not before my first kiss," Wanda wailed, and Lauren joined her.

At the same time, everyone started talking, crying, and swearing. They were hopeless. They all knew that as soon as the next log came loose, the bus would sink and so would they. Everyone gripped their seats and then it happened.

The last log rolled out from under the bus.

Saturday, November 28th
Chapter 5 Close Call

Rooter was nervously proud that he avoided that semi-truck. He blamed the semi fully for being there when he was coming around the corner. Mr. Haugen and his team didn't know what just occurred or who was at fault - it happened so quickly. They didn't completely trust Rooter at the wheel after he passed Ms. Kim for no reason whatsoever. They looked behind them and saw lights, so they thought the kids were OK. What followed Rooter's bus was a double-cabbed construction truck that had all lights on from top to bottom, which resembled the bus's lighting.

Haugen's team was all trying to boot up their cell phones to check on the weather and call Ms. Kim to ensure the students were all right. Haugen wished he were aboard their bus. If anything happened to those kids, he would never forgive himself, not to mention his career would be doomed. He dialed Shannon's phone. Her mother programmed Shannon and her phone number in his cell while they were being briefed back at the plaza. There was a constant busy signal and no answer. He looked back at the vehicle behind them and it put his mind at ease, knowing that soon he would see each of their bright faces.

One of his colleagues brought her tablet up and sat next to Mr. Haugen. Shauna got a snapshot of the weather and its worsening conditions.

"I don't know if we are going to make it to Minnechanka," she said distressed. "This blizzard is supposed to pile two or more feet of snow."

They pulled out a map and tried to see if there was a place to pull off and wait out the blizzard. It would have to be somewhat of a major town with a hotel to handle the amount in their group. As they checked from city to city, they knew that most were rural towns with a small motel at best. The only thing they could do was to try and make the trek to their destination. Mr. Haugen internally cursed the weatherman who said the major snow would miss New York.

27

Chapter 6 Help Us

The last log rolled from the undercarriage in the back of the bus to the front of the bus, where it snagged on something and was held on by a thread. Water gushed in, filling the back of the bus quickly. Lauren and some of the other kids were struggling to open their window latches. Ryan and Vaughn tried to push open the front door lever, but it proved futile. The outside pressure was too great to open it. Ms. Kim, still affixed to the steering wheel, knocked out cold, had no idea that they were in their final moments of doom.

There was chaos and screaming all through the bus as they tried to claw their way out, which wasn't working. A moment came when they all realized they were going to die and the commotion stopped. The water was climbing to their chins and the only part of the bus that was still thrust into the air was where Ms. Kim sat. The students knew if they made any last-ditch movements, it would be the last time they saw each other.

"Clunk," the bus hit what felt like a wall. "Clunk, clunk, clunk, clunk."

Nobody knew what was happening but apparently, the bus stopped spinning and was now stuck in some sort of rut. They could hear faint voices from the shore yelling commands. The water first rose above Brianna, who did not come back up. Arcado saw her go under from the corner of his eye and swam to her area. He dragged her to the spot nearest Ms. Kim and she took a deep, choking breath as she came up and out of the water. Right now, she had to focus on taking the next breath, so she did and hung on to Arcado like he was a flotation device. Everyone made their way to the front because all they cared about was keeping their head above water. Ms. Kim's head was now under water and they knew they would be next.

The blizzard still obstructed the kids' view outside the bus. There seemed to be a log jam that stopped the bus from floating away and they continued to hear people yelling commands. Then, out of nowhere, the bus was yanked towards the land. Soon water was draining out of the bus as it reached the bank's shore.

Ryan quickly moved to get the front door open. It was a blur outside; the only thing they knew for certain was that if they stepped outside, they could somehow get to snowy land. Ryan and Vaughn made sure all of the students got off first. To get out, they all had to leap to the shoreline. To add to their already injured, hypothermic bodies, most of them fell flat on their knees or faces after they leaped.

They could barely see but noticed figures of people and animals fastened to what looked like ropes attached to their bus. That's exactly what saved them. They put together pieces of the scene before them: men waded into the water holding chains and ropes and attached them to the bus. They also had a rope around their waists to prevent them from being dragged away by the currents. The chains on the other end were hooked up to a team of a dozen oxen that had pulled the bus out of the rapids and onto the shore.

Not knowing if she was dead or alive, Vaughn unbuckled Ms. Kim, which was harder than he thought because her wet, fat rolls hung over the seatbelt. One of the men jumped onto the bus and signaled for the students to jump off as he dragged Ms. Kim from her seat. They obeyed, and in no time, everyone was off the bus and into the blizzard.

They were completely numb from their injuries, shock, and hypothermia, but they followed the men up the snow bank to a place where they could get shelter. Lauren and Darcy passed out from the cold and fell right to the ground. Two of the men picked them up and carried them. They brought one sled and Ms. Kim overfilled it as it took two men to pull her to safety. As they did so, she sputtered out a bunch of water and gasped for air, coming back to life. The students were on autopilot - all they could do was follow the men to a large log cabin with a covered porch and fogged-up windows. The inviting smell of chimney smoke was abundant in the air as the howling winds blew here and there. The students never craved anything more than a roaring fire on the other side of the door that had suddenly appeared before them.

When the door opened to the shelter, there were women and children there ready to help them into the warmth. All the students fell to the floor and lay there. They absolutely couldn't move another part of their body. While the crackling of the fire emanated from deeper inside the shelter, they were far too frigid and tired to move.

"Listen up please," declared a lady in her mid-forties who clapped her hands to get their attention. "I know you are exhausted, but you need to get out of those wet clothes and warm up. Hypothermia is our biggest enemy out here and it will kill you."

One by one the students got up and followed her to a set of rooms. One was for the boys and one for the girls. There were different sizes of clothes set on chairs. The lady followed the girls into their room. The girls all looked at each other with discomfort written all over their faces.

"I am a doctor, so I've seen it all ladies," she said in a soft but mother-like voice. "I know you don't have a lot of strength so I can help pull your clothes off."

That sounded dreadful to all of them. Only Lauren was desperate enough to speak up.

"I need help," Lauren begged.

The doctor came over and gladly tugged until she was in her underclothes. Then Lauren looked at the smaller-sized clothes and took them. She swiftly changed and instantly felt much better.

"Oh my gosh, these clothes are so warm, and these socks are so comfortable. Thank you," muttered Lauren meekly.

"Well, a little trick that I learned was to put your clothing by the fire and heat them before you put them on, and man it works wonders," the doctor said and smiled. "Kind of like getting them out of the dryer."

At that, all the girls wanted help tugging their clothes off and getting into the heated ones. The clothes seemed rather old-fashioned and rugged. It's like they were dressed right from an L.L. Bean country catalog. The insides of the pants were warm, soft, and flannel and the outside was a cotton khaki. They all wore a white t-shirt and then another cottony long sleeve over it which was looser fitting. The socks were

30

made of thick, soft wool and felt like heaven. There were even rugged half-boot shoes that they put on.

Soon, all the students were dressed in clothes that wiped away the evidence of the ordeal they had just gone through. Their wet hair and damaged faces seemed to be the only traces left. They were instructed to sit by the large hearth at the fireplace to thaw. Adam was the only one that was still shaking uncontrollably. He had severe hypothermia that needed attention. They took him to a different room where they had what looked like a bathtub. He had to strip down and submerge in the hot water until he brought up his body temperature. Through all the turmoil, his yarmulke was tattered but still attached by pins to his head. When Adam stopped shaking violently, another Jewish workman, named Samuel, escorted Adam back to the fireplace and told Marta he would watch over him. He spoke a little Yiddish to put Adam's mind at ease.

The kids sat in woven rocking chairs by the fireplace as it crackled and emitted comforting heat. The fireplace was grand - it went from the floor to almost the ceiling. The warmth radiated through their bodies like sunshine on a hot summer beach. Marta introduced herself as the village doctor and readied her examination room where she performed a short physical on all of the students. She bandaged Brianna's head and then cleaned, stitched, and wrapped her leg. Marta sewed stitches on Lauren's face, Vaughn's lip, and Shannon's head. Ryan, whose left elbow needed resetting, had a split-second alarming scream when the doc corrected it. Adam would, ironically, need to put an icepack on the bump on his head whenever he warmed up. After all was said and done, the students were content that they lived to tell the tale and began to notice the people and the place that seemed to be a little unsettling.

Shannon was the first to observe that they were in a building with no electricity. Lanterns were glowing everywhere. It was only one o'clock in the afternoon, but it looked like nightfall since the Nor'easter had blocked the sun.

Each of the students seemed to have a moment of clarity realizing their cell phones or gaming systems were now gone.

Whether they were at the bottom of a river, on a bus soaked with water, or in a snowbank, they had all lost their lifelines to salvation.

Young children walked in and greeted them with hot oatmeal topped with sugar and cinnamon. Others brought hot apple cider. The five and six-year-olds wore similar clothing to the tattered bus students. As they sat and sipped slowly on their hot beverages, the little kids stared at them and smiled.

"Do you want a tip or something?" Brianna said abruptly to the little boy that brought her cider. "Why are you staring at me? Don't you know that's rude?"

"I wanted to make sure you didn't want anymore," the young boy said in his sweet precious voice and then walked away with his head hung low.

"Dang, that little boy was only trying to make sure you were all right," Arcado continued to give her a hard time.

"Leave me alone," Brianna sulked. "How was I supposed to know that?"

She thought a little bit more about what she said to the boy and began to feel remorse. It seemed to be a moment of opportunity to make amends with Arcado.

"By the way," she said with a pause trying to find the words to say it. "I wanted to thank you for helping me on the bus. You know.... get my head above the water."

"Yeah, I know," he said softer. "So, you do have a soul?"

As he said that, she cracked a smile for the first time. Arcado thought that she was cute when she didn't look so scornful.

The students were exhausted from the emotional and physical experience, and most were falling asleep in their chairs. They were warm, bandaged, fed, and comfortable. It seemed that they came such a far way than that of an hour ago. Lauren was one of the only ones that still worried if they would make it home tonight or tomorrow. She left her chair to find the doctor. The doctor was at a desk logging in the visitors. She already got each student's full name, date of birth, height, weight, and bus injuries. Charts were made in case there were any other issues that she would have to address. The doctor had her long brunette hair in a bun. Her caramel skin came from her father who was from Mexico and her green eyes came from her mother who was from Brazil.

"Sorry to disturb you, doctor, but I am wondering if you know when we can go home?" Lauren sheepishly asked.

"Lauren, you can call me Doc Marta," she said with kindness. "I think we will have a better idea of things once the blizzard settles down."

"Well let's say it settles down today, when can we leave?" Lauren asked a little more forcefully.

"I'm afraid that's not my area of expertise," Doc Marta replied. "Our city councilman will give us a full report soon and he will have a better idea."

"Where is he?" she inquired nervously. "Can I talk to him?"

"He and the men are tending to the livestock to make sure they are safe. They're also bringing in more logs for the fire," the doc explained. "They're very busy keeping us all safe and warm."

With that, Lauren walked back to her seat and sank deep. She didn't like being away from home and was desperate to get back as soon as possible. Contemplating what Doc Marta just told her, she assumed they were in a rural farming area. Her head was physically hurting from the accident and mentally aching from the thought of not being able to go home. It seemed fruitless to fight it. After minutes passed, everyone was asleep, even her.

Chapter 7 Frantic Parents

M r. Jekel's cell phone was ringing with texts and calls from all the concerned parents, coworkers, and even the Mayor of New York. New York City was getting a foot of snow due to the Nor'easter, but reports of how the weather was even worse upstate with four to six feet of unexpected snow, alarm bells were going off in everyone's minds. Nobody could get a hold of either their kids or Mr. Haugen. Mitch Jekel set up a group text so if anyone got through, they could report it to the other concerned parents.

There were warnings from Darcy's parents about suing the city if their daughter was harmed or lost any limbs from frostbite. Arcado's parents (who were lawyers) were some of the sanest of the group advising that everyone calm down and emit positivity to make the Earth feel the love and diffuse it to their kids. The group text buzzed nonstop for hours with daunting comments, updates on the weather worsening, or the busy signals each parent continuously received on calls out to their children. The hysteria only heightened.

Mr. Jekel requested that the mayor ask the governor to send the National Guard to locate the children and ensure their safety. Because of the unexpected snowfall, there was no collection of personnel gathered to do so. Generally, when a storm was predicted, an order would be given to have the National Guard on standby to deploy. They would kiss their loved ones, suit up, and report to their duty station awaiting commands. But these men and women were now at home, trapped in their houses or apartments waiting for the snowfall to clear to be recalled to duty.

The Mayor of New York City had already notified the Governor of New York who lived and worked in the state capital of Albany. The governor was the only one who could call up the National Guard. The National Guard Units were stationed all over the state of New York, mainly in the major cities. The Guard troops were activated by the governor in any state emergency. Some troops even helped with overseas combat missions with the military. Their skill sets varied to assist in all situations.

Albany had already received two feet of snow, so the National Guard Unit that would be recalled would have to be from the south, like New York City. The governor thought they could deploy faster, but the snow in New York City was piled up just as greatly as in Albany. It was not just the heavy snowfall that was the issue. The 30-40 mph winds blowing the snow prevented anyone daring to go outdoors, not to mention anything freshly shoveled would be buried in minutes.

The governor was in touch with the Tracking and Capabilities Command (TACC) and the Mobile Maintenance Company (MMC) National Guard Commanders. These units had large vehicles that could handle extreme weather. He wanted a status of when they could assemble and get on the road to find these students. The troop commanders hastily did a recall exercise to their men and women for status updates. But these accountability phone calls could take hours to get a full report, so everyone just sat tight and waited.

As the news trickled back to Mitch, he sat there in his recliner thinking about what the young man Arcado said when he introduced himself earlier. He wanted folks to think about an artificial Christmas tree. What a good idea, it seemed to him, now.

Chapter 8 The Councilman

A boisterous noise woke the students up from their sitting slumber. When they awoke, they were met by the councilman. He was in his early sixties and had a full head of thick, white hair with a manicured mustache and beard to match. His brown eyes and weathered face were friendly. His six-foot-four trim frame was a bit intimidating, but his voice seemed calm and mature when he talked. He never raised his voice, even in a debate. Doc Marta gave him the statistics on each student along with their names.

"Good afternoon, my name is Boyce Goodman," he looked at each one of them when he talked. "Please call me, Mr. Boyce. I would like to explain where you are and how we are going to try and help you get back home."

"Are you the councilman?" Lauren inquired timidly.

"Yes, I am," he answered.

"What does that mean?" asked Vaughn like he was left out of the loop.

"It means, Mr. Vetter, that I am in charge of this charter, and it's up to me to make decisions to keep everyone safe, clean, fed, and ensure they can pull their weight for work," he said in his confident, steady voice. "Our village is unique. I wish that the snow would allow you to see it more clearly, it's a remarkable place and we have amazing people here."

"It's not all that, you have no electricity or phones," cajoled Wanda putting in her two cents.

"Good observation, Ms. Womack," complimented Boyce and then continued. "We choose to live off the grid. We work hard, but we work together so we can appreciate life a little more. You see, the adults all come from some type of corporate job or a place where they were searching for something more out of life. We are all different in culture, race, and religion. We work together, play together, pray together, eat together, and have social events that bring us even more together."

An unexpected voice came from the back of the room. It was Ms. Kim dressed just like everyone else with a major bandage from one side of her face to the other keeping her nose in a steady position.

"Ya' a dang cult and now we're ya' prisona's!" she yelled as she walked towards Boyce and the kids in a defensive way. "Don't you lay a finger on anyone of 'em or I will give ya a nose like mine."

Subtle laughter came from the ten or so villagers that were in the room. Nobody seemed threatening to the students or Ms. Kim. She wasn't even aware of how many ladies it took to get her out of her wet clothes and into her warm, snuggly ones. When she finally awoke, the doctor introduced herself, did a full exam, and put her nose back into place. This would've had any normal person screaming, but Ms. Kim just sighed when it was finished. The bandaging would keep the nose stable. The doctor let her sleep in the clinic hospital bed with heated water bottles and blankets.

Standing within inches of Boyce with her hands on her hips, Ms. Kim glowered at him as if looking for a rebuttal, but he calmly took a deep breath and indicated with his hands to his people to stop laughing.

"Ms. Kim, neither you nor the children are my prisoners, I assure you," he continued. "Let me tell you how we rescued you. I think it's an amazing story."

"Yeah, you rescued us to become ya' cult slaves," replied Ms. Kim who was more than skeptical. "I've seen it all on reality TV. First ya' act all nice and then we find out ya' are as evil as they come."

"Please, have a seat," he insisted to Ms. Kim and pointed to another wicker chair by the fire. She sat but the unconvinced look on her face still hung. "You see, Charlie forgot his harmonica up in the tower of the campanile. He climbed 200 stairs to the top. Now, mind you, he just lit the lantern up there when the storm hit so it would guide anyone out working back to our village."

"What's a campanile? Why are you using fancy words on us?" Brianna remarked in her distrusting way.

"My dear, a campanile stands in the middle of our village. It's a rather thin, red-bricked tower that holds three large bells and a lantern at the top for signaling and warnings. It also has a large clock dial on the front," he continued. "Charlie lit the large lantern and accidentally left his harmonica on the ledge. After he reached the ground floor, he remembered it was back 200 steps up, so he climbed up again to claim it. When he reached the top, he took the binoculars that were stationed there and glanced around, looking for people out in the field, but what he saw was a bus a mile and a half floating right toward us on the river. This startled him so he rang the bell. This means there is important news to be shared, so we all gathered at the town hall. We didn't have a lot of time to get the ropes, chains, and especially the oxen. In case you don't know, oxen don't move fast, so we had to motivate them by dangling food in front of them."

"How did you know we were on the bus?" Lauren asked.

"Well, we didn't know if anyone was on the bus, but we didn't want to assume that nobody was on it or you may have kept riding the river or sunk," Boyce stated honestly.

This hit a nerve with everyone but Ms. Kim. They all knew they almost died in that bus and whomever this Charlie guy was they owed him a thank you. They all let Ms. Kim play the skeptic, but they all were grateful and open to listening.

"Doc Marta went to the clothing pantry with the others here and grabbed a variety of sizes and then set all the clothing by the fire to heat them. The young children that weren't doing chores accompanied the folks here and helped feed you," Boyce explained as best he could. "We plan to make you our guests until the snow subsides. Then we intend to get you back to where you belong as soon as it's possible. How does that sound?"

Vladimir and Sergei both stood and hugged Mr. Boyce.

"Thank you," they said in unison.

Ryan stood up, approached Mr. Boyce, and shook his hand. All of the boys did the same and some of the girls just gave him a polite "thank you".

"Ya' stupid kids are fools," Ms. Kim said cynically. "I got my eye on ya' Boyce. And that goes for all of you's."

"Sorry, you feel that way," Boyce stated and gave her a serious stare. "The next thing I would like to do is take you to the mess hall to meet the town folk. Afterward, we will have dinner. For sleeping quarters tonight, the boys will bunk on the second floor and the girls on the third floor of our lodging quarters across the street. I will have your peers show you that after we eat. Ms. Kim, we have a guest suite on the first floor for you."

"Mr. Boyce, I have a question," Darcy finally spoke up. "Does one find the bathroom facilities outside, at a fir tree, or in a bucket in a corner?"

Each kid and Ms. Kim thought about how they could use the answer right now.

"We don't have plumbing per se, but we do have compost toilets in all buildings. There are two in here and six in the mess hall. Shall we proceed there and I will show you?"

They all agreed.

There were warm cloaks with insulated hoods to put on before they headed out the door. Most were oversized but they protected them from the nasty, blowing snow. As soon as Boyce opened the doors to the outside, the loud howling of the winds shrilled through everyone's body. They moved in a quick shuffle, single file across the way, past the campanile to another building with double doors, and entered. Doc Marta was the caboose of the party and swiftly closed the doors, shutting out the whistling winds. They all stomped the snow off, removed their cloaks, and hung them on an empty hook in the entry parlor.

The students walked into the open mess hall and all the clamoring and chatter from the village folk stopped. The only thing audible was the wicked sounds of the wind whistling and howling outside. It was eerie as hundreds of people studied them - some old, some middle-aged, and children of different ages. They were diverse in race, ethnicity, and religion. Some wore turbans, hijabs, yarmulkes, and a few in bright orange garbs. The half smiles on the villagers' faces were not exactly warm and inviting but more of uneasiness.

"I knew it," Ms. Kim snarled her lip. "Dey' are gonna' convert us to some type of sick mixed religion."

Saturday, November 28th
Chapter 9 Meet the Townspeople

Councilman Boyce cleared his throat and introduced the kids and Ms. Kim as the bus group that was rescued a few hours ago, but everyone already knew that. They were just waiting to get a look at them and see what their story was about. They put on cautious smiles as Mr. Boyce introduced them, but some wondered what they were going to tell them about this place and their lives, should they ask. This place was a sanctuary to most who found comfort in living off the grid. They moved here to get away from the bad news stories, the politics, the worrisome economy, random crime, school shootings, and other various reasons that they kept private.

Unlike the adults, the resident children were desperate to see new faces. There were many kids that lived here, but now they had these new teens to hang out with and ask questions about things they were missing. Most residents worried about how long these rescued students would be there. Several of them had concerned looks and stares. They hoped that the councilman would get them to the city as soon as the storm subsided without delay.

The mess hall was quite large and each wooden table held about 20 people with four tall lanterns illuminating the gigantic space. There was a serving area, much like a cafeteria. Tonight, they would be served beef soup, turnips, cucumbers, and bread and butter. Water was served at every meal with the exception of fresh milk at breakfast.

After the general introduction, the student group looked for the compost toilets. They were surprised as they flushed, and it didn't stink as much as they thought it would. There were hand washing stations outside the toilet closets. Afterward, they all stood in line to get dinner. Most kids were hungry but unsure of the food. Darcy tried to be a vegetarian at home but occasionally ate meat when no one was looking. She started avoiding meat because a group of her friends was making a statement about animal cruelty. She found that she preferred plants and vegetables anyway. Now, the beef soup sounded wonderful to her. Keeping the vegetarian part to herself, she knew that she would never see these people again after tomorrow.

Adam thought about the kosher foods that he was used to and looked around for Samuel who had helped him earlier. He found him eating his soup and bread. There was no butter on his bread.

"Don't worry Adam, Joe here is the butcher and one of the cooks, he prepares the meat properly for us," Samuel said. "In the cold months, there is less variety, but everything tastes delicious. You should come join us to eat."

"Thank you. I might just stay with my group," Adam said looking around the table at all the older Jewish men staring back at him. The youngest man at the table looked 10 years older than Adam.

Adam went and stood in line with the rest of the students. The group was still unsure of their surroundings. Arcado should have welcomed the site. He always wanted to save the Earth, and these folks lived as pure as they could: no pollution, no wasting food, saving electricity, and just being in a place where he was one with nature.

Something about this place was unsettling to him but he couldn't put his finger on it. These people seemed fake - they smiled too much, he thought. With every ounce of his being, he was skeptical of their abundant happiness. He wanted to get to the truth of the people here.

Vladimir and Sergei almost had matching cuts on their faces. They didn't need stitches but the scrapes on their faces looked like they were sparring against each other. They didn't doubt the people as Arcado did. They were appreciative to be alive, safe, and warm, and now eating dinner. They both loved the fact that people were friendly and they smiled back at everyone. Doc Marta even struck up a conversation in Spanish asking how they were doing and letting them know that she was always available should they need her. They both thought she was intelligent and pretty and wished she would come back to the city with them and meet their single uncle.

Shannon, Wanda, and Lauren stuck together like new best friends. Lauren was a picky eater, but she was hungry enough not to do her routine of smelling everything before she ate it. She thought the bread was heavenly. It was fresh and warm. Wanda requested a little more soup in her bowl because she was a growing girl. Shannon inquired how the vegetables were kept and if they were fresh or frozen.

Ryan, like Wanda, requested more from the beginning. He ended up with two bowls of soup, no vegetables, and lots of bread and butter. Brianna, surprisingly, had no comment. She went through the line accepting whatever they put in front of her. Vaughn went through the line making sounds with his mouth, as if he were going to rap, but instead made thuds and beats. He too smiled back as he received his food. They sat down at a table with some surprisingly lively old ladies. Everyone in the mess hall took their turns staring at the new kids. They tried not to make it obvious, but the new students could feel everyone gazing at the backs of their heads.

After dinner, Mr. Boyce walked over to their table with a clipboard clamping down a thick stack of papers and looked up from his notes to the students.

"Say, listen," he said. "You are all able-bodied kids and until I can get you back to your folks, all of you will have to pick up some chores."

"Do what?" asked Darcy as if that was a foreign word and she wanted clarification. "I don't think you mean everyone, right?"

"I'm afraid to make this a community, we depend on every single person to pitch in," Mr. Boyce laid it out simply.

"What do you mean?" Vaughn asked.

"Well, tomorrow is Sunday, so we do have morning celebrations, which you are all invited to in the town hall that doubles as a chapel across the street," Mr. Boyce continued. "But before.... well, I will just read the list and you can holler out when you hear something you can or want to do. OK, there's the sewing room – you know, making clothes, there's also mending and making shoes and boots, there's hunting, firewood gathering – which means cutting down a tree and branches and dragging it to the woodshed, oh yeah, and milking the animals. You can switch up and do different chores daily until we can get you home if you prefer."

"I'll milk," Ms. Kim readily volunteered without an attitude.

He looked around from student to student and they all looked horrified.

"Mr. Boyce, we don't mean any disrespect, but I don't believe any of us are familiar with the chores on the list that you mentioned," Shannon chimed in. "Is there any cooking or cleaning that needs to be done?"

Wanda and Lauren smiled and nodded their heads, glad that Shannon was their spokesperson.

"Well, you see, everyone is in charge of the cleanup," Mr. Boyce continued. "It's strictly forbidden to leave your space without cleaning your dishes, making your bed, and even washing your clothes. As far as cooking goes, I am afraid that the cooks go through years of culinary experience and we have special dietary needs such as kosher meals and gluten-free. So, cooking is out of the question."

"Hunting," Sergei and Vladimir said together and raised their hands.

"Me too," Wanda shouted without thinking about this task. She knew that if she were with the boys, she would be happy.

"OK – that's Sergei, Vlad, and Wanda for hunting," Mr. Boyce said, writing it down. "You will see Travis in the morning at 0500 for instructions and gear."

"I'll gather firewood," volunteered Ryan.

"Yeah, that's good for me too," said Vaughn.

"Very good, Ryan and Vaughn," Mr. Boyce wrote their names in. "You will see Wilbur in the morning."

"I will try sewing," Shannon offered. "I hope I can accomplish something there."

"Oh, you will be surprised how quickly you catch on," commented Mr. Boyce who wrote Shannon's name down. "You will see Cherise."

"Yeah, I'll sew too," Brianna said reluctantly.

"Uh, me too," said Lauren as knew she was running out of options.

"Sounds good," Mr. Boyce. "And I will put Adam, Darcy, and Arcado down for shoemaking. You will see Harvey in the cobbler shop."

"Wait, what?" argued Darcy who was NOT going to touch someone's stinky shoe. "I don't want to do any of this."

Arcado was about to second that notion from Darcy, but Mr. Boyce cut him off.

"So, then it will be milking the animals?" he asked. "I do have to warn you about milking the cows and goats. That must happen at three thirty in the morning. We need it fresh for breakfast."

All three of them groaned. Arcado thought that milking the cows would be the easiest and that his work would be done for the day, so agreed to it.

"I'll stick with doing the shoe thing," Adam offered, shrugging his shoulders.

"I will go to the shoe shop, but I hope your expectations aren't high," Darcy said, knowing that getting up early for milking was out of the question.

"All right. Done and done," Mr. Boyce smiled at the kids. "Arcado and Ms. Kim, Jesse will wake you for the milking shift. Adam and Darcy, I will put you down for the cobbler shop and you will see Harvey."

"Speaking of sleepin', where ya' putin' us?" Ms. Kim asked in a voice that was still cynical.

Lauren went over and sat next to Brianna. Brianna almost shoved her to the floor but felt Lauren shaking nervously.

"Can I bunk with you, please?" Lauren whispered to Brianna. "Nobody will mess with you and I know they will pick on me. It happens wherever I go."

Brianna felt annoyed on one hand but complimented on the other. She also knew that nobody would mess with her. Feeling sorry for how pathetic Lauren was, she agreed. She wanted to demonstrate what a strong woman looked like.

Mr. Boyce had them stay seated as he explained the history of the town that used to be an old textile mill back in the late 1800s through the mid-1960s. He described how some buildings were made out of wood and some from brick depending on the year built. He explained how there used to be some plumbing, but the occupants never had electricity. Finally, in the 1960s, the founder, Harold Shunderfoot, refused to run the textile mill without the state of New York investing in it. The problem was that the school was so far away from the major roads that the electric companies refused to accommodate it. And so the buildings became abandoned for 40 years until Boyce and four of his hunting buddies stumbled upon them.

They used some of the buildings when they hunted, mainly the lodging and kitchen. One year they went up to Albany to see who held the deed to the property. The land was owned by the state but was for sale for only $50K. They all pooled their money together and bought the whole property. In total, they owned 40 acres of land including all the existing buildings on it. There were no restrictions on building on the land, farming, or having livestock. The five owners were a Jewish butcher, a Catholic priest, a dairy farmer, an auto mechanic, and Mr. Boyce who was a contractor that built houses. It took them a year to get the place to be habitable.

Before they even moved their wives and children into the place, word hit the street that they were going to live off the grid and be their own bosses. This new place out in the sticks was not advertised but strangers approached the five owners for a chance to join them in the remote lifestyle. All owners gave consent only if the requested parties agreed to work the land and be providers for the group.

This formed their community and the rules were made and voted on by the majority. The previous name was Textile City, which hardly seemed a good fit anymore, so they renamed it the Village of Ourstory. It was kind of a pun for the word 'history', but it seemed sexist that one would say "his" "story", not "her" "story", so they nominated the one-word town of "Ourstory". Soon, they had titles and jobs for everyone. Mr. Boyce became the councilman because he had a gentle way with people. He was firm, yet kind.

The people that lived there chose to live there. They could leave the village at any time after they turned 18. Nobody moved there thinking that this was a vacation spa. Everyone knew that pitching in every day would be required. There would be a trip made several times a year to a warehouse a few hours away for materials for clothing, axes, and other sharp tools, more compostable toilets, rain barrels, and other miscellaneous items. This was done by horse and carriage. The village was self-sustainable making their lye for soap, and food from the spring, summer, and fall gardens, digging new wells for water, hunting all kinds of animals for meats and furs, and cutting wood for housing and keeping their hearth warm.

There were houses for families and then there was the three-story lodge with windows that bunked many of the children, adults, and in-betweens like Ms. Kim. In the lodge, the top floor housed the girls, the second floor housed the boys, and the main floor housed singles and some couples. There were bunk beds all lined up in a row with warm wool blankets and a pellet stove that needed no electricity. There were compost toilets on each floor and a showering room. In the summer, everyone used the river nearby to bathe, but in the cooler weather, there was a different system. On rotating days, there would be an allotment of two gallons of heated water that was waiting near the shower stations. One would wet down, wash, and rinse. It was a quick shower but the system worked.

Next to the lodge was a building almost identical to it. It had three floors. The main floor was the textile room. All the sewing machines, textiles, and accessories were housed there. On the second floor, there was the shoemaker's shop. All of the machines and apparatuses were in different areas on the floor. On the top floor was the school. There were four different rooms up there. A nursery school, an elementary school, a middle school, and a high school. All of the classrooms had traditional school desks facing the front. There was the traditional American Flag, wide circular clock, and chalkboards at the front of every classroom along with the teacher's desk.

The building on the other side of the lodge was the town hall. This building was as large as any of the three-story buildings next to it. But instead of three floors, it was a magnanimous open space with acoustics that any opera house would envy. There were rows of chairs and then at the front was a stage. Each religion used this space for worship, so symbols were replaced for each celebration. There was one Sunday celebration that all faiths were invited to. It was the 11 a.m. celebration. There would be readings, words of inspiration, and contemporary music.

At the end of the road were two huge barns. One held the horses and oxen and the other the cows, goats, chickens, and pigs. In the attics of the barns, hay bales were stored and worked into the animal's bedding. There were barrels of feed everywhere, mostly scraps here and there from the corn that was grown, different grasses, hay, and wheat.

In the summer, acres upon acres would be rows sewn with seeds for all sorts of vegetables and fruits. No matter what job you held, farming was always a part of the community job. There was a food shed that stored meats, milk, wheat, vegetables, and fruits. This was situated directly behind the mess hall with a large padlock that only the butchers, which happened also to be the cooks, had the key to. Occasionally, an animal from the woods, including bears, have been known to help themselves, so the shed was always closed and locked.

Everything about the food was manual production - planting the seeds, watering, weeding, picking, and finally processing them to eat. This took much of the villagers' time from spring to fall. In one way or another, everyone was proficient at food preservation, such as drying out fruit or pickling cucumbers to temperature storage of meats and fish.

Nothing was thrown away. Any scraps went to the animals and were composted for the large gardens. This was a way of life. Any city slicker who came to the village might think that it was a lot of work to maintain such a lifestyle. They wouldn't be wrong, but when everyone pitched in, the work went quickly and efficiently. The most difficult part was picking and harvesting. In the cold months, the workload slowed down, so the village would focus on things like repairing or making clothing, shoes, and weapons, and preparing the garden tools for the spring season.

Even after hearing all of the histories of the city, Ms. Kim still could only see this as a cult.

"So, Boyce, let's say I wanted to leave tomorra' at first light, you wouldn't stop me from going?" she asked and took a deep breath only through her nose. "What is ya' real intention with us?"

"Ms. Kim, may I remind you that we cared enough to risk our lives and rescue you strangers," he reasoned. "Furthermore, it is another by-law that we have to let you leave whenever you feel that you need to. We set a rule that if someone leaves, no matter what Mother Nature throws our way, we let you go...well as long as you are of age to make that decision."

"Well, I guess I meet da' criteria," Ms. Kim begrudged. "Why do I feel like ya' just saying that to please me?"

"Well, if you do decide to go, we can't stop you. However, we won't follow you either," he continued. "Meaning, if it were the worst blizzard in the world, you would be on your own if you step out that door."

"Has anyone ever left before?" Arcado popped his question into their back and forth.

"Yes," Mr. Boyce said. "Last year, one of our young fellows had a dream that his mother was dying and he wanted to say goodbye. He requested a horse and carriage ride to the main road and we took him the next day. Now, granted that was in the summertime and there was no blizzard. How he got to his mother's house after that, I couldn't tell you. Most likely hitch-hiked and hasn't returned since."

At this time people were rising from their seats to clean their dishes and head out of the mess hall. Mr. Boyce and the students stayed behind to keep their conversation going. The students and Ms. Kim were intimidated by their surroundings, but they also noticed how friendly everyone treated each other. They slowly started to buy into the group as just normal folks living off the grid.

"After we clean our plates, I will take you to your quarters where you will sleep. After dinner, we generally have a game and recreation night, but that's up to you," he added. "I know it's been a long and trying day for all of you, and if Doc Marta had it her way, she would tell you to get more rest."

48

"Sure, uh huh, put us ta' sleep," said Ms. Kim being snarky.

By this time the kids were getting tired of her paranoia comments. They now just wanted to fit in until the storm ended. Most of them trusted that they would be on some type of sleigh ride out of there within a day or so. Arcado seemed to agree with Ms. Kim and wondered what would happen if they fell asleep tonight.

Saturday, November 28th
Chapter 10 We're Stuck

Rooter put his foot on the pedal steadily so as not to go too fast and spin or too slow and get stuck in a tire track. The visibility was still poor with snow blowing from all directions and they hadn't seen the other bus in hours. They were on a country road, but the feet of snow covered the gravel that was normally there.

Mr. Haugen tried to call the cell phone numbers of the students on the other bus while Mitch, back in NYC, sat nervously in his cozy home. The other gardeners had given up hope of contacting the students, but Shauna was determined.

"Listen, Mr. Haugen, we need a plan," Shauna continued. "We haven't seen the other bus in hours. We all know that this road is leading nowhere. The other bus driver would not have sped off, that would be reckless."

"You're right, Shauna. I've been so focused on trying to reach one of the students that I lost sight of the bigger picture. Can anyone provide a status check?" Cyril spoke, sounding like a wreck.

"How much gas do we have?" Josh asked Rooter.

"We got 'er less than a quarter gallon left," Rooter reported back, staying focused on the road and daydreaming of his next ciggy, forgetting to be gas vigilant.

"I say the next house that we see, we turn in and request shelter," said Shauna calmly and wisely. "We can pool our money together and offer to pay them. We aren't going to make it much longer."

Everyone agreed by nodding their heads. Rooter wondered what she meant by saying that everyone could pool money together. He only came with ten dollars and the way things were going, he may have to use every penny on another pack of menthols.

Mr. Haugen turned back to his phone and continued to redial a few numbers as his stomach felt ill from the futile effort. It was nothing but busy signals. Out of nowhere, his cell phone died. Along with it were the important numbers to the students and Mitch. Desperation was written all over his face.

They slowly rolled down a road that had fields of nothing on both sides. There were wooded areas and a lot of farmlands, but no creatures nor houses in sight. Mr. Haugen thought things couldn't get any worse. Just as he was thinking that, the bus made a kerchunk-chunk noise and then stopped dead on the white drifty road.

Saturday, November 28th
Chapter 11 Sleeping Arrangements

They all managed to clean their plates, silverware, and cups to the proper shine and then donned their cloaks and headed over to the large three-story building that held the lodging. They followed in the previous footsteps of the others before them as the howling wind blew. When they stepped into the building, they removed their shoes and cloaks which were wet.

Folks were waiting for them so they could show each group where they would stay. Doc Marta escorted Ms. Kim to a single room on the main floor. It looked like a cozy cabin for one with a bed, nightstand, and a dresser opposite the bed. There were warm quilted blankets and fluffy pillows. There was a lantern on the nightstand that was already lit. Doc showed her the shared bathroom area that only the ladies used and then invited her to play Gin rummy in the central common room on that floor.

Next, a tall, slim, eighteen-year-old escorted the guys up the stairs to the second floor. There were bunk beds almost everywhere. There were a few private rooms like Ms. Kim's at the back of the room, but the boys would stay in the central area with the others whose ages ranged from five to 20. The girls went up to the third floor with the exact setup as the boy's second floor. In the back of their large open room was a community bathroom. They had five toilet stalls and three showers with private curtain areas. There were five sinks that had limited plumbing and buckets of water were nearby from the water tank.

The boys took the open bunk beds nearest the stairs. The girls took almost identical bunk beds a floor up. Each bed had a fitted and flat sheet, one pillow, one thick, gray, wool blanket, towel, and washcloth. There was a footlocker at the end of their bunks for each person, but there wasn't a lot in there. There were sets of pajamas placed along one wall, so they could select their size. Also, there were gym clothes set out which consisted of a white t-shirt, sweatpants, and a thinner pair of white socks. Since the townspeople fabricated all their clothes and shoes, the students were surprised to see what resembled athletic shoes with rubber soles. The tops of the shoe were the regular brown fabric that most of the boots were made from, but the other parts were sporty.

All the town's kids seemed to change into their sports clothes for what appeared to be playtime in the recreation room on the first floor. The New York City kids followed suit and went down to the rec room. On the first floor, in the back of the dormitory, two large doors led into a two-story, open-aired, large gymnasium.

For having no electricity, the room was amazing. The huge gymnasium had a basketball court on one side and an empty court on the other side for other activities like volleyball or badminton. There was even a rock-climbing wall, albeit small. There were large blue mats that kids could tumble on or play chess or checkers on and an art table in the corner. There were four different skylights in the ceiling, but they were covered dark with snow. The room had incandescent lighting from the solar panels that absorbed the light. This was the only building that was designated for solar power.

In no time, all of the boys were shooting hoops with the rack of basketballs nearby. The girls went over to an area where some others their age were jumping rope. This was Wanda's favorite activity to do with her sister and cousins back home in the summer. She jumped right in and amazed her peers with her fancy footwork and endurance. Shouting out a childhood limerick as she jumped, all the girls watched her and clapped along.

Brianna got a glimpse of the adults all sitting at card tables playing Gin rummy and decided to join them. She honestly never jumped a rope, climbed a wall, played chess, basketball, or anything else that happened in the gym, but she loved playing cards. She asked to play and they all moved so she could squeeze in another chair. Ms. Kim was highly competitive and her New York manner made her look like a mobster talking about taking everyone to the cleaners. They weren't actually betting, but Ms. Kim acted like they were.

When Adam saw some boys in the corner playing chess, he dropped the basketball and headed over. Even though the boys were half his age, they were brilliant at the game, as he would soon find out.

The twins wanted to try to climb the wall. It was meant to start on one side and get to the other by grabbing onto the rubber knobs of different shapes that were embedded into the wall. Others were on the course but invited them to take a turn.

Ryan was making three-point shots and Vaughn was rebounding the ball. Ryan sank most of the shots without effort. When Vaughn had his turn, he missed almost every basket. He decided to take shots from different spots closer to the basket. Ryan gave him a hard time and teased him that even girls could make better shots than he could. A young lady who was shooting at the opposite net overheard Ryan and made a point to introduce herself.

"Hey, I'm Bianca," a spunky girl with dark, ebony skin said, looking Ryan eye-to-eye with disdain. "So, what did you mean by girls could make better shots than him?"

As Bianca asked that question, she shot and sunk a three-point basket. She smiled smugly and walked away.

"Wait!" Ryan shouted and ran after her. "My name is Ryan. They call me Hoops back in NYC."

He thought this would impress her along with all his basketball skills. Bianca was a year older than Ryan, but they were similar heights. They were both tall for their ages. Bianca thought she would challenge the hotshot, so she grabbed a basketball and started playing one-on-one with Ryan. He was up for it and started his defense. She drove the ball to the right and he followed her every move. She stopped hard on a dime, backed up, shot, and sunk it for two points.

This became a noticeable challenge and anyone dribbling the ball stopped to watch the two battle on one side of the court. They both talked smack when they had possession and each of them scored consecutively. Soon, both kids were sweating profusely.

An hour and a half went by and all the kids were having fun playing their games. Ryan's left elbow wasn't feeling the best and he knew when to call it. Both he and Bianca left the court and sat with their backs against the wall watching Arcado and Vaughn shoot around.

"I take that back, what I said earlier about girls making shots," Ryan commented. "You really have game."

"When you have nothing to do but practice a sport every day, you can master it," Bianca explained. "So, I take it you're an All-Star for your basketball team?"

"Well, I have been known to be the feeder of the team," he continued. "Meaning if you get possession of the ball, feed it to me, so I can sink it for three."

"How do the other guys on the team feel about you being the hot shooter?" she asked abruptly. "Does anyone else score?"

"Occasionally, if they make a quick steal and they are already down at the other end before I can get there," he said logically.

"Here's a suggestion, if you want to open your mind," Bianca said maturely and turned to look at him. "A team is not a team if just one person is the star. Teammates can get resentful if they have real talent and it never gets shown. You are stealing their limelight."

"Dang, that's cold," Ryan replied, offended at her speaking so condescending. "It's not up to me, it's what my coach wants."

"Maybe you can be a leader and help your team be a team," Bianca got philosophical. "Help make it enjoyable for the guys that support you. You can feed them too when you know they are in position. Switch it up. The other team will never expect it."

"I don't know," he thought before he revealed himself. "I need to look good out there. Scouts come to our area all the time to recruit for college teams. I need that more than I need to be a leader."

"Tell me, while you are gone and your team has to play, are they going to miss you?" she asked snidely.

"Uhhh yeah, I am the score maker," he said like it was a silly question.

"Really?" Bianca was getting into his head. "I wonder if they could win without you?"

"Maybe they could, but not by the numbers I put up," Ryan said smiling, but inside his confidence was dying.

"Hmmm, I am sure that's important to your teammates who are waiting for an opportunity to shine. Perhaps you could start with Vaughn," Bianca knew all of their names. "Instead of teasing him, you could stop and give him some pointers."

She was putting Ryan in an uncomfortable position. He just met this girl and she already asked a lot of deep questions that he needed time to process. He felt that she didn't know him well enough to be doling out advice. She knew nothing of the dire straits that he, his dad, and his brother lived.

The lights started to flicker, which meant that playtime was over and everyone headed to their quarters. Ryan stood up and helped Bianca to her feet. He disliked her for criticizing him but knew it would only be a few days of putting up with her bad judgment. She, on the other hand, was grateful that she got to play against a worthy opponent and let him know. Being straightforward and never sugarcoating anything was just her way. Being protective of the kids in her village would become evident over the next few days. She always stood up for the little guy as fairness was important to her.

It was nine o'clock and it was time for bed. For most kids their age, it would've been an early bedtime, but the students were looking forward to their warm beds. A few stayed up chatting, but the early morning hours would come soon enough. As they slept, the winds hollered and the snow remained steadily falling.

Saturday, November 28th
Chapter 12 White Out with Nowhere to Go

Shivering on the bus, Shauna was the first one to let out a little whimper. Generally, she was the resourceful gardener, but she sat there with her watery eyes closed in misery thinking about how lucky her coworker Danny was for declining the job. The best she could do was reach into her backpack and grab a pair of dry socks to replace her wet ones. When she found two pairs, you would have thought she won a million dollars. She wore them both. Jessica and Joshua dug into their large rectangular camera trunks. There were four padded cloth tarps used to cover some camera and recording equipment. After digging out the coverings, they passed them around. Paul, who was the heftiest, moved to sit next to Shauna and shared the blanket tarp with her. Shauna was happy to learn that his body heat was better than the blanket. Jessica and Josh also shared one so Mr. Haugen and Rooter could each have their own.

The wind whipped around every angle of the bus and they all tried to push the feeling of utter despair out of their minds. They all sat near each other, even Rooter. The coldness had him with no appetite for either food or smokes. He tried to think about the truck that barreled down the road that he swerved and missed. He wondered if Ms. Kim had to suddenly stop to let the truck pass and then couldn't start the bus back up. He blamed whatever vehicle was behind him for not stopping to help her. He would never admit this was his fault. He wasn't even scheduled to work this weekend. He thought he should be at home with his two roommates who appreciated him. Luckily, his roommates had a food and water dispenser and a kitty litter box that he emptied before he headed out that day.

Inside, Mr. Haugen felt like he was suffocating. He had never experienced this feeling before and thought he was having a heart attack. His body was numb from his thoughts and he didn't feel as cold as the others because the chill wasn't on his mind. The faces of each child that boarded the bus occupied his mind.

The bus was silent. The snow covered the sky to the ground and there was no visibility. The whole event had everyone on the bus drifting off in a nap. Sleeping for Shauna was difficult because her body wouldn't stop shivering, so she half slept and half dreamt about her toasty heating blanket that she turned on before hopping into bed at night.

The quietness was interrupted by gasps for breath. He couldn't breathe anymore, he was suffocating. The only thing you could hear now was the wind holler and Mr. Haugen wheezing for his last breath.

Saturday, November 28th
Chapter 13 The National Guard

First Sergeant Maxson, from the Mobile Maintenance Company (MMC) and Sergeant Major Sharp from the Tracking and Capabilities Command (TACC) called everyone on their personnel rosters and nobody had chains on their vehicles. More than half of them didn't even own a car. They took the subway or a cab to the drill site. There were two soldiers that First Sergeant Maxson couldn't get a hold of that were housemates, Chauncy and Tolbert. They were young, hard partiers, and he didn't hold out on any hope talking to those yokes (as he often referred to them) once he did. Maxson just needed to check a box to say that he reached all of his personnel.

Maxson and Sharp reported their personnel status up the chain of command, who in turn updated the governor. They both were under a lot of pressure to get someone to their garages on the drill site.

The subways were running on a storm schedule, which only moved back and forth to the underground stations. Many stranded workers who just got off shift, couldn't get home. Taxicab service halted. Cars were stuck in snow banks all over the major city. The streets of New York City held only winds and snow. Due to the lack of notification, there were only two snow plows in the city and one could barely tell that they were doing their job at all. The snow would just pile behind them as they shoved it forward into a bank. Most people in the city evacuated their work sites or social events and headed home after the first six inches hit. History was their guide to knowing that the city shuts down in blizzards. Some were in denial even after six inches of snow telling friends that it will subside soon. Those in denial were now stuck in places they would rather not be.

First Sergeant Maxson and Sergeant Major Sharp wanted the glory of finding those New York City students. They both harassed all of their enlisted personnel on the roster. They both wanted someone to buck up and get to the drill site.

Unfortunately, Maxson was home watching his granddaughter of six months while his wife was stuck at the hospital working. His daughter and son-in-law went to Atlantic City for the weekend, so he was in charge. Every time Maxson yelled into the phone at one of his soldiers, the baby would giggle uncontrollably, which took away from his threatening First Sergeant man card.

The mayor, the governor, and Mr. Jekel were all apprised of the situation as were the parents, families, and the ever-forgiving media. There would be no hope of a search and rescue that day.

Chapter 14 Last Breath

Everyone could hear Mr. Haugen gasping for air, but Shauna was the most awake and alert. She instantly went to his seat and tried to help him.

"Mr. Haugen, are you OK?" Shauna asked in a panic. "What can I do?!"

Joshua jumped into action moving Shauna out of the way. He looked Mr. Haugen in the eyes and grabbed his upper arms straight on, staring him in the eyes.

"Mr. Haugen, follow my breathing pattern," instructed Joshua as he took a deep inhale and held it, and then exhaled. "Keep breathing with me."

Mr. Haugen nodded and tried to take deep inhales but exhaled right away and then fell back into panting again. Josh coached him into another deep inhale until Mr. Haugen finally caught the rhythm and slowed down his breathing. After a minute Mr. Haugen coughed a few times and was back to normal breathing.

"Are you asthmatic?" Joshua asked him.

"Not that I have ever known," replied Mr. Haugen in exhaustion. "I just felt a tightness in my chest and then my breathing went sideways."

"Oh my gosh, you just had a heart attack," Jessica said stunned.

"No," Joshua corrected her. "More like a panic attack. They can be similar, but Mr. Haugen doesn't have a history of heart disease, so I am sure it's just the stress of the day."

"You think?" Mr. Haugen said sarcastically. Everyone knew that Haugen was as fit as a fiddle from all of the city walking and because he bragged about taking no meds and having no histories of diseases at his age.

"Nonetheless, I feel like you should get medical attention as soon as possible," Shauna insisted as her breath could be seen frosting in the air.

"Sure, as soon as Santa and his elves pick us up and take us to a warm hospital," Mr. Haugen snapped back. "Thank you, Josh, for bringing my oxygen level back up. How did you know what to do?"

"Believe it or not, I was pre-med, before I changed to horticulture," Josh stated. "I did some runs with a paramedic team and saw many panic attacks."

Mr. Rooter just watched and observed. He thought about what would've happened if Haugen had died. This made him rethink smoking and drinking, at least for the next few minutes.

It was dark out and the wind and snow were still blowing hard, but the bus was past the point of going anywhere even if it had a full tank of gas. The wind had blown the snow to block the exits out the front or back door. They settled on eating snacks that they packed for the trip. Everyone shared peanuts, pretzels, granola bars, and water. As they ate in silence, they heard howling, but this wasn't the wind. It was difficult to make out, but Joshua noticed something moving about outside. Everyone observed Joshua's stare and they got up to see what could take his attention to his side of the bus. As they looked out a small portion of the window, they saw it too. A pack of wolves slipped in and out of the snow, banging the bus with their bodies and howling. They wanted a snack too.

Sunday, November 29th
Chapter 15 The Chores

The next morning someone gently shook Arcado awake. He was sound asleep from the hard day that almost made him non-existence. At first, he didn't feel a thing, so Jesse shook him harder until he awoke. Arcado forgot that he wasn't in his warm, safe bed, but now out in some woods in upper New York. This thought disturbed him and he protested getting up before the sun had risen to help with chores. But Jesse wasn't leaving and Arcado found himself doing the right thing, as usual.

Milking Cows

The cow and goat milking group gathered in the vestibule, gathered the pails, and dressed smartly in cloaks, hats, boots, and gloves. There were 11 of them total, which worked out nicely with the 33 animals to milk. In one swift motion, the doors were yanked open and the milking crew headed single file into the predawn darkness that was lightened by only the white earth. Jesse went first to block the fierce wind and make a trail so others could follow. For Arcado and Ms. Kim, it was so ridiculous to be out in this weather. To others, it was just part of being self-sufficient.

Jesse opened the barn doors and held them open until all were through. Once inside, the only things that weren't present were the snow and wind. It was still below zero and the chill hit everyone even inside.

"The sooner we start, the sooner we finish," Jesse remarked in a loud voice.

At that, everyone went to it and grabbed a stool and sat down low on the cow's left side. Ms. Kim thought it was like riding a bike and started squeezing one teat and then the next. Arcado knew the premise of milking but never had done so. Jesse came to his side after he sat on his stool by the cow. Arcado took his gloves off and blew his hot breath on his hands like he watched everyone else do and then he started squeezing one and then the other of the cow's udders. Jesse stepped in just to correct him a little and showed him that squeezing and pulling down helps the milk come out more. As much as Arcado didn't want to be there, one thing for sure was that his cow warmed up his numb hands. Some citizens milked so fast that they took on the extra cows and goats and finished milking both by the time Arcado had milked his one.

They completed it within 30 minutes and were set to carry the milk to the mess hall. Arcado stood up and looked his cow in the eye after he finished. He wanted to show appreciation to her after she gave her all into his pail. He petted her by her ears.

"Thank you, Bretta," Arcado said aloud.

"Why Bretta?" Ms. Kim inquired in her sassy way.

"Well, my Great Aunt Bretta is the only big girl I know besides this one," said Arcado with a smile.

"At least ya' didn't call ya' cow Ms. Kim," she chuckled after she said it.

"No, Ms. Kim, you're slender compared to my great aunt," explained Arcado and then he quietly thought, "and you're not as kind."

"Goodbye, Eun," Ms. Kim said to her cow and then patted her on the head.

"Who is Eun?" Arcado inquired back.

"Oh, just one of my honorable, olda', richa' family members who is skinnier den' a toot'pick, but gets milked by all of her kids," she chuckled.

Everyone put their gloves on and carried their milk until they reached the barn doors. They braced for Jesse to open the doors. Soon enough they were back into the mighty winds that were trying to rob the residents of the liquid that rocked from side to side in their pails. They sluggishly walked single file again until they reached the mess hall.

When the door opened, the cooks were already inside awaiting the milk drop. The pails were passed through the doors quickly and the milkers went back for one more milk haul. After the third drop-off, they all continued back to their sleeping quarters.

Arcado shook off the chill and crawled back into bed. With just the little bit of work he did, he was exhausted in one way, but his adrenaline was pumping in other ways. As he was trying to find his comfortable sleeping position, the others started clamoring to begin their chore routine.

The guys on the second floor could hear the ladies on the third floor shuffling about as the floor creaked above them. Everyone was changing from pajamas to their everyday clothes. The lanterns were on and conversations were growing loud. Arcado was still happy he was in a warm and comfortable bed, but sleeping was definitely out of the question.

Hunter/Gatherer

Soon Vlad and Sergei met up with Wanda and their group to head out to hunt. They were first guided into the gym where Travis spent 25 minutes giving instructions on how to hold a spear, shoot a slingshot or twirl a bolo. They went over all the "do's" and "don'ts" of hunting. Travis handed each their hunting apparel. Their outside clothes were slightly different from the cloaks they normally wore. They suited up in what looked like black snowmobile suits with an orange patch on the back and the front for hunter visibility. They also wore black ski masks, which Vlad and Sergei put on first, laughing and pretending they were Lucha libre wrestlers. These suits were warm and form-fitting.

All the hunters gathered by the door. Travis gave a spear to all the younger ones and a rifle to the older and experienced ones. Wanda was the only female hunter. She grabbed her spear and turned to face the crowd.

"Wanda Womack," she said with one hand on her hip and one holding the spear ground up. "Yeah, that's right, like Wanda Woman, but better. Let me at those animals, I will jab one in a jiff. Hey, do you have a lasso? Wanda Woman uses a lasso."

"I'm afraid these are the only hunting tools we have," Travis said. "Also, please be careful. There have been mountain lions and bears that sneak up on us sometimes. Always stay with a partner."

Travis pointed toward the men behind him. "We are going to the edge of the woods. We generally find rabbits or deer there. We motion with our hands if we see something. Animals are keen on noise and our body smells, so we try to take them before they hear or smell us," Travis said as he opened the door to the snowy landscape.

Wanda tried to lift her arm to sniff and make sure the deer wouldn't smell her coming, but the suit made it difficult to maneuver. It was a little tight on her, but she thought she looked hot in it. She smiled at the twins as she showed off her curves. The twins nodded to her and muttered the word "bumpy" in Spanish.

It was still dark outside and the whipping, wild winds had stopped blowing. The snow had drifted here and there but it wasn't impossible to walk in like the day previous. It was calm, cold, and white everywhere with the snow measuring up to some of their hips. The front men plowed through the snow with their bodies making a trail for the others to follow.

It took significant effort to wade through the feet of snow, but they finally arrived at the tree line in the woods. Travis motioned for half the team to break off and go to the south, and then he motioned for the other group to go north. He and two others would stay central with Vlad, Sergei, and Wanda. Travis took his binoculars out and started searching in the woods and around the perimeter. Wanda felt adventurous and took steps inside the tree line and peaked around the woods. Sergei and Vlad followed her to make sure she didn't get into trouble.

Wanda thought it looked darker and scarier the further she went in, so she turned around and started walking out of the forest. Vlad and Sergei suddenly stood frozen in place staring beyond her as if a boogeyman were there. Wanda saw the look on their faces.

"What?" she asked and stopped in her tracks but then thought she would have some fun. "Ah, is there a mountain lion or a bear behind me? Because if there is, they better run before I show them the wrath of Wanda Woman."

In one move, she turned around and gave the loudest growl you ever heard from a girl or, for that matter, a grown man. Unbeknownst to Wanda, a big black bear was standing directly behind her. After her loud outburst, the bear turned and scampered back into the darkness. Wanda, in shock, fell to the ground, passed out cold.

Travis and the men ran into the woods and found Sergei and Vlad on the ground tending to Wanda, trying to wake her. Wanda opened her eyes and found that she was surrounded by five men, and for a minute her memory lapsed of why they were giving her so much attention. She could see their lips moving to ask different questions, but for the first time, she had no answers. Sergei and Vlad could see her struggling to speak and comprehend the situation.

"Wanda, are you fine?" Vlad asked with his eyebrows raised in concern. She looked him in the eyes and then smiled.

"That's right, I heard you. Wanda fine. Yer' right," she heard what she wanted to hear and she was back to her normal self. "Help me up boys, we need to go chase Yogi."

"I think you've had enough hunting for the day," exclaimed Travis. "Charlie and the twins will help you back to the quarters."

When they were assisting Wanda off the ground, they heard a gunshot a few clicks south as several dozen birds fluttered out of the top of the forest. They all tugged and yanked Wanda to her feet. They ran out of the woods, dragging Wanda with them, to see what was happening. In the distance, Travis could see his men using rope to tie a tarp around something.

Soon enough, the men marched through the snow dragging a deer wrapped inside a canvas. Only the antlers were poking through at the top. The two men in the front pulled a thick rope that was attached. They all walked to the central path where they met up with the remaining hunters and headed toward the town. Just as they were nearing the back of the mess hall where the meat shed was kept, the winds picked up fiercely. The hunters went back to the living quarters.

As they pushed through the doors of the lodging hall, Travis collected the spears, slingshots, and guns from the crew that came through the entryway. Wanda and the boys were peeling off their snowsuits when the other groups came through and finished with their morning chores.

Shoe Cobbling

In the shoe cobbling shop, Adam sat there with four other cobblers. They inquired about Darcy's whereabouts.

"I am afraid she isn't coming," Adam declared. "Rumor is that she needed more sleep."

"Thank you, Adam," the head cobbler, Harvey, replied. "We'll have someone make sure she is OK."

They began their cobbling, showing Adam how to pull the sturdy leather fabric onto a form and stitch the fabrics together. One of the cobbler women went to look for Darcy.

The room was quiet and dark and Darcy enjoyed catching up on sleep after her body went through the trauma of the bus crash and freezing water. She was used to being an only child with nobody to answer to, nobody issuing chores or bossing her around. In the middle of her perfect reflection of slumber, she heard a door slam and someone approaching.

"Darcy?" the older cobbler asked. "Are you ready to do your work for the day?"

At first, she didn't answer. She didn't want the accountability. Knowing the old lady wouldn't leave, she turned her head to look her in the eye.

"I'm too tired," she proclaimed. "I didn't sleep well last night."

"I believe Mr. Boyce let you know that we can't operate without all hands working," she said softly. "We need your help."

"No," said Darcy who kept it simple. "I'm not going anywhere. You can't make me."

Darcy put the cover over her head, hiding from the world. The older lady let her stew for about a minute.

"Well, I guess you will have to deal with the consequences then," she gently said. "No need to come to the mess hall today. There will be no food for you. It's plain and simple, we don't feed those who don't work."

Darcy was starting to feel a pang of hunger just when she heard she would get no food. Her meal wasn't abundant yesterday and now she craved a nice piece of toast with a pile

68

of jelly on it. She pulled the blanket off of her face and again was eye to eye with the cobbler.

"That's not fair," remarked Darcy. "I am a guest here. I didn't choose to be here, you guys rescued me."

"Your definition of unfair seems a little misplaced," the older lady's face seemed more and more patient and wiser by the moment. "If we allowed special treatment for only you in this village, that would be unfair."

"But I don't want to touch shoes," continued Darcy. "It's gross. Feet are gross."

"You could milk cows or sew," she replied reasonably.

"Yeah, right," complained Darcy. "Nobody should have to do these weird jobs. It's ridiculous."

"It's up to you," the cobbler all but whispered. "If you don't come within the next 15 minutes, you forfeit meals for today."

She departed. When the older lady returned to the cobbler shop, nobody even inquired as to what happened in the dormitory with Darcy. They were busy tightening up and stitching shoes. Adam was happy that he picked up this tradecraft rather quickly. He was making a men's ankle boot, size 11, for everyday wear.

Darcy sat up on her bed with a frown. She was not used to being treated so unfairly. School was always her main focus and as long as she got average grades and behaved, her parents left her alone. Nobody ever demanded more than that from her and she wasn't ready to be subservient to anyone, especially strangers. While she sat there brooding, her stomach started growling. She was only 110 pounds and never ate much, but the thought of eating lots of food now consumed her mind.

She thought about it and then a grin came over her face. The word sabotage popped into her head. She would go and make shoes, she thought. However, she would make them fall apart. It would be a win-win. They will see how bad of a shoemaker she was and she would still get to have some toast.

The cobblers stretched fabric here and there and made sure things on both sides were even before they stitched. As they were sewing away, Darcy cracked the door open and stepped in, and announced herself. The older lady cobbler gave her a slight smile and motioned for her to join Adam.

She showed Darcy how to pick the fabric and pull it over the form. She threaded her needle with the appropriate color of thick thread and demonstrated how to sew the seams. Darcy was making a women's size seven moccasin for the spring and summertime. The cobbler showed her what the end product would look like.

Darcy took a deep breath to try and get rid of the disdain she felt, but when she did the smell of new shoe leather and fabric filled her nostrils. Instead of a stinky shoe factory, this room was filled with an aroma of new clothes that she secretly liked. She reluctantly took the needle and pushed it through the fabric. The form allowed her to sew without stopping from joining the seams together. As hard as she thought about sabotage, she was trying to do her best to make the moccasin. After her seams came together, it was time to put the bottom of the sole onto the fabric. The older cobbler woman demonstrated how to do it. For Darcy, this was the hardest part and when she finished, she thought it looked all right, but not great.

She happened to be a size seven. The shoe fit, but Darcy knew that the sole could've been done way better. She picked up more fabric and made another one. This time, she was more meticulous about the soles and they looked better, but still not great. She was no longer on a mission of sabotage but oppositely, perfection.

Adam and Darcy struck up a conversation about how lucky they were to pick this task and that in no time, both of them would have flawless shoes. Even though Adam talked about improving his shoes, he had already done well. He had a knack for this task and felt like he found a substitute for his video games.

After Darcy finished another pair, she walked around looking at the different shoes and styles on the shelves in the back of the room. She wondered if they ever thought of making anything stylish for the girls and women to wear on a special night. There were only small, practical sole heels and nothing with a higher wedge, kitten, or stiletto heel. The materials were labeled on the shelves. There were boxes labeled sole, insole, outsole, midsole, heel and vamp, lining, tongue, quarter, welt, and backstay. The elder cobbler woman mentioned these words when she was giving instructions, but Darcy only remembered the steps and not the names of everything. But now she was ready to learn. She approached the elder lady and looked at her for another readied lesson.

Sewing

Shannon, Brianna, and Lauren never even threaded a needle before. When they got to their sewing duty station, there were two areas. The first area was manually hand-stitching items and the second area was full of sewing machines. The machines were the old fashion, manual kind where you would pump a device with your feet to make the arm go up and down. You could also spin it with your free hand on the side of the machine. It was more physical labor than the girls thought.

All three girls went to the head seamstress who showed them a pattern, the materials needed, and the mannequin to help the fitting process. They all took notes. Their first assignment was to take a pattern to the material and cut it out. The manual cutting process was tedious and their hands were cramping. Brianna enjoyed learning something new. She thought about how proud her mom would be to know that she had learned a skill set. She hoped she wouldn't criticize her for taking on a staple that was pigeonholed as "women's work". After she thought about it, there were almost more men, clothing designers, out there than women. Making a child's shirt would be the starting point. She hoped she would learn quickly how to make more things.

Lauren was tired after she cut the pattern. Shannon was re-cutting some pieces to make sure they exactly matched the pattern. The next step was to take the pieces and pin them. They had to line them up exactly to the seam. Brianna and Lauren matched, but Shannon had to recut the pattern again. She trimmed too much and the material got smaller and smaller until it was uneven to match up.

Within a few hours, they each made a wonky child's shirt. Brianna came the closest to an acceptable product. The other sewers, both men and women, congratulated them on a good day's work.

Firewood Gathering

Vaughn and Ryan put on the snowmobile-type suits similar to that of the hunters and then pulled on the full ski masks. Vaughn and Ryan laughed at each other when they put on the ski masks because they knew in their neighborhood, that this would have a totally different meaning. There were sleds with long wooden slats on top to hold the wood in place. It looked like a wagon on skis. There were buckets that held axes and machetes.

They went into the opposite woods that the hunters pursued. Wilbur waited until they were out in the wooded area and demonstrated how to handle the ax and machete safely. The machete was used more for the smaller branches. Both took a lot of effort to chop the wood into manageable haul sizes. Ryan used the machete which was a little less painful than swinging the ax. He injured his left elbow in the crashing bus ride down the ravine. He thought it felt good to work out the soreness, but mainly used his right hand to hack branches to a manageable size. Vaughn took to the ax. He used it like he was swinging a bat in baseball which was his second favorite sport to play.

Intently, he tried to chop the tree at the same point without deviation, which was hard. In the end, both boys chopped a good amount of wood.

The chopping action kept the men warm. They stopped chopping when all of the sled buckets were full. This caused both pleasure and pain. It was nice to head back to the town with the workload, but painful because of the sweat build-up. The torturous wind froze their sweat.

All in all, the chores took a few hours for everyone to finish. Hunger crept up and they couldn't wait to hit the chow line. All through breakfast, the students anxiously talked about their first time doing these types of chores. The volume of talking was elevated at their table and the other students smiled as they enjoyed having these young visitors understand their way of life. Everyone nearly fell off their chair laughing listening to Vlad and Sergei tell the story about Wanda and the black bear. She owned it and laughed along with the group.

The students went back to their lodging to relax. Outside, it started snowing and blowing again. As they looked through their window, they knew there was no hope of returning today or tomorrow. They wished this place had some sort of radio so they could figure out the forecast. They thought today was different and exciting but were still ready to go home to their families. Their guts told them that maybe they should all attend the Sunday service and pray that they make it home soon.

Sunday, November 29th
Chapter 16 Stranded

It was sunup or rather eight o'clock in the morning when Rooter fell off of his seat onto the floor. The noise startled the gardeners. They all found a way to sleep through the chill, the wind, and the howling wolves. There were only a few windows that they could see out of clearly, most were frozen over, not to mention their breaths fogged the insides of them too.

Mr. Haugen had to scrub at the window before he was able to see that the wolf pack was gone. Everyone stood up to stretch and twist away all the pain in their necks and backs. It was not a comfy sleep for anyone.

A buzz could be heard through the snow whistling. Everyone stood still to hear the buzzing noise. At first, they thought it was a chainsaw, but the noise drew nearer. In an instant the lively clamor was loud and then it ceased.

Someone - or something - was brushing on the front door. The bus riders didn't know if they should be frightened or elated. Paul was the brave one and went to see what the commotion was at the door. He put a scowl on his face and stood in a fierce stance to attack whatever crept up to the door. He didn't mess around.

Soon, the door was cleared and there was an older couple with snowsuits, hats, mittens, and goggles knocking at the door.

It took both, Paul and Josh, to push the lever to open the door. The couple climbed the bus stairs, bringing with them the snow and wind.

"How many of ya's are in there?" the woman asked.

"Six of us," Paul responded curiously.

"Well we each can get two of ya's on at a time," she said impatiently to get back to warmth. "We'll have to come back for the last two."

Before anyone could say a word, Rooter grabbed his satchel and was out the door sitting on a snowmobile. Paul and Joshua volunteered to stay and the others grabbed their gear and headed outside.

"It's just up the road, so it won't take long," the old man said slowly.

Off they went. They were in so much pain with the cold and the wind on their face, but they kept reminding themselves that warmth was around the corner. The boys were picked up next. In no time they were all soaking wet in front of a fireplace inside a semi-warm house.

"I guess introductions are in order," the old woman said cheerfully. "I am Myra and this is Valley – short for Valentine."

Mr. Haugen introduced everyone and thanked the couple for their rescue.

"Yeah, we didn't see ya's until I woke up this morning and saw a big yeller thing sticking out of the snow," Myra said pointing out of the window. "We both thought maybe there were children on the bus, so we got dressed as soon as we could."

"The electricity is out too," Valley said in a serious tone. "We have a generator, but we try to conserve it for the ice box. There are no lights in the house, but we have candles, two flashlights, and one lantern. We have a fireplace and a wood-burning pellet stove in our bedroom and on the opposite end of this room. We have a second bedroom, but no heat, just blankets."

"Ya see, we are used to losing electricity out here," Myra explained nonchalantly. "Bad storms hit in the summa' or in the winter, so over the years we prepared."

"The plumbing still works and the stove is operated by propane," informed Valley. "We don't have a landline either and cell service only works occasionally."

"I am making fresh scrambled eggs and cheese toast for you this morning," Myra said and smiled, then turned to make it.

"Thank you," came from everyone but Rooter.

"Do you brew coffee at all?" Rooter asked in a bad mood, smirking.

"Does a wolf howl at the moon?" Myra joked back.

"I dunno," Rooter replied irritated because he honestly didn't.

"Of course, we have coffee," Valley chuckled. "We'll put the brew on and step outside for a little smoke and then come back in to drink some joe."

Rooter's ears perked up as did his eyebrows. His appetite for life returned in those magical words and he suddenly felt social. While Rooter and the owners went out to smoke in the blizzard, Haugen and his team assembled for a meeting. They all stood in a circle in the family room by the fire and began the discussion.

"Boss, believe me when I say that I am grateful to be here and not on that bus, but this feels a little Twilight Zone-ish for me," Paul said darkly.

"Yeah, this is definitely going to take some adjusting," Shauna remarked in agreement. "But I'm not shivering to death."

"Let's try and make the best of this. We do owe them a lot of gratitude. I think we have to come up with a plan for once the snow stops," commanded Mr. Haugen dutifully. "With limited electricity, we can try and charge our phones. Although, I know service out here is still bleak. They do have snowmobiles, so maybe Paul and Josh could get to a nearby gas station to use a landline phone."

"I hope those poor kids got as lucky as we did," Jessica said, shivering at the thought of being back on the bus.

"Knowing Ms. Kim, she probably carried every kid to safety," Mr. Haugen hyperbolized. "She is a tough cookie."

They all were convinced that the kids had some type of rescue, so they focused on their mission.

"When this blizzard lifts, what's our next move to pick out the Christmas tree?" Joshua asked, devoted to the idea of work.

"Well, it's getting too late to make another weekend trip," Haugen replied. "And because we lost the kids, we're not going to be able to have them decide."

Out of nowhere, Paul started laughing. Then Jessica and Shauna joined in, and finally, Joshua and Haugen rolled up laughing so hard they started crying.

"We lost the kids," Jessica blurted but could hardly get the sentence out laughing.

"All of them," Shauna added amused in laughter.

"Oh boy, are we in trouble," cracked Joshua and laughed more heartily.

They laughed for a good while until they could all breathe normally again.

"We are so screwed," Paul said in a serious tone.

"Nobody is screwed," Mr. Haugen assured him. "Perhaps, I might be, but I fault nobody but myself."

"And Rooter," Joshua sarcastically added.

At that, the wind flung the door open and the three of them stomped in. Myra had gathered a dozen eggs in a carton from the nearby coop. Her pride and joy was keeping the chicken coop warm and full of light in the winter. While this had been more of a challenge lately, she was proud that Valley's invention worked. He bought a heat lamp that both warmed and added light to the coop, which was needed for the hens to lay their eggs. Valley figured out a way to change the power to work off of batteries instead of electricity.

"I can smell that coffee," Rooter said merrily. The sweet relief of smoking a cigarette after going so long without one had made him chatty. "Can I pour anyone a cup?"

"No, go on and help ya' self," Myra said in a friendly tone. "We can fend for ourselves."

One by one, everyone helped themselves to a cup of coffee. It warmed up their insides, so they felt almost normal again. Valley made another pot, which would soon be emptied again. Myra started on the scrambled eggs. Jessica and Shauna felt the maternal urge to help Myra, so they did.

By this time, it was late morning, so they all sat down and ate brunch together. They became more acquainted by recounting the story of why the gardeners were in upstate New York and how they had gotten stuck. They told the couple about the children and how important it was to find them as soon as the Nor'easter lifted. The couple knew the sheriff in town and would contact him at the first available opportunity. All and all, each of Haugen's staff knew the couple was a little strange, yet hospitable, nonetheless.

After the dishes were cleaned up, try as they may continue their meeting, every one of them fell asleep in the family room;

some in chairs, some sitting on the couch, and some relaxing on the floor. Apparently, the caffeine couldn't overcome the stress from the bus.

Sunday, November 29th
Chapter 17 The Mayor and the Governor

Mitch Jekel had the mayor of New York on speed dial and had already spoken with him several times. In turn, the mayor was in constant communication with the governor. While New York City was assaulted by the blizzard, the mayor thought surely the storm upstate had subsided; however, the governor assured him that Albany and everything in between was still a windy blanket of snow. He couldn't even see his bird feeder 10 feet from his kitchen window.

The governor was on speed dial with the commanding officers for the TACC and the MMC Regiments in New York City. He also talked to the Army Reserve Unit in Albany. So far, because of the lack of notice of the blizzard, nobody could make it to the armories. They were in their warm homes looking out their windows waiting for an emergency vehicle to pick them up so they could execute the recovery mission. That never happened.

No car was able to drive to the Reserve Centers without getting stuck in the snow. The only vehicles that could handle this weather were dry inside the garages of the TACC and MMC. The Army Reserves in Albany had a few all-terrain vehicles, but they were in the shop being serviced. They were normally deployed in January or February, sometimes even March, but had never been used in November and rarely in December.

Jekel had his assistant make a website for posting information about his continuous efforts to find the children. His assistant emailed all the families once he finished making the website, so they could check on the updates. There was also a section for asking questions or posting a comment.

Soon, the press got wind of the missing students and made it their second story after the blizzard. Jekel knew the students were OK because they were with Cyril, who was resourceful and conservative. He had a hunch they were buckled down in a cheap hotel waiting out the snow, or at least he hoped it was cheap, he didn't want to pull too much out of the budget to cover it.

The hottest news in town was the blizzard. The governor and the mayor pressed the television studios to get personal updates on any changes to the weather. Unfortunately, the forecast was that the Nor'easter was going to bear down on the northeast for days to come.

Sunday November 29th
Chapter 18 Sunday Service

After eating and relaxing, everyone scampered down to the hall where the Sunday service takes place. Some of the students had never been to church, some only on important holidays, and some like Brianna and Vaughn were practically raised in the church.

After shuffling through the white tundra just to go about 50 yards to the building, they decloaked the snow and their winter capes. Music was the first thing they all noticed. There was an adult choir with all ethnicities and religions singing. It wasn't based on one religion, but on popular songs to uplift one's soul.

The citizen's grabbed the first rows of seats near the stage where the choir and band were. The students sat and blended in with the other residents their age. There were sheets of music in the vestibule that the students grabbed in case they wanted to sing along. Vaughn was mimicking the sounds of the bass drum and nodding his head. He and his dad normally played in the church choir band. His dad played anything brass and Vaughn either played piano or electric guitar.

Brianna liked the music. She and her aunt were in her church choir and they did some heavy gospel singing for hours every Sunday. After a few songs, a reverend got up and read a verse from the bible's New Testament. He then gave a pensive homily to support the words. It didn't last long, but nonetheless was impactful and then the choir was onto their next song.

After a song, a member would stand up and say something that inspired them this week. Many were thankful that Charlie had a bad memory, obligating him to climb back up the campanile for his harmonica, which led to the saving of the students. When the last song was sung and the service was over, Brianna, who was moved by the holy spirit, wanted to comment.

"Lord, I just wanted to thank you for this village and the members who saved us," said Brianna in a grateful tone.

The students nodded, feeling the same.

"Lord, may you lift this blizzard and return us safely too," Brianna said and then sat back down.

All the students nodded in agreement. Darcy, who had never attended a service before, thought that this wasn't as bad as she thought it would be. She thought going to church meant people speaking in Latin and singing old songs played on a stuffy organ. This was contemporary and the students were glad they went. They all noticed that Ms. Kim didn't make it this morning. The students were getting tired of her skepticism. They knew they only had a few days there and wanted to fit in until they could go home.

After the service, they went to the mess hall. The students were already familiarized with the community's routine of going through the line, eating, and then heading to a wash station to clean their dishes and wipe the table.

On Sundays after lunch, it was all free time until dinner. The students headed back to their dormitory and started getting to know the other students.

A fifteen-year-old named Christopher introduced himself and talked about the summer when they had to plant the crops. He admitted that the work was steady but told them stories of the fun they all had as a group. He told them how Ourstory was in its prime in the summer with fishing, swimming, and playing all kinds of sports. The other boys gave their summer accounts of Ourstory and the Mini-Olympics that were held every late August.

Someone brought up Major League Baseball and asked who the New York students thought were the best ball players. There was quite a huff between Vaughn and the López twins who disagreed on the best hitter. Christopher remembered favoring Betts, Turner, and Trout a few years ago. Baseball was Christopher's hobby before he came to Ourstory. He missed it every day, man the things he would do for a portable transistor radio to listen to a game in the summertime. He loved tracking any team he could get on his radio, normally the New York and Pittsburgh teams.

A tinge of jealousy was building in Christopher. Baseball was the one thing that took his mind off growing up in the system and not having any blood family to call his own. He grew up an orphan. He loved immersing himself in the announcers play by play calls and the excitement in their voices when a player would hit a home run. After intently listening to the announcers rattle off players' stats, he cataloged them on a score sheet and then analyzed how he would have them bat. He envied that these guys would leave soon and go back to their loving families and have access to things he treasured. He kept his cool composure throughout their conversations but planted inside were his own dreams of leaving this place.

While the boys were talking, Arcado noticed that two rooms at the back of the floor had their doors closed. He wondered if some guardian slept there to make sure they didn't get into any mischief, but he didn't recall seeing anyone enter it. He walked over to one room and he could hear someone moving around inside.

"Best if you just leave the room alone," said Charlie assertively. "You shouldn't disturb what's in there."

Charlie was a dark-haired, dark-skinned boy, originally from Pakistan. He looked to be around Arcado's age. Despite Charlie's warning, Arcado could not let it go.

"So... Do you keep a caged madman in there?" questioned Arcado, dying of curiosity. "Or is this a room for just the privileged who can't be bothered sleeping in a bunk bed with 30 other cats like us?"

"No, it's nothing like that," Charlie tried to change the subject. "Do you play any sports or have any hobbies?"

"Yeah," Arcado went back to it. "Guessing mysteries."

Charlie knew he was never going to give up but didn't think it was his place to talk about what was in the room, so he walked away.

Arcado, knowing he wasn't going to get anything out of Charlie, walked back to the boys arguing over the biggest fish caught and who had done so. Another resident boy, David who just turned 12, asked question after question about living in the city. Vaughn and Adam fielded the answers to most of the questions. The twins loved hearing about farming from another group of boys.

On the girl's floor, Bianca introduced herself. She was the leader of the group, even though there were a few older teenagers. Lauren was intimidated by her but knew that Brianna had her back.

At first, Bianca came across as mean and preachy about not touching other people's stuff. But after she laid out the rules, she softened up and the girls all went around the room and introduced themselves and a fun fact for an ice breaker.

The older girls wanted to know what was popular in the world now and for some reason, Wanda seemed to be the spokesperson for their group.

"Zombies," she said without a thought. "Zombies that eat you, zombies that chase you, and even zombies that fall in love. It's all about the zombies."

Shannon was about to disagree with Wanda, but she found it oddly true. Even Darcy talked about how she dressed like one just last month for Halloween. She admitted that her best friend did her makeup and thought she looked like the zombie in the last love story movie. Lauren didn't talk about zombies because the thought of them scared her, especially out in an isolated place.

The conversation got Brianna heated. She talked about everyone she would bite if she were the queen zombie. This included the chauvinistic store owner down her street. The resident girls listened to their new roommates go back and forth on whom they would bite and whom they would save. All in all, it wasn't what the girls, who hadn't seen a big city in a few years expected to hear, but all the same listened intently.

The topic flipped into biting as a vampire versus biting as a zombie. Then it took a romantic turn into biting the hottest movie stars or singers. Most agreed they would bite Harry Styles, the Hemsworth brothers, Michael B. Jordan, and Manny Jacinto. Wanda threw in the López twins, but that was no surprise to anyone. The resident girls didn't know some of the famous guys but agreed that if they had to live forever it may as well be with a hot guy.

They all talked and laughed until dinner. While everyone built up an appetite, they didn't look forward to bundling up to walk a few feet to the mess hall. Because the students started to get to know their floormates, they all intermixed at dinner, talking to different people for the first time. Lauren stuck by Brianna but opened up a little when the other girls asked her questions about New York City or her home life.

Again, after dinner, they went back to the lodging building for playtime. Ryan looked for the mean girl, Bianca. He didn't want her confronting him again. On the court, the usual guys were shooting around including Christopher and Charlie. Bianca was nowhere in sight. Ryan took his three-point shots as Vaughn tossed him the ball and rebounded. Vaughn was a strong point guard and his ball-handling skills were good, but his shooting skills needed improvement. It was Vaughn's turn to shoot and he stood around the free-throw line. Ryan looked around the gym, once more for Bianca, and didn't see her. He approached Vaughn and backed him up to the three-point line.

"Dude, you know I can't make the throw to the basket," Vaughn looked him in the eye and thought Ryan was being cruel.

"Do you mind if I give you a few pointers?" Ryan asked earnestly and then looked once more, triple checking that Bianca was not around.

"Uh, sure, but remember, I am not you," Vaughn explained elementarily.

"OK, hold the ball over your head," said Ryan, demonstrating without a ball. Vaughn held the ball with two hands over his head as instructed. "Now jump straight up and release the ball with this hand and follow through after you release it."

Vaughn had never tried to shoot a three-pointer in the way shown. He always brought it up from his stomach and made an arc to get the height. He did as was instructed and the ball was short of the net by about five feet.

"Nah, man it's no good," Vaughn said hopelessly. "I can't shoot like you, I'm not that tall."

"I have been shooting this way since I was smaller than you," Ryan jibbed. "I just watched my brother and perfected my shot. Try it again but try snapping your wrist at the height of your jump."

Vaughn repeated the steps as he tried again. He released the ball and this time it almost went in.

Ryan gave Vaughn a fist pump. For the next half hour, Ryan fed Vaughn the ball and he made about 50% of his three-point shots. Ryan wasn't sure what feeling was inside his stomach. On one hand, Vaughn was sopping up his advice and it was working, making him feel relieved and a tinge proud, but on the other hand, he hated that he would have a burden to care for other team players by doing the same for them. He thought that this could make him look weak or worse, make his game look average. He hungered for being the best and looking unmatched by any other player, especially anyone on his team. Weighing the decision to be a leader with being the best player would require more thinking.

Darcy and Adam noticed that the head shoe cobbler, Harvey, was doing magic tricks for the young kids in a corner by the art table. They sat on the blue mats and Harvey had a small table with a black cloth over it. He continuously pulled out a blue scarf from his hand that seemed to pile up on the floor and then it turned orange. The little ones loved Harvey's magic. Adam and Darcy watched in amazement as he performed other tricks with his black top hat. This drew the attention of Shannon and Lauren who joined the crowd.

Brianna played cards again with the adults, the twins tried their luck at chess with Adam's friends, and Wanda jumped rope again. Wanda had the fastest and tightest footwork. She dominated the rope as usual.

When it was time to head back to the sleeping quarters, there was nothing but loud talking on all floors. Everyone was excited about making new friends. The village kids hung onto every nuance happening in New York City. Wanda showed the girls the new dance moves to songs they never heard before. She had them doing the shuffle in no time. Everyone wanted to learn it, even if there was no music playing. Darcy explained how the smoky eye with neutral lipsticks was all the rage. Brianna talked about the different cities that she traveled to in the last few years to attend rallies.

On the boy's floor, Christopher explained to Sergei the fishing that happened in the fast-moving rapids. Vlad listened to a seven-year-old talk about chess strategies. Ryan and Adam described Time Square to David and others who liked the city. Vaughn was beatboxing and showing Charlie how to rap and rhyme while Arcado watched. Charlie excused himself to use the restroom and this had Arcado scheming. He sat quietly, imagining what life would look like here. In the midst of his daydream, he realized that the door to the mystery room was ajar. A chill pricked his neck and his heart raced as he remembered the conversation with Charlie earlier, and his stern warning to keep out. Without even realizing it, Arcado found himself right in front of the door. It was as if he had no control over his body and was being moved over there by pure curiosity and the desire to solve the mystery. He knew that any minute Charlie would return and scold him for being mischievous, it was now or never. Arcado took a deep breath and then quickly slipped inside the room. His eyes widened in shock as he discovered what was waiting for him on the other side.

Chapter 19 Discoveries

"Ms. Kim, wait up," called out Mr. Boyce who jogged a little to make sure she didn't disappear into her chambers for the night.

"Yeah?" she asked curiously.

"I have in my hand some of the best mystery books in the library," he said out of breath and excited.

"Huh," she didn't want to sound disrespectful. "I don't read books. I am more of a, ya know, a TV gal."

"Oh but, I think you will like these," said Boyce like a salesman. "You see, if you don't have anything to do most of the time here, you might go a little stir-crazy. Reading helps me focus and think of all the possibilities."

She looked at him as if he were a crazy countryman with no appreciation for the city girl in her. She took both books from him as a kind gesture and also so he would leave her alone.

"Thanks for da' books," she said, fibbing. "If I think I am going stir crazy, I'll crack one open, how 'bout dat'?"

"That's fine, that's just fine," Boyce said smiling. "Oh, and if you want someone to discuss your theories on the killers in these novels, I'd be happy to hear them."

"Sure," Ms. Kim said unamused, and turned to head in for the night.

As she was settling into bed, Ms. Kim's lantern flickered like it was begging her to use it to read a book. She had rarely gone to bed without noise from either the streets below or her TV blaring. As the silence deafened her ears, it became a little uncomfortable.

"Stir crazy indeed," she said as she opened her first murder mystery story.

Upstairs on the boy's floor, Arcado peered into the mystery room and saw a regular bed, rather than a bunk bed that the rest of the kids had, a table and a few chairs, a bookshelf filled with toy cars, and a nightstand with a lantern glowing on it. Standing right in the middle of the room was a boy all of seven years old that was smiling at Arcado. For most, this would have meant nothing, but there stood a four-foot replica of Arcado. This light-skinned boy had an afro relative to the size of Arcado's. His newly grown front teeth were gapped in the middle just like Arcado's used to be at that age. He ran his tongue across the top of his teeth where his braces sat tightly for over two years until just six weeks ago when he got them removed.

"Hey, I'm Gabriel," the little boy said with a smile. "Who are you?"

"Hey little man, my name is Arcado," he tried to give him a fist pump, but Gabriel wasn't sure what to do. "What are you doing in this room by yourself? Are you sick or something?"

As he was asking the question, Charlie walked in to see the two had already met.

"Arcado, did you wake him up?" scolded Charlie, who was protective of Gabriel.

"No, Charlie. I was up. I opened the door, it's all good," replied Gabriel kindly.

"Am I not supposed to be in here?" Arcado asked. "The door was open. That's the only reason I walked in here."

"No, you are welcome in here anytime," Gabriel said as if Arcado was his new best friend. "I don't get that many visitors, but Bianca did come to read with me tonight."

"Why do you get your own room?" Arcado asked in a gentle but direct way.

Charlie looked at Gabriel and the boy motioned for Charlie to leave and so he did.

"I have narcolepsy," Gabriel explained. "That's what Doc Marta tells me. I can't seem to stay awake for too long and it throws my whole sleeping schedule off. At times I am up from two o'clock in the morning and I fall asleep at five o'clock. Then I sleep until after breakfast and then I am up again."

"Do you ever eat or go to school?" Arcado asked assertively.

"Of course I eat," Gabriel chuckled as he answered. "Lately, Charlie brings me food after every meal. All because it's too cold to go outside right now. But I am homeschooled. I tried to go to class, but I just fall asleep suddenly out of nowhere. I guess they say I am too distracting."

"That's too bad," Arcado uttered, feeling sorry for him. "How does this happen? Is it hereditary or something?"

"I never knew my biological parents, so I don't know," Gabriel said and sighed. "Doc Marta says it has to do with my nervous system and some type of auto-immune problem. But I am a normal kid that does normal stuff, it's just that I can't control when I might lay my head down and crash. Charlie told me all about you guys on the bus and how you got here. That's so cool."

"Well, one thing is for sure, I am happy we are alive," said Arcado in a serious tone. "I really didn't think we were going to make it, and then out of nowhere, people from your village pulled us out."

"I am going to go brush my teeth now," Gabriel said and grabbed a towel and a little kit that held his toothbrush, toothpaste, and soap.

"Hey, Gabriel?" asked Arcado who couldn't stop thinking of their similarities.

"Yeah?" he responded as he was gathering his stuff.

"If you ever need someone to talk to or hang with, come get me," Arcado stated, feeling a strong connection to this stranger. "That is if I am not sleeping. I gotta' milk those dang cows early."

"That's kinda nice. Not too many of the guys say that to me. They say I have a wild imagination and talk crazily," Gabriel said and took off to brush his teeth.

Monday, November 30th
Chapter 20 Stress in NYC

By now the website created to update loved ones had 30 posts from families. Stressed out with no new information, Jekel ate lots of his wife's cookies until he felt nauseous. He had weak information about the mayor and governor of New York requesting assistance from the Army Reserve and National Guard units. He also admitted that they couldn't deploy until the storm let up a little and that they couldn't get to their battle stations.

There were posts of hope from Adam, Wanda, and Arcado's families, but that's where the optimism ended. There were doomsday posts from Lauren's mom and threats from Darcy's parents. Other parents made demands of unreasonable measures. The twin's mom posted a prayer to Saint Anthony of Padua, the patron saint of lost things. Even though it was in Spanish, the families got the idea.

Mr. Jekel used the website now as his platform and advised that he was keeping his cell open to only the mayor and the governor for updates, so he wouldn't be taking any more phone calls. This eased the burden of not having to make excuses to parents repeatedly. The parents saw this as him blowing them off. Jekel did update the website however, he was getting tired of writing the words "no new updates".

First Sergeant Maxson from the MMC called all his personnel to check if anyone's status had changed to get to the reserve site. An abundance of negative replies was received. He still couldn't get a hold of Chauncy and Tolbert, the two goof-ups in the unit. It didn't surprise him that the slackers were out of touch. His expectations of their helpfulness were low, but he couldn't report that he got a 100% response on his recall. This frustrated him to no end.

The Sergeant Major from the TACC had a similar status except he could report 100% of his troops could not make it to the reserve site. Looking outside in the miserable snowy wind, he only hoped that the students had some type of survival skills if they weren't already holed up in some cozy hotel.

Monday, November 30th
Chapter 21 First Day of School

After the morning chores were completed and breakfast was devoured, all of the students went to school. It was so different seeing kids of similar ages all sitting and taking instruction from one teacher. The classrooms were divided into ages. Ages 4-6, ages 7-10, ages 11-13, and ages 14-18 were in their own classrooms.

"My name is Mrs. Beersly, but you can call me Mrs. B," said the five-foot, middle-aged, pale, white-skinned woman with brown and graying hair. She stood confidently at the front of the class. "I don't tolerate tardiness, talking in class, or wisecracks. I do expect you to complete every assignment that I give you. I do expect you to ask questions if I am not clear. Do you understand?"

The students quickly answered "yes".

All of the New York City students sat near each other in the classroom. Shannon took to the teacher straight away. The teacher asked each student to give a little introduction about themselves, in which everyone had their take on what they disclosed, but Lauren nervously only stated her name, her age, and that she had a cat named Shamoo. Others were more elaborate. The day's lesson would be in English composition. The whole day concentrated on the sentence structure of a short story. The topic sentence, the body, and the conclusion.

They were given time in class to write a short story about a time when they learned something that stuck with them like an "aha" moment. Shannon wrote quickly. Everyone else needed to brainstorm. They were given 30 minutes to do so and then began writing. During this time, talking was allowed so the students could bounce ideas off each other. The twins laughed hard at many 'aha' moments, which made the others smile with anticipation of hearing their stories.

After the time expired, everyone was nose to paper writing their story. Darcy and Ryan struggled with their writing skills but had their ideas intact. Arcado had a collage of ideas that he had to talk to the teacher to whittle down to just one. Wanda had to be shushed for speaking everything she was writing.

All of the Ourstory kids couldn't wait to hear about the outside world and the stories that would soon be revealed. The writing continued with breaks in between. After the lunch period, the students stood and took turns reading their papers.

Shannon volunteered to go first and began to read hers aloud. The classroom was silent except for the wind hollering past the windows while the snow twirled fiercely in circles up and down the buildings.

Shannon confidently began her paper by explaining how she joined her parents at a distinguished professor's house for a party. Her sentence structure was impressive as she read on proudly reporting that she was the only child in attendance. She continued with her pointed remarks and even used some onomatopoeia and alliteration in her paper. She concluded that her "aha" moment was when she felt inspired to become a teacher from that part.

Everyone clapped at the end and nobody wanted to follow her amazing performance of writing. A few of the Ourstory kids went next. One explained how his "aha" moment was viewing the birth of a baby cow and the effort it took Mr. Boyce and the others to wrangle the infant beast out of the mother. Next was Bianca and she explained how the choir coach taught her how to use her diaphragm and belt out her song, so it didn't sound so timid. She demonstrated as she read. Ryan's eyebrows raised in distaste as he thought about how she liked to brag about herself.

Next, was Adam. He explained how he learned to code at a camp this past summer and then built a game on his computer. Since that camp, he had researched on his own how to add better graphics and improve the game. He mentioned how he couldn't wait to get back to it. Some thought it funny that that was why Adam wanted to get back to the city. Most wanted to get back to their loved ones, pets, a hot steamy shower, television, or their own bed. Arcado followed with heavy pauses for effect. He talked about saving electricity by making different efforts at home like turning off lights, unplugging appliances that weren't in use, and installing solar panels to help save the world. The Ourstory kids didn't think his tale was that big of a deal because they already lived that way.

Brianna acted like a preacher giving her speech. She ranted for a few minutes talking about the injustice of women making less money than men. Again, this was a topic too irrelevant for most of the students, so they yawned while she spoke. Darcy stood up and talked about how eating desserts could be disastrous for teenagers. Her mom stressed it to her constantly, but Darcy's tiny frame could have used a donut or three. Again, the Ourstory students weren't impressed by someone not eating sweets. They only got real desserts a few times a year.

Wanda read her paper full of dos and don'ts around relatives. The topic didn't meet the requirement, but it broke the mind-numbing that was happening in every seat. Laughter rolled throughout the class after every sentence. She told story after story about how she and her cousins got into so much trouble because they were overheard by this aunt or that uncle who told another aunt or uncle who finally told their parents. By the time the story would reach one of their parents, it cascaded into a bigger story than it ever was. She concluded that the moral of the story is to make sure no one is in the next room when you cause trouble.

Lauren followed by reading her paper as fast as she could and like a robot. She didn't look up once and after she was done, nobody remembered what she said. Ryan stood up and gave more of a demonstration than a story on how his brother taught him the three-point shot technique. He read the summary for points of clarity. When he finished, he caught sight of Bianca, and her face looked disappointed. He thought it was so frustrating that she judged him constantly. Because he had no sisters, and for that fact not even a mother, he brushed it off as maybe some girls were just impossible to please.

Vaughn stood up and out of nervousness began to push beats back and forth from his mouth like he was about to rap. A few girls giggled at him as he cleared his voice to begin. His "aha" moment came to him when he was feeling lonely one night. His dad taught him how to play several instruments, but the piano was his favorite. He explained how his mama moved out to cope with some issues and he experienced a lot of heartbreak from that. He would drown his sorrows by playing music. One Friday night he started writing words and generating notes on the piano, creating his first song. He spent the entire night and finished around 4 a.m. Expressing how he turned his pain into something meaningful was a feeling that he didn't get until later. He sat down after he read his paper and everyone pegged him as a deep guy. The resident girls shook their heads as if they wanted to hug him.

Finally, the twins went one after the other explaining how the kindness of the strangers among them was inspirational. They each had a different example, but the theme of their papers was the same. It was about their gratitude to the people of Ourstory. It was simple but heartfelt. As each boy read it aloud with their deep accent, it added to the endearment. By the end, you could feel the temperature in the room was full of warmth and high spirits.

It felt like a lifetime in class. In some ways, it was the best icebreaker the kids had ever had. The Ourstory students intermingled with the new students more and more.

At the end of class, everyone turned their paper in to be graded by their teacher. Mrs. B asked Shannon to stay behind for a moment for a small conversation.

"If I were to grade your paper right here and now, I would give you a C," said Mrs. B sternly.

"What?" asked Shannon in shock. "But mine has all the elements of composition in it. What reason could you give for a C?"

"It's not the writing, it's the content," said Mrs. B, seeing right through Shannon's practice of giving them what they want. "I think your writing is a little generic when it comes to content. I am just underwhelmed."

"Compared to the other students, I thought my content was good," admitted Shannon.

"But is it *your* best?" asked Mrs. B looking into Shannon's soul. "I don't know you all that well, but I think you can do so much more if you challenge yourself to be more creative."

"I don't see you calling other students out for having a lame paper," said Shannon defensively. "Why me?"

"The literary elements in your paper are praiseworthy for sure," Mrs. B continued, "But I want to push you to be more creative. I believe you have the potential to be one of the best writers for someone your age if you could only be true to yourself."

Shannon was miffed. She liked being the best in everything and it came to her easily. Now this lady wanted her to challenge herself further and become someone whom she didn't know how to be. She knew she outwrote everyone in that class with her story and was criticized for it. Try as she may to see what Mrs. B was talking about, she left her class without uttering another word. She thought if she said anything it would not be very nice. She caught up to her peers at the cloak rack.

Going outside was like preparing to walk in outer space. Everyone was sure to don their thick woolen cloaks with the hood over their heads, while the mittens were the last thing to handle. The boys mainly complained about the process until the door opened and the wind slammed them with snow.

Shannon couldn't shake the bad mood thinking further about Mrs. B's criticism. The other students didn't care about their grades, they considered it a good way to get to know their counterparts. At dinner, the resident kids sat intermixed with the new students and talked and laughed all through their meal. Pre-existing friendships were growing stronger and new friendships were blossoming too. Lauren felt a little more at home when she found other shy girls that also wanted to chit-chat but couldn't work up the nerve.

After dinner, they bundled back up and held on to each other as they crossed the blizzardy street. As they hurried, some fell, but the others pulled them back up and they laughed all the way into the vestibule of their housing. They undraped their heavy coats and prepared to go to the gymnasium for the nightly exercise.

Again, Brianna preferred to stick with Ms. Kim and played Gin rummy in the adult room off of the gym. Brianna appreciated Ms. Kim's no-nonsense approach to everything and began to mimic her style. Ms. Kim saw Boyce out of the corner of her eye and debated about whether to mention the murder mystery she was reading. All day when she wasn't reading, she yearned to hurry up and get back to the book. This was a new addiction for her, but she would never admit it to anyone.

The other kids fell right back into their favorite sport or game. Adam wanted to beat the eight-year-old that had beaten him two nights in a row in chess. The twins timed each other to see who could climb the wall the fastest. The other kids promptly joined in the counting. Wanda jumped rope like she normally did, but this time two ropes were swinging back and forth. She was brilliant and nobody else could match her swiftness in and out of the jumps. Almost everyone in the gym stopped and watched her as if she were putting on a show, even the twins hopped off the wall.

Shannon read to some of the younger ones with animation in her voice. Gabriel loved being read to and became one of her biggest fans. Gabriel told her that there was no one like her in the whole wide world. She had been complimented by several adults, but never by a child because they were too honest and normally found her boring. Shannon thought that was the best kind of praise. What he really meant was that he had never seen anyone with red hair before. He stared at her red hair and wondered if her head hurt because of it. He thought he could ask his new friend Arcado later.

There were several players on the basketball court that night. Christopher, Charlie, Bianca, Vaughn, Ryan, and Arcado. They played three on three using just a half-court. It was the Ourstory kids against the New York City kids. It was all fun for about 30 minutes until Bianca and Ryan started playing hardcore ball like they had something to prove to each other. Their faces looked angry as they dribbled or shot. The other kids just wanted to have fun, but the game became so intense that they dropped out, leaving just the two competitive players. After the intense one-on-one game which left the score at an even 32 to 32, the lights started to flicker. As Ryan was distracted by the light flicker, Bianca shot the ball and made it in, beating Ryan by two. He thought that was something a cheater would do but acted like it was fine and congratulated her. He walked out with the guys grabbing his left arm which was more than sore from his bus injury. Tomorrow he would shoot more three-pointers and just win quickly, he thought. Friendly attachments were being made in every activity with the new students and residents. It gave everyone something to look forward to and helped pass the time until the weather lifted. For the inconvenience of being stuck somewhere until the snow subsided, this wasn't so terrible, so they thought.

Monday November 30th
Chapter 22 Gardeners Getting Anxious

Haugen was grateful to Myra and Valley for rescuing them and providing shelter. What he didn't realize is that the hosts were more of Rooter's kind, meaning they smoked and drank and carried on like this was one continuous party. Every day the lady of the house would make a new creation in her crockpot for all to have for lunch and dinner. The best part was that she made fresh bread from scratch each morning. They put out pickled and canned vegetables and fruits from their summer garden, so every day a jar was opened for a new adventure of taste.

They had a large chicken coup that, luckily, was flush with the house. Through the blizzard every day, the owners made it a priority to make sure the tarps were battened down tight on the coup and the chickens had fresh water and grass. There was a small, battery-operated, space heater that went on and off intermittently to keep the coop at a temperature above freezing. A few chickens didn't survive. But the ones that did, produced eggs on the daily, just like it was a spring day.

To keep from boredom, there were three puzzles on the floor in various places around the family and living room, which was their entertainment during the day. At night, the hosts slipped into their routine bedtime of eight o'clock. This was fine by most because sleep was always welcomed.

Their cell phones were still out of reach in the mountains. Mr. Haugen conducted morning meetings with his staff, but after the first day, it was hard to come up with much to say. They unanimously decided that when they all got back to New York City, the tree would still be chosen by the students by showing them pictures of each of the final tree nominations and giving the history of the fir.

All of them watched out the window and when there was ever a small break in the harsh wind blowing the snow, Paul and Joshua would suit up to head out the door. But as soon as they got to the snowmobiles, the weather would howl up another windstorm and they would return indoors.

Mr. Haugen was becoming a frazzled mess. He didn't sleep much thinking of the worst outcomes. Pacing the floor constantly, his staff worried that he was losing it. Haugen talked to himself, out loud, mumbling about the kids freezing to death. Even Rooter was starting to think he was weird. He cursed at himself over and over. Not being a risk taker served him well for 60 years, and now his big idea might either put him out of a job or even worse, in prison.

Tuesday, December 1st
Chapter 23 Tolbert and Chauncy Awaken

Tuesday morning, Chauncy and Tolbert lay in a stupor from the weekend drinking binge of a bachelor party that they were supposed to host. A high school friend of theirs was getting married and they volunteered their place above their car repair garage on 14th Street. It was a central location for everyone invited. The garage was their workspace that Tolbert inherited from his father who passed away two years ago. He and Chauncy, his best friend, were business partners. It was a big piece of real estate in the city that serviced all sorts of vehicles. On top of the garage were two large condominiums, one for Tolbert and Chauncy to share and one they rented out that more than paid the bills. Their condo had a huge living area that was staged for the party that never happened.

The two met when they were in elementary school and played on the same soccer team up through high school. Chauncy had moved from American Samoa when he was eight. His two older brothers were big and sturdy like his father and mother, while Chauncy was tall and scrawny like his grandad. His curly black hair was groomed in a military way which complimented his brown eyes and olive skin. Tolbert was a mix of his father of German descent and his mother from Algeria. He was tall like his dad, but his mother's dominant features gave him dark brown hair, eyes, and an olive complexion. Most passersby thought the two were brothers.

The boys were only 24 years of age. Right out of high school, they both joined the National Guard and went to a specialty school for Track Vehicle Repair, which was the closest thing to a mechanic's degree they could get. Secretly, Chauncy wanted to go into forensic science and solve mysteries, but he never wanted to part from his best buddy. They worked hard and played hard and had all sorts of expensive toys to prove it.

The party that was planned was a dud because the only ones there were Tolbert and Chauncy. When the snow came down, they decided to consume a few beverages and watch the blizzard on their large screen TV. When they awoke, it was Tuesday. A few days of drinking and dehydration had put them in a serious sleep mode. The place looked like it was hit by a tornado. They couldn't find things, like Mr. Skittles, Tolbert's cat, their cell phones, and most importantly, the TV remote. They sobered up and ate the stale, cold pizzas that were in oily stained boxes. They were slowly returning to normal.

"Dude, I don't think I ever drank like that before," Chauncy mentioned as he squeezed his skinny gut that was not feeling well. His head also pounded. "I don't ever want to feel like this again."

Tolbert passed him the headache medicine and a glass of water. They found their phones. One was in a bag of Doritos and the other was in the cat food dispenser, which was nearly empty. With the cat gone, Tolbert wondered who ate all of his pet's food. They honestly didn't remember any of the shenanigans that made the condo such a mess and both wondered who created such mayhem.

"Did you ever install the video camera inside the condo?" Chauncy asked.

"Not inside, but I have one outside for anyone who tries anything stupid," Tolbert answered.

"That's too bad," Chauncy said with a laugh.

"Dude, you smell," Chauncy commented as he thought the body odor mixed with his head and stomachache didn't blend well.

Tolbert leaned over him and sniffed.

"That's you, not me," Tolbert argued. "I don't smell me."

"No, it's you," Chauncy gave him a nauseous look.

The truth was that both of them smelled bad. They conceded that it was time to take a shower.

First, they took their phones and played all of the messages. Tolbert went first and put it on speakerphone. Most were the guys from the bachelor party stating that they wouldn't make it. Ten were from his mother threatening to walk from her condo, by Central Park, through the tundra to make sure he was still alive. They both laughed hard until the next message. It was from First Sergeant Maxson doing a recall for the National Guard Unit.

Chauncy played his messages and again, Maxson called him a few times too. By the third message, Maxson got a little hostile about both blowing off the recall drill. Nobody could make it to the National Guard drill site to get their all-terrain vehicles on the road to look for a group of missing school kids.

"Easy peasy," Tolbert said. "Let's get cleaned up and suited up for the ride to the drill site."

"OK, but first, can we finish the video game that we started on Saturday?" Chauncy asked, trying to get his priorities straight. "I don't like to leave things unfinished."

"How old are you, seven?" Tolbert criticized. "There are lost kids out there and it sounds like only we can find them."

Chauncy gave him the look of "really"?

"OK, one game, and then we go," Tolbert gave in.

As they lifted the game controllers, Tolbert's keys dropped to the ground. They were his keys to everything he owned – the garage, his apartment, and his truck. He wondered what else he would mysteriously find as he carried on his day. He gave Chauncy a look, suggesting that they play.

After what ended up being two hours' worth of gameplay, they realized they were hungry and thirsty again. In the middle of eating the next box of three-day-old pizza, the phone rang.

"Hello?" Tolbert was ready to take his beatings from Maxson. "Oh, hi mom. Yeah, I'm good. I, I mean, we were doing a little drinking and sleeping for the last few days and I lost my phone....... yes, obviously I found it because I'm talking to you. Oh...you took Mr. Skittles? On Friday? Wow, I forgot you were taking him to the vet for me."

Chauncy's phone rang. He thought it was most likely his mom too.

"Hello mom and yes I'm all right," Chauncy said as if it were routine.

"I am not your mommy!" Maxson yelled on the phone. "Where have you been?"

"Hey First Sergeant Maxson, Tolbert and I were just suiting up to head over to the drill site," Chauncy said like he was in a hurry. "Sorry, we can't talk too long, we have to go."

"Click!" There was nothing but a dial tone on Maxson's end.

Maxson wondered if they would get to the drill site and start the search and rescue before the TACC started theirs. The next call would not be as easy - he had to tell the governor that the rescue mission was a go, finally.

Chapter 24 Joining the Choir

During Tuesday's class, Mrs. B went over the agenda for the day. They started with the next math lesson on integers. The teacher explained the definition and then gave examples. Next, it was time for the students to prove they understood.

"Mrs. B, you're a great teacher," Vaughn said out loud as he turned in his assignment. He was about the last one done. The teacher smiled and nodded as she corrected his paper on the spot.

After the last student turned theirs in, she stared at her students with curiosity.

"Vaughn, you paid me a compliment earlier," she hesitated but continued. "Did you not take to math at your high school?"

"All of my mat' teachers are, you know, okay, but nobody ever got through like you do," as Vaughn talked, a lot of the city students were nodding in agreement. "I guess I never understood mat' so it must be the way you explain things. I am catching on now."

"Do you think it was your teacher? Could it have been external factors like noise in the class, your classmates, and their expectations of learning, or could it have been that you weren't in your best mind to accept instruction?" Mrs. B asked.

"Why you put dis' back on me?" Vaughn asked. "I gave you a compliment because I get you. But to answer your question, I think all those could be a factor maybe."

"I will tell you a little about myself and maybe that will help you understand my curiosity." Mrs. B started from the beginning. "I grew up in the projects. I had one teacher in elementary school who would have fundraisers to buy new books every few years, so we could experience what it was like to be treated nicely like the big-money school districts. Her expectations of every student were high and she wouldn't accept any excuses from anyone. Even though we were just kids, she treated us like adults with an important job and allowed absolutely no slang words, whatsoever, which was harder than you could imagine. I can remember that every student in that class talked better, behaved better, and made it a priority to do the homework to the best of their ability not to disappoint her. There was no class that I had in any of the grades later that would compare to hers. From that day, I knew I had to be like her when I grew up. You could say that was my "aha" moment."

She looked around the classroom and all eyes were on her intently.

"When I was in high school, I remember applying for a college scholarship. It was important because it was the only way I could go to college. I had to write an essay on my hero," she said pensively.

"I bet you wrote about that grade school teacher?" Wanda interrupted.

"I wanted to, but she thought she lived a mediocre life and forced me to go outside my comfort zone and look deeper for what she called 'more deserving people'. She was a private and modest person but was happy to be my mentor in life. She told me to look at my neighbors and people in my community."

"So you wrote about a bunch of people?" Wanda blurted again. "That's a lot of work."

"I thought so too until one day I was walking home from school and cut my fingers opening a can of soda," she continued. "I slipped into a nearby Asian food store to see if I could nick a Band-Aid from the owner. I'll never forget it. The owner's wife was in her early 50's and she treated me like I was her own daughter. She grabbed my good hand and dragged me to her office and cleaned and bandaged my hand."

"So you wrote a story about a lady who put a Band-Aid on your hand?" asked Vaughn, incredulously.

"Well, there's more to the story," stated Mrs. B patiently and dramatically at the same time. "I kept thinking of my mentor pushing me. I asked the shop owner's wife about her life growing up and what she revealed to me could have filled a novel. She grew up in Cambodia and when she was a teenager her whole country was torn apart by a dictator who punished and killed professionals like teachers, doctors, and lawyers and tore the whole country down in mayhem. She and her brother escaped into the dangerous jungles to reach Thailand. I sat at

106

the edge of my seat the whole time listening intently as she talked for over an hour about her journey here. She opened my eyes to a history I never heard of before."

"You would have never known if you didn't ask her that one question," remarked Shannon in a solemn mood. "So your paper was about the Cambodian lady, I assume."

"Well, the more I thought about my scholarship essay, the more I wanted to keep digging," said Mrs. B in her storytelling voice. "The next day I visited the seamstress at the dry cleaners and listened to her tale of sewing for the Queen of Lesotho, South Africa where she grew up. Her accounts of the queen and her extravagant wardrobe was thrilling. The next week I visited the park where I met an immigrant from the former Yugoslavia, and he told me about serving in the war there. Then, I went back to the basics and asked my neighbors about their childhood and how it was growing up in New York, the south, the north, the west or wherever they came from and again my notebook was full of tales of wonder - some happy and some sad. After a whole month, I had a collection of stories of my neighbors and my community."

"Which one did you write about?" inquired Arcado.

"I decided to write what I titled "Current Heroes, the Forgotten People"," she said with much fervor. "I made a point of writing about real people who, in my eyes, were all heroes and had incredible stories. After I submitted my scholarship essay, I found out that everyone else who applied for it wrote about Martin Luther King, John F. Kennedy, Cesar Chavez, Susan B. Anthony, and well-known heroes that could be fact-checked. I knew I most likely wouldn't get the scholarship. As interesting as my people were to me, I knew that it was a long shot to write about the unknowns."

"But you became a teacher anyways," remarked Bianca with a smile.

"That's because," she paused for effect. "I won the scholarship."

Mrs. B strutted to the blackboard and wrote on it as she said the words. "Remember, that everyone has a story."

"The people that surround you all have a story," she reminded them. "What they look like on the outside may not

107

reflect their experiences on the inside. And sometimes, all you must do... is ask."

"I still don't understand why I get what you're teaching more than my teachers back in the city," said Vaughn curiously. "It's not like I don't like to learn."

"There's a secret to learning," said Mrs. B. "And you might have found it here."

"What's the secret?" asked Wanda in further anticipation.

"It's rather simple, but it works," stated Mrs. B.

"Are ya' going to tell us?" Wanda impatiently asked.

"OK, but prepared to be shocked," Mrs. B paused. "It's called paying attention."

Everyone groaned.

"I'm not kidding," she said seriously. "If you can stop your mind wandering and engage in what's being taught, you'll get what I am teaching. Asking questions keeps your mind involved and yearning to learn more. Like the story I just told you. You followed me all the way to the end to find out the answer. If you have other priorities occupying your mind, your interest will be lost."

"That sounds way too simple," stated Vaughn in disbelief.

"It's happening right now," she said. "Everyone in this class just found out the secret to learning because you paid attention. I hope you let me keep proving my theory."

"It's more than just that," said Vaughn and most nodded their heads in agreement.

"One thing I do know is that I will always fight for you. I will always challenge you. I will always be there to mentor and guide you," she said confidently. "My passion is to open your minds and expect that you are hungry enough to want to solve the impossible."

"I'm hungry!" shouted Wanda, moved by her teacher. "I'll solve world peace right now!"

A few laughed. Shannon thought that Mrs. B was specifically talking to her. She wished she could rewrite her paper because she just experienced her biggest "aha" moment. No one had ever pushed her to be a stronger writer. She, like Wanda, wanted to solve the impossible.

Hours flew by as they solved more math problems. The students' stomachs were growling like angry bears and were relieved to be released for lunchtime. They had only been there a few days and already the mess hall seemed to be routine and most sat in the same seats. Everyone socialized and laughter was plentiful.

Choir practice was next. The students shuffled across the frigid, dark clouded, and windy street to the large building next to their quarters. Inside was a large hall with rows of chairs and a large stage at the front. They attended Sunday Service there and were familiar with the layout. The smaller platform before the stage looked like an altar that was fashioned with a cross symbol on the side. To the right, there was an Ark that held the Torahs' for the Jewish services. Atop the Ark was a menorah with white candles standing at attention. There was a smaller room off to the left front that was used as a Mosque. It was a much smaller room with a beautiful carpet over the hardwood and a large stained-glass window in the back. This room required shoes to be removed before entering, so it was only used for Islamic Prayer and Friday's Khutbah.

In an ideal world, all three houses of worship would be in separate buildings, but a consolidated structure was all that the small town could afford. The large hall was used for other gatherings for social events or plays that the students would put on a few times a year. The town had to use every space available to them. But to the students now the worship building converted into a choir hall for practice.

All of the students except Brianna were in the large hall. Brianna insisted that she sing with the adult choir who would rehearse in the gym today. The students gathered on the stage. The choral director, Mr. Chad, had the new students, one by one, sing a bar of "Happy Birthday" or whatever they knew to sing. He divided them up into their proper sections putting Arcado, Ryan, Vlad, and Sergei in the baritone section. Shannon and Darcy went into the sopranos. Lauren was a mezzo-contralto and Wanda was a contralto. Adam and Vaughn were tenors. The music director was truly gifted. He had an ear for tones and harmonies. He made the children's choir sound majestic and heavenly. He knew how to work with the tone-deaf and have them sing in a quieter pitch, so they added more than they took from the beautiful harmonies.

The students grabbed a folder from a box in the front of the stage that held the song choices. He instructed as he played the piano. Eight students played violins and violas. They sat in their seats and readied their music sheets on their stands. Before they started, Mr. Chad asked the new students if they had any talent with musical instruments. Vaughn said he could play any instrument, but played the piano best, while Adam confessed to playing the violin.

He gave them a choice to play or sing. Vaughn felt more comfortable behind an instrument, so he decided to go to the piano. Adam loved working with his hands more than anything, so he chose to play the violin. A young lady kindly handed him her violin, which was already in tune, and left to join the sopranos. It was a win-win for everyone.

Mr. Chad sat with Vaughn on the piano bench and made sure that the young man knew his way around the large instrument. The sheet music was on display in front of them. Out of the blue, Vaughn began to beatbox until he found the beat and then he spread his fingers over the keys firmly and started playing. Mr. Chad closed his eyes to absorb the notes that he knew by heart. Even though the beatboxing stopped when Vaughn started playing, he couldn't decide if he wanted to incorporate anything fresh like that into the program. He would have to think about it. Meanwhile, he thought Vaughn's piano playing was exceptional.

This was the first time since he started the choir that he could actually stand like a conductor in front and lead instead of directing from the piano. He took advantage and lined up the sections to sing. They warmed up to "White Christmas". The students took out the sheet music to sing, even though most knew it by heart. When Mr. Chad pointed to each group they sang and then he flicked his music baton so all groups would sing at once, which created near perfect harmonies. The new students were blending in in no time. Darcy's eyes widened as she realized how remarkable her voice could harmonize. She had never known this was possible and wanted to sing more.

Ryan and Arcado gave it all they had in the back row with their deep voices. While most kids smiled while they sang, Shannon had the most serious look on her face, as if it would be graded. Lauren felt comfortable for the first time without Brianna being there to take care of her. Wanda insisted that she stand next to the twins because they had similar voices. Mr. Chad had to address her personally as one who needed to take it down a notch in volume. She stopped focusing on the twins and more on how to make her voice quieter. Vlad and Sergei couldn't help but bob their heads slightly in unison when they sang. Wanda thought it was cute, but she had to concentrate on her singing, which was almost a full-time job. After an hour went by, they had a water break and finished the afternoon with more songs. A few Christmas songs were introduced to the New York City students, which they loved more than the others. They worked on a new song for the last hour straight. When it was time to wrap it up, there was disappointment all around.

Meanwhile, Brianna was in the gym singing with the adults. She thought that their music had to be much more soulful than the kid's music. Singing in the choir with her aunt was one of her favorite things to do and so this came naturally to her. They practiced the Christmas songs that their music director wrote. Their choir had a saxophone player, trumpeter, drummer, guitarist, and pianist. They started with "Silent Night" and then moved on to the original songs.

Brianna seemed to soften with the group as she sang in harmony. There was even an occasional smile from the group. Ms. Kim sat and watched. She could never hold a note and never had the courage to do anything but hum along poorly. Tapping her foot subtly, she felt an unexpected and rare sense of enjoyment. This had Ms. Kim secretly wondering if she should try her hidden yearning to sing. She teetered back and forth on whether to walk up there and grab a music sheet. In the end, her backside stayed seated, but her mouth moved with the lyrics and her feet tapped with the beat. Both groups spent the whole afternoon rehearsing. They had to prepare for the annual Christmas concert coming up and it was a huge deal. The girls would braid their hair with ribbons and the guys would wear a tie with their button-up shirts. Afterward, the cooks would have an extravagant spread of desserts and punch. The adult choir band would play dance music, and all would have the opportunity to show off their moves. The Christmas Gala was one of the best days on the calendar for Ourstory.

At dinner, the New York City students found themselves sitting in between the resident kids who were sharing stories and laughing. It felt like summer camp with new friends that they were getting to know better each day. The adults stared at the kids making friends and thought that the new children would like it here, permanently.

Tuesday, December 1st
Chapter 25 Revelations

Vaughn was getting ready for his turn in the shower. He was thinking of abandoning getting clean because he was cold and he wanted a hot, steamy, long shower. Wishing he was home in his old, run-down, but functional house made him smile. What he saw next brought bewilderment and shock to his whole body. He acted like nothing was out of the ordinary and slipped out of line to shower next.

Ryan, Adam, and Arcado were sitting across bunks just reminiscing on the day's activities and laughing about the chores that were done in a sophomoric way. The twins jumped down to join them when Vaughn shuffled over and glanced to make sure no one was within earshot. He looked at everyone as if he were going to spill a secret. They all got quiet and gathered around in a tighter circle.

"I think we need to get out of here, sooner than later," Vaughn shuttered as he said it. "We're not safe here."

"What are you talking about?" Ryan was tired and didn't feel like dealing with drama tonight.

"They beat these kids," Vaughn spoke slowly when he said it.

"What do you mean?" Adam asked, confused. "Like beat them at chess or checkers?"

"No, dumb-wit," he said impatiently. "They beat these kids with a whip or something that leaves raised scars on their backs."

"Dude, are you sure?" Arcado asked. "I mean was it one or two? Was it just the older kids? Like what?"

"This is serious," Vaughn whispered sternly and then dropped the conversation when Christopher came over to see why they were in a huddle.

"Hey guys, what's happening?" Christopher asked in a joking way. "Are you planning your escape into the cold tundra tonight?"

"Ahh...no way," Sergei said with an odd laugh.

"We dun't wanna die," Vlad said nervously.

"We were just getting ready for bed and reviewing the day," Vaughn said. "It's been a full, long day and we're beat."

Everyone gave Vaughn the stink eye for saying the word "beat".

"Well, just wanted to tell you all goodnight then," Christopher said and walked away to his bunk across the room.

Ryan got up and headed toward the bathroom. He nonchalantly acted like he was looking for something in which the guys in line acted a little suspicious of his intentions to do so. He saw it too. One after the other as they finished showering, they toweled off the deep lines in their backs that didn't seem to hurt when they touched them as Ryan thought. Ryan acted like he found what he was looking for as he bent over and picked something off the ground and held it in his fist and left.

He walked casually over to the bunks of his mates and opened his closed fist. They all looked at it like he was going to release something. When he opened his fist, it was empty, but just in case anyone was tracking him, he wanted to make it look like he found what he was looking for in the shower room.

"OK, we need a plan," said Ryan, whose face was serious but calm.

"I can't believe they beat these guys," Adam declared. "We should see if they beat the girls too."

"Well, I really don't care if they don't beat the girls and just the guys, we have to go," Vaughn remarked and pointed at the door.

"Well, obviously, we can't leave in this blizzard on foot," Arcado said. "I don't want a beating, but I don't want to die out in the snow."

"We fight," Vlad said as he did some boxing moves. "We punch left and right."

"There has to be an explanation," Adam replied and shook his head. "Maybe it's a branding thing, not a beating thing."

"Dude, that might be worse," Arcado retorted.

"Anyway, I don't think it's a branding thing," Vaughn mentioned. "Some marks were high and on the side of the shoulder and some were lower and across the center."

While the boys tried to come up with a plan, something similar happened when some of the girls were in line to take a shower. Darcy, Wanda, and Shannon were in their lines to shower when Shannon noticed some scars on their shoulders and cigarette burns on their upper arms. Unlike the guys, girls cover up immediately with their towels because it's cold and also because they're girls.

Shannon whispered something into Darcy's ear who after she heard it and then saw it too, gasped. She, in turn, tried to whisper into Wanda's ear, but it was no use because she was so ticklish when it came to a whisper. Wanda started laughing loudly and looked at Darcy who was not laughing whatsoever.

"Just tell me," Wanda said in what she thought was a whisper, but in fact was just a regular conversational voice.

She never could whisper. Whenever Wanda needed to say something in private, the whole room and the other room knew. It just wasn't in her DNA to speak lightly. Shannon and Darcy gave up on her and she seemed clueless about the markings on the girls as they left the shower room.

After each had showered, they met back at their bunks where they gathered the other girls around and told them about the raised scars on their skin. Wanda seemed amazed that she didn't notice, but in truth, she was used to being around crowds of family or friends and never deeply looked at the surface too closely of anyone. She was more of a conversationalist and listener. This concerned Laurel the most. She was fragile physically and knew she didn't stand a chance, so she inched up closer to Brianna.

"Anyone who tries to, I mean just even tries to...I will mess them up for life," Brianna said confidently. In the back of her head, she wondered how the older, taller, and bigger girls let anyone hurt them.

As they were discussing things, a knock on the door happened. It was Gabriel who walked right over to Brianna and gave her a note and scurried back to the door.

"Hey there, you can't just walk in the girls' room and think we don't notice," Bianca said as she looked into his cute, brown, adorable eyes. "Next time, you stay at the door threshold and speak to me or else."

"Or else, she's gonna beat you," Wanda said as she thought she was whispering to her friendly group, but instead the whole room heard.

"Nah, I would never beat anyone," Bianca said. "But I will withhold minutes of our reading time."

At that, he raised his eyebrows, smiled at all of the girls, and ran back downstairs.

"What did he give to you?" Bianca walked over and asked.

Brianna read the note quickly and then smiled at the rest of the group.

"This is private," Brianna said. "I think someone's got a crush on me."

"Who?" By then all the girls in the room wanted to know about her potential love life.

"Maybe Arcado," she said thinking quickly, but after she said it, instantly regretted it.

"Ewwww," the girls all said in unison, wanting to know more. They all stayed and stared for her to reveal additional details.

"All right everyone, go away, I'm tired," she rudely said and made shewing hand gestures to the girls. "There's no privacy around here."

When they all walked away, she motioned back for a huddle with her close classmates.

"It's a note from Ryan," she whispered. "He wants us all to meet up tonight, after everyone is asleep, in the stairwell."

Shannon told the girls that she would stay awake and when everyone was asleep, she would awaken them for the meeting. Everyone blew out their lanterns, nodded, and crawled into bed.

Tuesday, December 1st
Chapter 26 Blizzard Killer & Snow Slayer to the Rescue

Chauncy and Tolbert showered, shaved, ate, and went down to the garage to pull down the snowmobiles. They had two stored up in a rafter that could be lowered down by a pulley system. After the snowmobiles were lowered, they gassed them up and got ready to go. It was all too easy for Tolbert until he realized the large garage door opened by a switch and there was a seven-foot bank of snow blocking the exit. It was still blowing and snowing like crazy and now the inside of the garage started to accumulate the white stuff.

Chauncy hit the button and closed the door. Tolbert happened to have a toy just for the problem. In the corner of the garage was a bobcat snow remover. After gassing it up, they attempted to open the door and plow through it. It wasn't easy. The process of shaving off the top layer of snow and placing it on the side was a lot of work. While Tolbert bobcatted, Chauncy took a snow blower and tried to make a dent in the snow. In all, it took three hours to dig a path out of the parking lot to allow the snowmobiles to exit. As soon as the snow moved, more blowing snow replaced it. The effort seemed futile and by the time they finished, it was after 9 p.m. They were exhausted and Chauncy was soaking wet.

They regrouped in the garage and Chauncy took off his snow clothes. As he stood in the garage in his t-shirt and boxers freezing, Tolbert shook his head in despair.

"Dude, this is crazy," Tolbert stated the obvious.

"Yeah, you could be right," Chauncy agreed and grabbed some work overalls hanging in the office and put them on.

"What do you mean "could be"?" Tolbert asked.

"I mean, we play video games and solve impossible situations," Chauncy got philosophical. "This snowstorm is our real-life challenge."

"You mean you want to try getting to the armory?" Tolbert asked, shaking his head no.

"Oh yeah," Chauncy replied, shaking his head yes.

"Hmmm..." Tolbert was thinking out loud. "If we do this crazy thing, we need hero names, like we do for our video games."

"I'll be Blizzard Killer," Chauncy replied, naming himself and then stood in a muscle man pose.

"I will be the Snow Slayer," said Tolbert dramatically raising his fists.

Chauncy changed into warmer, drier clothes and packed his gear bag with more clothes. Tolbert packed more food and water, just in case.

The garage door opened for the last time. The men rode out on the two snowmobiles with the most powerful two-stroke turbo engine and used the remote to close the door behind them. Their helmets protected their faces from the whipping wind all around them. The winter storm dulled the streetlights leaving them with little illumination. Nobody was on the snow-drifted streets of New York City, which was eerie. The most populated roads in the state were now vacated, surrendering to the storm of the century. Besides the howling of the winds, one could hear the faint, noisy motors of two foolish boys who thought they could make a 17-mile death journey.

Chapter 27 The Womacks

Ernest Womack remembered the 1986 Mets' win over the Boston Red Sox at Shea Stadium. He was only 10 years old but saw it with his own eyes from high atop the busy announcer's box. The excitement in the air, the loud cheering, and his father who did audio/visual for the announcers. He spent so much time in the boxes helping his dad that his voice developed professionalism at an early age. He practiced mimicking the announcers in his bedroom at night.

Not only did he watch the professional game, but he also played on a little league team. When his team would bat, he would take the opportunity to report the game from the bench as if he were in that box, high atop the field making play-by-play calls. At first, his teammates and the families watching would laugh it off, as if it were some type of gaff. But, after a few years, everyone expected and enjoyed the colorful picture he painted with his description of plays.

In high school, Ernest was called upon to read in front of the student body. Juanita loved his voice and his seriousness. She flirted with him from the earliest of grades, but Ernest never took her seriously until after they met up in their first year in college. She invited him to a family gathering and met all her relatives who lived in the same neighborhood. If there were any tests to be passed by family members, he more than exceeded them. Everyone loved Ernest.

After a year of dating, Juanita was the one who proposed. Her family wondered if it was because a rowhouse on the block was going up for sale in a few months, or that she was just an aggressive woman. Either reason, they were glad to have Ernest as a new family member. Still in school and now married, Juanita's uncle helped them buy the rowhouse. This meant that Juanita and Ernest would live on the same street as eight of her relatives. It wasn't long before they both graduated and started having a family. Ernest got a job doing different voice-overs for several cartoon characters at the downtown studios in New York, which paid more money than he could imagine. His voice was in demand for all sorts of commercials on a local and national level. He did that for almost 20 years while they grew their family starting with Ernie Jr., then Wanda, then William, then Serita. Recently, he was offered his dream job to announce baseball at the former Shea Stadium, now the newer Citi Field.

The job offer went through on the Friday before Wanda departed on a bus to pick out a Christmas tree. The Womack family was about the happiest that you could ever engage with. Ernest was the conservative one, who ironically never did much talking at home, while Juanita livened up the place. They were in the midst of a block party at the Womack house celebrating Ernest's new job when the weather report hit. When there was no communication with Wanda or any of the students, it turned into a prayer vigil. Juanita expressed her pain and grief just as loud as she did her other emotions.

Wednesday, December 2nd
Chapter 28 The Midnight Meeting

When Shannon knew everyone was sleeping, she got up and gently awoke the others. First, she woke Brianna and Lauren. She was about to shake Wanda when Brianna stopped her. She shook her head no and let Wanda continue snoring. They woke Darcy and tiptoed to the stairwell. The door creaked if you opened it slowly, so Brianna took the door handle and opened it as swiftly as she could with only the sound of the air.

They shut the door quickly and crept down the stairs until they met up with the boys. Both groups shared the revelation of the other kids being scarred and burnt. Coming up with a plan was difficult, but necessary. While they were whispering amongst themselves, they could hear a man talking on the floor below and other voices too. It was odd because everyone had chores early in the morning and to hear voices booming this late was concerning.

One by one, they crept down the stairs and could see rays of light coming from the gymnasium area. Mr. Boyce was the lead speaker of the group. Ryan peeked through the small window leading into that room and saw 20 or so men and women holding a meeting. The door was ajar, so the students could hear the conversation. It was about them.

"If they tell the outside world, those kids will ruin us," one man shouted to Mr. Boyce.

"Yeah, we worked so hard to make this place a home and now it will be nothing but investigators and TV News trucks coming to find us," another man yelled. "I can't go back there."

"I didn't give up everything I had just to have some young kids mess up our home," a woman bellowed.

"I say we don't let them leave," an older man advised sternly. "They will learn to like it here."

Lauren's bottom lip started to quiver when she heard that. She was as quiet as a mouse with teardrops sliding down her cheeks one after the other. Adam shook his head in disbelief and crept back upstairs. Everyone followed his lead until they met back in the middle of the second and third floors for their own meeting.

"This is worse than I thought," Vaughn said. "So, they beat their kids and now we can't ever go home."

"We just gotta stick together," Shannon commanded as she stepped up to the leadership role. "If any one of us is threatened, then we need to huddle in a group."

"Someone's got to tell Ms. Kim," Ryan spoke up. "But we can't have her acting like we know what's going on or they might lock us up or beat us too."

"I know a way to tell her," Arcado agreed. "When we do our morning chores."

"Maybe we should hide some hunting weapons," Sergei suggested.

"No, remember, they count them as they go back in the locker," Vlad said. "And then they lock them up."

"We will wait until the blizzard dies down and leave silently in the middle of the night," Shannon whispered in a high, intense, dramatic voice. "We should start hiding little bits of food like bread and non-perishable items to take on our journey. This storm has to be over shortly."

"We need a few different plans for different scenarios," Vaughn inputted. "We need a plan for when they come to abuse us, or brand us, or force us to do something we don't want to do."

"They haven't hurt us yet, so let's be cool and not act so defensive," Ryan added. "We need to remain calm but on the ready."

"I want to go home," Lauren said as she wept silently. "They want to keep us here forever."

"No way," Darcy said. "The plan may not be fully developed tonight, but now we all have to look for opportunities to prepare for an escape. Between all of us, we will be OK."

They could hear the meeting disbanding downstairs, so they separated and went back into their rooms. Besides Wanda, not one of the kids slept well that night. As they lay, each one of them stared at whatever was above them to try and solve an impossible situation.

Wednesday December 2nd
Chapter 29 Preparing the Track Vehicles

Chauncy and Tolbert made it to the Armory at midnight. It was a long and unpleasant journey that took them 30 minutes on a regular day. To get into the armory garage they had to put in an entry code. When the two arrived, they pretended like they were generals that owned all of the track vehicles. Track Vehicles were the tanks and other armored vehicles that were needed on a battlefield. Now, the blizzardy state of New York would be their combat zone. Tolbert crawled into the Bradley Tank and popped his head out of the top.

"Can you see me driving this through the streets of New York City?" Tolbert asked.

Chauncy climbed into an Armored Personnel Carrier that resembled a tank without the enclosed top.

"I will follow you through the storm, sir," Chauncy said dramatically.

They both saluted each other and then Tolbert's phone rang. He answered it on speakerphone.

"Are you knuckleheads at the Armory yet?" Maxson whispered so he wouldn't wake his sleeping granddaughter nearby.

"Yes Master Sergeant," Tolbert whispered back. "We just arrived. It was a difficult trip here by snowmobile."

"Snowmobile-eh?" Maxson spoke gently. "And why are you whispering? Never mind. The plan is to pick up the rest of the team at their homes and head north on I-87. I will call the crew and tell them to expect you before dawn. You will text each man or woman before you arrive, so they can prepare."

"Should I pick you up first?" Tolbert asked no longer whispering.

"Negative," Maxson whispered in his manly way. "I have diaper duty and there's no one to relieve me to help with this search and rescue."

Chauncy burst out, almost laughing out loud, but contained his noise. Tolbert had to hold the phone away from his face to silently laugh too.

"And Corporal?" Maxson commented as he knew these guys well. "Get out of the tanks and start prepping the Oshkosh's."

"We aren't in the tanks," Tolbert said as he was climbing out of his. "Oshkosh's will be ready soon."

"One more thing," Maxson ordered. "I will send you an email that will serve as your orders. I want updates sent directly to me every hour on the hour unless there's something to report any sooner."

"Yes, First Sergeant," Tolbert obeyed and then hung up.

Chauncy checked the condition of the Humvees and the large all-terrain vehicles called Oshkosh's. Each of the boys would take a Humvee to collect the crew and meet back at the armory for their orders. They put chains on the Humvee tires to make sure they wouldn't get stuck in the snow, even with the mighty weight of the rolling truck.

They set out at two a.m. to pick up their comrades. The Humvees rolled over the heavy snowfall down the empty streets of New York. They all thought that time was running out and their efforts would be in vain.

Wednesday, December 2nd
Chapter 30 Desperate for an Update

In the early hours of the morning, Mr. Jekel awoke hoping that the wind and snow would behave today. When he pulled the curtain away from the bedroom window, he saw the same relentless snowfall. He heard the winds roaring even before he saw the snow. Not wanting to wake his wife, he gently slipped downstairs to check his computer for emails and website updates.

On his website, Darcy's parents commented that their lawyer was starting a lawsuit against the city of New York City. They solicited other parents to join them. So far, no other family had done so. The López family started a prayer chain around the globe and posted the link to join. Arcado's father wanted to lighten the mood and created an animated Christmas tree that shook 11 cartoon kids out of the tree. Wanda and Lauren's moms were coordinating a 'Welcome Home' celebration. Adam's mom posted that she was on her 10th batch of her famous Babka Bread for the party. Both Ryan and Vaughn's fathers only posts were from that Friday evening saying that they hadn't heard from their sons in awhile. Brianna's mom and aunt had started a rally demanding the governor take action about their kids. They made signs and gathered participants, some even from outside the community. All would rally as soon as the storm subsided.

There was nothing new in any emails about the student sightings. Jekel saw that he had 22 text messages from the parents and families of the students. Not one from Haugen nor any of the missing students. He wanted to make another call to the mayor or governor, but it was too early for that.

He looked around his home - a refurbished, three story rowhouse with a red-brown brick facade, called a brownstone. As he walked through the family room to his office, pictures of his grown children and young grandchildren stood on every bookshelf. There were pictures of him and his wife shaking hands with political celebrities on the wall. He thought how happy that time was. He pulled them down, one by one and thought how irrelevant and useless those experiences were to him now. As he climbed the ladder to become Chancellor of the New York School Boroughs, he got to know many government officials. He had done them many favors and now when he needed it the most, nobody could help him.

The wicked, chilly winds blew the snow haphazardly all over New York City. It was a fretful night looking out the window from any home or business. The fear was especially palpable in a music shop in the Bronx. It belonged to Vaughn Vetter's father. His name was Vegas. He inherited the store from his uncle who knew Vegas was a hard-working man with a lot of discipline and talent for music. In the music store, guitars and violins were hanging on the walls for sale. There were music stands, sheets of music, and all kinds of instruments, old and new tacked up on all sides of the store. The pride and glory of the shop was the baby grand piano that sat near the front window. It was timeless. Its shiny, black exterior and smooth ebony and ivory keys gave the store its credibility.

When Vaughn was four years old, he sat at the piano next to his father and watched him play classical jazz songs. He observed his dad in full concentration mode as his eyes closed and he gently touched the keys that he knew by heart. By the age of five, Vaughn was taking lessons. His dad made him practice every day, rain or shine, for an hour. When Vaughn turned 10, he told his parents that he wanted to play sports. His mother, who worried about him getting hurt, agreed that he could play basketball, baseball, or even soccer. Vegas preferred him not to play sports at all. He wanted his hands untouched and unharmed so he could play the piano.

Above the music store was a small two-bedroom apartment. Because of the storm, Vegas hunkered down in his recliner and watched the storm through his large picture window. He listened to Billie Holiday on vinyl. The needle on the record crackled and her strong voice broke the deadly silence inside his home. Besides the howling winds, there were no other sounds in the normally noisy city. As Vegas sipped on his hot tea, he heard a noise from below in the music shop. Someone was pounding on the front door which startled him.

It was dark outside, but the snow seemed to soften the dimness. He didn't own a weapon, but he grabbed a baseball bat from Vaughn's room and headed downstairs to see what the noise was about.

At the front door, he saw a person covered in snow. The hood of a jacket covered his head, so he couldn't recognize him. As he got closer to the door, the person stopped pounding. The outsider dropped to the snowy ground and lay unconscious. Vegas tried to push the door open, but between the body that was slumped in a pile and the heaping snow, it took a lot of effort. After what felt like forever, he got the door to open as the snow bushelled through and blew throughout his shop. He pulled the body into his store by his underarms and laid him gently on the floor. He then shut the door to prevent more of mother nature from entering and then locked it. When Vegas pulled the hood from the face of the stranger, he recognized her right away. It was his wife.

She kept mumbling about how she was so cold. He took the wet coat off of her and set it aside. She was barely alert as she floated in and out of consciousness. The shop was cold, so he carried her upstairs and laid her on the couch. Her clothing was wet also, so he peeled away her shirt to find that she had several cuts that were covered in saran wrap. Knowing that she frequented a trap house, filled with people who fulfilled their addictions, he assumed that's where she got these wounds.

He gathered a bucket of hot soapy water, clean rags, and a towel and brought them to her. As he took the saran wrap off of her arm, fresh blood pooled up, so he washed the slashed area with hot water. He applied pressure with the soapy cloth. He thought that she was such a mess and should be in the hospital but understood that wasn't going to happen. As Billie Holiday sang in the background, he moved from cut to cut washing each, applying pressure, wrapping it in gauze, and taping it firmly. He dressed her in one of his old t-shirts and sweatpants to keep her dry and warm. Even through the dry clothes and two blankets, she shivered. Vegas knew that this may have nothing to do with the coldness in the air, but rather the drugs that she didn't have access to.

Billie Holiday's LP had ended and the needle dragged around the record. He selected Duke Ellington this time and replaced the record. He sat on his recliner and watched his wife twitch uncomfortably on the couch. She moaned here and there. Drinking his now cold tea had him reminiscing about the time they first met. He played in his neighbor's jazz club one night a week. Those nights, he always wore his blue velvet jacket with a black tee and freshly pressed blue jeans. For one hour, he gently blew his saxophone solos that put everyone in an easy place as they sipped on their $10 drinks and ate their $20 appetizers. One Thursday, after he finished his set, a new waitress brought him a glass of water with lime. She was five years younger, but her deep brown eyes and pretty smile had him hanging around longer than usual. When she revealed that her name was Veda, he got a lump in his throat. It was a sign. Everyone in his family's name started with the letter V.

Her five-foot-four trim frame, stylish, black weave, and her glowing smile had Vegas instantly hooked. His dark handsome face was disguised behind a trimmed, noir beard and mustache. He kept his brown, bristled hair cut neatly. After months of flirting, they both fell deep in love. Shortly after, he took her on a business trip to Reno for a jazz convention. They came back to the Bronx as Mr. and Mrs. Vetter.

Vegas had a lot of time to recollect as he stared out the window. He regretted the day last year when he sent his wife to grab their carry-out dinner. She had to walk through two blocks of construction. As she walked under a safety barrier holding scaffolding, it broke, toppling heavy pieces of steel and wood on her leg. The construction company took full accountability and paid her medical bills but what they didn't take care of was the aftermath of her addiction to the pain medicine. He stared out of the window into the abyss of snow and prayed that both of his lost family members find their way home.

In the next borough over, Mr. Jekel clicked on the website and hit the updates tab. He thought he could finally share the good news. His heart was beating fast, but a feeling of relief

128

came over him as he typed, 'The National Guard is on the way to rescue our kids!' It was short but sweet. He typed that the MMC National Guard from New York City was making this happen. He was sure to include First Sergeant Maxson's name for transparency of who was in charge. He added a few happy face emojis too.

His next email was to the local television stations and newspapers. As soon as he sent it, he received some quick replies from the different networks. They wanted brief interviews with him from home. This had Jekel pacing back and forth considering if he wanted that kind of network attention. If all ended well with the search and rescue, he would be a hero. However, if any of them were harmed, injured, or even frostbitten then he would look negligent for putting teenagers in the face of peril. He decided that he would do phone interviews. This way his voice would be heard and the expressions on his face couldn't be interpreted incorrectly. The media had a way of manipulating their narratives and he would steer clear of that.

Chapter 31 Milk a Cow or Two

That morning Vlad and Sergei were the first to gather in the vestibule for their hunting assignment. They were anxious to go out into the miserable blowing and frigid cold. The hunting crew started to arrive at the entry and then Travis asked Vlad to move so he could open the gear locker to the weapons. After Vlad moved aside, Travis put the combination into the lock and then pulled down to release the mechanism that kept it tightly closed. He set the lock aside and pulled out the everyday hunting items. As he did, the men stood behind him to take their assigned armament. He gave Vlad and Sergei their spears but decided that perhaps the slingshot would be best for Wanda today. Wanda didn't complain, but she didn't shut up about having a new toy to take her enemy, the bear, down.

Vlad and Sergei whispered something furiously in Spanish back and forth with serious expressions. Wanda thought they were trying to keep secrets from her, so she gave them the stink eye.

"You don't have to whisper about me," Wanda went on. "I don't know what you're saying but whatever it is, you can say it right in front of my face. Don't worry, Wanda knows what you're talking about. You're fighting over me. Good thing there's enough of me to go around."

She took her slingshot and pointed it to her heart. At that, the boys looked at her and smiled like she knew them well. The twins were too polite to say anything contrary to Wanda's continuous heavy flirting. Instead, they bundled up to endure the winter blast that would pound their eyes, ears, and mouths.

They trudged as they had done before following in the leader's fresh footprints in the snow. They used the same system to divide up and search the wooded area and perimeter.

The whole time hunting was spent in pursuit of a moose they spotted as they entered the field. They thought it would be easy to chase and catch because of its size, but it disappeared into the woods and was not seen again. The wind and snow picked up, so they had to stop their long pursuit and the hunters turned back to the village empty-handed

Sergei handed Travis all of the weapons as he put them back in storage. He waited until the lock was secured on the locker and then walked out with Travis. They both complained about the wasted time out in the cold and then split ways.

Before they ate breakfast, both Sergei and Vlad snuck down to the weapons storage locker and stealthily went to work. Vlad memorized the lock combination from earlier in the morning. They took one dagger and one short-barreled shotgun and relocked the storage cabinet. Hiding the items in their cloaks, they walked up to their room and stashed them in their footlockers. While hiding the weapons, Vaughn made a spectacle in the middle of the room beatboxing. Everyone surrounded him to watch the fun, except for the twins.

The plan worked. Sergei and Vlad nodded to the boys in their group that they accomplished step one of their mission. They would be ready to defend their group from any attacks. Going down without a fight wasn't an option. As they planned their next moves, they all thought that the enemies were acting normal still interacting with them. The thought occurred to the boys that maybe their sleep mates were all innocent and they only had to worry about the village adults. Still, they couldn't afford to trust anyone.

At some point during the day, they would slip Brianna the dagger to hide. They didn't trust the girls with the gun. They got dressed and headed to breakfast. Because all of the kids were now intermixed, they talked in code which was about Arcado's cow being milked. They told the girls Arcado had milked two cows this morning and it went fine. They also mentioned that Ms. Kim wasn't aware of the two cows but was aware of everything else. No resident thought twice about it and was glad that Arcado milked two cows. The girls knew it meant that they got two weapons, but Ms. Kim only knew about the beatings, not their planned escape. Now they would just have to meet at some point to retrieve one of the weapons from the boys.

At breakfast, a group of older folks at the table next to theirs glared at the New York students. One of the ladies in particular gave them the stink eye and pursed her lips as she talked to her tablemates. It was evident that she disapproved of them. This had every single one of them on high alert. Lauren scooted closer to Brianna and kept her head down low. The scowls only confirmed what the kids suspected; they were not wanted there.

As in their routine, they went to class next. Not one New York student paid attention to Mrs. B's lessons that day; they were all thinking about their defense plans. Unlike the Nor'easter that took them by surprise, they were ready to take on the village. While they were in class, Travis went back to the weapon storage locker because he had extra shells in his pocket that he forgot to unload earlier that morning. He was alarmed at what he discovered.

Wednesday, December 2nd
Chapter 32 The National Guard to the Rescue

Before Tolbert and Chauncy left to pick up their team, they put on the police scanners as was protocol. They didn't even reach a mile down the road when they heard a dispatcher requesting support from any contracted ambulances that could get to 5th street. They learned that a man was bleeding out from an accidental gunshot. Then they heard another request for a woman who went into labor in a breech position and needed immediate attention at any hospital.

It was time to make decisions. Tolbert and Chauncy used their citizen band (CB) radios to talk from Humvee to Humvee about their options as they drove. Tolbert really wanted to help because that's what they were trained for. He relived the gut-wrenching feeling of being unable to help his dad when he had a heart attack and wished someone were there to help him. That terrible fate of his father had him envisioning a different outcome if just one person were there to help. However, their sole mission at this very moment was to collect their National Guardsmen so they could head upstate, find the missing personnel on the buses, and bring them back safely. But they could not dismiss others that were in peril.

"We need to make a few stops before we pick up the team. Over," stated Tolbert with full assurance.

"Should we tell Maxson?" asked Chauncy. "Or do we take our chances? Over."

"Nobody will ever know that we helped," said Tolbert without hesitation. "You take the pregnant one and I'll take the gunshot. Over."

"We better get the tarps out and lay them on the seats. Over," recommended Chauncy.

At that, Tolbert dialed into the emergency channel, identified himself, and requested the full addresses of those needing a ride to the hospitals. Shock and amazement came from the dispatchers who had been talking to an empty channel for the last few days. In that time, over four hundred babies were born at home with guidance over the telephone,

133

deep cuts were sewn with needle and thread by family members, victims of poisonous substances were flushed out with home remedies and so on. This was the first rescue that would save lives that couldn't be done over a telemedicine call.

It was slow, but Tolbert arrived and parked wherever he wanted in front of the apartment of the gunshot victim. Two neighbors carried him down to Tolbert's Humvee and laid him in the backseat on the tarp that was unfolded only moments ago.

Likewise, Chauncy drove to an older neighborhood at the edge of Queens and Brooklyn. Even before he got to the house, he saw five men outside shoveling the sidewalk to clear the path for the woman. The blowing snow made it impossible. After Chauncy parked, the front door to the house slammed open and an irritated lady in a housecoat and boots barreled her way over to him with her husband trying, unsuccessfully, to help her. Chauncy didn't know if she growled out of anger or the hurt of the baby pressing to get out, but he made sure she sat on the tarp in the back seat. Her husband got in first and grabbed her hand and Chauncy assisted her up into the vehicle.

All the way to the hospital she wailed in discomfort. Chauncy wanted to drive faster but knew the vehicle limitations and so his stomach filled with anxiety from all of her excruciating groans. The husband had his wife do breathing exercises and Chauncy did them right along with her and found it helped.

On the other side of town, Tolbert got an earful of how the guy in his backseat was bored and decided to clean his revolver. He didn't remember chambering it and claimed it must've been his ex-girlfriend who did so. Tolbert wanted to make conversation but couldn't think of anything kind to say to a man who didn't know the first rule of handling a gun which was to always assume it was loaded. All he could think was that the man's ex-girlfriend made a good decision to change her status to single.

Tolbert radioed to the hospital to tell them to get ready as he approached the emergency room. After he dropped off the wounded man, a doctor hopped into his Humvee. Tolbert hadn't noticed because he was wiping his passenger's blood from his tarp as his backside was getting pounded with snow. When he climbed back into the driver's seat the stowaway smiled at him and begged him for a ride to his condominium. The doctor had been on duty for days without sleep and his 12-year-old daughter and 10-year-old son were home alone and scared. That weekend his wife was supposed to return from her mother's house in Jersey and never made it back. Since it was somewhat on the way to the highway, Tolbert agreed.

As soon as Tolbert dropped off the doctor, eight more urgent calls came in including someone having third-degree burns from a small house fire, a few more unexpected ladies in high-risk labor, a hook in someone's eye, accidentally severed fingers, and the clincher of two heart attacks that had Tolbert agreeing to every one of them. They divided up the runs based on the proximity to their locations.

For some reason, Chauncy got the three pregnant ladies. He coached them on breathing techniques as he had learned from the first lady's husband, secretly joining in too. One of the ladies' promised to name the baby after him if he hurried up to the hospital. As they were focused on the eight pickups, more requests came in, and Tolbert knew he had to decide. By now, it was ten o'clock in the morning and they hadn't picked up any of their team for their mission yet. Not to mention, both boys were exhausted. It was unsafe for them to be driving with barely any sleep under such dangerous conditions. They both trudged on to pick up more emergencies and take them to area hospitals.

After one o'clock in the afternoon Maxson and members of their National Guard Team called them to inquire what happened with their pick-ups. Tolbert hated making excuses, so he made a general statement that they had Humvee trouble and had to fix a few things. He admitted that Chauncy and he were too tired to continue and needed a nap before they pursued the mission.

The boys met up at Mercy Hospital and grabbed a vacant room. The nurses were too happy to accommodate them since they did with all their night runs. Tolbert even got a young nurse's phone number out of the deal. He cracked a smile before he fell asleep and thought from then on, he would visit more hospitals in uniform to pick up girls. It was cheaper than going to clubs. Chauncy closed the blinds but thought it was fun to play with the bed controls going up and down before he fell fast asleep in a reclined position.

When they woke up at ten o'clock at night, they were served a delicious meal of turkey with gravy, a scoop of potatoes, and a side of green beans. For dessert, there was vanilla pudding. The nurses, especially the one that eyed up Tolbert, were generous in providing extra food to the boys. Each took showers and was ready to head out to pick up their team. Only one thing was missing - their Humvees. During their naps, different members of Mercy Hospital took the job of being drivers to pick up more emergencies.

Chauncy and Tolbert knew this would never end, so they thought of a solution. When the drivers came back to the hospital around midnight, they would ask for a few volunteers to go with them back to the Armory and they would give them a few Humvees for their purpose. Not to mention, their Humvees were running on fumes, and they would have to gas up at the National Guard garage since the gas stations around the city were closed. Everything was a process in this wind-filled, snowy city. Three male nurses and one female nurse rode to the Armory with them to grab a few vehicles with snow chains on them. Then they headed out to make the runs that no one else in the city could do. Tolbert was making decisions like he was a Five Star General, with no hesitation in his voice. He might pay for it later when called to the floor to explain civilians using military vehicles for hospital purposes, but he was willing to put his few stripes on the line to save a life.

It was almost 24 hours ago that Chauncy and Tolbert left to pick up their team and now they would make a second attempt. Even though they most likely saved a few dozen lives that day, Maxson would have them pegged as trouble, lazy, and not fulfilling the mission that the governor was promised. Maxson would have to notify his leadership and the governor of the delay in picking up the rest of the team and heading to upstate New York.

Wednesday, December 2nd
Chapter 33 The Town Hall Meeting

Mr. Boyce couldn't wait a minute longer and had Travis ring the bell for an important gathering in the town hall. Students were in school, adults were tending to their other daily chores, and the cooks were in the middle of creating a new soup. Everyone knew to drop their activities and head over in the blustery wind to the hall. The seats in the hall filled up intermixed with the young and the old. There was not an obvious reason for the meeting and everyone was giving their best guesses for the middle of the day gathering in the rather chilly space.

At the front of the room, Mr. Boyce stood like an airline ramp agent signaling to park an airplane but rather to the crowd coming through the door to be seated and pointed here and there sharply. Vlad and Sergei were told to sit in the front row. They were so worried that their legs shook uncontrollably. They knew that they would be the first to get flogged, whipped, beaten, or whatever was done to children here. They got caught and now they would have to pay.

When Mr. Boyce thought everyone was there, he quieted everyone down so he could speak. The New York students noticed Lauren, Darcy, and Shannon were missing. Mr. Boyce began to speak softly, like a reasonable and trustworthy man, but the New York students felt with the three students missing and the twins in the front row, it was time to panic.

"Ladies, gentlemen, and students, I would like to take this time to clear a few things up," Boyce started his lecture before they started with the torture.

"Wait a freakin' minute Boyce!" bellowed Ms. Kim and she stood up and berated him. "Where did you put the girls?"

Everyone looked to see that some of the New York girls were not sitting with the other students. They looked around and noticed that the girls were not in the hall at all. They were curious too. Mr. Boyce took a minute to check the room and notice they were absent.

137

"Did anyone talk to thc girls to see if they needed to stop anywhere? The restroom perhaps?" he asked loudly. "Were they feeling all right?"

"They were OK when we left the school building," said Wanda as she recalled when they put on their cloaks to head over to the hall. They all left in a large group and she didn't notice until now that they were gone.

"I know you have 'em tied up somewhere," said Ms. Kim loud with anger. "Release 'em now and I won't hurt ya."

"Ms. Kim, I am afraid I don't know where the girls are," he said with a serious look on his face. "If they are outside, this could be a grave matter. We need to start an immediate search party for them, or they could freeze to death."

"Yeah, that's just how ya' planned it," Ms. Kim said snidely.

The town's people were getting used to Ms. Kim's wild accusations, but they gasped at her suggestion.

"Travis, I need you to take 10 men and head south, Wilbur you take 10 men and head north. I need every student to check the buildings. I need the cooks to check the mess hall and pantry. If they are found, please ring the bell, so we will all know," Mr. Boyce commanded.

They all got up and dispersed. Vlad and Sergei were so relieved that they were saved by the search. They wished no harm upon the girls but hoped the search would take days. Ms. Kim sat in her chair while everyone left. She shook her head knowing that one by one they would all disappear.

Chapter 34 The Venhills

If you asked either Lydia Grant or Darby Venhill if their
union was an arranged marriage, both would deny it. Lydia
graduated from Harvard with honors. Darby attended
Columbia in New York. He was a fourth-generation New York
businessman and he was ruthless. Stepping over employees to
make himself look like the top dog was not only acceptable in
the marketing company he worked for but admired. Lydia was
a smooth-talking businesswoman, who was normally the top
seller in her company. The Grants and the Venhills (their
parents and lifelong college friends) organized a fancy party
out in the Hamptons one summer weekend.

Lydia was petite and pretty and Darby was handsome and
charming. It was obvious after the two met and everyone
disappeared, that they were being set up. This was fine by both
Lydia and Darby who were too busy to date and felt an
attraction. A month later, they were married at a small chapel
down the street and bought a brownstone in downtown
Manhattan. Lydia was accustomed to fine, sturdy furniture
and art, so the inside of the house was valued more than the
outside. Darby hated the price tags of the lavish things, but he
loved to please her.

When Darcy came along, she was tended to by an au pair.
Their jobs ran their family priorities. They occasionally ate
dinner together, but otherwise, everyone lived their separate
lives. By the time Lydia noticed that she was missing out on
her daughter's young life, it was too late, Darcy turned 10 and
was too busy for her mother. She had made loads of friends in
school and a few in ballet. There were sleepovers and mall
drop-offs that made Lydia feel not needed. When Darcy turned
12, she twisted her ankle during ballet and couldn't dance
anymore. Lydia bought her the cutest Pomeranian to keep her
spirits up.

Now that Darcy was gone and Lydia and Darby were
forced to be in the massive house alone, they struck up a
conversation. They realized that they never even took a
honeymoon because their work schedule was too demanding.

Darby confessed that he always had hoped Darcy was a boy, but after meeting her for the first time in the hospital, thought she was breath-taking. He realized that he had been so busy over these last 15 years that there was some catching up to do with both Darcy and Lydia.

With Darcy gone and the uncertainty of her return, they both sank to the floor with their backs against the family room wall having their first heart-to-heart talk. It wasn't about his next million-dollar project nor was it about her last business meeting, they talked about themselves.

He wanted to know everything about Lydia from the time she grew up until she went to college. He wanted to know her dreams. She happily described that her dreams were about writing fantasy books about sea creatures. Writing was something she used to do before she graduated and got her busy job. As far as sea creatures, she was fascinated by Loch Ness and found the mystery exciting. He never knew this about his wife and now told her that she should quit her job and do it.

She, in turn, asked Darby what his dream had been. His voice was filled with excitement when he talked about his visions. He always dreamt of playing baseball professionally. In high school, his batting average was .500 and he was the fastest fielder out there. From grade school until high school, he tracked the New York Mets because he thought they were the underdog of baseball and was thrilled that he owned every player's trading card. The desk in his bedroom had one drawer designated for baseball stats for the Mets. His father never took him and his brothers to a game. Dreaming was not allowed in his family. Expectations of making money and being successful were ingrained in his blood.

They sat talking about their dreams like two eight-year-olds for hours. He realized this would have never happened if Darcy wasn't lost in the storm. Jekel's website that was created for the families to keep in touch made him realize that there were others who were in the same dire straits. Social status and all of the money in the world could not change the situation that was now beyond his control. The families responding on the website humbled him. Most were full of hope, while his comments were spiteful. He made a vow to Lydia right then and there. First, he begged his wife to forgive him and his business-like way of running their family. Second, he promised to be more of a family man and insisted that they do more family things. Third, when Darcy returned, they would start living a life based on carrying out their dreams and helping others achieve theirs too.

Wednesday, December 2nd
Chapter 35 The Village Search

Travis grabbed the shotgun and took 10 men south past the barn and into the woods. He didn't want to think about what could happen if an angry bear or bears wanted to haul some delicate kids away. He heard stories of it happening. Wilbur took 10 men, a spear, and a sled and headed north. He thought that if they made a run for it and were unconscious from the cold then they would have to carry them home.

Christopher organized the kids to separate and check the gym, the sleeping quarters, the barns, and every floor of the school building. Anyone left would search the town hall and all its spaces. They would all search for as long as it took until the NYC student girls were found. The priest stayed behind and knelt by the makeshift altar at the town hall stage and said a silent prayer so they would be found unharmed. Ms. Kim sat and watched him. In her mind, the priest was making a sacrificial offer to his god. She imagined the girls were punished and discarded somewhere out in the snow. Thinking that all she could do now was to fight back if they came after her, she would look for a book of matches. She would light this place up if they tried to touch her.

The New York students stuck together in the search. They were all in panic mode and wondered who would disappear next. They thought that taking three of the weakest kids was on purpose. The rest of them would not be taken without a fight. Wondering why everyone would put on a charade by looking for the missing girls had them puzzled. Everyone appeared to be nice and concerned. They wanted to know their plan. What waited for them around the corner? Why were the villagers taking their time?

Because the blizzard was so dense outside, the afternoon sky was haunted by darkness. Nobody knew how the girls would be found even if they were down the street in what would normally be plain view. Nothing was plain about their surroundings. Everything they could see was covered with snow, but they still couldn't see much due to the pounding wind. The students were glad that they were confined to looking indoors.

Arcado wondered if they shouldn't defy the order to stay inside. Maybe the guys should suit up for a search. He didn't trust Travis and Wilbur. After he thought about it, he decided not to mention it to the others. Going outside might make it easier for the townspeople to leave them to die in the snow. Nowhere was safe and nobody could be trusted.

Hours went by and every nook and cranny had been searched. Everyone met back in the town hall. Ms. Kim had never left. She did, however, find a pack of matches near some candles by the altar. Nobody was going to mess with her. Mr. Boyce stood in the front by the stage and did a silent roll call, making sure nobody else was missing.

Everyone except the cooks was present. This wasn't unusual since they had the biggest job in town. Travis and his 10 men entered the building. Their snow suits were packed with wet snow and they were shaking uncontrollably.

"Boyce, there was no sign of the girls traveling out to the woods," Travis reported. "There were absolutely no tracks leading anywhere."

"Thank you, Travis and everyone," said Mr. Boyce, grimly, as he could see they were in distress from being out in the cold.

After they peeled off their snow and iced-packed suits, they walked over to the pellet stove to warm their shivering bodies. Wilbur's group that went north returned to the village over an hour ago. Once they saw that no trail was made by the girls, they didn't pursue a more in-depth quest. They did head to the edge of the forest to make sure they weren't buried in the well-traveled path that had been covered in snow.

"Boyce, we didn't find them either," Wilbur stated.

"Neither did we," Christopher added.

Ms. Kim thought that either the girls had a great hiding spot, or they were most likely chopped up for tonight's stew. Either way, her large appetite was nonexistent this afternoon. The matches were uncomfortable in her front pants pocket. Her thoughts kept growing darker and she was getting edgy. The murder mysteries she read didn't help her paranoia.

"Ladies and gentlemen, we need to have a reckoning about how things went today," Mr. Boyce calmly stated. "I would like the New York students to head to the front."

The students knew this was coming, but they didn't want to give in so easily. They huddled to decide what to do. Before they had time to make a plan, someone started screaming. It was Ms. Kim. Everyone was in total shock at what had happened.

She set a hymnal book down on the floor and lit it on fire. The flash started so fast that it jumped to her pant leg and now she too was ablaze. Ms. Kim's ear-piercing screams sent shivers down everyone's spine.

Travis was the first to run over to Ms. Kim, with his wet snowsuit in hand. He tackled her to the floor and put the flames out. Doc Marta was right behind him. Her whole lower left outside leg was smoldering. Her pants stuck to her burnt skin. Ms. Kim, who was never at a loss for words, was in so much agony that she could only muster up a low moan of pain.

"We need to get her over to medical right away," Doc Marta commanded.

The men who volunteered to carry Ms. Kim sized her up. She was a big gal and the task of carrying her to medical wouldn't be easy, especially with a leg that they had to be gentle with. Wilbur and Christopher disappeared into a storage room and came out with a rectangular folding table. They brought it over and used it as a stretcher. It took 10 men to carry her through the hall down the steps into the windblown street until they reached medical.

The New York students followed. They all stuck together and wanted to make sure Ms. Kim was taken care of properly. Doc Marta had the kids wait outside of her examining room. She gently cut the charred pants away from Ms. Kim's skin. Pouring sterilized water over the affected area, she cleaned out any debris that was left on her leg. Doc Marta let it air dry. She unlocked a medicine cabinet and took out a pain reliever and filled up a glass of water.

"Sit up Ms. Kim," Doc Marta instructed. "This should take the edge off the pain for a while."

"How do I know you are not tryin' to kill me with poison?" Ms. Kim asked as she sat upright.

"I think you are doing a fine job all by yourself," Doc Marta answered smartly. "I am going to apply an antibiotic ointment to the area. You have third-degree burns in one area and second-degree burns in other areas. I know you probably don't feel too much pain, but that's only because you damaged your nerve endings. You could've killed yourself entirely, you know?"

"I didn't mean ta'," confirmed Ms. Kim. "I just don't like anyone threatening me or my kids."

Doc Marta lightly applied the ointment and then sighed. She sat thinking of how Ms. Kim would get around with an open wound to the different buildings. Gauze, scissors, and medical tape came to mind. Doc Marta cut a large piece of gauze and taped it a few inches above the burn. It draped over the burn down to her ankle. She left it loose.

"OK Ms. Kim, these are my instructions to you," she said sternly. "Keep the burn area open to air when you can. Try not to let your sheets or pants cover the burn. You don't want any lint or debris in the wound. The wound must not get infected. I only have so much medicine here to treat you."

"Yeah alright," Ms. Kim acknowledged. "I don't want ya' to fuss over me anymore anyway."

She slid off the table putting pressure on her right leg and hobbled to the door. When she opened it, the kids were sitting on the floor waiting for her. They all stood up and greeted her.

"Yeah, I'm gonna live," she said sarcastically. "For now, anyway."

Ryan and Arcado helped her, as best they could, to cross the street to her quarters. All of the kids made sure she got settled in her bed. Brianna took an extra pillow and elevated her leg onto it. They were surprised when they noticed all of the murder mystery novels on her nightstand.

"Ms. Kim, can we stay with you for a while?" Brianna asked. "We don't feel safe anywhere."

"Yeah, if they are coming after us, let's be together," Vaughn said.

It was tight with all the kids in her room, but she didn't mind. They all ran up to their quarters to get their pillows and blankets and returned to her room. They were scattered on the floor feeling safe for now.

Ms. Kim smiled as she felt the uncomfortable pack of matches in her front pocket.

Thursday, December 3rd
Chapter 36
Mobile Maintenance Company (MMC) on the Move

All in all, Tolbert and Chauncy collected 20 personnel from their National Guard Unit and brought them back to the Armory. They formulated a plan for their search and divided up their team into six different vehicles. Because of the heavy snow, they attached tractor snow plows to two of the Oshkosh's. They also gathered extra gas and put it in the reserve tanks. Because the blizzard was predicted to bear down for a few more days, other supplies such as flashlights, food, water, and sleeping gear were packed. Medical supplies and extra blankets were packed in anticipation of finding the kids. Each person had a two-way radio on them for communication. It was known that cell phone coverage was spotty through the mountains.

Even though it was daybreak, there was no proof of it in the sky. The gloomy, windy snow swarmed their vehicles as they left the Armory. Chauncy drove the Humvee that he was in all morning, while Tolbert switched up and drove one of the Oshkosh's. The convoy moved slowly down the empty streets of New York until they hit the highway.

As they trudged down the highway, something unexpected happened. People were stranded in cars, vans, and trucks. They had been tucked into the snow for days waiting for the snow to stop, or for a rescue. Now the occupants believed their prayers were answered.

There were four Humvees that could easily pick up the stragglers. Decisions had to be made quickly.

"Blizzard Killer to Snow Slayer, do you copy?" Chauncy radioed Tolbert.

"Go ahead, Blizzard Killer. Over," Tolbert replied.

The code names didn't surprise any of the personnel in the unit. They worked with these guys long enough to know not to take them seriously.

"If the boss agrees, my Humvee will pick up as many stranded motorists as we can," he said. "We will take them to the hotels right off the highway and head back out. Over."

"Roger. Over," Tolbert said, understanding that it was the right thing to do.

"Hey Blizzard Killer, this is uhhh...Yellow Snowman, I will be your wingman and pick up stragglers with you. Over," the driver from one of the other Humvees chimed in.

"Sounds good. Over," Chauncy replied.

"OK children, we have a mission to do," Crane, the female Master Sergeant in charge, finally chimed into her radio. "We will have only the two detach from the mission and catch up with us later. Over."

"Copy that Ice Queen. Over," Chauncy said, graciously assigning her a name.

Master Sergeant Crane smiled knowing that she could be called worse. The four vehicles drove by the stranded motorists. In their side view mirrors, they saw the two Humvees stop and help. That morning, the two Humvees made over 20 runs back and forth from the highway to the local hotels. The marooned motorists were immensely grateful for their help.

Once the two Humvees got to the highway leading to the mountains, they found no more stragglers. They were now three hours behind the convoy and the radio wasn't working with the many miles in between them. They sent text messages to First Sergeant Maxson until they got up into the mountains and the cell service dropped.

Blizzard Killer and Yellow Snowman inched their way around the mountain slowly. Blizzard Killer's Humvee stalled in the same location where Ms. Kim's bus went down the cliffside. He and his passenger got out to make sure the chains were on properly. The winds blew right through their warm bodies. In the other Humvee Yellow Snowman stopped ahead to wait until they were up and running. The snow on this wayward side of the mountain didn't accumulate as high as in other parts due to the wind direction. There were only two feet of snow. The boys inspected the front wheel chains which were still secured on the tires. However, the chain on the passenger back tire was broken and coming off. Chauncy and the other Corporal tugged on the chain to take it off so they could replace it.

It took an exhausting amount of effort as they both pulled. Finally, the chain broke loose sending both of them flying backward. Blizzard Killer hit the guardrail and it opened right up, sending him down the ravine. The guardrail snapped right back in place as if it had just eaten a hardy dinner.

Chapter 37 The Whites

The two-bedroom bungalow was small when all three of the Whites occupied it. But now it was just Shawn, a senior in high school, who stood almost eye to eye with his six-foot-seven father, Patrick White. Mr. White had just gotten off of the midnight shift from the electric plant that Saturday morning when Ryan left for upstate New York with the other students. He slept all day and when he woke up, Shawn told him about the Nor'easter and how he couldn't get ahold of Ryan. Patrick didn't know what he should worry about more, his son or not being able to make it to work that night. He held too much faith in the school system and the likelihood of the bus pulling into a nearby hotel for shelter. He only complained about the money he would lose from not working due to the snow.

Even though both boys were of age to hold down a part-time job, Patrick wanted them to give their full concentration to their education and sports. He wanted, no he needed them, to do more than he did. He saved every penny to pay for their new basketball shoes, practice jerseys, and tournament fees. He could only afford mac n cheese and sugary cereals, so the boys ate a lot of carbs. He figured they could get their fruits and vegetables with the meal programs at school. He could only afford one gallon of milk each week, even though the boys needed three.

Patrick worked at the electric plant doing everything from running tests, to custodial and maintenance, to sending reports of the grids to his boss. He sometimes worked on his days off and tried to pick up any overtime he could. He had been there for 20 years and worked the midnight shift for the extra shift premium. It was rare for him to watch either of his boys play a basketball game at school. He always promised that he would try to catch the next one, but that never happened. With his height, he knew that his sons would grow tall, so at an early age, he had them practice dribbling and shooting. That skillset grew over the years and now Shawn was recruited by the University of Syracuse.

The former Mrs. Ryan, who ran off with the dentist to Oregon, sent a card yearly for their birthdays hoping to reconnect with them. At this point, the boys had no feelings for their mother whether it be love or hate. They simply didn't know her and preferred that she'd not make any attempts. Their father never mentioned her and the boys knew not to ask anymore. They could tell by the stoic look on their father's face how much pain she caused him when her name was brought up. Patrick went on a few dates here and there, but women didn't hang around for too long when he couldn't spoil them on dates and they ended it when they saw his crowded bungalow. Instead, he found himself at the community center playing chess with much older men than he. They became his good friends.

After a few days of being snowed in, Patrick was getting stir crazy. He'd never been home this long before. It was Shawn that brought up how worried he was that Ryan was stuck on a bus in a blizzard. Feeling helpless, Shawn started up the computer that was a hand-me-down from the community center. The center also donated a printer and some refurbished flash drives. It took about five minutes for the system to get logged online and then he started to solve the mystery.

Both Patrick and Shawn researched the land between New York City and Minnechanka. They went into a forestry mapping website and printed the area around the main highway. Soon, every inch of their blank family room wall was filled like an atlas with the route the buses should have traveled. They created a spreadsheet with the phone numbers of all of the Police Stations, hospitals, rest stops, motels, and hotels in every county leading up to their destination.

They checked the website postings for families who had kids on the bus and documented the time of any significant update. Neither of them felt it was productive to air complaints about the school or to speculate what terrible things may have happened, so they never replied to the website chat. Their mission was just about the facts. They each made phone calls to the various places that they researched to inquire about the students. They documented the replies with the date and time, which were either negative in sightings, no answer, or a left message.

Over meals, Patrick and Shawn discussed the probabilities of the time they left, the rate that they likely traveled, and the zone they should concentrate on. Except for Shawn starting the computer, it was Patrick who pieced this nicely together in a logical fashion.

"Not too bad for two lugs-eh?" kidded Patrick to his son.

"Dad, our family room looks like a freakin' FBI office," replied Shawn. "Did you ever think about becoming a detective?"

"No, I'm too old for that," he said, chuckling. "Where I work, nobody is interested in opinions, just the facts. Whenever we do testing, everything is documented from start to finish with anomalies and all. The grids are complex and could fill more rooms than this one. When a sensor malfunctions, I have to find the point of origin and send someone out to see if it was a bad sensor or foul play. It's not that different from what we are doing, in a way."

"I guess I have never seen this cool, investigative side of you," admitted Shawn.

"Well, by the time we narrow down our search, the National Guard will have them coming home," said Patrick confidently. "But it sure gave us something to do to pass the time."

"Sure did," laughed Shawn, but then he grew serious. "Dad, do you mind if we keep searching and researching?"

"Son," he said sternly. "I am not gonna stop until I hear they're found."

Thursday, December 3rd
Chapter 38 The Campanile Rings

It was a long evening for everyone. The adrenaline pumped through the New York City students' veins, disrupting their sleep. They feared what would be on the other side of the door in the morning. The Ourstory children were sad because they wanted to talk to their new friends. They were also concerned when the girls went missing. The gossip on floors two and three was that the girls tried to run away in the storm and didn't make it. They would find them in the spring sometime when the snow melted. They were also perplexed at why anyone would want to run from their village. They thought everyone got along and it was a great place to live.

There was a knock on Ms. Kim's door at 3:30 a.m. It was Jesse. Arcado answered it since he was used to getting up that early.

"Time to milk the cows Arcado," Jesse said. "Ms. Kim gets a pass, but you don't."

"OK, I will be there in a minute," Arcado replied.

He woke the twins up and asked if one of them would go with him knowing there was safety in numbers. They both blinked the sleep out of their eyes and agreed. They thought about waking Wanda, but she was comfortably snoring. They left her to sleep.

As they bundled up to depart, the boys were glad they had a different chore so they wouldn't have to face Travis about stealing the weapons. From now on, they would milk the cows. They opened the door to an abundance of snow blowing through the street. Being miserable was the new normal. Everyone's mind was filled with fear - of going out in the blizzard, being threatened by the town to stay there forever, being whipped for getting out of line, and the biggest fear was that of disappearing without a trace.

They trudged to the barn. Once they arrived, they grabbed a bucket and stool and then went to milking cows. Arcado was surprised to see that the two boys milked like they were seasoned veterans. They both milked theirs faster and then

153

went on to the next cow before Arcado and some of the adults finished. When the twins visited their Abuela in their mother's native land of El Salvador, they helped out with the farm errands. They milked cows, fed the pigs, and cleaned the horse stalls out daily during the summer. Farming taught the boys a lot about being self-sufficient. They were done in no time and headed back to Ms. Kim's quarters.

Shortly after they returned, there were more knocks on the door to wake up the rest of the kids for the daily chores. Everyone obeyed so that they would not cause trouble. Wanda woke the twins up. When they told her they milked instead, she was jealous.

"Why didn't ya'll wake me too?" she said in a scratchy morning voice. "Hey, I can milk a cow any day of the week."

The boys tiredly looked at her and then turned their heads the other way to continue to sleep.

"Well, goodnight then," she said, expecting them to say something. "It looks like I'll have to go with Adam to make me some shoes."

She thought this would get a rise out of the twins or make them jealous. They didn't stir. She looked at Adam who rolled his eyes.

Everyone went to their chore station as usual, but Brianna felt out of sorts being alone with the other sewers. She admired Shannon for making girls look competent and smart. She missed Lauren, who was coming out of her shell. Having Lauren's back was becoming something she looked forward to. Brianna felt purposeless without her girls, but she would never show it. Being solid was in her DNA.

Meanwhile, at the cobbler shop, Harvey showed Wanda how to get started on making a summer moccasin. Adam jumped right to it and finished a shoe he had started the other day. When Wanda was done with instruction, she sat next to Adam and started a shoe. It was a disaster. Wanda couldn't get the fabric to come together to sew. She ended up ripping apart some of the material and then dropped her tools on the floor. She was like a bull in a China shop. At that point, Adam threaded a thick needle of fiber and asked her to sew together his almost finished shoe. He cringed as she sewed it crookedly but knew that it would keep her busy. He sighed when he thought about Darcy. They had become such great friends making shoes. His head hurt thinking all day and night about what could've happened to her and the others. Like the others, he hoped that they made it to another house up the road and would come back and save him and the other students. He pushed out his mind, the dim notion that chances of the three frailest girls could do so.

After morning chores were completed, they headed to the mess hall. The students and Ms. Kim had missed last night's dinner because their stomachs were too upset to eat. Now they wanted to make up for it, so most requested extra bread and jam. They sat by themselves eating and moping. Samuel walked over to Adam and gave him a bag full of bread, jam, and hard-boiled eggs that he prepared for Ms. Kim. No words were spoken, just an exchange of nods.

The kids stared at each other in silence as they ate. All of the tables that morning sat in silence too. It was a grim day for everyone. Bianca made sure that the other kids didn't bother the new students with questions. The cooks sensed the tension in the room and quietly started cleaning the pots and pans. One of the cooks accidentally dropped a pan and it made a loud crashing sound on the floor. Everyone turned to look, but then dismissed it and went back to the dreadful quiet.

Then it happened. The noise startled everyone. The chiming, the ringing, the clang, clang, clang, clang was heard throughout the mess hall. It came from the campanile. Mr. Boyce and Travis stood up immediately. The ringing of the campanile meant that all of the town folk would gather at the town hall, but everyone was eating now. Boyce took a quick look around to see who was missing, rather, the person ringing the bell. Travis did the same and they both concluded that everyone was accounted for. The clanging sound wouldn't stop, it kept going. Swiftly, the two got their cloaks on and headed out the door. Adam was desperate to know if it had anything to do with Darcy, so he leapt up to follow the two men. Brianna felt the same way about Shannon and Lauren, so she followed Adam. After getting their cloaks on, they headed out toward the campanile, following Mr. Boyce and Travis.

The door to the campanile felt like it was glued shut from the freezing weather, but they pushed hard enough to break through. The clanging stopped. The four of them stomped up the stairs until they came to a landing around the 100th stair. There they were. Darcy and Shannon were wrapped up in blankets as they lay still.

Adam and Brianna gasped. They looked as dead as door knobs. There was no movement even with all the commotion they made when they arrived. Brianna noticed that Lauren was missing and she bit her lip in despair. Mr. Boyce bent down to Darcy and felt her neck for a pulse, but it was difficult to find. Travis did the same for Shannon. They looked at each other and shook their heads, hopeless.

"Please, help us," a soft voice from above said as she walked down the stairs toward them.

"Lauren!" Brianna exclaimed, astounded, and then went to give her a big hug. This was unusual for Brianna who had always tamed her emotions.

Lauren had a cloak on and was wrapped in her blanket. She was shivering.

"I think they need to get warm," Lauren said weakly and then fell into Brianna's arms and passed out.

Mr. Boyce picked up Darcy, Travis picked up Shannon, and Adam and Brianna managed to carry Lauren down the stairs. They headed to medical so the girls could warm up around the same fireplace they had only a couple days ago. Once there, they laid the girls down next to the unlit fireplace. Travis immediately made a fire.

"Adam, go get Doc Marta please," Mr. Boyce instructed. "Brianna, please get Wanda and bring her here."

They both obeyed and left. Brianna wasn't sure what Wanda could do, but she knew that having more NYC students there made her feel safe. She wished that Ms. Kim could hobble over and be there too.

Soon Doc Marta scrambled through the door and ran over to the girls immediately. She pulled out her trusty stethoscope, which was always in her pocket. She found a weak pulse on all of them.

"Travis, start the tubs up please," Doc Marta instructed.

Travis finished making the fire and it was popping and glowing. He headed to the next room to start up the tubs that were used to fight hypothermia. First, he turned on the generator, then he turned on two tubs. The water started bubbling but it took about 10 minutes to get them to the elevated temperature needed.

"The good news is that they are alive," Doc Marta said as she moved from girl to girl adjusting pillows under their necks to allow their airways more access for breathing. "The bad news is they may have severe hypothermia. It looks like they are dehydrated and their blood pressure has dropped, especially Darcy's."

Mr. Boyce went and retrieved a gallon jug of water and some glasses from a cabinet in the medical office. As he returned, the door burst open and Brianna returned with Wanda.

"Wanda and Brianna, please try and sit the girls up and have them sip slowly on the water that Mr. Boyce is pouring for you," Doc Marta commanded.

Brianna knelt and assisted Lauren in sitting up and taking a sip. Wanda did the same for Shannon. Doc Marta gave her full attention to doing the same for Darcy. Each of the girls needed help to stay upright and hold the glass to sip from. They were too weak to sit up so they laid back down to sleep. Each shaked uncontrollably. When the water was at the right temperature, Travis notified the doc.

"OK ladies, we have to bring your temperature back up to normal, so we need to walk to the thermal tubs," Doc Marta instructed in a serious tone. "Let's go."

Mr. Boyce, Travis, Wanda, Brianna, and Doc Marta were all needed to make this happen. The tired girls could not get up and walk. Once near the tub, Doc Marta dismissed the men and had the girls strip off their outer garments and kept the undergarments on. Wanda proved key to this effort. She amazed everyone with her strength. Of course, she had to narrate, loudly, the whole thing as she did.

Shannon sat in her tub and Darcy and Lauren shared a tub. All three of them were coming around and they started crying. They were in pain from being tired, thirsty, hungry, and still shaking in the hot water from being cold. Wanda saw they were in pain and she started crying too.

"What are you crying about?" Brianna asked.

"I don't know, but it feels good," Wanda said and continued wailing.

Brianna shook her head as if she was their guardian. It was stressful and she wanted to join in too. Being the voice of reason was her thing, so she stayed strong. Doc Marta continuously took the girls' temperatures to make sure that they were improving. Everyone wanted to know what happened to the girls, but the doc knew that the priority was to get them back into a healthy state.

The crying stopped and it turned into occasional moans and groans from each of the girls. Wanda was down to a sniffle too. While the doc was taking their temperatures, Brianna and Wanda took handfuls of hot water and poured it over their faces and necks. It took almost 30 minutes before the three frozen students came back to life. The girls finally had the warmth and strength to get out of the tubs, dry off, and then wiggle into the warm clothes that awaited them.

Mr. Boyce waited for the girls to recover. He wanted the whole story from start to finish. The doc and the five girls walked out of the medical room into the main room where the fireplace was ablaze. Mr. Boyce and Travis sat rocking in their chairs. They both stood up to give the girls their full attention.

"So," Mr. Boyce hesitated. "What happened?"

Thursday, December 3rd
Chapter 39 Blizzard Killer - Over

It happened so fast that the Corporal hadn't processed it. After getting the wind knocked out of him from his fall, he did a double take and noticed that Chauncy was missing. As he rose to look for him, his side felt tender.

"Chauncy!" he yelled. "Where are you?"

There was a long silence and then he heard a faint yell back.

"Hey! I'm down here," Chauncy replied.

The Corporal peered over the edge cautiously and saw evidence of markings in the snow but didn't see Chauncy. Then as he spanned to the left, he saw movement out of the corner of his eye. Chauncy waved to him and it looked as if he was alright. It was a good drop down, but the snow seemed to cushion his fall. The Corporal ran to the vehicle ahead to tell them what happened and figure out a plan.

Yellow Snowman turned his vehicle around to position the front near the edge of the cliff. There was a rescue rope rig above the bumper in the front of his Humvee. He released the mechanism so the rope would dump out into a pile on the ground. One end of the rope was secured to the mechanism and the rest of the rope was in a heap to be thrown down the mountainside.

With the wind sharply blowing, Yellow Snowman's attempt to throw the rope down to Chauncy was off by 10 feet or so, but he was able to make his way over to get it. Chauncy secured the rope clips around his waist and raised his arm to show that he was ready. The Humvee rope rig went into reverse and pulled Chauncy slowly to the top. Once he reached the top and was unhooked, he went to the guardrail and stared at it. As he looked at it curiously, it almost looked like the guardrail was grinning at him. Chauncy loaded back into the Humvee and retrieved a spray paint can. He marked the guardrail with a bright orange X so that he could put it in his report to be fixed.

Between the two crews, they put another set of chains on the back tire of the Humvee. In no time they were on the road trekking onward. Chauncy and the Corporal compared aches and pains as they drove. In the middle of laughing at each other, their radios squawked out a familiar voice.

"Snow Slayer to Blizzard Killer, do you read? Over," Tolbert must have been closer than before. He advised their coordinates which were straight ahead about an hour away.

"I read you loud and clear Snow Slayer. Over," Chauncy replied.

"So far there hasn't been a trace of the buses or any comms from the missing subjects. We called their cell phones and not one person answered. We found a fire station that we are going to hole up in for the night, compliments of Ulster County, and the five firemen fixing us dinner. We are going to spend the rest of the afternoon drawing grids for a more in-depth search tomorrow. Some of the crew is refueling the vehicles now and adjusting the chains. Are you heroes staying out of trouble? Over," Tolbert jested.

"Well, don't tell the Ice Queen, but I fell down the mountainside," Chauncy said in a no-biggie kind of way. "I just want everyone to know that the rescue rig on the Humvee works. I am proof. Over."

"The Ice Queen can hear you," she broke into the conversation. "You did what? And is there any more brain damage than before? Over."

"My brain is fully functional," Chauncy teased. "I hope I am OK cuz' I'm driving a $100,000 vehicle. Over."

"You're a little low on the price tag, but glad to hear you're alright. Over," the Master Sergeant remarked.

"I can't wait to hear the full story. Over," Tolbert squawked.

"Yeah, it was odd," Chauncy recalled, seriously. "I think I may have a theory on the missing buses. Over and out."

Chapter 40   The López's

Felix had just made it home in time before the first snow fell. He was an Operations Manager for Delta Airlines at the LaGuardia airport and Maria worked at the Memorial Hospital. Both of their family origins were from El Salvador but had lived in the states now for a decade. They lived in a large brownstone in Brooklyn Heights. It dated back to 1885 and was used for a century as a guest house for West Point military graduates furthering their education in the city. Then it was used in the mid-1990s as a hostel for travelers. The beautifully remodeled house had four levels, a basement apartment, and a small patch of grass in the backyard.

On the main level was a grand room for the family to gather in. There was a large brick and stone fireplace that was original to the house. The furniture was dated too but came with the house when the family moved in 10 years back. On the other side of the hall was a large dining area filled with heavy oak tables and chairs. Pictures of the López family covered every inch of every room on that floor. In the back was a large industrial kitchen, with six gas stoves and three ovens. An oversized kitchen island was in the center with a rack of pots and pans hanging above. The refrigerator was obnoxiously large and still somehow overfilled with food, mainly bought at the Latino Food stores around the corner.

Felix's parents lived in the basement, which was an apartment all by itself. His sister and her family lived on the third floor, and his wife's brother and his family lived on the fourth floor. Felix and his wife, Maria, and their four children lived on the second floor, which had three bedrooms. Vlad and Sergei shared a room and their sisters Mya, 5, and Maca, 8, shared the other.

Every adult in the house worked to share the mortgage. Their lives blended in every activity from cooking to taking care of the children. The language in the house was usually Spanish with a few English words thrown in from time to time. It was a nice place for Vlad and Sergei to grow up amongst family and, more importantly, cousins who they could get in trouble with.

With their father's flight benefits, the twins spent the summers at their abuelo's farm in El Salvador. Their mother loved to visit her parents any chance she could. This was the place where she earned her Veterinarian Degree. After Maria's mother seriously cut her femoral artery on a sharp sickle hook, she used tourniquet procedures to save her life. After a month of Maria's wound and physical therapy treatment, her mother was up and about farming again.

The story made local news and Doctors Group for Care stumbled across the article. They offered her a scholarship in the USA to continue her medical knowledge in treating people and she did. Felix worked part-time as a supply stocker at the hospital in New York, which is where Maria did her residency and where they fell in love.

Maria wished her parents could visit New York more, but they couldn't easily leave their farm for a visit because they needed to tend to the animals daily. This is where Vlad and Sergei learned to live off the land, fish, and hunt. Their summers were busy with work and play, and they were genuinely sad to go back to New York in the fall for school.

Word got out to the abuelos on the farm about Sergei and Vlad being lost in the snowstorm on the bus. They posted their grandsons' pictures in the field out by the main road with a caption to pray for their safe return. Because it was a small pueblo, all the residents knew the twins, so they quickly became the talk of the town and were mentioned at every mass prayer.

In Queens, the families sat around the fireplace sipping hot chocolate and coffee, talking about the twins as if they were never coming back. Felix's mother and father both had their rosaries in-hand and mumbled the Hail Mary. Felix had the student website up on his phone and translated all of the comments made by different families. He noticed his wife had posted a note of prayer, not panic, like most. In Felix's gut, he knew his boys were alright. They weren't like some kids who might give up in a tragedy. They were survivors. He kept everyone positive knowing that they would be OK. He wished his wife were home so that he could have some help keeping everyone upbeat.

Maria went right from dropping the twins off at the plaza that morning to the hospital for work. It was her day off, but she wanted to do some follow-up on a client's request, and didn't make it home before the feet of snow shored her in. Luckily, her office had a couch and a small refrigerator with leftovers. She made the best of it, helping out around the hospital wherever she could.

Whenever she couldn't be with her family, she would look up at the stars. It was a family tradition to look up at night when they were apart. It gave her comfort. Even if the skies were now snow-filled, they would still look up and feel their family's love.

Chapter 41 Fire Station Strategies

By the time Chauncy and his crew arrived at the fire station, it was late afternoon. The vehicles moved through the snow slowly but steadily. The drivers couldn't see what was in front of them due to the snow and blowing winds. The National Guard vehicles were parked back-to-back to allow little snow to accumulate in between.

When they entered the fire station, in one area there were two large fire trucks and in the corner were poles to slide down from the second floor above. In the room beside it, was a lounging room with grids and maps of the local area spattered across all the walls. The maps covered the route they were on all the way up to the student's destination of the Friend's Inn Resort in Minnechanka. Tomorrow, they would divide and conquer, one group taking the local roads first and the other group heading to the hotel. The firemen suggested the popular roads, besides the main road they were on, to add to the grid search. Ice Queen was in the middle of the grid search when Chauncy arrived with his crew. After they shook off and removed their snowy clothes, they were briefed on the plan.

Tolbert approached Chauncy with their usual rascally, high-energy handshake and then he handed him a cup of hot cocoa. They were both going over the day's adventures when one of the firemen announced that dinner was ready. In a galley-style kitchen, food was set up on the long counter. There was a mound of spaghetti and meatballs in a large rectangular tin, garlic bread, and hot green beans. Each stood in line to serve him or herself and then retreated to eat back in the large fire hall where the grids, tables, and chairs were laid out.

Tolbert described the long journey from New York City, that, on a normal day, may have taken an hour and a half to two hours, but today took five plus hours having made a lot of outdoor pit stops for the coffee that they all drank. Happening upon the fire station was like finding a treasure chest. There was smoke billowing out of the station fireplace and the smell of bacon wafted right through their thick truck windows. Even though the fire station was right on the main road, it was the pot of bacon and veggie stew over the station pit that had the National Guard honec in on the location. The fire station was perfect because, despite the snow banks in the driveway, there was plenty of space to park.

"Dude, you fell down the mountainside?" Tolbert asked. "I am so jealous."

Everyone was seated, eating, and listening to their day's story.

"Yeah man, Smith and I were checking the loose chain on the back wheel and when we tugged on it, the chain came off, sending us flying. I happened to hit the rusty guardrail that opened right up and spit me down the mountainside," Chauncy described. "I wonder if the buses went off the mountainside too. Maybe we should start there."

A burst of laughter came from all around the room.

"Did you see a bus or buses on the mountainside?" Ice Queen asked in a serious tone.

"Well, no it was snowing and blowing hard," Chauncy replied. "But..."

"But what, your bruised ego thinks that just because you tumbled down a mountain, the buses also drove down a cliff?" Tolbert jested.

Again, there were jeers and laughter from even the firemen.

"Hear me out," Chauncy pleaded. "After I recovered from my fall, I discovered a hard rock below me, which was in fact a tire. Not just any tire, it was a 11R22.5 tire, the same type of tires found on buses."

"How odd," Yellow Snowman said sarcastically. "A tire down a mountainside."

Again, the chuckling carried on and Chauncy realized that he looked like an idiot for suggesting it.

"The thing is," Chauncy said in a defeated serious tone and the room went silent. "There was no rust on it. It was a tire in perfect condition with the exception of not being on a vehicle."

The National Guard didn't know how meticulous Ms. Kim was about her bus selection. She liked her bus to shine inside and out. Driving a bus with rust or scrapes was her pet peeve.

She would buff her bus out and make it shine at any opportunity. Number 324 was the yellow, long, diesel that she drove regularly, but the transmission blew on the way to the plaza that particular Saturday. Rooter was refueling all the buses that morning when Ms. Kim reported the problem. Picking out the short bus that she would drive took a good 30 minutes. She searched and found the bus that had the best tires, muffler, engine, and most of all, a driver seat that was in good shape. Now one of her tires lay on the snowy hillside.

Everyone dismissed Chauncy's discovery. They thought he was making a big deal about a stupid tire. If only he would have found a bus or a big irregular rectangular mass in the snow worth investigating. The team went back to the grids and confirmed everyone's role in the next day's search and rescue. Chauncy acted like he was interested in the grid search, but he kept beating himself up for not taking pictures of the tire, the scene, the guardrail, and the river below. He had to get back to the scene somehow. He forgot about the river. The snow was blowing so violently that he didn't get to check if the buses had sunk in the river. Now, the only thing to do was to convince the Ice Queen to allow him to go back and check on his theory.

Friday, December 4th
Chapter 42 Town Hall Part II

The previous day's events of finding the girls on the stairs of the campanile quickly spread to the whole village. They were relieved, but wanted to know what the real story was, and if there was anything nefarious to worry about. Mr. Boyce had some restraint and didn't press the girls until they were fed and got sleep. Doc Marta told Boyce that she thought it best to let it lie until the next day when they got their strength and wits back. He reluctantly concurred.

The next morning after breakfast and before school, Mr. Boyce pulled the girls into the medical facility. He lit a warm, cozy fire and they all sat in a circle in the rocking chairs. Comfort was what he was going for, so he seemed non-threatening. Doc Marta, Boyce, and the three girls sat and stared at each other for what seemed an eternity before Shannon confessed.

Shannon was the one with the idea. She noticed that the steam from the mess hall cooking vent blew outwards toward a vent in the campanile. In her head, she thought that the steam would keep them warm. Nervously knowing a few days previously when they were summoned to the meeting in the hall, they might have the New York students punished or worse, she quickly devised the plan. As everyone left the school building, she pulled behind Darcy and Lauren and told them of her idea to hide until the weather broke.

The girls, who were just as afraid as Shannon was, did not have time to think and thought it was fate that they were the last ones to leave the building. In the foyer where everyone had hung their cloaks for school, there were footlockers full of supplies. Shannon snooped around on the first day accessing the lockers. In there she found blankets, flashlights, water, and a first aid kit. When Darcy and Lauren agreed to hide out until the weather improved, Shannon led them to the footlockers to grab the supplies. When they left the building, they could see the back of Wanda heading to the gathering hall. That's when they made their move to the campanile.

In a rush, they opened the door to the campanile and one of Shannon's bottles of water dropped and broke instantly by the door. Within hours, the door was frozen shut. They inched their way up the stairs to a landing where the vent poured in warm air from the kitchen steam from next door. They found this to be 100 steps up where they all fit snugly. Within the hour they could hear shuffling outside looking for them. This intensified their belief that they did the right thing. They could hear men in the snow calling the girls idiots for trying to leave. Each girl took this to mean that they would be beaten if caught.

Shannon was half right when the steam would come through and warm them up, but it only lasted minutes and it was a wet steam that would only make them colder in the end. Even with the blankets and huddling together, they were freezing. But they were in survival mode and they tried to put mind over matter. In her pocket, Shannon managed to skim extra bread off the table over a few days. Between the three girls, it was gone after two determined meal times. They were hungry, thirsty, cold, and utterly miserable.

There were times when Darcy changed her mind and would get up to leave, but it was Lauren who talked her into waiting it out. She knew that the storm would let up soon and they would escape. She was the most petrified of them all. When they awoke the next day, Lauren noticed that Darcy was weak and not doing well. Then, Shannon collapsed on the floor after she tried to stand up. As solid as Lauren wanted to be, she could not be strong for all three of them, so she made a choice. First, she went down to open the front door, but could not pull the door and break the ice that had formed. With the little energy that she had left, she slowly climbed to the top and rang the bell. There would be consequences she knew, but having her friends die right in front of her was too hard to bear. She mentally prepared herself to take whatever beatings as long as Shannon and Darcy would live. And they did.

After hearing their story, Boyce came to understand that they were afraid to be there but shuttered to recognize why they felt like they had to hide. He knew that the NYC students had a misconception of the people in the village. First, the new

168

students steal weapons and then three of the frailest girls hide in fear. It was time to air the story and set the record straight.

Mr. Boyce couldn't wait a minute longer and summoned Charlie to ring the bell for an important gathering in the town hall. Students were just arriving at school, adults were tending to their other daily chores, and the cooks were in the middle of peeling potatoes. Everyone knew to drop their activities and head over in the blustery wind to the hall. For the second time in a few days, the seats in the hall filled up, intermixed with the young and the old. They hoped Mr. Boyce would clear up the scare of the missing girls and his plan to have them stay or go home. At the front of the room, Mr. Boyce stood, signaling the crowd coming through the door to be seated. Ms. Kim found strength and hobbled over with her gauze-wrapped leg.

Soon, everyone was seated, but they continued to talk and make predictions on the purpose of the assembly. Mr. Boyce cleared his throat a few times to grab everyone's attention. It worked for the front but the sides and back were still full of chatter.

"Hey, be quiet!" Ms. Kim stood up from the center of the room, whistled, and talked in her commanding loud voice.

This settled everyone down and they turned their attention to the front of the room. You could hear a pin drop in the hall, giving Mr. Boyce an opportunity to start.

"Thank you for joining me here in the hall to make an announcement," he continued in his soothing voice. "A few days ago, we caught two of the New York students stealing weapons and hiding them in their footlockers, and then the same day, we had three young ladies feel that they were not safe in Ourstory, so they hid in the campanile."

He paused as the crowd gasped. Every New York student now had a deep pit of fear in their stomach, making them feel sick, even Brianna. Ms. Kim rolled her eyes at the stupidity of the whole scenario. There was no way she would stand by while this group punished her kids.

"I would like to call a few students to the front where I am standing." Mr. Boyce calmly said. "Charlie, Bianca, and Christopher."

169

Lauren thought that they would have their peers come to the front and lure their group up next for their beatings. She knew better and locked arms with Brianna, who in turn, locked arms with Arcado, who then locked arms with Adam, as he followed suit with the other New York students. The three teen residents called by Mr. Boyce soon stood beside him and stared out into the crowd.

"Everyone understands we are off the grid and there is much work needed to run this place. But, we each have so many of our own reasons for living here. It's no secret to us, but to our new young ones, it may appear to be a secret," said Mr. Boyce, who took his time trying to think of the right words.

"Don't you touch my kids!" Ms. Kim stood up and yelled at Mr. Boyce, pointing her finger angrily at everyone else in the hall. "I will hurt each and every one of ya's."

Everyone in the hall was puzzled and waited to hear what Ms. Kim would say next.

"Ms. Kim and students from the bus," Mr. Boyce said and then paused to make sure he got all of their attention. "Like I was saying, we all have our reasons for living in this old village. It started as a hunting retreat for a few friends. Then family members joined us and then certain circumstances landed others here."

"What I am about to reveal to you is absolutely heartbreaking and well, unless you live here, we didn't think you had the right to know," he looked at the three students and continued. "In upstate New York, there was an orphanage run by a rather peculiar husband and wife. Children were disappearing every six months or so. They were children of all ages. The children were intimidated and beaten."

At those words, Ms. Kim sat down and looked concerned for the kids standing in the front. Charlie and Christopher turned around and lifted their shirts to show the scars on their backs. Bianca lifted her sleeves to show the cigarette burns and scars on her upper arms and shoulders. The residents shuddered, even though this had been revealed to them already. Mr. Boyce told the story from start until finish.

The orphanage owners told each of the children that they might disappear if they told anyone about the abuse. They clearly implied that 'disappear' meant 'swimming with the fishes'. They truly believed the owners because kids were disappearing. The police would come around to take statements about the missing children. The owners would have some type of planted proof that the kids wanted to run away. They put on a good show because the cops would write it off as if orphans were troubled youth who didn't like to stay put.

There was a local priest that would visit the orphanage and knew that something was off-kilter with the kids. The priest noticed occasionally the marks on the girls' arms or bruises on the boys when their shirts would shift here and there. Their one-on-one conversations could be overheard by the lady of the house at any time, so he would point to their scars and stare them in the eye until he knew something wasn't right. The kids would never reveal what happened at the house but would nod yes whenever he gave them the stare. He had the older kids make private notes in a journal and take pictures of when the abuse would happen and when they gathered enough proof, he would save these kids. But he knew without proof, these nasty owners would make a scandalous story about the priest in the paper. He was told by a parishioner that the owners were heavy gamblers and that they would lie, cheat, and steal to pay off their debts.

One night Christopher overheard the owners talking about which one of the brats they would sell next. From the crack in the door, he watched them lay out on a large table, pictures of each kid and their statistics, like baseball cards. It listed their height, weight, and age next to their picture. He saw them point to Bianca. He was all of 12 years old and felt a total shock of fear move from his head to his dry throat. The owners made a phone call to someone and confirmed the drop-off would be on Friday night at midnight. They confirmed they would use chloroform to knock out Bianca like the others they sold and make the trade happen when the kids were asleep.

Christopher quietly stepped around to the back door and opened it like he just arrived. The couple quickly hung up the phone and shuffled the pictures under a newspaper and welcomed the boy home with a fake smile. He ran up to the room he shared with five other boys. It was Tuesday night and they needed a plan to save Bianca.

The next day Charlie and Christopher visited the priest before school and told him about their guardians selling Bianca on Friday night. The priest, in shock, picked up the phone to dial his friend who was a detective. The boys made one request from the priest and that was that the 20 of them weren't separated into different orphanages. They'd become family and protective of each other. The priest agreed even though he wasn't sure if he could uphold that end of the deal. Safety was his priority for all of them.

After the boys left and the priest shared their story with the detective, they made a plan. They both knew the sleazy orphanage caretakers had connections all over the city to make sure they always looked clean, so they had to handle this delicately.

That evening when everyone sat down at the orphanage to eat dinner, you could hear a pin drop. Everyone seemed to be nervous and couldn't make eye contact with the owners. The owners knew something was up when they looked at Bianca and she started crying uncontrollably.

They needed a new plan. The brats knew the gig was up and they would ruin everything they built. They suspected the priest was involved too. The owners left the room and made phone calls. They came back with a sloppy, frozen cake they defrosted in the microwave and sliced a piece for each kid and gave them a creepy smile. But no one was hungry, not even the small ones who were now crying too. The dessert was laced with sleeping medicine, and no one would eat it.

The owners brought out the whip and demanded that the kids eat a piece. They flogged everyone so hard that their shirts ripped and blood was dripping from their backs and arms. Each owner yelled at the kids as they moved around the tables with their whips. The little ones didn't want to get whipped so they ate their cake and minutes later they slumped under the table asleep. The owners demanded that they go to their rooms immediately. The older ones carried the sleeping little ones.

A few hours later, Christopher overheard foreign voices in the foyer saying that they would take them all. The owners said they needed some bodies to be found in the house fire. Christopher grabbed the emergency ladder out of the hall closet and shuffled everyone quietly to the girl's room in the back of the house. One by one, they climbed down the ladder to the back of the house and crept in the darkness to the side of the detached garage. The bigger kids carried the smaller ones, who were still sleeping, down the ladder gently. The goal was to run four blocks down to the church. After 10 of the children were safe a couple blocks away, the owners went upstairs to their locked doors and demanded that they open them. They warned them that if they tried to escape the bad men in the house had their pictures and would find them one by one and take them away.

Their threats only made them climb down faster. Soon, the few that remained could see and smell gasoline under the bedroom door coming through. Next, a match was lit and the house was in a blaze. The owners and the human traffickers escaped through the front door. Neither could have their business ruined, so leaving no witnesses behind was the only thing to do. When the firefighters got to the scene, it was just the distraught owners in the front sobbing uncontrollably that the kids were trapped in the house and they were the only ones who made it out in time.

After that morning's conversation, the priest and the detective couldn't think of anything else but the children. The officer had a few guys set up surveillance in an unmarked van across the street from the house. They took videos all day and all night of anything they could. They captured anyone who entered or exited the house from the front door, including the human traffic mobsters. They also captured some of the whippings through the windows.

When they saw smoke billowing from the house, two of the three men exited the van and ran around the house, even before the owners escaped. They saw the kids climbing down the ladder and escorted the remaining few to the side of the garage. When all were accounted for, they ran as a group through the back alley to the church.

The orphans entered the parish rectory and were led down into the basement which was a storage area for goods and clothing. The priest advised the two undercover officers not to say a word about the children to anyone except for his friend, the detective.

There was no time to lose. The moving van that was ordered for next week's food and clothing drive, appeared in the church alley within the hour. One could hear fire trucks, police cars, and ambulance sirens speed by the church. From the basement, the clothing, food, and blanket donations were brought up so they could be packed into the vehicle. The truck was backed in nicely to the back door so no one would see the cargo loading. Next, the children piled into the windowless compartment of the moving truck toward the front. They sat on blankets and huddled together behind boxes of donations. Soon, the tug of the truck inching forward let the children know they were on the move.

It was a brisk fall morning when the moving truck pulled into a warehouse. The kids lay asleep in the back of the vehicle until late morning. When they awoke, they could smell bacon wafting in. Many of the orphans still had a knot in their stomachs from the previous night's events and weren't that hungry, but the aroma of breakfast started to change their minds one by one.

Mr. Boyce was the first to greet them and invited them to eat breakfast. He assured them that they were in a secure location and nobody would take them away. Christopher was the first to indulge. He carried a six-year-old girl on his hip and a five-year-old Gabriel on his back to the table. Everyone slowly followed him. It was buffet-style. There were scrambled eggs, toast, bacon, sausage, orange juice, and muffins. This was something they never experienced before. The money allocated for the orphanage wasn't spent on any good food. It was no-name-brand raw oatmeal for breakfast every morning, bologna sandwiches with week-old bread, and something from a can for dinner with frozen veg-all.

They all ate until their tummies were full. The mood changed from heavily suspicious to cautiously optimistic. The warehouse was huge. It was stocked with aisles of shelved items, mostly for farmers. There were even riding lawn mowers and a few tractors. Mr. Boyce and the two men that brought the kids to the warehouse were doing some logistics to move the children to a location that the moving truck couldn't go.

Mr. Boyce, even though he was tall and intimidating, softened his look with his soothing, calm voice. He stood at the edge of the long breakfast table.

"Children, I want to introduce myself," his composed voice drew all eyes to him. "My name is Boyce Goodman. Well, you can call mc Mr. Boyce. There's a village about a few hours from here that I would like to take you to. You will be safe there. We have over 100 people, including children, living there now. It's a little off the grid, so we have to take alternate transportation to get there."

"Sir, what does alternate transportation mean?" Christopher asked.

"Well, I'd rather show you," said Mr. Boyce and waved for them to follow him.

The warehouse's large garage-like door opened and there was a carriage hooked up to a team of horses. The wagon was covered.

"Wow, like in the movies," remarked Christopher. "Cowboys and Indians."

"Well, hardly any of those around, but I'm afraid it's a small wagon, so we will need to make two trips," Mr. Boyce said and then saw the children start to panic as they didn't want to separate.

"Mr. Boyce, if it's all the same to you, sir, we would like to stay together," Charlie spoke for the group. "I can walk behind and so can some of the others. We don't want to be separated."

Mr. Boyce looked at every one of their earnest faces begging him to keep them together. He knew it had been a traumatic ordeal, so he gave into their suggestion.

"Well, I think we can work it out," he said and grinned. "But it may be a long walk."

The children felt like they had won a small victory. They hugged each other. The warehouse was set back off a major state road in which the horse and carriage would have to cross.

That was the only risky part of the plan. This area was heavily populated with Amish towns and many of whom had never spoken English. Anyone driving through would expect to see a horse and buggy or sometimes just horses on the road.

That fall day was the first day 20 upstate New York orphans felt cared for and safe. That was also the day they joined the town of Ourstory.

After the children were safe in Ourstory, a few days later, several videotapes were distributed to the Police Chief, the editor of the Daily News, and one to the FBI division that investigated human trafficking. What they found on the tape were videos of the orphanage, the owners, the faces of the human trafficking mobsters, and videos and pictures of scarred orphans. It included that night's flogging of the children from an outside window. It showed the owners as they left the house without rescuing one child from the fire. The husband put a few large duffel bags into the trunk of his car parked on the street. It showed him returning to the house lighting a cigarette and waiting for the fire department to arrive. The audio captured the wife on her cell phone calling to cancel their bowling lane for that night. She fussed about getting charged extra for not calling earlier.

All of this would be brought up in the arrest warrant. The owners surmised that the priest was behind the covert tape and put a friendly hit out on him. They knew ruthless mobsters who would handle even taking out a priest. Nothing was below them if the price was right.

The way Mr. Boyce retold the story to the whole crowd in the hall was mesmerizing. Each of the kids remembered that day as if it were a national holiday. But it still had everyone in tears, especially the New York students. They couldn't believe in this day and age that someone could get away with treating children so badly.

"We have no intention of hurting you or anyone. There was some abuse, but it was never done here. The orphans that were mistreated are just some of the residents that fled here from bad situations," he continued. "You see, there are others here that were in abusive relationships or failed witness protection programs. This world can be mixed up at times and this is a little bit of sanctuary for those who just want to live a normal life. We all don't have the same story or even the same reasons for living here."

"But we don't have a reason to stay here," Shannon stood up and spoke. "No offense. This is a nice place for all of you, but we want to go back to our families. We heard that you don't want us to go back."

"The weather should be clearing up soon. I would say even a few days. I intend to take you back home to New York City. I am sorry if you heard that we would keep you here longer than needed," Mr. Boyce paused again searching for words. "I know I can hardly ask a group of young teenagers to keep a secret for life, but it sure would honestly mean life or death for some of the residents here."

The whole room was silent and somber for minutes.

"We won't tell anyone," boomed Wanda's voice, who was so moved by the story. She looked from student to student when she spoke up. "We can't tell anyone."

She looked around at each of her classmates who nodded in agreement, except for Brianna whose eyes examined the floor instead.

"We don't say a thing," Vlad stood up, and then Sergei did to show solidarity. They were so relieved they weren't in trouble.

"Well kids, I can only imagine that having your story of where you have been just might make front page news in New York City," said Mr. Boyce nervously. "Not one of you would consider getting some attention, or heck even some money out of it if the story was really good?"

"How much money?" Ms. Kim stood up, chuckled, and looked around the somber room. "Just kiddin'."

The quiet crowd couldn't gauge if she was truly joking.

"I can't promise anything," Brianna shouted. "I can't lie to my mom or aunt."

"Honesty is one of the best traits to have and I admire that," Mr. Boyce shook his head.

"The owners of the orphanage went to prison, but they only nabbed one of the four human traffickers. The firemen reported that there were no bodies found in the burnt-down house, so I know for a fact that, along with the FBI, those thugs are looking for these orphans. They still have pictures of each one of these kids from two years ago. So your truth may have 20 of your peers hunted down like animals and forced into human trafficking or even killed."

"I've always given everyone the choice to leave this town when they are old enough to make that decision," said Mr. Boyce somberly. "But I never thought that I would see the day where news stations find us and exploit who we are to the world. There's nothing I can do about it, except to beg for your mercy to understand that lives are at risk."

"I'll have to think about it," Brianna said in an unbiased way. "I'm not saying I will keep a secret, but if I do, I need a cover story and it's got to be something mostly truthful and solid enough that we can all remember by heart. So, I will need you to think of something like that for me. I can't make stuff up easily."

"That won't be a problem," Mr. Boyce smiled at Brianna, knowing that he had her by a thread. Inside, the real threat that he worried about was Ms. Kim. She tended to be a bit outspoken.

After the town hall meeting, he dismissed the villagers, but everybody seemed to linger and talk. It turned into hours of reconnecting with the new students and even old neighbors. There would be no school or other activities that afternoon. The New York students apologized to their friends for the suffering they went through. Ryan was upset knowing that Bianca was almost sold into human trafficking. Down in the pit of his stomach, he thought she was sassy and bossy, but after discovering she was orphaned and a victim of abuse, he wanted to take care of her. After a few minutes of thinking, he knew that he could never tell her that outright. She was strong and proud and didn't need his pity or his protection.

Travis pulled Sergei and Vlad over for a side conversation. The boys expressed regret for stealing the weapons and agreed to put everything back. They thought he would reprimand them, but instead, Travis sympathized and said he thought they acted bravely to protect the other students when they feared for their lives. He convinced them to keep hunting with their crew until they were ready to leave their village. They both felt a heavy burden lifted off their chest. They smiled and agreed to hunt the next morning.

Before they left for lunch, the door to the hall opened, a little boy walked in, and everyone turned to see who it was. It was Gabriel. This raised a lot of eyebrows because he rarely ever left his room, except for choir practice or the Sunday service. He walked to the front of the room and onto the stage where Mr. Boyce had just told his story of the orphanage.

"Excuse me, ladies and gentlemen," stated Gabriel in his adorable young voice. He waited for the room to quict down. "I just wanted to say that I had a vision of us living in peace. This will happen because it has to happen."

At that, he stepped down the stairs and walked back out of the building. Everyone was confused and nobody understood what he meant. While what he meant wasn't evident, his goal was always to make people think a little deeper. And that is exactly what everyone did that day.

Chapter 43 Rescue on the Way

The next day when morning broke, the soldiers woke up with a vengeance. The Ice Queen helped the firemen make breakfast so everyone could hurry up and move faster.

After breakfast, the Ice Queen stood in front of her guardsmen and went over the plan. They would divide and conquer into three groups to cover the whole grid. One group would continue down the road straight until they reached the Friend's Inn Camp. A few would detour and go down 17 offshoot roads, from the main road to the south. The last group would take 21 offshoot roads to the north; most of which led out to Amish country.

They secured all of the bedding and gear and put it back into the trucks. They refilled their water jugs in the kitchen. Some were tasked with refueling the track vehicles. Some were assigned to remove the snow and make a path for all the vehicles, which, luckily, there was no ice holding them down. Things were moving along and daylight was sneaking through. There was no sun, nor for that matter any moon present, but the day did get a little brighter.

Chauncy wanted to go back and investigate the mountainside, but it was a 'hard no' from any leader. He hated to be dismissed for his theories. One day, he would be a criminal investigator and hoped maybe people would take him more seriously. Until then, he was in the vehicle heading toward the Friend's Inn.

The troops thanked the firemen for their hospitality and warned they may be back. All the vehicles had started and were idling. Once everyone boarded their vehicles, a radio check was completed and then they rolled out in a convoy. Chauncy and Smith turned left and were on their way to the Friend's Inn. Tolbert turned right with his crew to search one of the 17 feeder roads. The Ice Queen's team went left to tackle the 21 feeder roads.

As they trekked through the whipping winds and snow, they made their own road wherever their wheels rolled through. Each vehicle went no faster than 20 miles per hour. It would indeed be a long day of searching. Hours went by and Chauncy saw a house with a barn behind and a garage the size of an airplane hangar coming up on the left. He made a turn into the street off the main road. This alarmed Smith.

"What's going on? We are still over an hour's drive to our destination," he asked.

"Look at that big garage," remarked Chauncy. "Two buses could be in there."

The track vehicle turned into a lot that had seen no snow removal in days. The truck rolled over a few feet of fresh snow until it was right up to the front porch. The nicely sized garage was perpendicular to the house and it wasn't attached. An outside light from the house turned on and a man could be seen at the front door studying his visitors.

Chauncy and Smith got out and were wind blasted as they trudged up to the house. The man opened the inside door, but the outside door pushed open just slightly due to the mound of snow piled in front of it. As Chauncy got to the porch, the man handed him a shovel to do the honors, so he could open the door properly. It took more effort than he thought to shovel a little space for the opening. When there was ample space to open the door, the man invited them inside.

Snow-covered, Chauncy and Smith entered carefully, making sure they didn't bump anything to prevent sending piles of snow to the ground. They glanced around at the simple house with a fireplace lit behind the owner.

"Sir, we are looking for two school buses with students and gardening staff from New York City," Chauncy said. "Have you seen either the buses and/or the children?"

"No, I haven't," the older man said, pulling on his suspenders. "I heard about 'em on the radio. I wished to God I had seen them. We have plenty of room to host them."

The older man's wife came into the entryway with a dish towel drying her hands.

"You boys should take your coats off and let me fix you some breakfast," she said with a friendly smile. "We just finished having some grits and toast."

Chauncy looked at Smith with questioning eyes. It had been two hours since they ate last, so they weren't hungry. The place just seemed so cozy that they wished they could strip right down to their long johns and chill by the fireplace. Smith was the conscience of the two and shook his head "no".

They turned around and were about to leave. Chauncy stared at the enormous garage and his wheels started spinning.

"Sir, we are going to have to search your garage," insisted Chauncy. "We have to be thorough on all avenues with this mission."

"It's been two years since the children were in the warehouse," the owner's wife said mistakenly.

The owner's head snapped and stared at his wife as she misspoke. Chauncy and Smith were confused and suspicious of what she meant.

"I mean, it's been years since any visitors of any age," she went to correct herself. "Oh never mind."

"Let's go," said the owner and grabbed a key.

The older man inhaled deeply, signaling his distaste for being accused of any shenanigans. But he understood that they wanted to eliminate this residence as a possibility of refuge for the missing group. He grabbed his coat, stepped into snow pants, put his boots on, and then a knit hat and gloves. They pushed the door open and then climbed a few feet of snow to a side entrance of the garage.

He turned the key in the door and then shoved it open. They all piled inside bringing a nice amount of snow with them. Smith thought about it and wished they would've radioed the group to advise them they were entering a resident's house and garage. If anything nefarious happened, they would track them there. He remembered that each vehicle did have a tracking device inside to give off its GPS, which relaxed him slightly.

After they stomped off the snow, they looked around. It was as quiet as a vacant library. Chauncy was amazed at how sizable this garage was out in the middle of nowhere. There were huge pieces of machinery. There was large industrial shelving with farm supplies, animal feed, people food, hunting apparatuses, housewares, canoes, kayaks, horse saddles, lots of lumber, tools, nails, paint, brushes, hoses, blankets, cots, furniture in plastic, and just about anything a local store would house.

They walked around the rows of shelving and products. This seemed odd to Chauncy to have so many of these kinds of things when the population had no demand for them. This made him more suspicious. There were a few closets and a washroom but no back rooms or loft rooms, it was all open bay. Hiding in this warehouse was not possible. After a few laps around, Chauncy admitted defeat.

"Sir, why do you have so much junk for such a small community?" he asked.

"I wouldn't ever call this junk. There are all sorts of farmers and Amish folk that live around here," he answered. "They need these things. To travel through the mountain and into the city is time-consuming, so I order it and have it handy for them. I am not in it for the money, it's more to be the center of the community and help out. Living 'round here is different. People know each other and their families. Also, I bid online for the big industrial machines and some of the other stuff. I know what they are worth and I underbid. If I win the bid, I know that nobody else wanted to bid on it. So my clearinghouse is good at every angle you look at it."

"There's nothing illegal about this Chauncy," Smith stated.

"Yeah, I know," said Chauncy, cynically. "It just seems odd."

The older man chuckled at the young kid who he thought had most likely watched too many TV mystery shows. He and his son had managed the warehouse for years. It was a legitimate business, although some of his dealings were more barter than sales. If he were asked to produce a ledger of sales, this would most likely be a problem. Luckily, these kids were only there for a search and rescue mission which had nothing to do with his warehouse dealings.

Chauncy and Smith seemed to be satisfied with their search. Chauncy left the man with his business card with his cell phone number on it, in case they should see the bus load of students and staff. They bid farewell to the house owner and climbed back into their track vehicle and got back onto the road they were traveling on.

"I can't put my finger on it," Chauncy said as he thought out loud. "But something bothers me about that guy and his convenient warehouse overfilled with everything and the kitchen sink."

"Wow," remarked Smith. "You are so out in left field. I am starting to worry about you. Keep your head in the game man. We are looking for students, not bootleggers."

They drove off and continued toward the Friend's Inn Camp. Chauncy barked on the radio about what he and Smith checked out and that they were back on the road. The Ice Queen didn't appreciate his decision to make a side stop. She gave him implicit instructions to get to the camp with no more deviations. Chauncy explained his strong hunches. She remarked something back to indicate that he was no "Sherlock Holmes" and to quit acting like it. He retorted back in his best old, British voice acknowledging her in his sarcastic yet respectful tone.

Tolbert and Corporal Farmington were on their second vacant road. The farmhouses that they passed did have large barns and after Chauncy plead guilty to deviating to check out the large garage, he thought that was a good idea if they wanted to be thorough. But he had already passed over 20 barns and to backtrack would take hours. He felt less satisfied just driving down streets without chatting to the residents at every house. Tolbert squawked over the radio, asking to exhaust all possibilities and stop at every house with barns. The Ice Queen shot it down, saying that the buses would be in plain sight, not hidden. Most of the unit thought the buses most likely got stuck in the snow and they were either still in them or a kind resident took them in for shelter. Tolbert and Chauncy were out-of-the-box thinkers in all sorts of ways and found that they were looked at as causing trouble for it.

It was a long day for certain. The speeds were slow and the winds were unforgivable. Some got out of their vehicles to search a truck or a trailer pulled over and covered in snow. Some vehicles were down roads so far that took them to another trail and then another mountain road. The day was coming to an end and only a few vehicles were making their way back to the fire station.

Chauncy and Smith finally made it to the Friend's Inn. It looked like a ghost town of snow. No lights were on in any of the cabins and the registration building was closed. They accidentally drove through a boom barrier and broke the red and white pole that prevented just anybody from driving onto their property. The snow was piled too high to see it. They decided to drive the circular path of the campground to check out the cabins and see if the owners were around. In the back of the property, they discovered a larger cabin that housed the owners. They pulled up as close as they could and startled the couple with a knock on their front door.

They allowed them to enter and then invited them to stay. It was four o'clock in the afternoon and it was getting darker. Chauncy and Smith were tired and yawned, deciding to radio the group to tell them they were going to hunker down for the night at the Friend's Inn. They did report that the owners hadn't seen any of the buses nor heard from the students or gardeners. The owners were on their third day of venison stew, which to Chauncy's surprise was one of the best things he had ever eaten.

Tolbert drove to where the top of the mountain road led back to New York City. There was an Inn with no vehicles in front. Across the street was a dark gas station with a sign flipping back and forth from the howling winds. There was another offshoot road nearby, which Tolbert claimed to be their last one before heading back to the firehouse. After they turned down the street, he thought the darkness made the road look eerie. They crept along trying to be observant, but it was useless seeing farther than a few feet in front of them.

"Let's go back," said the corporal in the passenger seat. "We can't see jack."

"I agree," remarked Tolbert. "It's hopeless. We can come back tomorrow and start fresh."

Tolbert stopped the vehicle and maneuvered to turn it around. When he made the broad turn, the vehicle hit something solid and it stalled the Humvee.

"What was that?" the corporal asked.

"Dunno," he said. "But it didn't sound good."

They both got out in the tundra and went to the front of the vehicle. It was smashed. Still standing was a five-foot tall fire hydrant made of a solid metal alloy on the side of the road, covered in the snow. Eyeing the dented-in engine, they thought surely the engine was damaged.

"Seriously Tolbert," exasperated the corporal angrily. "I knew I should have ridden in the other Humvee."

"I didn't mean to," admitted Tolbert. "How was I supposed to know a gigantic fire hydrant would be out in the middle of nowhere?"

"Now what?" asked the corporal as Tolbert put his hand to his chin. "What are you thinking?"

"I am thinking," replied Tolbert who couldn't resist cracking a joke. "They must walk some big dogs out here."

It took the corporal a minute to put together the gag and finally gave a chuckle-like sigh. They both returned to the vehicle and sheepishly turned on the radio.

"Snow Slayer to Ice Queen. Eh- we may need a rescue. Over," said Tolbert and then winced.

"What do you mean by rescue? Over," reprimanded the Ice Queen.

"Our engine is damaged from running into a 10-foot fire hydrant," Tolbert hyperbolized. "Now she won't run. Over."

There was silence on the other end. Both Tolbert and the corporal knew that the Ice Queen was swearing up a storm.

"Well, unfortunately, it will have to be tomorrow," she replied angrily. "Hunker down boys. We will radio you tomorrow when someone is on the way. Over."

"But," injected the corporal on the radio.

"Good night," the Master Sergeant said in her condescending voice. "Sweet dreams. Over."

Saturday, December 5th
Chapter 44 Storm Subsides

Before daybreak, the students got up for their chores, all tired and cold. It occurred to Arcado as he was milking Bretta that he wasn't whipped with wind and snow when the crew walked over to the barn. The air as crispy cold as it was, held no blustery wind or blinding snow. He didn't want to get his hopes up but he thought this might be the day he can go home.

When Travis woke up and realized the snow had stopped and the winds weren't whipping, he became optimistic and thought he would show the new students how to handle new weaponry. He gave Sergei and Vlad a bow and arrow and Wanda a bola. The weapons were interchanged between the hunters, so they all had the opportunity to improve their skill sets.

"Boleadoras," Sergei and Vlad said to Wanda, meaning bola.

"Yeah, I think ya'll are adoras too," Wanda flirted back.

Travis took Sergei and Vlad to a place to practice before they headed out to hunt that day. Because of the early morning rise, there was little light in which to hit the target, but after the back wall of the barn was dusted off, they could see plenty of bullseyes drawn on it. Both boys were hitting targets within minutes of starting. They felt relaxed in the outdoors and were able to control their breathing and muscle movements.

Wanda trailed behind the boys. Travis taught Wanda how to hold the bola and throw it to trap the prey. He whizzed it around overhead and tossed it, wrapping it around a wooden fence. While Travis gave the boys more tips, Wanda spent the entire time untangling the rope and stones from the fence. This was not her favorite weapon. She kept getting the bola tangled even around her legs or the weapon itself, so she finally started carrying it by the weights as opposed to the ropes.

The teams were ready to hunt and divided into three groups as usual. This time the twins went off to the north, the experienced team went to the east, and Wanda and Travis's team went to the south. They would hunt in teams and meet to carry their prize back to camp. This was the first time Wanda and the boys didn't hunt together. In some ways, it was a relief to Wanda because she felt that she hadn't helped at all yet. The boys would occasionally get a squirrel or a muskrat to contribute. She wished they would fish. Her grandparents fished recreationally and had some of the neighborhood's best fish fries in the summer. Wanda had never fished but knew she could do something like that. She desperately wanted to show that she could pull her share of the work.

Her team entered the woods together and walked gingerly, hearing far-off twigs breaking from animals moving. Wanda was off in her world thinking about making her own fishing pole with some line. She thought she might need someone to put the worm on the hook though. A few of the guys took the path to the right after hearing some noises. Everyone followed and as usual Wanda was the last one.

Wanda saw a large stick on the ground that would be a perfect pole. She went to grab it, but some of it stuck, frozen to the ground. The others were now further ahead, but she wanted that stick. Getting down on her knees to loosen up the end of the icy stick, she fervently pulled until it broke free, sending her flying to her back. The tight snowsuit required her to roll from her back to her belly so she could position herself to stand up. As she rolled onto her tummy, she cast her eyes on a big tree that looked like it was moving.

It changed shape. A deer, she hopefully thought. She quietly got to her knees and grabbed her only weapon. She was afraid to grip it again because it would get tangled around her body, as usual, as she tried to handle it. Wanda picked the weights up first as the rope dangled. As she did so, the deer was moving faster until it was running at her full speed. She panicked. She took the bola correctly by the ropes and swung it above her head in a fast-circular motion. It was heavy and difficult, but she didn't want the deer to ram her. Closing her eyes and letting out an exhausted scream, she finally let go of the bola and in an instant, the galloping sound coming toward her ceased.

Bullseye, she got it. The men on her team ran back to see what the commotion was about. The team gathered around and looked at her strangely.

"What the heck did you do?" Travis asked in shock.

Wanda felt a wave of acid race from her throat to her stomach and felt sick.

"I mean how in the blazes did you do it? You must be really strong." stated Travis, puzzled.

"Well, you see, it was either him or me," Wanda reasoned. "That deer was gonna' barrel me down."

"Wanda, that wasn't a deer," Travis exclaimed.

In a panic, Wanda walked 20 feet to see the beast lying on the ground. It was the black bear. The bola weights hit his head, killing it instantly with the force. Her jaw dropped and eyes widened in amazement. She was in shock.

The team rolled the bear onto the tarp. They dragged it to the edge of the woods where the other teams arrived to assist. Wanda was so glad to see Sergei and Vlad.

"Guess what?" Sergei asked Wanda when they met up together. "Vlad and I shot rabbits."

Vlad and Sergei both were trying to show off their new skill. They knew this would impress Wanda, although they didn't have to try hard.

"Oh, that's nice," Wanda brushed it off. "Oh Sergei, guess what?"

"What?" Sergei inquired with a smile.

"I bagged the black bear that we're carrying," Wanda chuckled and strutted away carrying her new fishing pole, leaving them wanting more. Both boys' mouths hung open in disbelief. The teams started laughing as they dragged the heavy tarp and the twins carried their little rabbits.

Back at the village, as the team dragged the tarp to the butcher's station in the back of the mess hall, everyone stared like they were watching a parade. All 600 pounds of this beast were pulled to the door. There were only two chefs that could prepare the bear properly. If you didn't cook it well, it could make you as sick as a dog. This would take the two of them days to do their magic in the butcher's shed.

Arcado and Lauren were the only ones not happy about seeing the tarp come through town. Arcado was a vegetarian before he came to Ourstory. He thought hunting was wrong. Lauren never thought about it until she came to this place, but seeing poor helpless creatures hunted down put it in a different perspective. Being vegetarian here was difficult because the only meals so far with protein included meat. There was no tofu, beans, or protein powder to supplement. So, try as they may to snub the meat, the reality of staying healthy was to eat their portion and complain when they got home eventually. The students never thought that they would witness the full process of making a meal, starting with hunting.

At breakfast that day, two things happened. First, the beautiful weather didn't go unnoticed. While working on their chores that morning, everyone observed the change in the weather and the opportunity to go back to New York City. Mr. Boyce knew the kids would be asking to go home as soon as possible. He had arranged a team of men to make the trek up the path and see if it was passable. The snow was piled up so high that the horses wouldn't be able to walk down the marked path easily.

Secondly, Wanda told her bear story to anyone who would listen and the story grew more and more dramatic every time she told it. She was the talk of the village and retold the story several times throughout the day. She hoped that the twins would see her in a cool, hunter-provider light that would be desirable. Some of the local boys asked her for details about the kill which made the López boys a bit jealous. The twins were finally starting to make a connection with Wanda. Whether it would be a romantic connection or not would remain to be seen.

After everyone ate and washed their dishes, Boyce made an announcement to everyone regarding his intention to get the New York City kids back to their homes as soon as he got the assurance from his team that the horses could handle the road path full of snow. He indicated that it might take hours to know and there would be a cutoff to when he and the kids could make the journey for the day. He wanted to keep it real just in case they had to leave tomorrow.

There was excitement in the air for all the New York kids. They had been in Ourstory for eight days without hope of the snow letting up. Now, they would finally get to go back to their comfortable homes and see their parents, siblings, pets, and neighbors. Ms. Kim in her sarcasm kept saying she couldn't wait to write her "tell all" book of her tale of the crashed bus. Truth be told, she got knocked so hard in the head, that she barely remembered any of the details of the semi-truck she almost plowed into. She would never admit that to anyone. The kids had recounted to her the story numerous times that she knew the details of the incident and how to embellish things to become newsworthy.

Saturday, December 5th
Chapter 45 Yippee

Mr. Haugen was the first to rise that morning. After he stumbled to the kitchen to get a glass of water, he thought of the agenda for the day. He thought about his wife, daughters, and the students' families. As he sipped from the glass over the sink, he looked outside and stared at the whiteness and the forest that was at the back of the property. He thought it odd that he had never noticed the forest before. He didn't mean to, but, out of shock, he dropped the glass in the sink and it shattered.

"Oh my goodness," he realized. "It's over, I can see the forest as clear as day!"

Everyone was still sleeping somberly on the floors, couches, and recliners. He wasn't sure if he should wake them but would explode otherwise.

"Wake up everyone," he shouted. "The storm has subsided."

Shauna was the first to open her eyes and sit up to confirm it. She slowly got to her feet and stared out the front window. She saw blue skies peeking through the clouds. Snow still shifted from the wind here and there, but it was nothing compared to the whipping winds of the days earlier.

"It's true," she said to her coworkers, still comfortably sleeping.

She looked at Mr. Haugen who was impatiently childlike in wanting everyone to rise and get going. Paul and Josh would need to take the snowmobile and get to a phone to notify the sheriff of the missing children and request the police department rescue them from that house.

"Well, I'll be," said Myra entering the room and scratching her head that held curlers under a scarf. "Looks like we have ourselves a day to ride into town finally."

"Maybe we should have a celebratory smoke," said. Rooter in a yawn as he walked out of the guest bedroom.

"Let me get these rollers out of my hair and I'll join ya," she said, almost embarrassed at her appearance.

Jessica and Shauna made coffee while Paul and Joshua folded sheets and blankets to get ready for the day. Nobody talked, but just enjoyed the blue skies that were breaking through. Rooter went out the backdoor by himself and reappeared with a basket of eggs. He placed them on the counter carefully and went back for more. Everyone had fallen into a routine to contribute to the chores of the house. Mr. Haugen decided that there was no reason to finish the different puzzles on the floor so he picked them up and put them into their respective boxes. His staff seemed unhappy that their hard work on the floor had now been ruined, but they knew they had to focus on getting back to New York.

After breakfast, Paul, Josh, and Valley decided they would go on the two snowmobiles to the sheriff's office. Dressing warmly, they departed. They didn't see their whole team waving goodbye furiously from the window in excitement.

The snowmobiles puttered down the road. Valley started yelling descriptions of his neighbors and pointed at their houses, but the boys couldn't hear them, nor did they care. They just nodded their heads in kindness. They passed their mostly snow-covered bus, seeing only some yellow on the top. There was no reason to stop at the bus, so they continued onward. After another mile down the road, they saw a vehicle that was blocking half the road, so they stopped. They were curious to see if there was anyone inside and, if so, if they were alright.

Joshua brushed the snow off the front passenger side window and peered inside the front seat of the Humvee. There was a body in the driver's seat in an almost full recline. Paul cleared the back seat window and found another body fully stretched out and sleeping. Valley knocked on the window loudly. This had both boys jump up in a scare. Tolbert noticed the men stare at him through a clearing in the window and it felt a little creepy.

"Dude," said Tolbert in his morning hoarse voice. "I think the neighbors noticed we got stuck."

The corporal opened his eyes and sat straight up like he was late for something. The temperature in the Humvee was just a little warmer than outside of the vehicle. Each boy was

193

bundled in blankets. They pushed them aside and got out of the Humvee, pulling themselves together.

"Hello, I am Corporal Tolbert and this is Corporal Farmington of the MMC," introduced Tolbert. "We hit a fire hydrant and got stuck last night."

"Yep," said Valley. "The only fire hydrant on the road for miles. Did ya' damage it?"

"No," replied Tolbert a little perturbed. "It's pretty sturdy. So sturdy that it damaged my Humvee."

"Well as long as the hydrant is OK," continued Valley. "You never know when you might need her, but it's the only one we got."

"Of course," said Tolbert in a sarcastic tone. "Glad we didn't damage it with our now cracked V8 engine."

"We are on our way to the sheriff's office," mentioned Paul.

"The National Guard will pay for any damages," said Farmington. "You don't have to get the sheriff."

"That's not why we're heading there. Our bus broke down on the way to a camp about a week ago," replied Joshua. "We need to let them know we are OK."

At that, Tolbert took the black, warm watch cap off his head and threw it in the air. Both he and Farmington started jumping up and down in almost a dance.

"We found you first," yelled Tolbert. "I mean, we found you."

"Is everyone alright?" inquired Farmington.

"Yes, just fine," said Valley. "I had them holed up in my house until it was over. The rest are waiting for someone to pick them up. That's why we're headed to the sheriff."

"I can radio my Guard Unit and we'll pick them up," said Tolbert in more than an insistent way.

"Sure that'll work," stated Paul. "Do you happen to have a cell phone? We would like to let our families know we're alright."

"Our cells don't get service around here," mentioned Farmington. "We need a good landline, but there's a lot of wires down."

"Snow Slayer to Ice Queen do you copy? Over," said Tolbert anxiously as he spoke into the radio.

"This is Ice Queen, go ahead. Over," she said unenthusiastically about using that handle.

"We've found the bus people and they're alright," he announced. "Come get us so we can go home. Over."

"You what?" she said, but in the background, you could hear cheering. "I don't believe it. We're on our way. Over."

Saturday, December 5th
Chapter 46 Ourstory Making Music

Everyone was in a celebratory mood after breakfast. There was choir practice scheduled for both the adult and children's choir. Brianna and Ms. Kim walked over to the gymnasium together. By now, the burn on Ms. Kim's leg was healing nicely. She left her skin exposed to the air without any gauze. Truth be told, Ms. Kim's body temperature was known to run hot and she liked her shin exposed so much that she rolled up the other pant leg to match. Ms. Kim sat in a chair to watch, but Brianna, who was in a fiercely good mood, dragged her to stand next to the choir to sing.

"I've watched you every time we practice," remarked Brianna. "I think you have a songbird in you that you need to let out."

Ms. Kim grabbed a folder with the music in it and gave Brianna a sly look as if she double dog dared her to sing. Everyone was in their places and the electric guitar started up. It was the song "Shackles" by Mary, Mary. They let Brianna take the lead in vocals and she sang in-tune and pure. Ms. Kim did sing in the refrain with the choir and moved from side to side like everyone else did as they sang. The choir chuckled internally watching Ms. Kim get down and sing at the same time. It was so uncharacteristic of her, but Brianna thought it was time for Ms. Kim to feel free. The casual vibe was exactly what Ms. Kim needed to get on the stage. After a few songs, most wished she didn't feel so free, but the beast was unleashed.

Next door in the town hall, Vaughn played the piano as the children's choir warmed up their vocals. Bianca sat next to Vaughn on the piano and flipped through the song selections. Mr. Chad hadn't shown up to direct the choir yet, so she took the opportunity to pick some songs. She chose the song "Mary, Did you Know?" and Vaughn studied the music sheet to familiarize himself with the pages and notes.

It started with Charlie singing the first verse and then Bianca joined in with the children harmonizing. The New York

City students didn't know this song, so they sang off the song sheet and after getting the hang of it during the first refrain, blended in with the others. Ryan thought that Bianca had a beautiful voice and cursed her because it was just another thing that she did well.

After the song ended, Bianca asked Vaughn if he would play and sing the song that he claimed he wrote when he gave his narrative in class. He admitted it wasn't a Christmas song, but everyone egged him on to play it. The silent hall was soon filled with the soft sounds of the piano playing at first, and then an easy melody of words rolled out of Vaughn. It was a tender song about love, but to him, it was about losing his mother and having her find her way back somehow. There were no harmonies or other instruments played, just Vaughn baring his soul on the piano singing.

He knew how to carry his voice, sometimes it was gentle and other times it was intense and sharp. In the end, as the song tapered down to the last chord, everyone cheered and clapped. Girls of all ages were instant fans and already dreamt of him singing to them someday. Mr. Chad entered as Vaughn was finishing his song and clapped along with everyone. The director knew that one day if he ever went back into the city, he would buy Vaughn's album. In the meantime, practice was needed.

They practiced for hours like they normally did. When they broke for lunch, Ryan caught up with Bianca before heading across the street.

"Hey, I was wondering if you wanted to play one-on-one on the court tonight?" Ryan asked, trying to overcome his sour view of the talented and pretty girl.

"Why?" asked Bianca, not wanting to form any attachment to a boy that was rude, cocky, and most likely leaving in a day or two.

"Because you are a good opponent," he stated and then felt stupid for trying to be nice.

Bianca's light brown eyes looked into his searching for a man that he didn't know he could live up to, making him feel absolutely uncomfortable.

"I figure that you are the best one to practice with here and I have been a little impolite letting you know it," he said truthfully. He stood there awkwardly waiting for her to answer and then shook his head when she didn't say anything. "Ahh...forget it. Nevermind."

They both put their cloaks on in silence and Ryan was about to walk out the door.

"Sure," she said, not wanting to seem ungrateful for his efforts of admitting his bad manners. "I won't be easy on you though."

Ryan couldn't resist a smile as he faced the opposite direction. Exhaling a deep breath, he felt like he had just won the game even before it started. He looked forward to that evening.

Bianca tried to fight the feeling too, but in fact, she couldn't wait either. Neither of them knew why they might be starting a game they couldn't finish.

Chapter 47 Gardener Pick Up

Because they only had two snowmobiles, the plan was for Josh to motor the guardsmen back to the house and Paul and Valley would head to the sheriff's office. The word spread quickly around the fire station that the buses were found and everyone was alright. The morale was high and the firemen brought out the best-tasting bacon from the freezer to celebrate. However, the Ice Queen declined her team any sort of breakfast that would take longer than 10 minutes. The new mission was to gather gear, pack up, and head out. They did so, complaining of eating only flapjacks.

Valley and Paul made it to the sheriff's station. It was a small one-story building and the entrance was covered in snow. You could hear a loud buzzing sound around the side of the building, so they went to investigate. There was the sheriff and two officers in plain clothes digging out the parking lot. They had two snow blowers and a shovel. When the sheriff saw the two men coming, he put down his shovel and greeted them. The back door was accessible, so he ushered them through to discuss business. The electricity had just come back an hour ago, so the inside of the building was chilly. It would take a few hours to heat up.

The sheriff was aware of the missing New York City school buses and was eager to get some credit for his station. He led Paul to his desk so he could make phone calls. Paul picked up the phone and, per Haugen's instructions, made the first phone call to Jekel. The School Chancellor didn't recognize the phone number, so he didn't answer it. He couldn't tolerate talking to any more press or citizens who wanted an update. Paul left a message that Jekel would regretfully not play back anytime soon. Paul had a list of phone calls to make, but the second one would be to his girlfriend to let her know that he was alright and coming home soon. He wanted to say so much more, but he had an audience. The list included a call to Haugen's wife, Shauna's husband, Jessica's daughter, and

Joshua's mom, which he did in that order. Every single one of them answered and gave a heartfelt sigh of relief.

Paul and Valley let the sheriff know that the National Guard was on their way to pick them up and take them back to the city. Not wanting to get slighted out of the credit for contributing to the rescue effort, the sheriff made his own phone call to the Police Chief of New York City to let him know that his office was assisting the National Guard. He left his officers alone so they could keep digging out the parking lot and reopen the station. He was going to head over to Valley's to assist in the rescue. When the officers heard that, they left their blowers in place and tagged along. In the station's garage, they had an SUV with chains on the tires and they all jumped in for the ride. Soon, they were following along Valley and Paul with the lights of blue and red flashing but the sirens off.

It was an exciting escort that looked like a parade. When they reached the house, Joshua, Tolbert, and Farmington were shoveling out the driveway so that it could be easily accessed. They were full of sweat. It was a long driveway and there was much more to shovel out. Luckily there were shovels in the back of the SUV. The officers pitched in and helped the effort. Soon, there were two Humvees and three track vehicles rolling down the street. Their tire tracks made the snow drivable for any regular car without chains. The Ice Queen and her staff got out of the vehicles and started a discussion with the sheriff.

The Ice Queen had contacted First Sergeant Maxson before they departed the fire station to let him know that they found the lost buses and everyone was alright. He let the governor know of the rescue and dialed the mayor and his press secretary next to let the world know the missing group was found and reported in good shape.

Mr. Jekel had the news station on since the snowstorm began. He was doing a crossword puzzle from an old New York Times to take his mind off everything. The news reported updates about the Nor'easter. It wasn't lost on Jekel that it was clearing up outside, but he could not get anywhere due to the heap of snow outside his door, so he waited by the phone for any familiar number to come across his display. An urgent sound came from his TV and the reporter sounded serious alerting there was breaking news. He curiously looked up at the TV.

"Found," the newscaster stated while a picture of the students and gardeners before they departed on the bus a week back showed on the TV screen. "The busloads of students and gardeners were found upstate New York and are reported safe and sound. We expect their arrival sometime this afternoon or evening."

That's all that Jekel needed to hear. He knew it all along. His wife came out and gave him a huge hug and smiled. Jekel's computer was booting up so he could post on the group web board that the students were found and to listen to the local broadcasting for more updates. The news reporter continued with details about how they stayed in a house with a couple who fed and housed them. This was another victory for Jekel's budget. He updated the group text as well.

"Today is a great day," declared Jekel to his wife. "Thank goodness for kind people."

First Sergeant Maxson, the mayor, the governor, the police chief, and all who were in charge were just as relieved as Jekel. The good news spread to the student's families, to strangers across the country, and across the world.

After hearing the news each student's family cheered, cried, and celebrated that soon, they would see their loved ones' young faces. The mayor geared up for a celebration to welcome the gardeners and student's home. He demanded the MMC to drop them off at the New York City Hall. There would be a press frenzy and he would have his writers send him the appropriate words to say for their arrival.

After Valley's driveway was more than shoveled, he invited everyone inside. The Ice Queen thought it would be quite cramped in the house with everyone, but she wanted to meet the staff and students. She also had an ulterior motive to take a photo and send it to the TACC with a caption of "in your face". There was an unwritten rivalry between the two guard units. The TACC always seemed to be a more successful unit than her MMC unit over the years.

It took a couple of minutes for everyone to take their boots and jackets off and walk inside. They were all greeted enthusiastically by the gardeners who were so happy to see every one of them. They all stood or sat in the family room, which was the biggest room in the house, and looked from person to person. The Ice Queen looked perplexed. She noticed no students. It didn't take long for the sheriff, officers, and the guard staff to pick up on it too.

"Excuse me, but where are the students?" asked the Ice Queen thinking that there was a logical explanation.

"What students?" asked Jessica, her smile quickly disappearing.

"You haven't found the students yet?" inquired Mr. Haugen with an alarmed look on his face. "They're still missing?"

"You mean they're not here?" asked the sheriff in surprise.

"What on earth?" asked the Ice Queen with an accusatory voice. "You traveled in buses together. How could you not know where they are?"

At that, the garden staff all turned and looked at Rooter. He felt it was unfair that he was blamed for the students missing. It was the weather's fault, not his. He grabbed his coat and exited the back door to think about it while smoking a cigarette. Everything was clearer when he inhaled and exhaled a long billow of smoke. The longer he puffed, the more he convinced himself other people were guilty. The National Guard didn't find them or the local sheriff, so why did they think he was to blame? He knew better than to accept blame for things he couldn't control. His conscience was clear as he looked inside the coop and told the chickens all about it.

Mr. Haugen explained how the snow came down so furiously and the student's bus lagged behind their bus. He reiterated the zero visibility and the distance between buses. He recounted that the student's bus followed close behind until it turned down the exact street they were now on. Because it took a large effort to turn their bus in the snow, they lost them. He wrapped up his story by retelling when they went down the street and got stuck in the snow and were rescued by Myra and Valley the next day. The gardeners all assumed that the students would have been found by now or at least had taken shelter somewhere.

The Ice Queen was irritated. She had already spread the word that the buses, plural, were found. That was all but an hour and a half ago, so she hoped that the word did not get out yet. The cell service was poor and the land lines were down on that road. The radio only reached a certain radius, so they all loaded back in their vehicles and headed to the sheriff's station to use that as a base to make phone calls.

They subsequently left the gardeners at the house to shift their attention to rescuing the children. Mr. Haugen felt suffocated. He could not be there one more night, not to mention that he wanted to assist in finding the students. When Haugen opened the back door to curse out Rooter, he was sitting on a snow-covered chair discussing his life with the chickens and complaining how nobody respected him. Not one more night in this crazy place, thought Mr. Haugen, as he went back inside.

The sheriff's office was now almost 64 degrees. He invited them all in, but there wasn't enough room to give everyone a desk. There was a conference room with a speaker phone that the Master Sergeant and her team could work from. The first call was to Maxson who shouted so loud that the sheriff heard it from outside the station. Maxson was not kind and ordered them to do a thorough patrol up and down the street they found the gardeners on. He hung up the phone on her mid-sentence, stressing that she screwed up. Now he had the irksome job of calling the governor.

Soon, the new word spread like wildfire that the gardeners were found, the students were still missing, but the MMC was still on top of it. The Ice Queen set up another grid search because, according to the sheriff and the house owner, the road Myra and Valley lived on eventually forked out to a few more roads. Before they departed the police station, the gardeners showed up, some on snowmobiles and some in the owner's truck with chains on it. They demanded to help in the search because they felt restless and needed to do something.

The Ice Queen reluctantly agreed and soon, all of the Humvees and track vehicles were full. The only Humvee out of the loop was Chauncy and Smith. They heard on the radio that the buses were found, so they took their time heading back. Smith rolled his eyes when he thought how skeptical Chauncy was at every turn. They were singing tunes on the radio when they heard the Ice Queen deliver a new order.

"OK troops, if anyone finds the bus with the students on it, radio me immediately," she commanded. "Be thorough. This time, we will stop at each house and ask each resident if they have seen them. If they have a barn, we will search it with or without their permission. Over."

Tolbert found this amusing because that was his suggestion that she disapproved just yesterday. Everyone knew their area of the grid to search and they all acknowledged on the radio.

"Blizzard Killer to Ice Queen. Copy?" squawked Chauncy.

"Where the heck are you guys? Over," inquired the Master Sergeant unamused.

"We are about 20 minutes away from your area. Over," he said back. "What do you want us to do?"

"You can be the sweeper," she insisted. "You can come behind us making sure we don't miss a thing. Over."

Back in New York City, the mayor phoned the governor and they argued about who would call the press and the families. They both agreed to push the family updates to Jekel and the governor ultimately knew he had to be the one to deliver the disappointing news to the press. It was a joyous day gone sad.

"I will order the TACC to take over the student search," the governor decreed. "The MMC is ordered, after today's search, to go back home, rest, and let the big guys handle it."

The governor was miffed that the TACC wasn't on the job in the first place. He heard they had better equipment and people. This would be over as soon as they got a handle on the search. He picked up the phone to call Sergeant Major Sharp and demand his troops deploy within the hour. His next call was to his press secretary to formulate a statement delivering bad news with a hopeful twist. He would make it seem that they had to comb every square foot of the mountain forest to find the students.

Saturday, December 5th
Chapter 48 Move Over for the Track and Capabilities Command (TACC)

Sergeant Major Sharp didn't mince words when he activated the TACC National Guard Unit recall for all of his troops. They were to muster in one hour at the drill site in New York City. Apart from a few men out of town, he had 71 members of his guard packing up equipment to head out and search for the students. There was nobody in his unit that dared to be like the jokesters Tolbert and Chauncy, this was strictly business.

While the MMC was searching every house, barn, and any large snow lump in the vast fields, the TACC rolled up the mountainside in a convoy. One would think they were headed toward a battle with the exception of no weaponry. Sergeant Major Sharp wanted his group to find the students and he knew they would. He had tools that the MMC didn't possess. There was the Forward-Looking Infrared which used shortwaves to detect any non-visible heat and a thermal imager that displayed body heat coming from inside a room. Once they were in place, he would order their helicopter to comb the area looking for a stranded bus.

The MMC had other resources too, but they had to make do with the bare minimum of personnel and gear until the weather cleared. And now that it had, they would miss their shot, because soon they would be ordered home. The TACC reached the sheriff's office at three thirty in the afternoon. The crew set up a large tent on a field behind the parking lot. First, they drove their track vehicles to flatten out the snow-covered field. Most parked in the sheriff's parking lot, but some parked outside of the tents. The tent was big enough to hold a circus. There were different berthing rooms in the tent – one for enlisted men and one for the women, one for officer men and one for the women, and a few for the senior leaders. The largest room was the multi-purpose hall-like room that was used as a mess hall with a makeshift kitchen nearby. There were trailers for toilets and showers near the mid-section of the tent. Every table, chair, cot, storage locker, and light fixture were smartly stored in mobile trailers. The unpacking of those trailers took all hands, but they had done this several times before, so it went fast. The last thing to hook up was the central heating system and lighting that would need a power source. The TACC ran five long, thick, industrial black cords to the electric receptacle plugs outside the sheriff's office and plugged them in.

It was five o'clock in the evening and the sun was disappearing from the clear overhead skies. The Master Sergeant from the MMC was summoned back from all searches to brief Sergeant Major Sharp. She cringed. Her crew didn't find any trace of the students despite having a thorough search. Most residents were not only hospitable but caravanned with them to the next house to help in the mission. Their actions allowed their neighbors to feel comfortable with the National Guard's inquiry. By the time the unit covered their grid areas, almost every resident was on the trail following, like the pied piper. Everybody united in the desire to find the kids safe. When the MMC drove back to the TACC tent area, the parade of cars from neighbors disappeared off to their homes.

Once the guardsmen from the MMC went inside the tent, they ate dinner and co-mingled with their counterparts from the TACC. Afterward, the Master Sergeant prepared to give her brief. The Ice Queen was face to face with Sergeant Major Sharp. It was a showdown. In some ways, she wanted to go home and get a good night's sleep. In other ways, she knew it would turn into a recovery mission and she couldn't bear finding the students in a state that would scar her for life. Her own three boys were all teenagers in high school and throughout the search she was eager to bring these kids home safely. Losing even one of them would be devastating.

Sergeant Major Sharp was behind a table that he turned into his command post desk. He dialed up First Sergeant Maxson and put him on speaker phone in front of the Ice Queen. He wanted her to humiliate herself and the unit in front of her boss.

"Master Sergeant Crain, what did you find today?" quizzed Sharp, motioning for her, the Ice Queen, to speak into the speaker phone. Her unit stood behind her in formation.

"The MMC found the gardeners and their bus on route 215, also known as Berry Road," she continued. "Today, we pursued a grid search on that same street extensively with the assistance of pretty much every resident that lived on that route, but we did not find the second bus, nor the students. The gardeners were witness to the student's bus going down that road in the snowstorm, but they must've either gone off the road somewhere or the gardeners were mistaken."

"In other words, you got zip?" asked Sharp and then he directed his voice to the speaker phone. "Did you hear that Maxson? Your unit is worthless. Also, the way I heard the story, the gardeners found and rescued your guardsmen, so that's pretty embarrassing."

The Master Sergeant retained a calm appearance, but she boiled with anger inside. Maxson, who was still at home babysitting, almost blew a gasket.

"Master Sergeant, please remove your unit from my tent and crawl back to the hole you came from," Sharp said indelicately.

"Wait!" shouted Maxson's voice from the speaker phone. "I say we battle for it."

"First Sergeant, what are you asking?" Sergeant Major Sharp questioned, confused as ever.

"If we beat you in a competition," Maxson paused for effect. "Then my unit stays and helps in the rescue."

"What kind of competition?" smirked Sharp interested.

"Anything you want," replied Maxson with a nervous laugh.

"No," said Sharp in a snarky manner. "I will let you make the call. We will match you man for man in whatever event you think you can beat us in."

The MMC Master Sergeant huddled her unit together and they threw out ideas. At first, Chauncy suggested telling jokes, but that was shot down. Tolbert recalled last summer during their two-week summer training that they did a fun group activity and became quite good at it. They all agreed.

"Alright, we have our competition suggestion," the Ice Queen stated shakily.

"Yes?" inquired both Maxson and Sharp at the same time.

"A five-layered human pyramid," replied the Ice Queen. "To win you must have 15 people, but four of them have to be women. The top layer is a person who has to stand straight up, with both knees locked."

"That sounds dangerous," shouted Maxson from the other side of the phone. He knew that his group was a bit danger prone. "How about a target shoot?"

"Too dark for that," replied Sharp. "But a pyramid build it is."

"We start in 15 minutes," commanded the Ice Queen.

She gathered her men around her and began to strategize. They did this over the summer, but as she thought back now, their unit never won, not even once. Sharp's men and women had never attempted this activity before, but they were all superior athletes, so a simple approach was put to paper. The biggest guys would make the base, followed by the next biggest, followed by the thinner guys, followed by more thin guys and a girl, followed by girls, followed by the shortest girl they had to make the topper. Sharp laughed looking at the Ice Queen in her desperate huddle. He knew that he had an advantage but loved rubbing her and Maxson's face in it.

In the village of Ourstory, the students and residents had just finished dinner and wandered over to the gym for their nightly recreation routine. Lauren waited for Mr. Boyce. When he finally arrived to play Gin rummy, she approached him.

"Sir, may I have a word?" asked Lauren softly.

"Of course," he exhaled. "What is it?"

"Do you think anyone is looking for us?" she inquired. "How will they know we are here?"

"They won't know you are here," he answered honestly. "We intend to take you to a place where you can be found."

"Will you just leave us on some roadside?" Lauren worried.

"No," he said, chuckling. "That would be highly unsafe. I have a friend that lives on a major road. He and his wife will take you in until you are picked up or they may even take you into the city themselves. They are the nicest people I know."

"I guess that would be okay," she said as he put her mind at ease.

Ryan and Bianca's one-on-one intense game started. He stared into her eyes as he bounced the ball here and there. Trying as he may not to notice her beauty, he blinked to concentrate on his game. She gazed into his eyes when it was her turn to dribble and something strange happened to her breathing. It wasn't steady like it normally was but shallow here and there like she couldn't get any air. They did play the game intensely, however, a new challenge was starting to take shape. Each tried to figure out what the other was thinking.

That Saturday evening, the gym was filled with more merriment than usual. The students and their Ourstory peers decided to sit in a circle on the blue mats and talk. It started with Arcado, Shannon, and Vaughn and then all of the teenage residents came over one by one. Brianna left the adult Gin rummy table to join as well. They all had a sense that their departure was drawing near and wanted to immerse themselves in each other's company for perhaps the last time.

Ryan and Bianca, not concentrating on their ball game any longer, decided to join the group in the circle. Ryan asked Bianca to kindly move over so he could take a seat next to her. She rolled her eyes and scooted over making room for him. As Ryan sat on the floor, his knee brushed Bianca's ever so slightly and his stomach flipped. He tried to breathe normally and hoped nobody noticed that he was having a hard time doing so. But everyone's attention went to Vaughn who started to beatbox. Then, Charlie started rapping to it. He and Vaughn had practiced nearly every night before bed and now they had an audience. Afterward, everyone clapped and then broke into separate conversations once again.

Wanda started out by making up a story of what would happen when she got home. To her, she painted a serious scenario about all her cousins, uncles, and ti-ti's who would not let her be until she told them all about her journey. She was in deep thought as she talked, but everyone was rolling on the floor laughing because her descriptions were hilarious.

Every New York student took turns describing what would happen when they were returned to their parents and extended family. But nothing compared to Wanda's tell-all. Vaughn didn't really say too much. He knew his dad would be losing his mind with his whereabouts but was deeply hurt knowing that his mother probably hadn't a clue.

Some of their village peers spoke about how they adjusted when they first got there. It was difficult for them to have to wake up early every morning of every day to pitch in, but after a while, they wouldn't have it any other way. It's what made the days rich there. They loved interacting with the whole village whether they were young or old. There was a lot of pride contributing to survival and thriving. There were some that complained, mostly about the sweets or television that they missed. The New York students noticed that there was no bullying and no leaving out someone because they were different.

High above them, through the skylight, they could see the full moon as clear as day for the first time. Sergei and Vlad were relieved that finally they could stare at the same stars that their family back in New York City would be looking at too.

Miles away, the full moon shone over the tent next to the sheriff's office where the competition would begin shortly. Each team supplied a judge that would have to agree on a winner together. On the MMC side, it would be Farmington. Even though he may have done well as one of the biggest guys on the bottom base, his team knew that under pressure his stomach got upset and he could puke easily. They would not let him be their weakest link. On the TACC side, it would be a young female lieutenant, who felt jipped at the opportunity not to be on the third tier.

The judges announced "GO" and the timer began. The TACC quickly went to it. Their five big guys were methodically put on the bottom as the base and they built their pyramid fast. The MMC couldn't stop arguing about who should be on base middle and ends. They were a mess. The TACC were on

210

their third row, and finally, the MMC got their base down and began on the second layer of bodies.

"Who is winning? Someone, answer me," yelled First Sergeant Maxson through the speaker phone.

"Who do you think?" laughed Sharp from the base of his own pyramid.

A few curses came across the speaker phone. Even though Farmington wasn't participating, the yelling from First Sergeant Maxson, the excitement of it all, and his unorganized team had his stomach bubbling up into nausea. He swallowed hard so as not to get sick. His co-judge made snide comments on his unit's incompetence, cracking a joke that MMC stood for many, many, chances to get it right. Farmington's stomach flipped and flopped.

Somehow the MMC team caught up to the TACC teams and both teams were now going into the fourth level, which had only two. Both teams' bases were shaking and struggling with all the weight on their shoulders. The second tier was also groaning through the pain. The teams were tied and the only part left of the competition was for a single person to complete the top layer and stand with locked knees.

The five-foot-seven, slender Ice Queen, who had 20 years of experience, was faced against the slim, four-foot-nine teenager from the TACC. They both eyed each other up and the 19-year-old soldier smiled knowing she would easily climb up and win. They both began their climb to the top level. The big difference was the way they each chose to climb. The little one, from the TACC, climbed up from the side. The Ice Queen went around the back to the middle and climbed from that angle. One would think the 105-pound feisty girl would feel like a kitten on the climb, but she was more like a clumsy Mastiff. As she climbed, she stepped on her teammate's hand or put her knee in their face or back. Nothing about her climb felt gentle.

Then it happened. Farmington tried to look as cool as a cucumber standing in between the two pyramids knowing that he couldn't help it. He let it rip, loudly. It wasn't so much of the long, lingering noise as it was the foul smell of gas. All of the MMC unit laughed hysterically because they were used to the famous Farmington flatulence factory. The laughing led to

211

more of the tower shaking. The TACC looked to be in deep pain, whether it be from the queasiness from the emissions in their face or the petite monster climbing like King Kong, nobody could say.

The Master Sergeant, on the other hand, climbed swiftly up the middle back rows with finesse ignoring the stench of Farmington as she had done several times before. Somehow, they both got to the top level at the same time. Now, the only thing to do was to stand up and lock their knees. Again, they eyed each other down, before attempting to stand up fully to take the win. You could hear the groans and the straining everywhere from the TACC and the uncontrollable freshman giggling from the MMC. Maxson was still screaming out of the phone and cheering the MMC on to victory. The little soldier was wobbling about to stand straight up and she gave her competition the nastiest smirk as she did. Suddenly, her base broke underneath her and everyone went tumbling down. It was not a pretty fall. All eyes turned to the Ice Queen as she was in a crouched position about to try and stand.

"If she falls, then it's over," groaned Sharp in a lot of pain from the foot that kicked the back of his head in the collapse. "We don't have time for this."

With one steady yank of her body, she stood up tall and proud with her knees locked. They waited for the judges to say it. The MMC were declared the winners. Farmington excused himself to go find the portable and hoped it wasn't too late. The winning unit slowly disengaged the pyramid, from the upper level to the bottom so that nobody got hurt. The MMC tried not to gloat, but they all felt that they deserved some satisfaction on this unfulfilled, long day.

"Well done Master Sergeant," congratulated Sharp. "We will make room for your team tonight. I think you cheated in an unconventional way, but I guess some could call that strategy."

She wanted to tell him that the success came from crossing and linking hands on each level. She also wanted to rub in his face that she did gymnastics for over 20 years of her life too. In the back of her mind, she was also satisfied that Farmington could produce on demand. But all she did was shake his hand

and prepare for bed that night. They both agreed that the briefing would be best in the morning when they would have all hands awake and ready for the search and rescue. Sharp accidentally bumped the phone, abruptly ending Maxson's hooting and hollering.

"Ooops," said Sharp, not sorry. "It's time for bed anyways, we have a bus of students to rescue in the morning."

Sunday December 6th
Chapter 49 Standing for a Cause

The men sent to scout the path back to NYC the day prior were only able to get a few miles. The snow came up to the horses' knees and leading them through it exhausted the beasts. They let Mr. Boyce know that it would be a slow ride back to the main road, but it could be done. After chores and breakfast, the students headed over to the town hall for Sunday services. Mr. Boyce kept the New York students behind for a chat. He let them know if they were up for it, they could leave right then and make it to the main road by mid to late afternoon and be back home in New York City for dinner. Their faces went from happy to giddy and everyone agreed to leave as soon as possible. They were instructed to collect anything of value from their bed lockers and meet back at the barn to load into the wagon. Everyone knew it was a possibility to leave today, but they were not prepared for such an abrupt departure.

The teens were so excited to go back to New York City that they ran to get anything they wanted to carry back with them and gathered at the barn as Mr. Boyce requested. The students, Ms. Kim, Mr. Boyce, Travis, Harvey, and Wilbur loaded everyone up in the wagon and started on their journey home. There were four horses pulling the wagon. The students were cold but ready to finally go home. The team of horses worked hard with each step to pull their cargo in the thick snow. This trip would take hours because of the large snow drifts that made the road nearly impossible to trot on.

They weren't even a mile out of Ourstory, when it hit. They didn't get to say goodbye to the friends and people that they met. Lauren was heartbroken that she didn't get a chance to say how much she appreciated the doc, the cooks, the teacher, and the kids that she met. Ryan was annoyed that he would have liked to have said goodbye to Bianca because it was the polite thing to do. He convinced himself that leaving without saying "good luck" was the only reason he was upset.

Adam and Darcy wished they would have finished making their design for the perfect shoe but were satisfied that they took the sketches with them. The twins were silent. They've always been adventurous and thought this brought out their skillsets of being able to adapt. Shannon was the most excited to go home. She hoped she would continue her journey of soul searching as she wrote. She would never forget Mrs. B and wished she could write and send her a manuscript that she would be proud of. Arcado loved saving Mother Earth, but secretly, couldn't wait to get back to technology. Wanda was thinking of ways to stay in touch with her two new boyfriends. Depression sunk into Vaughn's head. He wished he could stay through Christmas so he wouldn't have to face his broken family. Ms. Kim sat in silence and seemed the most uncomfortable in the constant tugging of the wagon. She hoped the horses wouldn't drop from the heavy pull.

The horses worked overtime to pull the wagon. Mr. Boyce wasn't worried because these young plow horses were meant for tough work. He would reward them with food and water soon but wanted to get at least halfway first. An hour went by and the students were getting restless.

"Are we making good time?" Shannon asked Mr. Boyce.

"We are just approaching the bridge," he replied. "Once we cross it, it'll be a few hours until we hit the interstate."

They came around the bend and the horses stopped. Mr. Boyce climbed out of the wagon and cursed at the world. Ahead where the bridge should have been, only one side of it remained, haphazardly dangling from their edge of the canyon to the other edge. The right side and the bridge floor were now down at the bottom of the ravine.

Everyone climbed out of the wagon to see for themselves. They all looked 50 feet down and saw the remnants of the bridge under a monstrous oak tree. Mr. Boyce walked over to the left side of the bridge that hung in position. The top of the one side was in good condition, but the part that should be attached to the missing floor was damaged in some areas. He thought that some of the teens could scale across and make it to the other side, but then gasped when he realized the risk. If any of them slipped and fell, they would die. The only alternative would be to rebuild the bridge for safe crossing.

Boyce, Travis, Harvey, and Wilbur huddled to discuss rebuilding of the bridge and how long it would take. The students and Ms. Kim wanted to be included in the discussion.

"So how many days will it take ya's to get 'dis bridge back up?" Ms. Kim thundered in.

"Days?" Mr. Boyce asked condescendingly, his eyebrows lifting. "I am sorry to say that this could take months."

"What?" the kids almost yelled in unity.

A hornet's nest of different complaints arose. Travis got out a notepad and wrote what was still standing and estimates of wood and any leftover steel beams that might be reused. The students and especially Ms. Kim's grumbles didn't stop, but it fell on deaf ears. The men knew that this was the only way back and learned in life making remarks without solutions did no good. Mr. Boyce turned the team of horses around.

"Load up everyone," Mr. Boyce demanded helplessly. "We will go back to the village and plan with the building team. We will need absolutely everyone in the village to help rebuild, but we will do it as fast as we can. I don't want to get your hopes up about leaving this week or the next. I am not sure with the manpower and materials if this can get done quickly, but we will get you back to the city as soon as we can. I promise."

Nobody moved. The students, in shock, slowly absorbed the devastating information. As Mr. Boyce looked from face to face, he knew that if there was a word stronger than disappointment that would be the word to describe them. He turned once more to look down the ravine and to study it a little better.

The bridge was a symbol of connecting the past to the future, the old to the new. The bridge was their freedom to go home. Now, they all stared at the gap from cliffside to cliffside. The feeling of despair set in as they thought that there was no way to cross it soon.

"I know you kids want to go home," said Mr. Boyce grimly. "I just can't believe our luck."

He looked into one despondent set of eyes to the next. His heart was heavy. He knew that this would cause them not to be home in time for Christmas. Evaluating the dire situation, he closed his eyes and thought of a proposal.

"I am going to throw something out to you all and see what you think," he continued. "We can lower each of you down the ravine tied by a rope and then we can have some of our guys climb up the other side of the cliff and pull you up, one at a time. But once we are up on the other side, we will have to walk the rest of the way. All of this will be a monumental struggle and I estimate about five hours of work to reach the main road."

They all looked down the ravine and then up the other side. Most of them thought they could manage it. It put a little hope back in their faces.

"Well, what do you think?" asked Mr. Boyce.

"Yeah, let's do it," Arcado answered straight away.

A few more nodded their heads yes.

"No!" Lauren shouted, steadfastly. "We will stay and help you build the bridge."

"I don't think so," contested Brianna.

"Yes, we will," stated Lauren more firmly. "You say that you stand for causes, then stand for this one."

"You calling me out?" asked Brianna angrily. Then, she thought like a proud mentor that Lauren found her voice. She turned her question into a statement. "You're calling me out. Well.... alright."

"This group of people saved us from drowning," said Lauren, sincerely. "We have become part of their family and now they need help. We should always help family."

Brianna walked over, gave her a side hug, and stood next to her, suggesting that she agreed. The twins moved over and stood next to Lauren.

"We'll stay," they said in unison.

Wanda said nothing, but the way she marched over to stand next to the boys, said it all.

"I'm totally in," remarked Ryan, who desperately wanted a reason to go back.

Vaughn almost thought God had granted him his wish to stay through Christmas.

One by one, they all stood behind Lauren, with the exception of Arcado and Ms. Kim.

"We could be back in our cozy homes with our loving families," he pleaded with the group to reconsider. "Really? Lauren, how are you going to help build that bridge?"

"I can support them in other ways, like milking cows, so the ones that can build it can be here," she said smartly. "I will hunt if I have to."

Nothing could stop Lauren. She never felt so fearless.

They all stared at him standing solid in their desire to return. He could tell that they were not going to see his side, so he took baby steps until he also stood behind Lauren. Brianna, who was next to him, did something unexpected and held his hand. He looked at her pleasantly and she smiled coyly back at him. The only person left was Ms. Kim.

"Well don't look at me like 'dat," she said, chuckled, and walked over to stand with the rest of them. "Ain't no way you'd be able to haul my asss...piration up 'dat mountainside anyway."

"Mr. Boyce, we are staying until the bridge is built," said Lauren in an assured voice.

Mr. Boyce felt humbled and wiped away the tears that welled up as he looked up to the sky for words to say. He cleared his voice and composed himself enough to address the students.

"Thank you for your trust, your patience, and your support," he uttered "This is the best Christmas gift you can give Ourstory."

They loaded up on the wagon and headed back to the village. Darcy thought about the questions she had for the cobblers. She was excited to get the princess wedge finished and now she had her chance. Adam was thrilled to have an opportunity to see if their design for the shoe would come to fruition. He loved working with Darcy. He tried not to show his crush on her and kept it professional and friendly, but he lived for any time spent with her.

Ryan couldn't wait to go back. He felt something die inside when he left without saying goodbye. God forbid she would accuse him of being rude for not saying so. Wanda was easy.

She liked whatever the twins liked. Going home to her family would be exciting, but if she could prolong their visit, her charms may eventually wear one of them down. Vaughn wanted to see his dad, but the connection to his newfound friends and the choir made him feel like he fit in better than in any place he'd known before. Shannon wanted more time with Mrs. B. Nobody pushed her to elevate her way of thinking and writing as much as this teacher. Brianna and Arcado sat next to each other, in the wagon, with his arm around her. They didn't know if they would keep talking after they got home, but the excitement of this moment felt like heaven.

Deep inside, Ms. Kim was excited to go back and read another book and milk her cows. This was about the most thrilling thing that ever happened to her. Soon, she would let the world know it. The only bad thing was if they were to make a movie out of her exciting story, there weren't a lot of Korean actors to choose from to play a lady of her girth. She smiled and thought that maybe if Zendaya gained about 10 pounds, she could pull it off.

Chapter 50 The Search Continues

After breakfast, the MMC and the TACC observed Sergeant Major Sharp and Master Sergeant Crain standing in front of the whiteboards and maps printed of the area. It was mostly Sharp barking out orders, giving the plan of the day and how the teams would divide up the grid searches. Sharp had also authorized air support to deploy their HH-60 Helicopter. He was confident that by dinner they would find the kids. The Master Sergeant stood nearby knowing that they had already thoroughly searched a lot of the grid areas he assigned. She had no confidence in him and, obviously, he had none in her if he was going to search her grids again.

She volunteered her group to head north in the direction of the Friend's Inn. Everyone was packing their gear for the day to include water, extra fuel, radios, and meal packs. Right before they headed out, the governor called on the op's phone and Sharp put him on speakerphone for the Master Sergeant to hear.

"The MMC is to retire from the mission and head home," the governor commanded. "The TACC will take it from here. I thank you for your service, so go home and get some rest."

The phone conversation was only heard by the two in charge. The Ice Queen felt punched in the gut by the governor. They were the first ones on the scene to search when no other could.

"Is there an option to stay and help search voluntarily?" asked the Master Sergeant respectfully.

"No, that is not an option," he said emphasizing the not. "Please bring our gardeners home today."

The next call was from the Ice Queen to First Sergeant Maxson to advise him that their mission was over. He kindly requested to be taken off the speaker phone.

"Master Sergeant Crain, you and the rest of the MMC made me proud," he continued. "Hold your heads up high. This has nothing to do with your leadership or our team, we are just pawns in the governor's game of quietly blaming us."

"What do you mean?" she asked, confused.

"When the students weren't found, the whole country would blame the governor," he said delicately. "By telling the world that there is a new team searching, it indicates that the incompetent team won't be in charge anymore. My dear, that's just how it works. Those words would never be said out loud, but implied."

"That's bull," she stated irritably.

"The best thing to do is to pack up and get back to the city," commanded Maxson. "That's an order with no deviations. I know we have some squirrely guys in our unit that may try some shenanigans. Don't let them. Don't add any more fuel to the fire."

"Yes sir," she said numbly on the phone and hung up.

The Master Sergeant called her unit together to deliver the news before they headed out to their vehicles.

"This is a direct order," demanded the Ice Queen. "Let's load up, pick up the gardeners and head back."

"But we won the pyramid challenge," protested Tolbert. "That wasn't easy on Farmington's digestive system."

"All of his talents wasted on nothing," added Chauncy, feeling defeated.

"I mean it," she said harshly. "I am talking mostly to the two of you. Don't get any ideas about staying behind or coming back here. It's the TACC's mission now, we stand down."

Sergeant Major Sharp enjoyed thinking about how terrible the MMC would feel learning that the TACC would find the students easily and quickly. He packed up his bag and departed, leaving the MMC to do the same. They walked to their track vehicles glumly.

"I will be submitting you both for the New York Aid to Civil Authority Medal," she said tactfully to Tolbert and Chauncy. "I think that your efforts to get to the drill site deserve at least that."

"Well, I nominate Farmington for the Guard Air Medal for letting it rip in the air and directly hit the target," joked Tolbert to the group as they exited.

The whole unit laughed emptily as they reached their vehicles. The first stop would be to Valley and Myra's for the gardener pickup and then back to New York City.

Chapter 51 The Building Team

They arrived back in the village during lunch. After they parked the horses and wagon, the students walked through a town they did not recognize. After breakfast that morning, the decorating team wasted no time transforming the drifty snow filled streets into a Christmas village. The town smelled like an evergreen tree and looked festive. The students strolled down the street slowly in awe. It felt like they stepped into an enchanted wonderland that imitated their favorite childhood Christmas story. Fresh fir tree clippings adorned every lamp post, door entrance, and even high up in the campanile had swags of the fir draped around it. The town hall could have passed for Santa's toy shop with two nutcracker soldiers standing at attention on either side of the door. The sleeping quarters were decorated with fir trees and clippings with ornate decorations too. Grand red bows were hung throughout the campus quarters inside and outside. Silver garland strands swooped from window to window. The joy of the postcard-like community would be imprinted on them forever.

As the students entered the decorated mess hall, most of the villagers, especially the children, got up on their feet to greet them. In the corner of the mess hall, a stringed quartet played Christmas music. It was a holiday tradition in Ourstory to have the quartet playing during all three meals to enhance the joyful feeling. Everyone was in cheerful amazement to see them walk through the door except for two residents. Christopher wished they hadn't come back. He thought it was excruciating to listen to their stories of their families and happenings back home. His face was just as stoic as Bianca's. Her facial expression seemed to be that of hurt and scorn, but she tried to hide it with a blank stare. Most village students hugged, and fist pumped the returning city students.

They grabbed food from the line which had holly hanging everywhere. As they did, Lauren made sure to comment on how grateful she was to every cook that prepared the meal.

Everyone ate and gabbed apart from Mr. Boyce. The wheels were spinning in his head on how they could make this a safe but quick repair. He didn't want the kids to be disappointed and lose faith in his words. Another important view that he needed to keep in mind was to protect the village. He thought that the longer they stayed there, anxiety could turn into resentfulness, not to mention a search party of National Guardsmen might make their way there. This wasn't healthy for either group.

After lunch, the students went to choir practice while Mr. Boyce held an emergency meeting with the building team. This included an architect, civil engineers, a construction team, and welders. They had to formulate a plan to quickly build a solid bridge that would last longer than just getting the kids over.

They already knew the specs of the bridge. It was 30 feet across, and it spanned 10 feet wide. The bridge existed when the hunters first found the village off the beaten path. It was a little rusted and at one time a few years ago, they reinforced the bridge with additional steel plates and welded high-strength bolts. Now, the only thing standing on the bridge was one complete side span that needed to be connected to a missing side and a missing floor.

The engineer and welders would test the durability of the existing side to ensure it could be used. Next, they would have to check their stock of steel for the new span side, and they would have to get treated wood to build the foundation of the bridge. A tool and die maker knew that he would need to make the triangles that would make the arch of the bridge. This allowed the weight load to transfer so it's not all in one spot. There were lots of details to get the task started.

A timeline was drawn for the best- and worst-case scenarios. In the best-case scenario, the bridge could be built in three weeks. The worst-case scenario, factoring in possibly more bad weather or the lack of supplies, would be five to six weeks. Either scenario could put their homecoming close to or past Christmas.

They needed to survey the bridge and collect data. The civil engineer and welders went by horseback to the bridge. The construction workers went to check on their treated wood. The tool and die maker lit up the cupola. This melting pot device needed a few days to heat up to the exact temperature to bend metals. He worked on a diagram to outline the various steel templates that would be needed to make the bridge come together.

As the Ourstory men began reconstructing the bridge, each of the students daydreamed about the possibility of making it home before Christmas. Even though they volunteered to help build the bridge, the thought eked in each of their minds of the likelihood of being stranded there throughout the holidays. They saw the crumbled bridge and knew they were in a place of little resources. But they were enjoying their temporary visit and had faith in the people that were more than capable of making things happen.

After choir practice, Ryan cornered Bianca at the back of the hall before she left the building.

"I was really upset today," admitted Ryan who had been practicing what to say, all of the ride home. "We left in such a rush this morning that I didn't even get to say goodbye to you...or the others."

"It's alright," Bianca played defense, but inside her heart was heavy. "Not like it really mattered to me."

All the students passed by them to depart the building, leaving the two of them to casually walk behind them. Ryan stopped turning face to face with Bianca.

"For some reason, it mattered to me," Ryan said seriously, staring hard into her strong, yet hurt, eyes. "I guess what I am saying is when the time comes, I want to be able to say goodbye."

Ryan's face turned into a puzzled look because he didn't know how to say how he really felt about her, and so far, he hadn't said what he'd rehearsed. It took him leaving this place for good to realize it.

"What I meant to say is," he took a deep breath. "I'll miss playing basketball with you and you know seeing your face...as I sink a three-point shot over your head."

At that comment, her face winced unfavorably. Then they both laughed, breaking up the tension that had built up. He stared into her light brown beautiful eyes and he wanted to steal a kiss. As he moved in to do so, she cleared her throat.

"I'll admit, getting to know you really has me thinking about my future," she said, trying to keep her breathing steady. "When I become old enough to leave, I might come find you. I expect by then, you'll grow taller, be wiser, and hopefully become handsome."

"Ewwww, burn," he said smiling, acting hurt.

"I also expect that you will have dated every cheerleader on the squad because each one got tired of you bragging about your three-point shot. But hopefully, on that day, there might be a little room in your busy life for you to show me the city," she requested in a sincere manner.

"So what you are trying to say is that you will miss me?" Ryan said in his cocky way because he would miss her too. "I'd love to show you the city. Visit anytime, although my house isn't in a nice part of the town and the place is always a mess. There're three guys that live there and we don't really clean a lot."

"Home isn't about the building," said Bianca as she put her hand out and touched his chest where his heart was. "It's about the people inside."

For the love of God, she did it again, he thought. How could she be so cruel and be so critical? It took a moment to sink in but after he sighed, he turned his scowling face into a grin. Nobody ever confronted him like she did. She spoke the profound truth and it forced him to think deeper about his potential in life. He needed to start living like there was more than just a life of basketball and she opened his eyes to it. Ryan needed someone like her in his life to challenge him and make his world bigger.

For the rest of the day, he was glued to her side. He thought about Mrs. B's earlier lesson and simply asked Bianca the question, "Can you tell me everything about you?" They walked to the mess hall hours before dinner. They sat in chairs by the yuletide logs ablaze in the fireplace discussing their childhood as the flames flickered, creating a warm, amorous atmosphere. She told him about growing up in the care of her grandparents until they became ill and no other relatives claimed her. What happened to her biological parents was never explained and someday she would conduct her own inquiry. The orphanage in upstate New York was her home since the age of four. Her struggles from that point had made her the tough, no-nonsense, confrontational, yet protective and loving person she was today. The orphans she grew up with were now her family. After she allowed Ryan a glance into her world, she regretted leaving herself vulnerable to a guy that would be leaving soon. Bianca shied away from continuing on about her life story as the quartet set up their instruments for dinner. Ryan wanted to know more but the crowd arrived, invading their privacy.

After dinner that night, Mr. Boyce made an announcement of the plan that the building team made for the bridge. He had Travis make a large timeline on a large sheet of paper and hung it in the dining hall. This was for transparency, so the students could see all of the work that needed to be done.

The students saw that the projected date of completion was in two and half weeks for the best-case scenario. This was right before Christmas. That was a relief to most students, even though they wished that it would be sooner. There was also another list that could add more days to the project, making it close to or after the 25th of December. So now the real question was, could they really be home for Christmas?

Sunday, December 6th
Chapter 52 Saving the Bus

The MMC were back at their drill site in New York City and as they stored their vehicles, Tolbert rolled his window down choking. Farmington did the same as he apologized, admitting that his stomach was excited about returning home. Family members showed up to collect their guardsmen and gardeners. Reporters were there to interview the gardeners and ask questions they would not be able to answer. Only the family members were allowed inside the gate as the reporters lingered outside of it. The reunion was heartfelt as spouses, significant others, parents, and children hugged their missed family members. It appeared that everyone had someone there, except for Tolbert and Chauncy. Their snowmobiles were still in the same spot they left them. In no time, they put their helmets on and drove home, leaving all the drama behind.

The TACC could hear the helicopter in the distance pounding the sky looking for the bus. Sergeant Major Sharp and 70 guardsmen had been looking for six hours and found nothing, not even a clue. All his vehicles, manpower, unique tools, and helicopter and still there was no trace nor clue that would lead them to the missing students.

"This is Mosquito to the TACC. Copy?" a helicopter co-pilot squawked.

"We read you Mosquito. Over," responded Sharp.

"We may have something in a gully near the northeast Chonart Mountain base in a ravine. It's rectangular in shape, covered in snow," he reported. "There's something metallic reflecting off of it. Over."

Sharp's eyes widened. He thought this was the break they needed, unfolded the large map, and put in the coordinates that Mosquito sent to him. Then, he doled out orders by radio for his Bravo Team, who were closest, to meet him there. He felt this one in his bones. If he were allowed to, he would bet a million to one on this discovery. His own Charlie Team was 30 minutes from the site, but he told his team to continue their grid search and he and his driver, a corporal, disappeared in his designated Humvee.

He wanted to be there with the Bravo Team to save those students. Everyone knew it was not protocol to ditch your team for the rescue glory and their disdain for him grew stronger. Sharp was known to step on his enlisted staff to advance his own career. The running joke in his unit was to watch out not to get Sharped by the prick.

The TACC allowed the helicopter to return to base. They were low on gas and had exhausted their search grid. The unknown target would be reached soon. The Bravo Team was only minutes out but Sharp gave orders to stand down until he arrived. Nobody took kindly to him giving orders that didn't make sense. If there were truly students in a ramshackle bus, under a blanket of snow, they would need assistance quickly. Sharp could see it in his mind's eye. He would be the first to reach the students and make sure they were cared for and given treatment as soon as possible. Sharp commanded his corporal driver to record the whole rescue on his, meaning Sharp's, phone. Editing may need to be done and who would be the best one for that job, but Sharp.

There were 10 Bravo Team vehicles all waiting near the bottom of the ravine. The almost non-existent road needed a path to get down, so the track vehicles were the first to plow through making a path for the Humvees. As soon as Sharp appeared at the foothill, he saw everyone standing by with stretchers and kits. He moved in with his corporal filming the whole thing. Sharp narrated like a newscaster while he walked toward the rectangular object. He got to the back of the rectangular-shaped object and brushed off enough snow to make sure it, in fact, was a bus. After seeing the exterior, he moved to the front door but to gain entry he would need to put effort into removing a lot of snow.

"Sir?" questioned the corporal urgently.

Sharp indicated, rudely, for the corporal to be quiet. He needed only his voice to be on the recording and no one else's. He wished he would've brought some sort of tool to brush off the snow, but instead used his hands to do so. He could see inside the long windowed, front door and it appeared dark inside. Scrambling wildly to make it look like he could save a life if he moved quicker, he brushed up and down quickly until he could push the door in. It was difficult because something was blocking it from the inside, but he couldn't see what it was.

He requested a Sergeant to help him push it open. They both gave it a forceful shove until they broke the door and it opened. At the exact moment the door opened, birds and bats flew out of it. They could tell that the bus was in water at some point because of the mildew smell that came rushing up their noses. It was almost too hard to breathe, but Sharp pressed on in his solo recording.

"I am now entering the bus," he continued intensely with his eyes widened. "So far, there are no signs of human life."

It was pitch dark in the bus because the windows were still covered in snow. As he stepped in, he could see the driver's seat was empty, so he turned the corner and moved on slowly. The corporal trailed behind him carefully, recording Sharp. He went deeper and deeper into the bus, but something did not feel right. Besides the damp, musty smell, there was a lot of sludge under his feet. He looked left and right, and the seats were empty of students but full of something that resembled mud piled on them. There was a movement in the back row of the bus and Sharp stopped in his tracks. Then he went further to investigate.

It appeared that the only thing he could hear and see was his breath fog which was filled with a tinge of excitement. The phone that the corporal held to record didn't shed much light on the bus, only the small amount that seemed to be absorbed by Sharp. As he attempted to walk to the back of the bus, Sharp felt his feet trudging and getting stuck in something gooey. His shoes were heavy with something that prevented him from taking another step either forward or back. Outside the bus, the rest of the guardsmen stood by impatiently awaiting his word. Nobody expected to hear the high-pitched, shrilling scream that resonated from the inside of the bus. The corporal, who was taping Sharp, dropped the phone and jumped off the bus. Something in there terrified the living daylights out of him and now had a hold of Sharp.

Tuesday, December 8th
Chapter 53 Hope, Goodness, and Light

It had been two days since the TACC began their search. Sunday went into Monday and there was still no reported finding of the students. On Tuesday, the governor of New York made the decision, recommended by his military council, to announce the recovery mission. There was not a soul out there that could survive 10 or more days without food, water, and shelter especially in this weather.

Regularly scheduled programs on all TVs in New York were interrupted by a news report flash. A picture of the governor of New York appeared next to a statement that read in a grave tone about how the status of the students went from rescue to recovery. The high expectations of the TACC who turned over every stone and still couldn't find them were the basis for the decision. It was presumed that if they were in the custody of a New York resident that they would have come forward by this time.

When the families heard this, they were in shock. First, they found out from a news report, not a phone call or website update. And second, the hope still flourished that their children would be found. Mrs. López knew her boys were alive; she sensed it. She knew that her boys were resourceful and strong. Most parents felt the same with the exception of Lauren's and Adam's parents. Even Darcy's parents knew her daughter was scrappy and would fight to survive. Mixed emotions filled the family web board. Nobody was having it. In a group text without Mr. Jekel, Mr. Venhill invited the families to meet at his house as soon as possible. They would take matters into their own hands if the city and state could not do their job. Helpless was not a word that any of the families needed to feel.

After the news broke out, Mr. Jekel added to the website that he hadn't known there would be an announcement. He was in just as much shock. The families dismissed his feelings of shock and sadness. They were in pain and he would never understand their agony of losing a child. Jekel posted an important question to the families that the mayor of New York and many of the gardening staff needed to know. The Christmas tree that was supposed to be the focus of the trip was now at their mercy. He asked them if they still wanted the tree to go up this year in the plaza in memory of their children or not at all. He would await their answer.

Tuesday's chores were done by the Ourstory village as usual. There were some men missing here and there, preparing the wood and metals for the bridge. The sewing and shoe mending crew got smaller as they helped milk the animals, hunt, and cut wood for the fires. At breakfast, the New York City students asked why the men weren't at the bridge repairing it yet. Mr. Boyce told them that the first few days to a week would require the materials to be produced and it took time to line up the bridge assembly. He assured them that they were working just as hard on the preparations which were critical for the plan to run smoothly. Even though some requested to assist, it was a task that Boyce thought would slow down the process if they had to be taught. He told them it would be best to head off to school to keep their minds busy.

Mrs. B did keep the students busy with geometry. They did lines, rays, segments, planes, and angles. This was repetition for some students, but brand new to others. The way Mrs. B explained the practicality of using geometry was like a story that took their minds to a place where they could apply it. Again, the students hung on her every word and then worked on the problems that she put on the board. By now, Vaughn challenged himself, after he returned home to the Bronx, to try harder to hold onto the key to learning and pay attention.

Perhaps the only one that didn't have his mind on math was Ryan. He sat behind Bianca and finished his work quickly. She slouched back in her seat and he leaned forward and played with her hair like a cat with a ball of yarn. She turned around and gave him a curt stare, as if to say "knock it off." After she turned back around, he blew puffs of air into her hair, which made her roll her eyes. He didn't care if she scolded him, he liked flirting with her and looked forward to getting a reaction out of her at any turn.

After lunch, it was time for chorus practice again. Everyone was eager to gather together for their favorite activity. There were many individual great singers in the group, but the whole collection of their harmonies made it angelic. Vaughn had a few suggestions and pulled Mr. Chad to the piano to share his thoughts. They spent 20 minutes trying out melodies with the string section, which turned into a full-blown choir practice.

During the refrain of the first song, a loud screech came from the sopranos.

"Mouse!" screamed eight girls not all at the same time.

Hysteria stopped everyone in their tracks. The 30-some students all scattered to find higher ground, except for Sergei and Vlad. They had mice for pets and didn't want someone to accidentally whack them. That is where Wanda drew her line from the boys. In no time, she was standing on a chair screaming for her life. There was some irony noted that Wanda, the black bear slayer, was terrified of a mouse. The twins explored the entire stage but there was no sign of the mouse. The boys knew that if they didn't find it nobody would be able to concentrate, so they cleverly acted like they found it and let it outside. It took 25 minutes to get the students back in position. Everyone went back to singing their best, while Sergei and Vlad kept an eyeful watch on the floor. The hall door opened and up walked Gabriel, removing his jacket.

Mr. Chad was happy that Gabriel made it to practice today. His little voice was in high demand for parts of songs that required a high, angelic voice. It was remarkable how long he could hold a high note. Right in the middle of the song, Gabriel bent down and picked up the mouse that ran across his foot. He calmly put the mouse on his left long sleeve and it scurried up and sat on his shoulder. At first, some nearby students jumped and eked, but when they noticed Gabriel's peaceful face and the obedient mouse just roaming back and forth on his shoulder, they settled down. His new found pet remained steadfast on his shoulder throughout the rehearsal. Near the end of rehearsal, Gabriel moved to the side of the stage and laid down too tired to continue as his new pet watched over him. One thing for sure was that the seven-year-old, charismatic boy made people believe in goodness and light that made every day feel like Christmas.

Chapter 54 What's My Prognosis?

Sergeant Major Sharp woke up in the hospital. He was still dazed, confused, and in pain. There was no recollection of how he got there and why. When the doctor stopped in and saw him stirring, he approached him to see how he was doing.

"I see you're awake," said the doctor grinning dutifully.

"What happened?" asked Sharp, noticing he was in a full hospital gown with no uniform to identify his rank of importance.

"Your unit saved you from what was on that bus," he answered. "You got some healing to do. You have injuries spanning from your ankles to the cuts on your face."

"I remember not being able to move my feet," stated Sharp recalling the events. "It felt like a rope tied around my ankles. And then, and then, something or someone attacked me."

"Oh yes, something did attack you," agreed the doctor wholeheartedly. "But in all honesty, you had it coming to you."

Sharp wondered what he meant. Many of the members in his unit were jealous of his title and position and he wondered if any of them had told the doctor he had it coming. He imagined his unit tying his legs and ankles together and attacking him. There were bruises and cuts all over his face. He would make sure they would pay.

"Do you know what attacked you?" the doctor inquired after Sharp's long pause.

"I assume the personnel from my unit," he revealed his dirty laundry. "I am sure they were angry that I would get the credit for finding the students, but I have it all on video that I discovered them first."

The doctor chuckled, almost wanting to keep Sharp in the dark about what really happened. He had seen his kind before and knew the egocentric bully type. But he felt he had a moral obligation to let him know what happened. The phone was plugged into a charger by his bed, so the doctor disconnected it, and put it up to Sharp's face to unlock it. Afterward, he found the video from the bus that the corporal recorded.

"This is what truly happened on your mysterious discovery," the doctor said and handed Sharp the phone as the video played.

Sharp judged himself for seeming a little too ambitious from the tone of his narration. He watched himself walk onto the bus and in the background, one could clearly hear peculiar sounds from the back of the bus over his talking. The memory of his feet being pulled by something as he moved forward flooded his mind. Then he heard his screaming, which was a higher pitch than that of a five-year-old girl, before the phone was dropped on the floor. The recording continued when the phone dropped into a pile of sludge, but it was at a perfect angle to capture the incident. A nest of large snakes had covered the floor and squeezed his feet so much that he fell flat onto their pit. In the back of the bus was a nursery of raccoons that attacked Sharp viciously. He screamed through the whole ordeal until he blacked out.

His team, outside the bus, were absorbed in so much fear that they did not come to his aid. The soldier that helped Sharp opened the door mentioned that there could still be students on that bus and they still needed to check. The corporal that drove Sharp disagreed. He noticed that the bus was a dark color of black, not the yellow school bus color and design specs from the operational picture given them. This is what he was trying to let Sharp know before he wasted his time on the bus, but he was shushed.

In the recording, Sharp could hear his team arguing about who was going in to retrieve him and make sure he was alive. Every single one of them declined to rescue him and care for his safety. They would pay for that in their next performance evaluation for dereliction of duty. Eventually, the team went in with heavy-duty flashlights and then retreated after they saw the animal kingdom that took over the bus. Tools from their track vehicles were brought back to the site. This included body shields and batons normally used for riot protection. A few went in and protected the other few that pulled out Sharp. The corporal noticed the phone stuck in the sludge and grabbed it hoping to tell the story. He lifted the phone up to record the back of the bus, with flashlights shining to show there were no signs of life, except for the annoyed raccoons. Knowing that Sharp would swear the students might have been back there, he wanted to be thorough.

After Sharp was pulled from the bus and loaded onto a Humvee, the videotaping ended. The corporal was clever enough to send a copy of the video to his email just in case the Sergeant Major created an alternate story. The doctor put the phone down and stared at Sharp.

"They just let me go into that death trap and they knew," said Sharp bitterly and felt pain throughout his body as he groaned.

"Nobody could've known what was on that bus," the doctor said candidly. "In the winter, snakes go into brumation and raccoons go into torpor. It's their hibernation. When you disturbed their environment, I think they got a little angry."

"What's my prognosis?" asked Sharp, growing impatient and irritated.

"Well, you have been on some heavy sedation meds because of the pain. You pulled muscles in your ankles and legs," the doctor continued. "Also, there are contusions and abrasions on your face, but what we are watching are the bites from the raccoons."

"Do I have rabies?" asked Sharp in a panic and then paused for a moment in reflection. "Am I going to live?"

"That's hard to say," said the doctor trying to rile him. "You never know."

"Just give it to me straight," said Sharp glumly. "I want to prepare myself."

"Well, you don't have rabies, but we are keeping an eye on infection," remarked the doctor calmly. He thought he had tortured him enough. "Two more days here should do it. We'll send you home with some salve treatments, antibiotics, and you can attend physical therapy to get your ankles in shape."

"Oh what a relief," smiled Sharp and took a deep breath.

The doctor didn't have the heart to let him know that the governor dismissed his National Guard unit off the case.

Chapter 55 Families Gather

Darcy Venhill's parents got the families together to come up with a plan. Family members of the missing students were invited only. They did not want Mr. Jekel, the media, or any outsider in attendance. Even though everyone met on the morning of the student's departure in the plaza, they only became familiar with each other through the comments on the webpage or texts that were posted. So when they arrived at the Venhill brownstone, they all introduced themselves again.

Wanda's mother and father showed up first. Mrs. Juanita Womack was boisterous, like her daughter, while her husband, Ernest, was quiet and pensive. She acted like she was in a museum making comments on how beautiful the paintings and bookshelves were. They were seated in a love seat that faced a couch in a living room. There were chairs brought in from the dining room and scattered to form a circle in that room.

One by one, the parents entered the living room taking an agenda and a seat. The meeting was just about to start when Vegas Vetter straggled in late with his wife, Veda, hiding behind him looking sickly and tired. She knew in her heart that she had to be there, but things were still hazy to understand at times and her head and body hurt a lot. She thought she would soak in the words and hope that Vegas would speak for both of them. After everyone was seated, Darby Venhill stood at the edge of the circle and began the discussion. He ran this meeting like his business meetings.

"First on the agenda, we need to discuss hiring out a private company to search for our children," he began. "I have contacted an old friend who did dark ops in the military and has committed five of his men. Children just don't disappear."

"I beg to differ," Brianna Germaine's mom said. "Did you see that story about minority children disappearing?"

Her sister agreed with her and it caused a commotion of chatter around the room.

"Nobody is gonna disagree with that, but this discussion is for our children," said Juanita loud and clear. "Let the man talk."

The noise settled down.

"Thank you, Mrs. Womack," he continued. "Now the cost of this is as follows. It's $200,000 for the first seven days. Then after that, we re-evaluate if we need them further. The price then goes to $100,000 for an additional five days and so on and so forth upon re-evaluation."

The noise went back up to a frenzy. Most stated that they didn't have the money and that the state of New York should foot the bill.

"I know it may appear that my family may have money, but our assets are frozen at the moment due to an auditing issue," stated Mr. Venhill regretfully. "But I can help repay at a later time."

Vegas who hadn't uttered a word in all the chatter stood up to make a comment and the talking ceased.

"I don't have that kinda money in a bank, but I would sell my music store if it meant seeing my son again," he remarked without hesitation. "Count me in on my share."

"We could pass the hat at the church," Ms. Germaine said confidently. "The members always step up for a cause."

"Now you're talking," replied Juanita. "I got a 401K at work that I was saving for retirement, but my baby comes first."

"What if we don't have a church, a store to sell, or a 401K?" asked Patrick White humbly. "I can barely scrape by affording my rent and feeding my boys...well, now just one boy."

The frenzy returned with people suggesting bake sales and taking out loans.

"Quiet everyone please," declared Sergei and Vlad's mother Mrs. López. "I will pay for the first installment of $200,000. I have been saving to open my own practice, but this is too important. It must be a sign because that is how much money I need to put down on the building lease. I know they're out there and they will be found."

237

Everyone showed their appreciation, thanking Mrs. López for her generosity. The second item on the agenda was a lawsuit against the city and state. They all agreed that if money were won, it would first pay off Mrs. López or any of the money put toward finding the children. The next item of business was to vote on whether the Christmas tree should go up in Rockefeller Center. This hit everyone with so many emotions. In the end, they agreed painfully that the tree should go up in their kids' honor and as a symbol of hope.

After the family meeting, there were refreshments. Everyone broke off into different conversations within their new group forming bonds that would hold them together forever. Mr. Vetter got his wife a cup of tea and some biscuits. She was quiet and looked glazed over and drained. Mrs. López saw her from the time she got there and approached her gently out of concern.

"She's alright," Vegas said to Mrs. López. "She's going through some issues, but I think soon she'll be good."

Mrs. López led them both to a small office that she noticed by the entry. She wanted to talk to them in private. When they were seated on a leather couch, Mrs. López approached Veda with a large work bag that she always carried with her. She took out a pen flashlight and studied Mrs. Vetter's eyes. She had her mouth open and checked up and down. A stethoscope was brought out and used to determine how her lungs and heart were. She saw the cuts on her scarred arms as she tried to take her blood pressure. Her blood pressure was low. This didn't surprise Dr. López one bit.

"I don't suppose you would have any opioid samples for me, would you?" Veda asked desperately.

"So that's your poison?" Mrs. López asked. "I think you should be treated for withdrawal."

Mrs. López did have samples of different things. She gave a pack of methadone to Vegas to help with the cravings. Then she wrote a prescription for more and also antibiotics for the cuts. She suggested a tetanus shot as soon as possible too. She handed Veda her card with her office hours for a more intensive physical and bloodwork and then handwrote the times for a support group that she runs. Looking from Vegas to

Veda with compassion, she was so adamant about her recovery that she vowed to pay for her roundtrip taxi to her office.

Nobody really noticed the offshoot physical that Dr. López gave to Veda as they were too consumed in their own conversations. Lauren Fairview and Adam Bray's moms found common ground in their feelings of guilt about making their kids go on this trip. By the end of the meeting, they were hugging in support and exchanging recipes and phone numbers.

Arcado Michaels's father, Arcado Sr., approached Ryan's father, Patrick White and they talked about their sons and what the future held for each in a melancholy way. Through a lot of conversation, they realized that they went to the same elementary school in the Bronx. Of course, in those days, Mr. White was at an average height. It wasn't until late high school that he sprouted to six foot five and was the star forward on the basketball team.

Mr. White went into detail about all the research that he and his son did while holed up at home. Patrick wasn't trying to brag but just show him what he did with his time. On his phone, he displayed pictures of their so-called "FBI wall" of upstate New York and the geography of the mountains and wooded area. With all the in-depth information, Mr. Michaels was impressed at his thoroughness.

Arcado Sr. just lost his researcher that he relied on for everything at his firm. He desperately needed someone like Patrick White to work for him which led to a job offer. The starting salary was higher than Patrick White ever made. Ryan's father didn't go there that day looking for a job or a handout, but Mr. Michaels needed someone like him, so his offer kept rising higher until he finally accepted. Shaking his head at the unbelievable job offer, he knew where he lived the neighbors were all stuck in the same rut jobs at minimum wage. He fondly shook his hand in acceptance and a 'too good to be true' excitement.

Shannon Dartmouth's parents found Brianna Germaine's mother and aunt fascinating ladies. Ms. Germaine graduated with a journalism degree at Howard University and wrote for the New York Times and her sister attended the same school with a degree in social work. Mrs. Dartmouth was an English major at Syracuse and now taught composition at Columbia. They decided they would team up and write an article on how this tragic event affected the families of their missing children. Shannon's father was tasked to obtain a few photos of each student from their group of parents.

Darcy's and Wanda's parents were having a heart-to-heart conversation while Lydia Venhill sat on the couch holding Darcy's dog, petting him lovingly. Juanita talked about their four children and her extended family that lived on the same street. Mr. Womack rolled his eyes at her oversharing. As she was telling one story after the next, Mrs. Venhill wondered why they didn't have more children. Of course, she thought that nobody could ever replace her sweet Darcy.

Their husbands were noticeably quiet. It was Ernest Womack who piped up and asked Darby Venhill about his job and line of business.

"You know Ernest, if you would've asked me about my job before our daughters went missing, I would've given you a boring earful of what I do," he continued. "But I don't want to talk about my work anymore."

"What do you want to talk about?" Ernest asked Darby respectfully.

"When I was growing up, I loved to play sports," explained Darby. "I especially loved baseball and would love to play again, coach or be an umpire. Do you know my father never took us to see the Yankees or the Mets? I would love to go to a game, bring my mitt to catch a foul ball, buy a score sheet to track the plays, and have my family sitting next to me eating hotdogs as I drink a cold one."

Juanita smiled at Ernest as if they had a secret between them.

"I can do you one better," chuckled Ernest as he handed Darby one of his newly made business cards.

"What's this?" asked Darby as he read his card.

"It's an invitation to sit with me in the announcer's box as my guest when I present the games at Citi Field," replied Ernest. "I can even get you a complimentary hotdog and a cold one."

Darby was shocked and then felt so much excitement in his body that it overwhelmed him, rendering him speechless. He felt as if he were 10 years old again and someone just handed him a golden ticket. Then he felt guilty for being so excited while his daughter was missing. He gave Ernest a sincere hug that normally best buddies only give. Darby had never even hugged his father or brothers, but this would change.

"Thank you," said Darby, shaking his head, not believing anyone could be that generous.

The families were bonding. Some laughed, some cried, and they all comforted each other. Hours went by and when it was time to wrap up, Juanita asked everyone to stand in a circle and hold hands. You could hear a pin drop when her quiet husband spoke like a reverend and said the most thoughtful prayer. They almost didn't want to drop the hands that they were holding on to; it was such a powerful moment. Despite the change in status to recovering the students, they felt they still had to keep hope alive.

Chapter 56 The Bridge Solution

It was day five of the bridge building project when Mr. Boyce decided that he would allow the students to help. He wanted to show them the level of difficulty. Ryan, Vaughn, and Arcado volunteered. The rest preferred to handle the extra chores and go to school.

Mr. Boyce started by taking them on a tour. He showed them the cupola shop where metal was being formed. Then, he took them to the lumber where the treated wood was already cut to form 10-foot five-inch planks for the bridge. Finally, they took the horse and carriage to the bridge itself. By now the trail was well traveled and the snow was packed down for an easy horse ride.

When they got to the bridge, they looked at the edge which was being prepped for steel beams to attach to the vacant side. The build started ten feet before the actual cliff. There was steel affixed to the ground with wood mixed in. Vaughn shuttered looking down the ravine, with a fear of heights. Ryan looked down and wished he had superpowers to fix the bridge, and Arcado wondered what he could do to make this move any faster.

"I wonder if we are doing this the right way?" Arcado shook his head as he stared down the ravine.

"What do you mean?" Mr. Boyce asked.

"I mean, we are starting from scratch?" Arcado continued. "Why can't we recycle the bridge below? We can haul it up and fix it."

"Not everything can be recycled," Vaughn shot him down. "And who is going to haul it up?"

"Well, oxen saved us in a one-ton bus, why can't they haul this bridge up?" Arcado asked.

Boyce looked at Travis with a questioning look. Travis put his hand to his chin and thought it was a long shot but agreed with Arcado. It was worth a try. The civil engineer was called over for speculation. After much discussion, he also agreed that there might be a chance of hauling it up the mountainside without chopping pieces off here and there to use it for rebuilding. Boyce and the other men wondered why they hadn't thought of it before. They were so consumed in the technical parts of building the bridge that the creative ideas were never thought of.

Even a straightforward idea needed preparations. The engineer designed the best possible places to situate the pulling forces to get the bridge up. They also thought that they needed oxen power, horsepower, and human power to ensure that this could happen. The villagers were part of the working plan to raise the bridge. Now they needed to build a strong chain that would be long enough to secure it to the fallen bridge and reach up and over the top to attach to the oxen. They would also use rope for pulling. The boys were told it would take a few days to get the supplies made for the heavy pull.

By now, they were used to lengthy delays in the project timeline. Arcado worked out the timing and knew that at least he would be home for Christmas which was his favorite holiday to spend with his family. The food that his mom and her four brothers made for his extended family had him eating for days. He had lost weight being in Ourstory. He could not wait to dive into the pecan pie. While they rode back to camp, Arcado was in his dream world, but Vaughn and Ryan were talking about their high school basketball team. Ryan did miss playing for sure, but this little adventure made him rethink his strategies once he returned to the team. He bounced ideas off of Vaughn, who felt flattered that Ryan asked him for advice.

Mr. Boyce and Travis went directly to the cupola shop with the engineer to inquire about making the lengthy, strong chains. By the time they returned, school was dismissed and lunch was over. The boys went to join the choir rehearsals. Of course, Mr. Chad was happy to see that Vaughn would take over the piano. Others were happy that they were back to join them and it was evident on their faces.

Over in Albany, the governor was over all the excuses. For days, he had been recalling any National Guard Unit that could assist in the recovery of the students. Since the governor's orders were sent days ago, there were plenty of excuses of digging out their cities first which needed to be done. Many of the guard sites were in remote areas, as were their homes. Not everyone owned a bobcat to dig their driveways and streets out and the county snow removal had other priorities to work on first. Today, the governor finally got responses from 11 guard units that would join the search. The battalions would come from Albany, Syracuse, Buffalo, Rochester, Ronkonkoma, and more from Manhattan. His confidence rose that between all of these battalions, there would be a recovery.

In NYC the first appointment with the bank manager that Mrs. López could make was at two o'clock in the afternoon on Thursday. She was lucky to get in because so many of the previous week's canceled appointments held priority. The bank manager recognized her as the mother of the twins that were lost in upstate New York but did not mention a word to her about it. She demanded $200,000 from her account and requested to have that money in cash as soon as possible. The bank manager was taken back from the request and asked her if she was in some sort of trouble that warranted the authorities. She assured him that the money was for a private family matter, so he hesitantly got the necessary forms.

She filled them out as fast as she could, not reading them at all, but just signing, dating here and initialing there. Handing back the forms, she smiled, desperately needing his approval to release her money. In her satchel were folded duffel bags to carry the cash. Her husband was circling the streets awaiting her call to help carry the money to the car. He even brought his brother-in-law who was big and muscular, in the event they ran into anyone with bad ideas.

"Alright, we will be in touch within five business days with your cash," the bank manager said after he looked over the forms. "Would you like all large bills?"

"What?" she inquired, confused in panic. "I need my money today."

"I am sorry, but the bank's agreement says that requests of any amount over $3,000 will take five business days," he calmly quoted from a pamphlet on the desk.

"Is there an exception?" she insisted.

"I will see if I can expedite the request, but it's already Thursday afternoon," he commented, feeling that she most likely had a good reason for the money, but it was beyond his control. "Technically, this business day is over so it may not be until next Wednesday, possibly Thursday, that it gets approved and is readily available."

"That's too late," she said, sounding desperate. "Please sir, I need my money now."

He picked up the phone and made a call to his senior manager. They talked about a special, urgent request for Mrs. López and a few minutes later he hung up the phone.

"My senior manager is working on your request," he looked at her apologetically. "As soon as I have word, I will call you instantly."

"Thank you, sir," she said excitedly. "I will answer your call anytime, day or night."

He escorted her to the door and bid her farewell.

Her next call was to Mr. Venhill to let him know that the cash would be ready in five business days. She recounted the bank manager saying that it would be next Wednesday at the earliest. Venhill relayed the information to his contact and pleaded in a gentlemen's agreement that they start their search immediately with the money to be paid on Wednesday. The man on the other side of the phone reinforced that next Wednesday his men would be ready and not a dollar before.

In the meantime, the families of the students would have to pin their hopes on the TACC finding their kids. Maybe by next Wednesday there would be no need for the expense and their children would return home safely.

After dinner, instead of going to the gym, Vaughn slipped out into the darkness and went to the town hall. He wanted to play the piano and let his stress flow out of his fingers. The lantern he had with him lit the vacant hall. When he sat down at the keyboard, he gently played Christmas carols without

245

lyrics. It brought his mind peace. He was happiest when he played without any soul in sight because he played for himself.

The door to the hall opened and about 20 people entered with their own lanterns. There were both men and women and he noticed Adam was with the group. Vaughn stopped playing. The oldest, Samuel, took the Torah out and spoke words in Hebrew and then took the shamash and lit the candle on the right end of the Menorah. There were responses, again in Hebrew.

"My friend, go ahead and play," Samuel directed Vaughn. "We are celebrating the first day of Hanukkah and your music is most welcomed."

Vaughn played some classical George Winston instead of Christmas songs because he didn't know what would be appropriate. It appeared to be the right choice. When Vaughn looked, he noticed that Gabriel was seated next to him on the piano bench.

"Where did you come from?" he asked Gabriel, surprised.

"I like to come here to think sometimes," replied Gabriel.

"In the dark?" asked Vaughn.

"Light or dark, it's all the same," remarked Gabriel philosophically. "It's a place where the mind can be at peace."

Vaughn thought that Gabriel could read his mind. That's exactly what he thought as well. Although, he preferred the mystery of playing at night. He thought it was more inspirational for whatever reason, he did not know.

The people were talking lowly around the Menorah and neither Vaughn nor Gabriel could understand what they were saying. Then after a few minutes, they all left the building.

"God gave you a gift," Gabriel said as he closed his eyes and listened contently.

"My dad taught me how to play," said Vaughn rolling on.

"Then God gave you two gifts," he said in jealousy, staring into Vaughn's eyes and soul.

At that, Gabriel smiled at him and then got up and left him to play in solitude.

Friday, December 11th
Chapter 57 Life and Death

The National Guard searched and researched all the areas they put up on the grid. Sharp was no longer in charge and sent home. Another National Guard Unit took over and that commanding officer was now running things from the tent that the TACC put up. Rolling through the towns were many more battalions. The commanding officers from all the battalions met in the tent deemed as the mission's headquarters. They spent the morning talking about grid searches and strategies. They were determined as ever to recover these students and give their families peace.

In the mess hall of Ourstory, the violins hummed the beautiful Christmas music as the students and residents ate breakfast. There was a new update in the foyer of the mess hall about the chains being made. Thirty-five men had worked through the night making the chains at 100 grade which was needed for the weight to be lifted. This was a thick, steel chain that took a lot of might and tools to shape. Men had to rotate out every 20 minutes because of the exhaustion and the heat of shaping the steel. They were making good progress, but they were now all asleep and would be woken soon to re-engage the effort. It was too dangerous for the students to help, but as usual, they took on extra morning chores.

While all the kids were in school, the sound of the bell ringing in the campanile startled everyone. All scrambled to gather in front or inside the town hall immediately. Alarmed, everyone put down their notebooks and quickly marched single file downstairs and, after putting on cloaks, walked right to a spot where the village was gathered outside. The residents thought how the campanile bells were never rung as much as in the last couple weeks. Some thought this was exciting while others thought it was exhausting.

Mr. Boyce was at the top of the stairs of the town hall waiting for everyone to assemble. There were some men in the crowd with wet eyes, so all supposed this would not be a happy

247

occasion. Most of the New York students assumed it had to do with the bridge and that they wouldn't make it home for Christmas.

"My friends of Ourstory, it's with regret that I have to tell you that our friend John Jones died today," Mr. Boyce said. "He was shaping a loop in the chain when his heart stopped working. We tried to give him CPR. Travis ran to get Doc Marta, but he was gone."

"On Sunday at the 11 a.m. celebration, we will remember him," Mr. Boyce affirmed. "Anyone who has words to say, that will be the time to say it."

The villagers hugged one another and the students were all in disbelief. Lauren felt a guilty tenseness in her throat down to her stomach. She thought if they didn't need to build the bridge so fast then maybe he wouldn't have exhausted himself to death. Most thought that death didn't happen here because it was supposed to be a place to live out a healthy and happy life. They looked around at the Christmas decorations and thought that life couldn't be more important than in this moment.

The students found their assumption was correct - the bridge would be further delayed because some men had to prepare a coffin and others had to dig through the snow and into the hard earth to prepare for Sunday. There was a cemetery between one of the oldest maple trees and the edge of the woods. There were three graves there already for one woman with cancer who chose to live as chemical free as she could in her last years, one for a man who lived to be 102, and one plot was for the faithful German Shepherd who got caught in a nasty bear trap.

Arcado, Vaughn, and Ryan cornered Mr. Boyce after lunch to express their sympathies to him for the death of Mr. Jones. They pressed him on another issue.

"We want to help build the bridge," demanded Arcado to Mr. Boyce. "We don't care if we miss school, we don't want anyone else to die on our account."

"Yeah, we can help," agreed Vaughn.

"It's not that difficult to point and tell us what to do," Ryan inputted. "We are stronger than you think."

Mr. Boyce thought about it for a few moments but did not fully commit to an agreement.

"Let me get with Travis to see how you can help," he replied. "I will get back to you."

After they met at the Venhill family meeting, Shannon Dartmouth's and Brianna Germaine's moms created a newsletter with all of their children's names, pictures, and a little biography of their lives. They did this mainly for their families to get to know each other's children. They uploaded everything to the website that was already created. There were a lot of goofy and funny pictures that Mr. Dartmouth collected from the families. He insisted that he wanted more than just a stiff school photo; he wanted any pictures that captured the essence of their children and told a story.

Mr. Dartmouth visited each family and wouldn't accept less than a dozen pictures. Mr. White and Mr. Vetter were hard-pressed to come up with that amount. They realized that they missed the opportunity to capture moments of their kids' lives. Luckily, Shawn, Ryan's brother had taken plenty from the games at the Malloy Courts and a few from school. Mr. Vetter combed through his wife's phone that hadn't been charged in weeks. She still had pictures from years ago of Vaughn at church playing piano and one that stifled him. It was the two of them playing the baby grand piano in his showroom. They were both caught in a laugh, looking at each other. He thought to himself, absolutely priceless.

The TACC still searched up and down the state highway. They did exactly what the MMC had done and went door to door. When the governor issued the orders that every New York National Guard battalion upstate look for the bus and the students, he did not include the MMC. They were still the fall guys. Every road and wood in upstate New York were filled with a Humvee or track vehicle. The area was so saturated with soldiers that the residents and sheriff were getting annoyed. By this point, the residents were getting insulted by the fourth or fifth search of their property with the innuendo of possibly hiding the kids.

At this point the snow was cleared off the highways and side roads, which made driving easier, but it still was a slow process. Residents going to the grocery store took twice as long because they were stopped in both directions for interrogation. Helicopters hovered over the skies all day and afternoon without result. Camps were set up here and there hosting the battalions. Not one iota of proof that the kids had even been in upstate New York was found.

Mrs. López called the bank manager that she had dealt with on the previous day to see if there would be any exception to her request. She stressed it might be a matter of life or death for her family members. The banker by this time was starting to believe that her sons were being held for ransom.

"I am trying my best to move things along," he said sympathetically. "Is there anything more you need to tell me?"

"No," she said curtly. "Call me as soon as the money is approved, or I will take my business elsewhere."

Friday, December 11th
Chapter 58 The Purpose

That evening at the gym an event was set up by Charlie. He called it "Ball Night". This would only be for the kids aged 12 and up. First, they divided up into three teams of seven. Then, they lined up behind a teammate to take a turn holding a tennis ball in between their legs and walking down to a designated cone, turning around and walking back until they reached their next team member to relay. If you dropped the ball, you had to start all over again. Names were picked randomly and teams were set up.

To start it was Wanda, Christopher, and Darcy each on separate teams. When the word "GO" was yelled, Wanda started hopping with hers and lost it on the fifth hop. Christopher, who played this game before, walked slowly. Darcy watched both of their strategies and decided to try Christopher's. Everyone looked weird and funny as they walked. Wanda went back and tried the slow walking but was super slow and super loud about it. The teams were cheering and laughing at the same time.

The whole gym, including the adults playing cards, watched and cheered along. Brianna decided that if there were another activity, she would play with her fellow students, and fold her hand in Gin rummy. This looked exciting and she was missing out, as usual. The game took longer than usual and when it was Sergei's turn, he laughed so hard he fell down. Surprisingly, Adam was one of the best at walking steadily and slowly to help Team Wanda out. Shannon got frustrated because she couldn't get a grip on the ball between her legs and had to return several times. Ryan was the anchor for his team, and he almost marched along to take the win for Team Darcy.

It took over 30 minutes for the game to play out and have a winner. The next game used a ball the size of a softball, but it was a round spongy one. This time because Brianna wanted to play, they split into two groups to have an even number on each team. The idea was to pass the ball under your neck to the next person down the line. The first team to make it down the line won. If anyone dropped the ball, it would have to go back to the first person and start all over again.

Bianca and Shannon were at the beginning of each team. When the word "GO" was yelled, Shannon had to pass it to Charlie, who was good at this game, and it was done in no time. Bianca had to pass it to Ryan and luckily, they were about the same height. They were both competitive, but the ball kept falling to the floor. Bianca felt strange being so close to Ryan and so she would pull back before he could nuzzle the ball under his chin.

"Come on, do it right this time," Ryan scolded Bianca with a devious smile.

She gave him a dirty look as he was the reason that she couldn't get it straight. So when they tried again, she put past the awkward feeling of touching him so close and just went for it. Bianca was reeling because of the closeness, but after the ball was passed, a sigh of relief came over her, until the ball got to Wanda. She had to pass it to Vlad and got over-aggressive and dropped it. The ball was brought all the way back to Bianca and Ryan. Ryan gazed into her light brown eyes and smiled as if he were enjoying every moment of it. She, on the other hand, acted like it was torture, but her competitive nature wanted to win. They snuggled necks up and passed it quickly and then Ryan turned to Wanda and did the same.

The ball dropped about eight more times and Bianca had to endure Ryan's cheesy grins relishing in the fact that they must do what they must do. In the other line, toward the end of the train, Christopher had to pass it to Lauren, and it turned out she was ticklish. There was no way in heaven that the ball would ever get passed to her. She screamed with laughter anytime Christopher would get close to her neck with the ball. He attempted repeatedly, but she just couldn't stop her squirming and giggling to hold it long enough. In the end, Adam passed it to Darcy, which he was only happy to do, and Bianca's team won. Everyone on their team cheered, including Ryan who picked up Bianca and spun her around in joy. This took her by surprise because she thought they had already been way too close on this competitive journey. For the next game, she would make sure they were on separate teams.

The next game was Four Square. Most of everyone stayed to play, but there were two extra people that had to sit out. Lauren and Arcado volunteered to sit out first. Arcado noticed the gym door open and close and then he saw him.

Gabriel walked in not causing any disturbance. Nobody knew he was there practically, except for Arcado. He felt protective of him. Although in truth, Gabriel never needed anyone to defend him, he spoke freely and wiser than most adults and never cared much about the consequences. Gabriel saw the glass half full even if it was almost empty. He couldn't understand why someone wouldn't be happy all the time if they didn't have an auto-immune disease. This was his wish, but he wasn't as blessed as others. He knew his limitations but lived as if he had none.

Arcado left the group and followed Gabriel to an art table in the corner. There were plenty of paints, markers, crayons, pencils, and blank sheets of paper. Gabriel stared at Arcado and then finally gave him a smile with the gap between his teeth showing. If he could, Arcado would pack the little guy in a suitcase and take him home, but the best he could do was enjoy this moment with him. The two were coloring with crayons making Christmas trees with presents underneath. Lauren walked over to join them.

"This looks fun," said Lauren, smiling at both boys. "I remember drawing the same kind of pictures at Christmas when I was your age."

She sat down and grabbed a blank sheet of paper. She made an outline of a Christmas tree that filled the paper from top to bottom. Then her smile turned into a serious, pensive look and she stopped drawing.

"What's wrong?" asked Arcado.

"I am thinking of the irony of trying to draw this tree," she said. "I mean that symbol is the whole reason we're in this mess, yet I still want to make it the most beautiful tree."

"Yeah, it's crazy that we're here because of some dumb tree," replied Arcado gazing at their drawings.

"You're here because you're meant to be here," interrupted Gabriel.

"We're here because of a hunt to kill a big tree," corrected Arcado, talking in staccato.

"Don't you know that God has a plan for you?" he asked as his little innocent face scrunched up in curiosity. "You were meant to be here. We saved you for a reason."

"What is the reason?" asked Lauren as she selected a few crayons to color with.

"I don't know," he declared in a frustrated child's voice as he colored his tree green. "God knows and, in the end, you'll know why."

"So, you think we came here on purpose?" asked Arcado, egging on Gabriel to explain more.

"Purpose," replied Gabriel as he kept on coloring. "Yes, that's the answer to your question. But only you know inside of yourself what your purpose is being here. It's not the same for everyone. Your purpose is different from Lauren's purpose. Even your family, missing you back home, has found a purpose."

"So, what you're saying is that we were saved for a reason?" asked Lauren, engaging him as she colored in her tree. "And each of us has our own purpose as to why we're being saved."

Gabriel didn't answer but just kept coloring. Arcado put his crayon down and gazed at his half-colored-in Christmas tree. He looked at the presents under the tree that he drew in and the stick-figured, happy faces that surrounded it. He stared at the tree and knew the reason for the season wasn't reflected, so he drew the manger scene under the tree and a star at the top. As he was coloring the star with a vibrant yellow crayon, the lightbulb flickered above them, and a beam of light shone directly on his star. All three of them gasped in awe and then the light bulb flickered out.

"If you ask me," Arcado paused. "I think we were saved by Christmas."

Saturday, December 12th
Chapter 59 Finishing the Chains

Arcado, Vaughn, and Ryan reminded Mr. Boyce to let them help with the bridge, even if it meant skipping chores or school. Mr. Boyce smiled and showed his gratitude, but he knew the danger of the heat and sparks from the cupola furnace used to form the chain. He wanted the boys to get home in one piece, not scalded or maimed. The men of Ourstory continued making the chains. It was so long that most of the chain was out of the building, stacked in neat rows. They had already made three chains of 100 feet and now the last one was 70 feet of 100-grade chain, and they needed at least 30 more feet to finish. The men worked rotating to take shifts so not all of them were there at once, which seemed to be a little more efficient.

Mr. Boyce put the students to work as they requested. He had them load up the completed three 100-foot chains in the wagon and take it to the camp near the broken bridge. The engineer went with them. Once they arrived, they unloaded the chains and hung some of them down the mountainside to reach the broken bridge. The rest of the chain was spread out on top of the mountain along a trail that the oxen would be taking the opposite way. When everything was properly in place, they drove a few stakes in the chain to hold them down on the trail.

While they were on the trail, the boys heard helicopters fly overhead. The first instinct was for them to run out of the woods and hail down the helicopter for a rescue. The engineer ran faster than they could to stop them from exiting the woods.

"Don't do it," he panted out of breath.

The three halted in their footsteps before they reached the sunlight. They almost gave their site away with a bunch of waving and yelling. When the boys stopped running and realized what they could have done, they shook their heads in shame.

"Sorry," said Ryan out of breath. "We weren't thinking."

The other boys nodded their heads in agreement. It may have not mattered. The area that the helicopters flew over, wasn't in their search grid, therefore, they flew over quickly to get to the designated areas for lookouts.

The state roads again were buzzing with National Guard troops and now they were combing the wooded area next to the roads. Many were up to their chest in snow or climbing snow banks in their search. The warehouse owner's door was knocked on for the ninth time and his warehouse searched again. He put a sign on his door that said: "Searched my house and my Warehouse" and then had a slash mark for every time one of them came back to do so. He now added a mark to make it nine times. The guardsmen felt embarrassed that they did so only because they hadn't been the ones to do so before.

"Do you guys ever communicate?" asked the perturbed warehouse owner.

He wasn't the only one that had treated the guardsmen rudely. The residents truly wanted the students found but felt like their lives and property were now under microscopes of anyone who felt like they hadn't seen the inside of their estate and felt they were privileged to look.

Inside the tent of the TACC, the commanding officers sipped on their coffees and wanted to change their strategy to now questioning the gardeners. They thought that after they departed from the plaza to drive up the mountain, maybe something nefarious happened and they got rid of the kids before heading up the mountain. The officers had seen some strange things in their days and wanted to make sure they looked at it from all angles.

In New York City, the families loved the project that Ms. Germaine and Mrs. Dartmouth started. Ms. Germaine was not satisfied with just their internal group knowing how great her daughter Brianna and everyone else's kids were and teamed up with Mrs. Dartmouth, Shannon's mom, to start a social media campaign and copied their project to a new website. They opened permissions for the public to view their site. Their hope was to reach anyone who may have seen the student's bus in the mountainous area at the time of the storm or even afterward. They rebuilt the public posting to include all 11 pictures and a little biography of each student. The minute after they posted, they got several hits. It was unbelievable the support that came through wanting to help and forward their posts to relatives in the upstate areas.

After hours had passed, several other odd things happened. The first is that it went viral and they had over 450,000 views. The second, was that pictures of other missing children were getting deposited in the contact portal of the website. Both ladies were in awe of the responses and the new pictures sent. They never knew the volume of missing children and were horrified to know that this website had now become a bottomless pit of desperation.

Mrs. Dartmouth sat down silently thinking that maybe God pointed his hand down on them for a much larger mission. She was barely up for her role of finding her daughter and some newly found strangers' kids. Thinking that the purpose just grew bigger, she wasn't sure she was the one that could do this. Writing and publishing words were easy, but to be actively involved in a nationwide problem made her feel uneasy. Oppositely, Ms. Germaine didn't flinch on acting on the new pictures that were deposited. She created more pages, in alphabetical order, posting the faces, names, ages, and the last location of the other missing children. Because she and Mrs. Dartmouth started such a webpage, she wanted to name it 'The Brianna Project' or the 'ShanBri Project' but settled on calling it 'The Missing School Bus'. It was the only name that might represent all missing children.

When Arcado, Ryan, and Vaughn got back to the village everyone was outside. It was a sunny, cold, and beautiful day. Behind the barn, several kids were building a snowman and some were building igloos. It was a whole snow village. The boys joined in the fun. Wanda was bossing the twins to make her a throne in the back of their fort. They punched through the snow and made a little seat that was fashioned for her to sit on. She stared at them in a serious way for a minute tapping her foot and pointed to the small seat. They laughed and added more snow to the seat.

Bianca and her girls made their fort. It was a wall of snow, with two windows. She called it their castle. When Ryan walked over to check it out, he got pegged in the gut with a snowball. He looked at who the culprit was and a face popped up through the castle window and Bianca started to laugh.

"Oh, you're so in trouble," Ryan said and picked up a handful of snow and ran in her direction.

She screamed and bolted around the back of the barn as he chased her all around until he caught her. He took the snow and slid some down her back, so it touched her bare skin and she shrieked and laughed at the same time. They both fell to the ground, out of breath, laughing. They both sat up and stared into each other's eyes. He thought she looked breathtaking when she smiled and it warmed his entire soul to make her laugh. He leaned in to get closer to her face. As he inched closer, there was a "whack". A group of kids came around the barn and pegged both of them with snowballs. Ryan was irritated. Bianca blinked her eyes in relief.

Switching gears, they looked at each other with strategic, competitive faces and rose quickly with snow in their hands. They formed a few snowballs and chased the kids around the barn and back to the snow village area. Everyone was hiding behind a fort, snowman, or igloo ready to launch snowballs at Ryan and Bianca. When they entered, they got pegged from every direction. Some hit and some missed.

"This is snow war," cried Bianca and she threw her snowball at anyone in sight and then created more.

Ryan saw a wooden barrel and rolled it over to where Bianca was losing her battle, so it would block the barrage of ammo. Sooner or later, everyone had a pack of snow embedded in their cloaks or hats.

The dinner bell rang from the mess hall. They all dropped their snowballs and ran to dinner. It was that kind of day full of energy and fun. Once they were inside and divested of their soaking cloaks, they took turns warming up to the roaring fireplace at the end of the hall. The quartet, who had dined earlier, played softly, "It Came Upon a Midnight Clear" as the crowd went through the chow line. Everyone was seated, eating dinner and chatting. Their faces were red in the cheeks from the fun of the day. Mr. Boyce stood by the fireplace and placed his hand in the air to make an announcement.

"Ladies and gentlemen, can I have your attention please," he bellowed and then waited for everyone's conversations to end.

"I am pleased to tell you that the last 30 feet of the last chain are complete," he barely got the last word out before all of the mess hall was in a cheerful chatter. He waited for the crowd to settle down.

"The plan is after the celebration of John Jones's life tomorrow, that we all head out to the mountainside to pull up the large piece of the bridge," again cheers and excitement filled the room, and Mr. Boyce gave up trying to say anything more.

Chapter 60 Investigations

There was a knock on Cyril Haugen's door bright and
early on Sunday morning. The head gardener peaked out the
window and saw two soldiers in their dress uniforms. Thinking
it highly unusual for him to get thrown in a brig for losing the
students, he wondered why they had come. His wife was next
to him wondering the same thing. She threw on a pot of coffee
and then went to get dressed. He was still in his pajamas but
answered the door anyway.

"Can I help you?" asked Cyril, a little intimidated.

"Sorry to bother you so early sir," one of the officers
politely said. "I am Colonel James and this is Major Bellerman.
We are here to ask you a few questions about the bus trip into
the mountains."

"Of course, please come in," said Mr. Haugen, stepping
back and opening the front door. "Please make yourself
comfortable in the living room, while I change quickly."

The officers wiped their feet thoroughly and proceeded to
the couch in the living room. While they were seated, Mrs.
Haugen came in with a tray of coffee, cream, sugars, and
cookies on the side.

"Good morning," she said brightly. "Please help yourself
while you wait for Cyril."

She disappeared into the kitchen biting her lip nervously
awaiting their questions that she planned on overhearing.

The only morning chore scheduled was the milking of the
animals that morning. There would be no hunting, wood
gathering, or the other things. Mr. Boyce thought it would be
best if everyone got a good night's sleep and used their energy
in a few hours to pull the bridge up the mountainside.

There would be just five milkers this morning and two
would include the cooks that would not make the journey to
the cliffside today. Cooking was a job that took all day and
when folks came back from the mission, they would expect a
hearty meal. Ms. Kim volunteered to help because she liked

the job. All the students were off the hook and allowed to sleep in this morning.

Breakfast would not be delayed, so everyone headed into the mess hall at the normal time. The stringed quartet played "What Child is This" as the students entered. The atmosphere of the day was one of anxiety and hope. Many ate in silence enjoying the soothing music in the corner. Most of the students chatted. Ryan, of course, stood behind Bianca in line and accidentally stepped on her heels as she walked through picking up her meal. She let him be silly, without the cold stares, because soon there would be no one to bother her.

They spent several meals sitting next to each other not saying a word. Bianca didn't want to speak because she was trying to keep space in her head and between them to make it easier when he left. Ryan was quiet because if he opened his mouth, he would say flirty things he had never spoken before and didn't want to sound like a dork. In the back of his mind, he reminded himself that he should just say everything he felt because what would be the worst thing that could happen? If she rejected him, he would be leaving soon, but if she said the same thing likewise, then he would feel so much better having his feelings validated. The whole situation was strange and Bianca kept the feelings between them tempered, so as not to get out of hand.

After the dishes were done, everyone went straight to the town hall for the celebration of the life of John Jones. Today, with the hectic schedule, it was earlier than usual. It started with a reading of 2 Corinthians 1:3-4 about comforting the afflicted. Vaughn was asked to play the piano as one of the ladies sang "You Raise Me Up". It was heartfelt and the residents that knew John Jones well wiped a tear from their eyes. Then afterward, Mr. Boyce gave a eulogy. John knew every baseball player since the year 1961. Boyce talked about John Jones being an avid Detroit Tiger fan and swore that Al Kaline was the best all-around player in the history of baseball.

"You have hit your grand slam and now may you rest in the dugout of peace." Mr. Boyce said, as his final words.

When the celebration was over, they slowly carried the wooden casket to the burial site. The whole village was in procession behind the six men that carried John Jones. The sun was out, but there was still a chill in the air as they trudged through a path in the snow. The six men lowered the casket into the earth and then gently laid dirt on top. All who wanted could shovel some soil into the grave as they said goodbye. The students watched but didn't participate knowing that they just met him and only really knew his face. In the spring, there would be a proper tombstone marker placed on top of John Jones. For now, it was just wooden sticks made into a cross.

"I think we should sing his favorite song," sniffled Travis.

Travis and some of the men started singing, "Take Me out to the Ball Game". Everyone, including the students, sang it. It was short and sweet, but it brought smiles to the villagers. They thought the oddness of singing such a tune seemed to match John Jones's life.

Everyone headed back to the village to change into their work clothes and head to the cliffside for the next task at hand. The cooks packed lunches and water and already put them in the wagon. They loaded the wagon also with food and water for the beasts that needed to be tended to. This left little room for anyone to sit, so just the older folks who couldn't walk fast did so.

Cyril Haugen returned to the living room dressed in a long sleeve dress shirt and khaki pants. He didn't want to seem too formal. He took a deep breath and sat across them on the love seat facing the officers, ready for battle.

"Mr. Haugen, why did you put all of the students in one bus and the adults in another?" asked the major who had his pen and pad of paper ready to record the answer.

Instead of answering question after question, Cyril decided to tell the story from top to bottom. He absolutely hated that he was the one to decide to keep the students together so they could start getting to know each other and have fun. He told them about losing phone signals as the snow came down the mountainside. Following Ms. Kim was the plan until Rooter passed her on the mountain. He swore that Ms. Kim's bus was directly behind them until it turned down a road, unexpectedly. The story repeated in his mind night and day since the time he lost the students, so he knew it like the back of his hand.

"Would you say the kids were a bother?" inquired Colonel James, suspiciously.

"I would never say that because I never got acquainted with any of them," he continued. "They seemed pleased when the introductions came about."

"So there was no malicious intent to get rid of them at any point?" Colonel James questioned.

"Rid of them?" asked Cyril, confused and then stated. "Nobody wanted to get rid of the students. We just lost them, that's all."

After Cyril said those words, he started laughing just as he and his team had done at Myra and Valley's house. He couldn't stop and was angry at himself for doing so, but this was a result of him being nervous. Mrs. Haugen heard the line of questioning and the odd laughter from her husband as she spied from the kitchen. She knew when a lawyer needed to be called and so she scrolled her address book on her cell phone until she found the number.

The team tied the horses up to the wagon and each of the oxen had a man leading them up the path. Over 200 people were making their way to the bridge with the wagon, horses, and oxen on the trail. The wagon got there quicker than the residents on foot, but the oxen took a long time. After a quarter of a mile, one ox would stop or lie down, and that caused a chain effect on the other beasts who did the same. After two hours of waiting for the oxen, they got the lunches out and ate. It was past lunchtime anyhow, but many were anxious to get the bridge up before lunch.

When the men finally arrived with the oxen, they watered and fed them. The oxen all laid down under a tree in the snow on a bed of hay. Some of the men climbed down the ravine to hook the four chains and four ropes to different parts of the bridge. They brought a rope ladder that helped get most of the way down. The rope ladder's lowest rung landed on a large boulder, so once they got to that point, there was still a bit of a climb down. It helped if you were taller to go do this part so you could reach the ladder from the boulder. A few stayed at the bottom of the ravine and guided the chains and rope once the pulling started.

At the top, the rope and chains were already laid out along a straight path from the cliff's edge. The residents all walked the path and took their spots ready to pull. The men hooked up the horses to the front of the ropes and lastly, the oxen needed to be hooked up to the chains. There was only one problem, the oxen did not move from their hay. Some dangled carrots in front of their faces to get them up, but nothing. They had just eaten all of their grains, so there was only willow and carrots to motivate them. It didn't work. After 30 minutes of failed oxen bribery, the council called a meeting. It was getting to be early afternoon and not only were the oxen tired, but the residents were yawning too.

Mr. Boyce called everyone to gather back at what they called the base camp near the cliff. After all was in place, he looked mostly at the students and shook his head.

"We decided to postpone the bridge haul until tomorrow," his voice boomed loud enough to reach everyone in the back. "We will leave the oxen here tonight and start again directly after breakfast tomorrow. I will need a few volunteers to camp overnight to keep watch over the animals."

Travis and the twins volunteered to stay. Wanda desperately wanted to, but she needed her beauty sleep which wouldn't happen on the ground.

"Alright," Mr. Boyce settled. "Let's tie the oxen down, head back and grab dinner. Then we will load up the wagon with hay, feed, water, and firewood. You guys can head back with the necessary overnight equipment."

The officers who interrogated Mr. Haugen had left after he couldn't stop laughing at their questions about the students. His wife got angry that he couldn't stop because this was a serious charge and she knew Cyril was innocent. The officers left thinking the head gardener was suspicious and would move to get a warrant to search his house, computers, and cell phone. Their next stop would be to the bus driver, Mr. Rooter. Surely, he would be a more reliable and trustworthy source.

When they arrived back at the village, the cooks had bear stew ready and served everyone a good healthy portion. After dinner, Vlad and Sergei departed with Travis back to the site. The rest of the community all met in the gymnasium for nightly exercise and social time. Bianca and Ryan challenged each other on the basketball court and then retreated to a corner to sit and annoy each other, playfully. Wanda had both Darcy and Lauren jumping rope together and chanting her playground words. Shannon challenged herself to climb the wall. Adam played badminton with Charlie. Arcado, Vaughn, and Christopher played Around the World with the basketball.

"If we get the collapsed bridge up, we might make it back a few days after Christmas," Arcado said as he shot. "I know once it's up, a lot more work has to be done to move it over the canyon."

"Yeah, I can't wait to see my dad's face," Vaughn went on. "I wish my mom would come to see me too, but I know she'll probably be stoned out."

"Oh boo hoo for you," Christopher said, cruelly. "At least you have a family to go home to."

"Yeah, but I only have one parent that knows I exist," said Vaughn wearily.

"Like I said, boohoo," Christopher was getting tired of the New York kids always talking about their parents. "You're lucky you have one parent to show you some love."

"Oh, sorry dude. I didn't mean to upset you," Vaughn said sensitively and then made the shot in the net. "Do you even remember your parents?"

"Really?" Christopher sounded frustrated. "Do you think any of us remember being loved by a parent or any relative?"

At that, he bounced the ball high and stormed out of the gym in a huff. Everyone took notice of the scene but left it alone. Drama didn't happen every day but knew they were in the gym to blow off the day's stress.

When everyone retired to their rooms for the evening, Christopher was nowhere to be found. According to Gabriel, who was the last to see him, Christopher grabbed a lantern and a backpack, filled it with clothes, and left. Charlie criticized the seven-year-old for not stopping him or finding someone to tell.

"I didn't make his decision and I don't judge him for his choices," he said innocently. "Things will work out, if you believe."

This wasn't a comforting thought to anyone.

Vaughn was upset that his words affected Christopher so much. He knew he was lucky to have a family that cared for him and he had been a jerk not to say it. Now being out in the cold wilderness at night was an unpleasant thought. With the bridge broken, there would be no destination of worth for him to head to. Even though Christopher wasn't 18 yet, this night would mark the day that he left Ourstory. The news spread like wildfire about Christopher's disappearance and the villagers were miserable because they knew the most likely outcome for his survival.

Monday, December 14th
Chapter 61 Heave and Pull

Hardly anyone slept well thinking of Cristopher's fate out in the wild. Vaughn blamed himself for the dumb remarks that drove Christopher away from camp. They did their routine morning chores almost in silence. The hunters were careful not to shoot at anything too distant due to the unknown location of the missing boy. Even Wanda, for the first time, was quiet and had a miserable time hunting without her "boyfriends", who were watching over the oxen at the bridge.

Breakfast was only a little livelier. People talked about the strong possibilities of working in unity to get the bridge up the cliffside. After the meal, they prepared to head to the bridge. The New York students were full of hope that this would be the day. If all went well today, the bridge would take about a week or so to be installed over the canyon, according to the civil engineer.

Horses and a coach were loaded up with the usual food and supplies needed. The elderly hopped into the wagon. The journey of over 200 residents restarted.

When they reached bridge camp, they saw the oxen laying on hay, not too far from the fire pit. Vlad, Sergei, and Travis were overwhelmed to have everyone there. Everyone took a 15-minute break and then they would begin the day.

After everyone rested, they took their places. Ropes and chains were brought in to tie to different parts of the fallen bridge. Bianca and Ryan volunteered to climb down the crevasse to ensure everything was fastened to the bridge and guide it during the pull.

On the path leading away from the cliff, there were women, students, Ms. Kim, and men gripping the rope or chain. Anxiety was high, but everyone needed to dig deep and find the adrenalin to lift the broken bridge. Mr. Boyce had one of the deepest and loudest voices, so he gave the commands.

"All right everyone, on the count of three we pull. One, two, three...PULL!" he shouted.

Everyone toward the very front couldn't hear Boyce, so people would repeat his words up the line until they all did. At the command, every person and beast moved forward. Bianca and Ryan in the pit guided the bottom of the bridge forward. The bridge inched upward. It wasn't a fast plot, but it was working. A half an hour went by and the bridge was flat against the cliff as it was being hauled up. A knot in everyone's tummy was starting to build in anticipation of their last heave and pull.

The bridge was in a dangling position. This strained everyone, including the oxen, because there was no ground for them to stabilize the weight as they pulled it. The effort to just keep it dangling was tremendous. People's muscles were starting to feel sore and wary. The oxen looked as though they might lay down any minute. Travis and Boyce knew they had to hurry, or they would have to redo it all over again.

The little ones came around and poured water into the adult's mouths, as they rested in between pulls. Even though there was a chill in the air, sweat dripped down every person. On Boyce's command, they would pull until it reached the top. He warned everyone to dig deep and not to stop.

"PULL!" he commanded.

They all did. They heaved and pulled in a rhythm. The broken bridge inched up and up for another 25 minutes and it was almost at the top. Bianca yelled from beneath the bridge that they were almost there. The people were concentrated, still in their rhythm. The hardest part was getting the bridge up and over once it got to the top. They continued to heave and pull and heave and pull. Finally, the bridge rose to the top. Now all they had to do was pull it over to land on their elevation.

What happened next came out of nowhere and so suddenly. During the heaving, nobody noticed some of the ropes unraveled and thinned out due to the stress of the weight and the rubbing on the corner of the cliff. In one second, two of the ropes snapped, leaving only chains bound to the bridge and oxen. The rope holders fell forward and injured themselves in doing so. This caused the oxen to fall on their hind legs, and then they were dragged back toward the bridge along with some of the men that were assigned to pull chains. The men had to let go of the chains, but the oxen were secured to them and were on their way heading down the long path faster to the cliff and ultimately down the ravine. At the bottom of the ravine Ryan and Bianca fled the scene so as not to get crushed by the now falling bridge. In her hurry, Bianca stepped into a hole, twisted her ankle, and got her foot stuck. She couldn't move. Ryan didn't notice until it was too late. The bridge was falling fast and soon would crush her.

Monday, December 14th
Chapter 62 Operation Tannenbaum

The call came early in the morning to Mrs. López's phone. It was the bank manager that she had talked to last week. He knew that he crossed the line asking her to give his wife the news story of the century. After his phone call, he went directly to the top manager and insisted that the money that was on request be released immediately for an urgent crisis. He vouched for Mrs. López as an upstanding citizen who would do a lot more business with the bank if she could get her money. On Monday when the bank manager logged on to his computer, the transfer for cash had come through.

"Mrs. López, your money is ready," was all he said. She acknowledged and hung up the phone.

Mrs. and Mr. López and his brother-in-law all traveled to the bank as planned and made the transaction. She called Mr. Venhill before he left for work to tell him that the cash was on the way. He, in turn, called his friend to drop-off the cash and a signed contract of work. They referred to this work as Operation Tannenbaum. There would be no other words to describe this mission.

No names of the men would ever be revealed. Unbeknownst to Mr. Venhill, one of the men worked on many different operations. He was also employed by a very unethical group that was involved with human trafficking. This group hired him years ago to locate a group of orphans that cost them millions of dollars in assets. He never did find the orphans; however, he had their pictures and kept one eye out for them on every job he did. This man did not know they were human traffickers, nor did he know the reason this mob wanted the children. All he had to do was disclose their location if he ever came across them and he would be paid a large sum of money. He never knew why the client wanted to locate someone, and he never asked questions either. This would keep his conscience clear.

Unlike the National Guard, there could only be success. The group had a 94% achievement rate for locating missing things and people. The only hard part about all of this would be bringing back the students in whatever state they were found. Five different colored SUVs with darkened windows drove to upstate New York for Operation Tannenbaum. They drove in a military-style convoy at full speed up the snowy mountains. These weren't your ordinary SUVs; they were equipped with spy-like gadgets and weapons.

Through means of hacking computers, they found out which residents and places of businesses, enroute had any type of video surveillance viewing the outside of their property and went and seized or stole it. They flashed credentials that appeared to be government-like, but they were just professionally fake down to the official seal. If residents weren't home, they jimmied the locks of their doors, snuck inside and uploaded the footage onto their media storage device, and then departed just as stealthy as they came. They would also first erase any trace that they were in the house.

The roads and woods were filled with the National Guard who got in their way. They were all over the place, pulling vehicles over to search and ask questions. Each man wore something to fit in and even had wigs and John Deere ball caps to wear in disguise. Their cover story was that they were from the city but wanted to check on their summer houses after the winter storm. They acted cool and calm and added that they supported the National Guard in their efforts.

An RV trailer for Operation Tannenbaum was already in place at a vacant farmhouse, almost a mile from the sheriff's office. Their sources assured them that the owners were already at their Florida home for the winter and had no security devices around the house, nor any neighbors.

The collection of all the data was uploaded to a master media drive and it held over 1,000 hours of tape. The men took shifts sleeping in the RV and working through the video footage. They would go through each surveillance tape and piece together the last time there was a student bus sighting. The trailer was equipped with high-speed internet and video technology that made the process faster, but not fast enough for the five men working on and off. There were hours of snow-blowing video that had nothing but forest animals. The men were too thorough just to fast forward. Any vehicle that drove on the road had the analyst slowing down the footage to ensure it wasn't a bus. Sometimes making out the type of vehicle was difficult due to the horrific snow blowing this way or that. But this is what they got paid for. This was the impeccable job that would find the needle in the haystack.

Days went by and The Missing School Bus project grew to be almost a full-time job. Ms. Germaine was fortunate that she worked from home and could give it her attention, but Mrs. Dartmouth had to head back to teach Composition at the University. Lucky for her, it was finals week and all she had to do was proctor exams. After one of the tests that day, a student walked up to Mrs. Dartmouth and thanked her. She assumed it was for the knowledge that she imparted.

Before she could even say "you're welcome", her student told her of how the webpage reactivated a story about her missing brother from four years ago. He was 16 when he went missing and there was no media attention. But someone emailed her parents with a last known sighting of him in Norfolk, Virginia. Her parents and she were going to leave immediately after her exam to check out the possibility that he could be alive.

Mrs. Dartmouth realized that this webpage provided hope. She knew in her heart that she had to be all in or nothing. After picking up the phone and dialing her new web partner, Ms. Germaine, she told her that they needed to increase the size of the webpage and ramp up for more postings. She was more than all in, she was determined to make this her legacy.

Chapter 63 Bridge over Troubled Canyon

The oxen were being dragged down the path and were nearing the ravine as the bridge was falling down the cliffside. Bianca realized that there was no hope and stared at Ryan as she took her last breath. He knew that he couldn't run back to save her. He fell to his knees and put his hand over his heart staring back at her.

Out of nowhere, the bridge suspended its falling motion right before it crushed Bianca's body. It started to ascend. Bianca thought it didn't make sense, but by the time she realized it, Ryan was at her side pulling her foot out of the hole. He carried her, walking carefully on the snowy rocks to a safe place.

From the vacant opposite side of the mountain, an industrial crane hooked onto the bridge and used a powerful magnet to adhere to the steel on the falling bridge. The oxen were no longer dragged. They all stood erect, bloodied and scuffed but alright. People from a half mile up the path ran to the cliff to witness the horror but now saw the saving grace instead.

"It's a miracle," Wilbur said in awe.

"No, it's more than a miracle," Mr. Boyce teared up. "It's proof that there is a higher power out there. Thank God!"

The mystery of who was in the crane and where it came from was on the mind of the villagers. Everyone stared curiously to the other side of the bridge where the crane operator was maneuvering the broken bridge that dangled and coming toward them. They moved out of the way as the damaged bridge rested firmly on the ground. The civil engineer and welders went over to the structure and started assessing the damage and the repairs required.

Across the other side of the bridge, two men got out of the crane and waved. One was Christopher and the other man Boyce recognized was the warehouse owner's son. Then, Christopher carefully guided himself over the single edge side of the bridge, which was too dangerous for most to cross, until he reached Mr. Boyce. The villagers watched in dread as he had to make skillful decisions to get across. He scaled the same bridge in the dark, the night previous, in his rage to leave Ourstory.

Vaughn walked swiftly over to where Christopher stood by Mr. Boyce. As soon as he got to him, he hugged him. When he realized that it wasn't a manly thing to do, he detached and gave him a fist pump. Then he acted normal like everything was cool.

"I am so sorry for anything I said last night," Vaughn apologized. "And just to let you know, I am grateful for my parents, as messed up as they can be."

"Vaughn, if it wasn't for you, I wouldn't have had the nerve to climb over the bridge, especially in the dark," confessed Christopher. "I've never lost my temper before like that. I was so freaking frustrated, I just had to leave."

On the other side of the canyon stood the warehouse owner's son awaiting orders and drinking water. Christopher waved and motioned that it would be a few minutes.

Christopher walked all night when he left the village. He walked right past the sleeping twins, Travis, and even the oxen with his lantern to the bridge. It was a tricky climb because there were missing pieces to the bridge that he had to maneuver around carefully. He wore his backpack and carried his lantern in his right hand during the climb. It was a good thing his lantern only shined upwards because as he just climbed back, he was horrified looking down.

During the night, after he got to the other side, he remembered from first coming to the town the warehouse that was over the state road. The path wasn't marked because of the heavy snowfall, but he followed the area where there was a clearing of trees. The snow was up to his waist as his body plowed through it. He was wet and tired. Several hours later, he happened upon the state road. After he crossed it and walked a little further up, he found the warehouse. It was early in the morning, so he didn't dare knock on the door to the house which sat on the side of the warehouse. Instead, he found a screened-in porch in the back, where he slept on a comfortable yet cold cushioned couch, under a warm tarp. He woke up to a shotgun pointed to his face. The warehouse owner had questions.

In no time, the owner was feeding Christopher breakfast listening to his plight. He knew of the missing children because that was the number one story on the radios and television and the National Guard 's recent visit. As Christopher was explaining the whole ordeal, he regretted leaving Ourstory and wanted to go back and help his family.

Christopher explained how the bridge collapsed except. The warehouse owner knew the bridge had to be fixed and thought the new piece of machinery that he bought at an auction might be able to help. This mobile crane didn't need to be hauled on a truck; it had its sturdy engine. It needed several engines to be able to move such heavy pieces. When spring came along, he was going to put it on the industrial websites to sell. He knew he could make at least $100K reselling it.

He called his son, who drove it back from the auction and was familiar with the mechanics of the machinery. He told him that he had another immediate project. Living right down the road, he arrived in no time. The son was briefed on the secret mission and then the warehouse door opened. The cab was only meant for one driver, but Christopher crawled in and sat behind his shoulder on a metal ledge as they drove through the forest.

On the way to the bridge, Christopher retold the owner's son all about the bus crash, the river, and the rescue. The owner's whole family knew about Ourstory, but the secret would die with them. They were loyal to Boyce and knew that many of the residents were hiding from evil people out in the world, especially the orphaned children. Unfortunately, the heavy crane moved through the forest slowly. The six-foot snow path was reduced to a foot by the time the crane rolled over it. He left an obviously visible path for anyone curious enough to follow.

When the crane arrived at the bridge side, nobody took notice of the large apparatus, even as it detached and swung its massive arm and hook to the bridge. The distance over the canyon, plus 200 people shouting and crying at the same time, might have muted the machinery noise.

275

An hour went by and the civil engineer made his last markings on the notepad and put all of his measuring utensils away. He called for a cliffside council meeting. The men that initially started the project gathered to discuss the new plan for the bridge. Boyce yelled across the bridge to the warehouse owner's son to show up at eight in the morning to help with the plan. The warehouse owner's son nodded and departed. He left the crane in place and motored back to the warehouse on a snowmobile that he had hooked onto the back of the crane.

With the completed bridge assessment and the use of the crane, the civil engineer advised that the work could be done in three full days, four days' tops. There would need to be eight welders on duty during this time to get the job done. The engineer showed Boyce on paper how the connection of the bridge would happen. The abutments, spandrels, caps, bearings, decking, girders, cables, and posts all needed to be aligned and fastened down on the bridge. Different welders would work in different areas to make the work more efficient. There would be three teams of eight men so that the work could continuously happen without a break.

By the time everyone got back to the town, it was almost time for dinner. The cooks prepared a simple meal of venison pizza with vegetables melted under the cheese. The sore and battered townspeople were famished. They burned a lot of calories on the job and told the cooks to keep the pizzas coming.

Ryan wanted to hold Bianca's hand and never let go. What happened today replayed over and over in his mind. The thought of him leaving her here in a few days upset him. They ate dinner away from everyone and sat on opposite sides so they could look into each other's eyes.

"You have to find a way to come with me to the city," pleaded Ryan. "I can't leave here without you."

Bianca finally let all of her ambitions go and admitted that she adored Ryan. That bridge almost crushed her and she never let him nor anyone know how much she loved and appreciated everyone. She wanted to leave this place tomorrow and never look back. Then she sighed and looked at the faces down at the other end of the table, the girls that she helped take care of in the orphanage and little Gabriel too. She couldn't leave them, not to mention that she wasn't old enough per their bylaws.

"How about in a few years when I turn 18, I will come find you," Bianca burst his bubble with a future plan. "I've never felt like this before about anyone. But...I can't leave these guys; they are my family."

"So how will this work?" Ryan inquired, focusing on the part when she leaves. "Do you just come knocking on my door?"

"Well, if you play your cards right, I expect that you may be recruited from some desperate college needing a three-point shooter," they chuckled together and she continued. "I will email you – hopefully there will still be email in the future - and tell you that I will meet you at a certain place at a certain time."

"What if I am married already?" Ryan threw a wrench in the plan.

"Not likely," said Bianca raising her eyebrows. "We will have a cup of coffee somewhere and catch up with each other. Even though we both waited years for this date, we should both know that things change, and we will have no expectation except to be good friends for the rest of our lives."

"No. I don't like it," Ryan refused her plan.

"Why?" Bianca asked, trying to hide her pain.

"Because...I hate coffee," Ryan replied. "I say for this reunion, after we email, we meet at the Malloy Courts and play one-on-one. The winner gets to decide if we should be friends or something more."

Bianca smiled with tears in her eyes.

Tuesday, December 15th
Chapter 64 Gala in the Gym

A knock on Rooter's door startled him. He opened the door to two military officers insisting to enter. At first, Rooter refused to let them in, telling them there was a conspiracy to blame him for everything. The officers invited themselves into his apartment regretting it instantly.

"Like I said, those chickens understood me," Rooter explained.

With their pens and pads of paper, they wanted to know why Mr. Rooter was being blamed for the student's disappearance. They thought they were finally getting somewhere.

"The coffee was good, you see," he blew smoke in the air and let his cigarette hang on the side of his mouth while he talked. "I helped gather the eggs, you know. I was a big help, I was."

"When was the last time you saw the student's bus?" asked Major Bellerman slowly, like he was simple.

"So what if I cut ahead of Ms. Kim, she was driving so darn slow," he rambled.

"The question was when was the last time you saw their bus," he asked again.

"On the road, I guess," he said, obviously. "Not my fault that I'm a good driver."

He was making no sense to the investigating officers. They also were disgusted that the whole apartment smelled like a cigarette and they were embedded in a hazy cloud of smoke.

"One last question," Colonel James asked this time. "Do you suspect that any of the gardeners wanted to get rid of the students and if so, was there opportunity?"

"Everyone knows that students are a pain in the neck," remarked Rooter, not realizing how it sounded as he blew out smoke from his nostrils and mouth. "Especially Ms. Kim. I don't know why she drove buses, she yelled at them kids non-stop. What was the question?"

"That'll be all," said Colonel James and they walked out the door to breathe some clean air.

Their take away from that conversation was that perhaps Ms. Kim was tired of putting up with driving students. The stress of the winter storm could have been the catalyst that drove her to hurt them. Maybe she drove off the road into a forest and caused an accident on purpose. They sent new instructions to the National Guard troops upstate to check the forests surrounding the roads at the top of the mountain.

The welders met the warehouse owner's son that morning at the bridge. It took almost an hour for the crane to put the broken bridge in place to cover the span of the bridge, from top edge to top edge. It almost fit like a puzzle piece with a few missing parts. The welders worked as the crane held the piece steady on the side of the bridge nearest their village first. After a few hours of welding pieces down and adding support beams here and there, they were able to cross the bridge. A few hours later the crane disengaged the bridge and it stood on its own, over the canyon. There was still much to do to secure the bridge properly so that foot traffic and wagons could cross without compromise. But the crane completed its job. The warehouse owner's son bid them farewell and drove the crane slowly back to his dad's big garage.

The timing was perfect so that no National Guard vehicles were driving about when the warehouse owner's son returned with the crane. After he returned, he took a few horses from his dad's stalls and had them trample down the snow, covering up the crane tracks that led into the woods. His father's house was a straight shot off the state road 32 miles from the sheriff's office. That area was hot with National Guard troops and checkpoints. There was no need for the National Guard to stop at his father's house unless one was lost and needed directions, otherwise, it blended in as a regular house on the side of the road with a barn behind it and a large warehouse beside it. After he returned the crane, he invited his parents over to his house to view the new table he fashioned. Many skills were learned from the Amish families down the road. He was a regular guest and spoke a little of their language.

One of the five men hired for Project Tannenbaum, Dino, parked his silver SUV and then knocked on the front door. The owners were out visiting their son who lived down the road. He took the liberty of casing the outside of the huge warehouse garage and noticed the surveillance camera. He couldn't believe his luck to find such a prominent place right off the state highway. If any place would reveal the bus comings and goings, this would be it. The heavy lock to the garage took a little extra effort to open. Inside, the garage held millions of dollars of every type of farm equipment and supplies, so of course, the owner would have a surveillance camera. After Dino snuck in, he found a closet where the recordings were wired into. He hooked up his media device and uploaded the footage. There were years of material in the system and now he owned it. Careful to erase himself off the tape, he set a timer to begin taping in five minutes. He slithered back to his SUV and nobody was the wiser. He headed down the road to gather more surveillance footage and then would return to the RV.

A camera crew went to Ms. Germaine and her sister's house to interview them about not only the missing New York students but also the Missing School Bus website. Mrs. Dartmouth and her husband were there too. Mrs. Dartmouth was in awe of how composed Ms. Germaine was as she talked about their project. This wasn't her first public speaking appearance as she was used to standing in front of a crowd and getting people riled up to do something important. Now, the mission was to spread the news near and far to look for all missing children.

When it came time for Mrs. Dartmouth to speak, she had written her words down and read them carefully to make sure she captured all the speaking points. She was a writer mostly and speaking off the cuff was something she needed to learn from her masterful friend. The news reporter told them that since their website, there had been two confirmed sightings of missing children. They loved making a difference, but inside, they were deeply jealous knowing it wasn't their children.

It was a stressful time in the village. All hopes were pinned on the welders. The students and residents took on extra chores and never complained. Mr. Boyce and the council held a quick meeting to brainstorm ideas to raise the spirits of the town, which they announced at dinner. He declared they would have a Christmas Ourstory Gala event in the hall that evening in the gymnasium. This kind of thing normally happened in the summer and the residents would talk about it for weeks after. Everyone was excited to clean their dishes and head over to begin the fun. The NYC students inquired about the event, but their peers told them to cross the street and find out.

When they entered the gym, the solar lights turned on as usual. In the corner of the gym, a small band was set up with fiddles, banjos, and a washboard. In the center of the gym was a step ladder which Harvey climbed until his elbows reached the top cap. He had with him a placard with words on it.

The residents were divided into groups of eight with all age groups from five to eighty-five. When the students asked what was going on, their peers finally admitted that the Gala meant a square dance. When Brianna and Ryan heard that, they both declined impolitely and sat down. Brianna thought there was no way she would entertain that kind of style of dance and Ryan proclaimed he didn't dance, period. But when the fiddlers started, Christopher went over and dragged Brianna on the floor to his square. She reluctantly gave in after a heavy sigh and an obvious eye-rolling. Bianca grabbed Ryan who profusely shook his head knowing she'd be sorry. When she stared at him with her large light brown eyes, he gave in and joined her.

All the students and Ms. Kim were mixed in with the residents in different squares. In no time at all, the fiddlers began playing, and then the banjo and washboard joined in and Harvey started delivering instructions.

"Bow to your partner, bow to your corner," he commanded in his booming voice. "Now join hands and walk in a circle left, now switch it up to the right."

He continued with some allemande lefts, do-si-dos, some right and left grands, and promenade homes. It was an easy dance to pick up and soon the students fit right in and followed along, except for Ryan. He had absolutely no rhythm and never caught on to any of the calls. Instead, he hopped around the whole time in his group. Bianca tried her best to guide him on every instruction and took his hands when they had to allemande or promenade, but he still hopped along as he did. Bianca's body convulsed for minutes as she tried to be polite until she finally exploded into laughter. She thought her laugh would dissuade him from staying on the floor, but Ryan laughed along too and stayed put. He loved making her smile.

Adam took to the dancing with ease. He would never reveal that his mother had him in jazz dance classes for three years. The twins also looked like professional square dancers with their partners. This type of dancing wasn't unfamiliar to them because at every family celebration there was always some type of Latino moves that were similar in some respects. Lauren and Darcy caught on quickly and couldn't contain their smiles as they ran out of breath in constant movement. Arcado was doing some type of moves that made square dancing look disco, but nobody seemed to mind. Brianna came to like the activity, but in her head, she didn't call it dancing.

Shannon was stiff trying to remember each call and lagged slightly behind her partner, but by the end of the night, she had it down. Nobody square danced like Wanda. She picked it up quickly and started yelling back at Harvey to call more of this or that. Vaughn went along with the dance and humored everyone but would make the guys swear afterward never to tell anyone back in New York City about this night. One would never know that Ms. Kim burnt her leg a week or so back. She was swinging her partner and "yipping" and "yee-ing" all over the floor.

After 30 minutes, everyone took a water break. Sweat filled the gym. It was like running a marathon but in dance. The students couldn't even imagine doing this event on a hot summer night. Vaughn approached Harvey and asked if he could do the calls for the next set. He gave Vaughn his placard of calls and let him have the step ladder. Harvey never thought he'd get the chance to have fun on the floor. The band played the same music with the same beat and rhythm, so Vaughn practiced beats in his head while he was on the floor before he stepped up on the ladder.

After 10 minutes, Vaughn stepped up on the ladder, put his elbows on the top cap, and started beatboxing. The fiddle bows started blazing through the speakers and everyone was on the floor. Vaughn yelled commands in a rhythm but mixed it up and rapped his originals. He quoted Dr. Suess or any nursery rhyme that he could think of. He called to swing and sashay, pass thru, separate and go home, weave the ring and do a wrong way grand. Anytime he could slip in a rap rhyme he would. When he ran out of rhymes, he quoted raps from JAY-Z and Eminem, and songs from Pitbull. His calling was clever and fun.

They took another break and Vaughn continued. Everyone switched partners at the break, except for Bianca and Ryan. He wouldn't dance unless she was his partner. Bianca wished she could take at least one break from dancing with her rabbit-like companion. Her rib cage hurt badly from the continuous laughter that she couldn't control. Every time she giggled at him, he looked at her as if he couldn't figure out what was so funny. But he knew.

They didn't know they were dancing their last set until the solar lights dimmed. The crowd wished the night wouldn't end and moans could be heard everywhere. As much as Vaughn enjoyed the calling, his voice was getting gravelly. Ryan thanked Bianca for showing him how to dance, and she gave him a wince as if she taught him nothing. Ms. Kim almost refused to leave and told everyone that they should keep going and bring some lanterns into the gym. In the end, Mr. Boyce accomplished his mission. The stress of having the students there, the heavy snowfall, the bridge project, John Jones' funeral, and now the upcoming detachment from their new friends was something tonight erased, at least for a few hours.

Wednesday, December 16th
Chapter 65 Old Geezer to the Rescue

They wore their superhero pajamas in their cozy condominium in New York City above their auto mechanic shop. It was Wednesday and both boys awoke early to do some chores before heading downstairs to work.

Tolbert and Chauncy picked up their game controllers in unison and sat down to play a car chasing video game. They were in the thick of it, speeding down the city, with the skyline in the background, smashing into guardrails and other cars. They jumped a bridge that was opening and then headed out to the country. They raced side by side, trying to knock the other off the road. Tolbert whacked Chauncy off the road and down a cliff. The smoke from his crash indicated that the game ended for him. Tolbert kept racing to the finish line for time.

It was at that moment that Chauncy flashed back to over a week ago when he tumbled down the hill and discovered the tire in the snow. He envisioned some car or truck trying to pass the bus in the heavy snow shoving the bus into the rail, which would have opened, sending it down the ravine. Tolbert continued to cheer for himself as he absconded obstacles trying to get to the finish line. Chauncy thought about those poor kids that were at the bottom of the gorge either dead or just barely alive. He couldn't figure out why he hadn't seen any figure that resembled a bus. But he knew in his heart that he had to go back and search one more time.

The finish line was drawing near, and Tolbert looked over at his distracted friend, who should have cheered for him.

"YES!" shouted Tolbert as he finished the race. "Best time ever."

"Sure," remarked Chauncy, searching the map application on his phone.

"You didn't even watch me," said Tolbert snidely. "Are you feeling alright?"

"I'm going back," replied Chauncy in the most serious tone Tolbert had known.

"You heard the Ice Queen," said Tolbert. "No more investigation. It's out of our hands now."

"I just can't wait around. I have to see it for myself," said Chauncy. "I need to search that cliffside."

"When do we leave?" smiled Tolbert. "I can't let you get into trouble without me."

"We both can't be on the naughty list," Chauncy replied in his cartoon voice.

"Maybe I want to see how stupid you'll look when you find more junk under the snow like trash or a toilet seat," laughed Tolbert.

"Wow now I really want you to come," said Chauncy sarcastically. "I don't care, you can come. Just don't."

"Don't what?" asked Tolbert as he put the game station away and turned off the TV.

"Don't ruin my concentration or my suggestions," he said. "Sometimes I have to be the bus."

"Sure," remarked Tolbert. "You be the bus. I might be the snowmobile. I say we bring them along, and if your thing doesn't pan out, we can at least get some riding in."

Chauncy was trying to be serious today, but his best friend was being the silly guy he normally was. They both packed differently for the trip. Tolbert was getting his thermal gear together, while Chauncy was rounding up blankets, heavy towels, jugs of water, and snack bars. The two separate trains of thought for the trip continued as Tolbert grabbed the keys to his truck that was formerly owned by his father.

"We're not taking 'Old Geezer', are we?" asked Chauncy. "We should take my Ram."

Tolbert inherited his father's 1989 Ford F150 double cab, four-wheel drive, 5 liter, V8 engine complete with a CB radio, and large fuzzy dice hanging on the rearview mirror. His dad said it was the best vehicle he'd ever owned. Tolbert teased his dad in detest of the old, wood-paneled, cream-colored truck telling him that was the reason his dad needed to own an auto shop. It was ugly and was always in the shop for something or another. The truck only had 80,000 miles on it because it was hardly ever driven. After his dad passed, Tolbert warmed up to Old Geezer just as his father did. He liked the way it could handle the mountain passes and it had proved it could haul heavy loads behind it.

"Old Geezer is a sure shot around those mountains," remarked Tolbert. "I don't trust anything that has a good Bluetooth stereo system, heated seats, and a nice suspension. We are rugged men."

They both chuckled as they went downstairs and hooked up the towing trailer to the truck. They proceeded to secure two snowmobiles onto it. They both piled into the front seat with Tolbert driving and Chauncy as navigator. Tolbert looked in the cab behind him that held a bench for at least three more passengers. It was filled with anything that Chauncy could scrounge including Tolbert's big warm, fuzzy, orange bathrobe. Tolbert looked at his best friend and rolled his eyes and then drove off toward the place they had just returned days ago.

The National Guard's new mission of searching the wooded area off of the state highway had soldiers making tracks all over the place. They were within twenty miles from the warehouse owner and closing in by the hour. Once they reached the owner's house, they would surely head into the woods across the road. The path couldn't be clearer from where the crane traveled.

Colonel James and Major Bellerman got a warrant to search Ms. Kim's apartment for any suspicious signs of intent to harm students. The manager of the place unlocked the door and the two men went in wearing gloves to search as if they were a forensics team looking for fingerprints or DNA. Everything seemed suspicious to them. The movie posters framed on the walls were that of Rambo and The Godfather, and some Korean Films such as Taxi Drive and The Warrior. They rifled through her desk, dressers, closets, and kitchen. There was not one thing written, printed, or any personal photograph that would have any normal-minded person think anything was amiss. But both officers thought she possessed violent tendencies based on her movie artwork on the walls. This would all be in their report.

It was one o'clock in the afternoon by the time Blizzard Killer and Snow Slayer got to the base of the mountain. As they cruised up and around, Chauncy pleaded with Tolbert to go slow so he could stop at a moment's notice if he recognized the guardrail. Driving slowly wasn't hard to do because of the slick roads. Chauncy didn't factor the heaping snow that was on every guardrail. His paint mark would be covered in snow.

Tolbert went ever so slowly around the bends, luckily with no trailing traffic behind him. They heard commotion and complaints on his CB radio about truckers getting stopped at the National Guard checkpoints somewhere at the top of the mountain. Some guardsmen were slow to search their vehicles which put them behind schedule. Tolbert and Chauncy could hear the impatience and sarcasm in their voices warning anyone who should travel on the state route.

"STOP!" yelled Chauncy.

Tolbert pulled over to the side, which wasn't easy with the trailer hooked up and sticking out in the road. Chauncy put on his gloves and hat and dashed out of the truck. He wore his snow pants and boots so that when he stepped over the snow-frozen rail, he could tolerate the almost waist-deep snow. After he climbed over and stepped down the side of the cliff, he looked left and right. Retracing that day, he fell down the cliff, he closed his eyes and remembered that there were big chunky things covered in snow which he assumed were bushes and trees. He also remembered a fast-moving river at the bottom of the gulch. There were possibly a few snow-covered bushes, but the river was so far away from what he remembered. He wanted to be sure, so he walked down a bit and stared at the scenery. Relaxing his mind for just a moment, he stood still in silence apart from the wind blowing. But then an annoying ringtone came from his phone, which was in his coat pocket. He peeled his one glove off to answer it.

"Any sign of the bus?" asked Tolbert cajoling. "I can't leave the truck hanging out on this roadway."

The call broke Chauncy's concentration. He was about to tell his friend off for disturbing his process. But as he stared out, it didn't feel right. The river was farther and there weren't as many lumps in the snow as he remembered.

287

"This isn't it," he said solemnly. "Be right there."

He made his way back to the truck. They drove on slowly around each bend. Chauncy knew it was on the east side that faced the river, so he would avidly perk up on those turns. They stopped three more times at similar-looking sites. All of them were disappointingly dismissed after he trudged around the top of the mount. He was losing faith, thinking that he either missed it or his imagination was on overload the day he fell off the cliff. They were almost at the top of the mountain when they turned the bend. Tolbert didn't have to be told, he slowed to a stop in a naturally formed recess on the side and Chauncy eagerly got out.

He was about to climb over the guardrail when he noticed that it moved as he touched it. This was it, he thought with renewed adrenaline, and his heart raced. He could still see Tolbert watching him and gave him a thumbs up, fervently nodding his head up and down. Chauncy climbed down the mountain and headed toward the clumps of snow at the bottom. It was not a fast and easy feat. It took him 15 minutes to get to the first snow-covered clump. He dug out a huge bush. Heading over to the next one, he figured this would take him quite some time, so he called Tolbert to tell him to sit tight and relax. Forty minutes went by, and Chauncy dug out his seventh bush all the way around, not finding as much as a piece of trash. He had plenty more to go. He looked at the trajectory from the guardrail down the hill. He envisioned the path that the bus would have made. He questioned if a bus was pommeling down a hill at a high rate of speed, where would it end up. His eyes followed from the guardrail down to the edge of the river. Then he remembered that the snow might have decreased the rate of speed and wondered if the bus would've made it to the river. There was a lump down by the river that he went to go dig out. While he plowed through the snow at the point right before the river, he noticed something shiny reflecting at the bottom of the snow pile. It was a headlight. His heartbeat shot up in excitement. Before he could excavate it, he heard a loud calamity coming from behind him. He turned around trembling, and he could not believe his eyes.

Wednesday, December 16th
Chapter 66 Oh Tannenbaum

The National Guard made rounds daily through the roads nearest where the gardeners were found. Behind a house near a barn, one of the troop's found the Project Tannenbaum RV with five SUVs parked near it. This seemed highly suspicious to the Master Sergeant. The armed soldiers stealthily surrounded the RV and through a bullhorn, identified themselves and told the inhabitants to slowly exit the trailer. Inside the RV, the five men, from Project Tannenbaum calmly, retrieved their pistols from their cases and hid them in their jackets. They didn't want any trouble but knew sometimes accidents happened where someone, from the National Guard, could get stupid. All five men stepped out looking perturbed that their work had ceased. They didn't have time to be interrogated or explain their mission.

"Why are you men here on this land and in an RV?" asked the Master Sergeant in command.

"We were sent to do our mission of finding the students," replied the leader of the project truthfully. "We are not in anyone's way."

The Master Sergeant thought if they had any good intel on these students, he wanted it.

"Do you mind if we take a look inside your trailer?" he crafted an excuse to search inside. "You know, to make sure the students aren't in there."

"I will escort one of your trusted men to search it under my supervision," the leader replied. "I don't want your whole troop stepping all over our expensive stuff."

The Master Sergeant picked out the Sergeant who was nearest him. Before he went in, his boss told him to look for anything that would help their team find the students. He told him to memorize the setup and the tools they had. The Sergeant nodded his head that he would.

The leader opened the door and the Sergeant followed him in. Luckily, they switched all of their monitors to the weather channel, or the news so there would be no guessing about the

289

footage they were investigating. The Sergeant opened all the doors, cupboards, and closets, but found nothing. There were a few small boxes of tactical gear, but the leader refused to have him open all of them. He allowed him to open the one with the long-range camera lens and a few that held binoculars.

"There's nothing in there," said the Sergeant after he exited the RV.

The Master Sergeant was getting agitated that this group of five men were doing their job. The leader and his men hoped the Master Sergeant wasn't going to do something senseless. But he did. He got right in the leader's face and they were almost nose to nose.

"I don't like you," griped the Master Sergeant.

"It's mutual," the leader griped back.

The five men held steady their pistols in their jackets.

"Are we going to have a problem?" the leader asked the Master Sergeant with fervor.

At one point, nobody knew who was intimidating who. One of the five men, Dino walked up to the Master Sergeant and looked him up and down with curiosity.

"I can't believe what a jerk you are," Dino said, with disdain.

The Master Sergeant turned his hard stare to Dino and then it became a staring showdown. After fifteen seconds both men started to laugh.

"So, this is what you do with your military retirement?" asked the Master Sergeant in a condescending way to his old friend.

"I had to do something to keep me busy," replied Dino. "Besides you know I am the best tracker you ever had in Afghanistan. I didn't recognize you without your bushy beard."

"That was some years ago," the Master Sergeant said drifting off to a place where they once both served on active duty together. He stroked his clean shaved face.

They continued catching up on the good times. The other four men breathed a little easier and went back inside the trailer. The Master Sergeant tried to get Dino to drop hints of any information on the students. But Dino told him honestly that they did not have any information yet that would lead to finding them. Dino wrapped up his discussion, bid his old military buddy farewell, and the group left in their Humvees. When Dino entered the RV, he explained how they served together overseas and that the guy had an ego the size of China. One of the men was a lookout in case any of them snuck back to their trailer. They continued sifting through the footage on the thumb drives.

The Sergeant described what he saw in the RV, but nothing seemed out of the ordinary, so the Master Sergeant had his group drive onward. He remembered Dino as a decent, quiet soldier who lost a lot of poker games. After departing Afghanistan, Dino owed everybody a lot of money, including him. Decisions needed to be made to either report that his team found the five guys or to stay silent. Having contractors come in and do their jobs made the guard look inept. He decided to keep this to himself for now.

The gardeners were all in the office talking about two National Guard officers that interrogated each of them at their homes asking odd questions about the students. They were all insulted by the questions and asked about their motives on that snowy day. The officers also asked which one of them in their group disliked the students the most. Funny, all of them revealed that Danny, who didn't even make the trip, cared for kids the least. Danny didn't find it amusing when the two officers showed up on his doorstep implying that he premeditated the demise of the students.

"It's true that I don't like children," stated Danny in disdain. "And I don't like men who act like them either."

At that, he slammed the door in their faces and called his lawyer.

They were weeks behind the original Tree Lighting Ceremony date and wanted to make sure the tradition lived on in New York City. This would be a complete rush to get everything set up in a few days. Mr. Haugen, who surprisingly wasn't fired yet, organized the families of the missing children to be there to honor them. The ceremony would be dedicated to each of them and they would be remembered as the tree lit up the plaza.

The gardeners were in a frenzy. The perfect tree choices that they had upstate New York were now too far away. They picked a Norway Spruce from nearby in White Plains, New York. It was only 70 feet in height and 40 feet wide, the smallest one in over 50 years.

When the tree arrived at the plaza, it was around-the-clock work by the gardening team, the construction crew, and the professional lighting artists. First, the tree was lifted by a crane and firmly put into the base, and then tied down on all sides. Next, a construction crew built a 10-layered deck of scaffolding from the base of the tree to the top. The arborists clipped off the dead ends and sewed in extra branches to make the tree look fuller to hold the illumination. Then the lighting team installed 50,000 led multi-colored lights. Everything was coordinated like an orchestra. A crane lifted the final adornment of three million dazzling crystals that made up the 900-pound Swarovski Crystal Star that was positioned on top. The star had 70 spikes that would light up in every direction - nothing but pure brightness. Every detail about the tree made it the most special symbol in New York City for the Christmas Holidays.

It was a close call, but Chauncy jumped out of the way, just in time. He heard it rambling toward his direction, but not until it almost hit him. Chauncy tumbled to the side and landed in the snow unharmed. He got up quickly, but he wasn't even sure what happened or what to do. Old Geezer splashed down hard and now sat crookedly in the water. He looked up the hill and saw a trail of destruction. The trailer holding the snowmobiles broke in two up yonder and the snowmobiles were laying on their sides haphazardly. He recognized Tolbert laying on the ground halfway up the mount. He panicked for a moment not knowing if his best friend was hurt, or worse, so he ran as fast as he could to reach him. Running uphill was difficult but his adrenaline had his legs working through the burn until he was in the range of reaching him and thankfully, there was movement. As

Chauncy approached him, he could tell that Tolbert was struggling in pain.

"Dude, are you all right? And what happened?" asked Chauncy in the most serious tone he had ever spoken around Tolbert.

"I got the wind knocked out of me," he replied, wincing in pain and not moving off the ground. "You know, like the time when Mary Margaret Sheehan knocked you out on the playground in the 8th grade?"

"OK, first off, Mary Margaret was a beast, and it was just a hard shove. I just happened to land on a broken, wheels-up, skateboard," defended Chauncy. "Secondly, why did you drive Old Geezer off the cliff?"

Chauncy put out his hand to help him up, but Tolbert reached up with only his right hand because the left arm was in miserable shape. He got him to sit up in the snow and Chauncy sat next to him.

"I was parked in the curve up the hill, perfectly," explained Tolbert describing the event with his one good hand. "I heard on the CB radio that a trucker was driving crazily on the downhill and almost ran another trucker off the road. I thought maybe I would be proactive and drive uphill to get out of the way. As soon as I put the gas on, he came around the corner, right in my lane. I swerved out of the way into the guardrail and next thing you know, Old Geezer broke through, and it was like I was teetering at the top of a roller coaster, except less teeter and more coaster straight down."

"Did he even stop?" asked Chauncy.

"I think he was around the bend before he knew I was through the guardrail," he explained. "I tried to push the brakes but when I broke through the guardrail, I damaged the undercarriage, and nothing worked. After the trailer broke off the hitch, I opened the door, jumped out, and landed on my arm."

"Is it broken?" asked Chauncy.

"Not sure. It just hurts, Mary Margaret bad," replied Tolbert. "It's not just my arm, my whole body hurts. Tell me. Is Old Geeze gone?"

"I'm not going to lie to you," he said with a sigh. "He's mostly underwater."

They both looked down in disappointment at the truck at the bottom of the hill. It wasn't easy to see Old Geezer's position, but there was no way it could be salvaged.

"My cell phone was in the cup holder," said Tolbert woefully. "My dad's probably rolling in his grave. Poor Old Geezer."

"We need to get you looked at. You may have broken some bones," Chauncy commented, bummed.

Chauncy rose and headed toward the closest snowmobile and shoved it with all his might to tip it over from side to upright. Luckily, they kept a spare key in a small storage box at the back of the vehicle. In no time at all, Chauncy motored down to Tolbert and helped him stand up and sit behind him on the snowmobile. It wasn't without a lot of groaning and discomfort, but he got situated to the point he could hold onto Chauncy with his right arm. They sped up the hill to the roadside. Once they reached the top, Chauncy had to open the guardrail and hold it while he also squeezed the vehicle through. Luckily there was just enough snow on the main road to allow the snowmobile to get traction and ride.

By now the boys knew the area. There was a hospital not too far up the top. Chauncy drove them directly there, and within 30 minutes they arrived. He ran in and requested help for his best buddy. Soon, two males in scrubs came out with a gurney and lifted Tolbert onto it and rolled him away. Chauncy followed him and took a seat in the waiting room. Before he got an update from the doctor, Chauncy made a call to Tolbert's mother. He never knew when his cell service would go out, and he didn't want to catch her wrath for keeping quiet. He had to hold the phone away from his ear as her frantic screaming was too awful to bear. There was a card at the reception with the hospital name and phone number and he gave her both. Then, he pretended that the phone was losing connection and hung up.

An hour later, the doctor came out to give Chauncy an update and invited him to visit Tolbert who was reclined in a hospital bed. After an x-ray and CT scan, he had broken his left arm, concussed his head, and heavily bruised his tail bone. Before Chauncy and he had a chance to talk, the phone next to his bed rang. It was his mother. Tolbert spent five minutes calming her down and helping her understand that he was going to live. She'd even offered to buy him a brand new, safer truck when he returned. He knew it wasn't necessary, but after he heard her say that he tried to seem more injured, adding a few more unmentioned aches. The doctor told him that he was to remain overnight for the concussion observation and would be released after an examination tomorrow. He convinced his mother to come around tomorrow afternoon to pick him up.

Chauncy reflected on the headlight he was about to pick up near the water, but now it was crushed completely by Old Geezer. He felt like he couldn't catch a break.

"Didn't Mary Margaret put you in the hospital too?" jested Tolbert. "I remember you showing up to school with some type of straight jacket."

"I went to an urgent care clinic, not the hospital," corrected Chauncy. "And it was only a neck brace for my whiplash from her push. As I mentioned, she was brutal."

They both sat there in silence half laughing remembering the good old days.

"I wonder what Mary Margaret is up to nowadays?" inquired Tolbert. "I bet you she's a bouncer at a bar."

"With her height and girth, I bet you she's a sumo wrestler or a shot putter for the Olympic team," stated Chauncy guessing wildly.

"No, I bet you she carries and throws bags of cement down on the construction site," Tolbert continued. "Then at parties, she drinks from the keg like it's her beer can."

They bantered back and forth about Mary Margaret scenarios for almost 10 minutes until they ran out of creative mammoth toppers. Chauncy could tell that Tolbert was getting tired from the pain medication the doctor gave him.

"Well buddy, Hoo-hah is on his way up with the company truck and trailer to help me get the snowmobiles back to the garage," said Chauncy with a large exhale. "It's been a day."

Hoo-hah was not a name that either Chauncy or Tolbert created. He introduced himself that way when he got hired.

Both boys loved going to any extracurricular activity that he would invite them to. Hoo-hah's favorite saying was "Guilty as Charged."

"You guys are going out and having fun without me, aren't you?" asked Tolbert with his eyes half closed. "Well, I hope Mary Margaret's working the door and throws you both out."

"I doubt we'll go out," insisted Chauncy. "Hoo-hah's wife has him on a curfew."

"Well one thing is for sure," said Tolbert, almost asleep.

"What?" inquired Chauncy.

"You are better than Sherlock Holmes," he allowed himself to get a few more words in. "Your theory was spot-on. The bus most likely drove off the cliffside and into the river below. I just proved you right."

At the mess hall that evening, the students and their resident friends were enjoying their meal with the heat of the fireplace nearby and the quartet quietly playing in the background. Shannon decided in the weeks earlier that she would attempt to sit with a different group of residents each night until she got to know most, if not all of them, and their stories. This was out of her comfort zone for the first few nights, but it became easier as time went on. It was like an addiction for her to listen to the villagers' stories. Like Mrs. B, she too could fill a novel with the remarkable tales of the residents. She also knew time was running out because soon, she would be back home with just her mom and dad. These villagers would disappear from her life forever.

The door opened and the welders and workmen noisily walked in and over to the long piece of paper on a corkboard that held the workload updates for the bridge. They were cheerfully laughing and making remarks. Everyone noticed the commotion that they made and a few of the residents got up to look at the board. The quartet stopped playing and everyone headed over to see what the ruckus was about. Mr. Boyce needed to make an announcement.

"Ladies and gentlemen please," Mr. Boyce said loudly but with a laugh in his voice.

The crowd settled down so Mr. Boyce could talk. The only thing you could hear were the cooks in the kitchen rattling the dishes.

"I am pleased to tell you that," he paused, and everyone looked at him in anticipation. "The bridge has been completed."

There were cheers, hugs, and clapping all around. They couldn't even hear through their commotion the rest of Boyce telling them that all inspections were passed and it was sturdier than Fort Knox.

While everyone was in their merriment, the New York students moved near the fireplace to talk about their departure, including Ms. Kim. The residents noticed that the news whom this most affected, had stepped away. The residents got quiet and stared at them out of curiosity. They hoped their group wouldn't request to travel tonight; it was too late. The students finished their huddle and stepped over to Mr. Boyce.

"Now kids," Mr. Boyce said before they even requested to leave. "I don't think it's a good idea to pack up tonight. It's just that..."

"Don't worry, we don't want to leave tonight," stated Arcado, smirking. "We have one request before we depart."

"What's that?" inquired Mr. Boyce.

"That you move the Christmas Party to tomorrow night," he said with his eyebrows raised high in question. "And then we will leave Friday morning."

"Yeah, we all worked so hard with the songs and the choir," stated Vaughn earnestly. "We wouldn't want to miss it."

"What do you think folks, move it up a few days for them?" asked Mr. Boyce loudly to the already agreeing crowd.

There was so much noise in a frenzy of agreement, that you could barely hear Boyce agree that the party would be moved to tomorrow night. The cooks heard the announcement and looked at each other in worry. They needed days to prepare for the party with all of the sweets to bake and did not want to disappoint. One of the chefs pulled the other two to the cold storage locker. He had woken up early that day to prepare cookie dough and shape the dough into fun-shaped

297

cookie cutters. There must've been over 500 cookies of different sorts just waiting to be put into the oven. Happiness was plentiful, now even in the kitchen.

It was dark after Chauncy and Hoo-hah picked up the other snowmobile. They motored down to where Old Geezer sat front end in the water and had a moment of silence. Chauncy felt bad bringing Tolbert's orange fuzzy robe and wanted to retrieve it out of the back cab but knew it was impossible. They secured the second snowmobile onto the trailer and headed back to the city. Hoo-hah tried to take Chauncy's mind off the bad day and switched on the radio. A Journey song came on and he sang it, poking Chauncy to sing along. Try as Chauncy may to do the backup vocals, something gnawed at him. It was something Tolbert said. He said that he knew that Chauncy was right and the student's bus must've gone down the hill and crashed in the water. He played out the scenario in his head a thousand times, but it didn't make sense. If the bus went down the cliffside, like Tolbert, the bus would be in the water just as Old Geezer had been. But there was no sign of a bus, no matter where he stood on the bank looking up and down the river. Chauncy admitted to himself that he only proved himself wrong. What Chauncy didn't know was that there were no logs floating down the river like the weeks previous, because of the heavy snowfall, the logger's union declared it was too dangerous to work until after Christmas.

Thursday, December 17th
Chapter 67 The Ourstory Christmas Party

The next day when Tolbert woke up in the hospital, his mother sat by his bedside sleeping. Sometime during the early morning, she crept in to watch her little boy sleep. She thought that he was always a good sleeper since he was a baby. Even though he was a grown man, she doted on him.

"Hey ma', thanks for coming to get me," said Tolbert in a sleepy voice.

"I came as soon as I could," she replied with an over-caring expression. "As soon as the doctor clears you, I can take you home. Don't worry, I will take care of you at my house until you heal."

Tolbert felt a new injury coming on called "mother-itis".

The five men of Operation Tannenbaum were growing tired of no leads. The last sighting of the buses was footage from a gas station at the base of the mountain, before they rolled up it. Any video tapings directly at the top of the mountain were not clear enough to tell if it was a bus or truck. The blowing winds had camera's moving wildly along with the snow. Their goal for the day was to finish going through the surveillance video that was newly collected from houses on the state highway. The tape that Dino took from the warehouse owner was next to be reviewed.

Everything had to be perfect. Gardeners, Shauna and Jessica made sure the large water trough under the tree was replenished. The lighting team finished their job of placing the colorful twinkling lights on every inch of the tree. The construction company was set to tear down the decks of scaffolding and clean the work site. The excitement of "their" moment was approaching.

Mr. Haugen was back in his office. He looked at the pictures on his office walls of the various Christmas trees and his staff from over the years. He had been head gardener for 22 years. It had been the best job he could have ever imagined.

Now as he printed out his resignation letter, he would hand one copy to the mayor and one copy to Mitch at the tree lighting ceremony. This would not give solace to the families, but at least they could see that the person responsible was stepping down. He was warned, in advance, that lawsuits would be next. Thinking that the financial implications would have him and his wife selling their house and moving out to the country where they could afford a modest home would be the answer. That was if he didn't get thrown in jail.

Adam's parents, the Bray's, Arcado's parents, the Michaels's, and Wanda's parents, the Womack's, volunteered to prepare the remembrance of their children for the next evening at the Rockefeller Center. They took Mr. Dartmouth's pictures, uploaded them from the Missing School Bus website, and made a celebratory pamphlet with biographies of their children. Their children's pictures would scroll at the bottom of the TV screen as the station aired the lighting ceremony. Also, a large 10 x 12 laminated picture of each child would be hung on the tree as an ornament.

The woods along the state highway were saturated with National Guardsmen on foot. They searched both sides of the road in the forest. There was no stone unturned. They brought shovels and other tools to dig out mounds of snow-filled bushes and trees. Time ticked away with the long hours they put in. There were hounds that got a sample of their scents and worked just as hard as the soldiers. Nightfall was right around the corner, bringing with it another unsuccessful day. The next grid to be searched was the wooded area across from the warehouse owner's home, which was scheduled for the next morning.

Everyone filtered into the main hall looking festive and cheerful. Up on the stage, there was the quartet playing Christmas songs before the concert. Arcado noticed that his twin little brother, Gabriel, entered the building with a box. Gabriel looked like a little businessman wearing his dress clothes. Nobody paid Gabriel any attention as he put his box down on a chair and moved it over to an arched doorway that led to a storage area halfway in the hall. Out of curiosity, Arcado went to find out what he was up to.

"Hey lil' man, what you got?" asked Arcado trying to peer in the box.

"It's to spice up this place for the holidays," replied Gabriel who took a branch of what looked like holly out and raised it high.

"What is that?" Arcado inquired.

"Well, it's holly, but with my sign that I am going to hang underneath, it'll be mistletoe," remarked Gabriel with the biggest grin. "You're taller, can you help me?"

Arcado took the holly and some branches whose ends were bound in wire, and then stood on the chair and wrapped the wires around a nail that hung right in the center of the arch. When he got off the chair, Gabriel took the chair and stood on it. He taped to the wall a piece of paper that he wrote in large, clumsy letters 'Mistletoe', with an arrow on the paper pointing to what Arcado just hung.

"So what does a seven-year-old want with mistletoe?" asked Arcado.

"I believe in love," said Gabriel, still smiling. "I read in Christmas books, all that kids want are toys at this time of year. Well, I want a kiss. I want to feel loved. Is that so wrong?"

"A seven-year-old should want toys," said Arcado, looking serious and sad that a young boy should have to beg for love.

He almost said that parents make us feel loved inside and that should be good enough. But then remembered that he was an orphan. Gabriel did have the love from his so-called brothers and sisters, but not that of a parent. He looked Gabriel in the eye, as he still stood on the chair, and couldn't resist giving him the biggest brother bear hug he could.

"Don't look so sad," Gabriel said as he detached from the hug. "I know these people love me because I am their family, but one day I want to know what real love is. You know the kind between a girl and a boy."

"Oh Lordy," was all Arcado could say. "There will be plenty of time for that. I am older than you and I don't even know how to get that."

"Yeah, well, you never know when things can be taken away," he countered. "So, I am alive and well and I am going to do everything I can because I can. Does that make sense?"

Arcado nodded. He knew that he would have to think about those words later and ponder if he really knew what he meant. Until then, they were summoning all the kids to the stage to get into position for the concert. Samuel lit the last candle on the Menorah to the right of the stage and told Adam "Happy Hanukkah". It was the final night of their tradition. Adam was grateful that he wasn't forgotten during the Christmas celebrations.

The chairs, facing the stage, were filled now with adults. The children wore their holiday outfits and fidgeted as they stood in their formation. The students stood still on a stadium-like platform that staggered from the bottom of the stage to four tiers up to the top. The smaller children were on the bottom and the tiers were filled based on height and vocal range. On stage left was the orchestra. Vaughn was on piano and there were eight children on violin and viola including Adam and one adult on drums. At the front stood the conductor, Mr. Chad, in his firm military stance looking over the sheet music and making sure it was in the proper order for tonight.

All of the students from the bus were mixed in their voice groups, with the exception of Brianna who sat with her grown colleagues in the second row. She and Ms. Kim sat next to each other waiting somewhat impatiently for this to start and end. Brianna thought that this was a pity concert to make sure everyone got their pat on the back. The adult choir was the reason this building had any soul. She wished that she and her cohorts were performing tonight instead. She looked at Ms. Kim and they both yawned at the same time.

Lauren was a soprano, so she was located stage right, and waved to Brianna and Ms. Kim, who both returned a nod. She had a tiny solo in the last song and she couldn't wait for her part. Her anxiety level was high, but like everyone, she practiced so many times that she couldn't wait until the singing started.

The twins and Wanda, who was surprisingly nervous, stood shoulder to shoulder in the contralto and alto sections. Ryan and Arcado stood in the bass section while Shannon and Darcy stood in the contralto section. Before they began, Mr. Chad did a deep breathing exercise to calm their anxieties. Nobody, except Brianna and Vaughn, had ever sung for school or church before. The possibility of knowing they would blend in and sound harmonious to fill the whole hall with music momentarily, made them all smile with excitement.

Everyone was seated and the back lanterns in the room dimmed, so the spotlight was on the front of the stage. The conductor tapped his podium lightly twice with his baton to queue the music. Vaughn's fingers spread out on the keys of the piano gently as the violins started in sync with the sheet music in front of them.

They began with the traditional Christmas songs of "Carol of the Bells" and "Christmas Canon". The youthful voices and harmonies were beautiful. They sang a few fun Christmas songs and then arrived at the finale. This song was practiced more than the others. A 9-year-old girl started "Born on Christmas Day" written by Kristin Chenoweth. Then another little girl sang the next part so strong yet soft that it stood out. Finally, a young man of eight with his pure soprano voice finished up his part before the choir of 36 children began their harmonious voices for the refrain. It was so heartfelt that it touched everyone in the audience, especially Brianna. From the first moment Brianna heard the children sing, something powerful happened to her.

Then Gabriel eased into his solo. His afro stood tall with few stray hairs and his imperfect, gapped front teeth contradicted the most sincere, honest look on his face. The soft melody that arose from the little voice made him appear like an angel sent to Earth. Brianna became so overwhelmed by his beautiful voice, then all the combined voices and harmonies, that her eyes welled up with tears. Finally, she just let the tightness in her chest out with tiny gasps of cries. Having suppressed so many years of acting so mature for her age, she felt like she might have missed out on some good peer interaction. Now watching the students make the most wonderful sound in the world made her feel like she had been saved and wished she was part of it. She let the tears flow and didn't care that she was acting like a child, because she was one. She raised both of her arms and hands in the air to let them know she supported them and to sing on.

Ms. Kim sobbed too. The sweet music and seeing Brianna weep brought her to her breaking point. She never showed a tender side until now, but the release of crying was out of the happiness of belonging to a group who didn't judge her.

The song continued as the piano and violins worked hard and the children sang in earnest to match their melodic efforts. By the end of the performance, both the choir and their crowd believed every word of the music sung. It was an incredible concert with the adults in the audience emotionally swept away.

The show concluded and they received a standing ovation. The conductor knew the kids nailed it and for the first time they saw him with a full wide grin, giving them the OK to take a bow. They bowed and then gave friendly hugs to each other in their happiness.

The children in the choir were charged with a lot of emotions. Some laughed and some cried, but it was all out of happiness. The atmosphere was filled with a soft glow from the lanterns and a lot of Christmas spirit.

After the concert, there was hot chocolate and cookies waiting at the back of the hall. Emotions were high, as everyone knew that tomorrow would be a completely different day. The teens held onto the notion of being in the presence of people who genuinely wanted a good life. Shannon looked around and closed her eyes wanting to savor these moments of Christmas with this family. Every student, including the twins, mixed in with the residents to have a conversation or dance to the adult band that was setting up to play for the evening party.

Arcado noticed Gabriel taking Brianna and Bianca by the hand and leading them over to his makeshift mistletoe area. He and Ryan followed him over there to see the action. Gabriel stepped up on his chair which he had brought over earlier and motioned for Bianca to come over and read the sign. She humorously gave him a kiss on the cheek and a big hug and told him that she loved him, which was true. Brianna looked at him, with her hands on her hips, as if he were some small player from the city. But she could not resist him and gave him a peck on the opposite cheek. She also hugged him, but not like the one just given.

After Brianna was done with Gabriel, as she went to turn, she bumped right into Arcado who didn't even ask for permission and planted one right on her lips. He didn't apologize for doing so and walked away in style, like he owned the place. This gave Ryan ideas and he went to grab Bianca, but before he could do so, one of the old ladies came over and tore Gabriel's sign down. She took a broom and knocked the makeshift mistletoe to the ground, picked it up, and walked away with it in hand. This ruined their moment.

The band played fast, dancing music. Ryan thought if he couldn't kiss Bianca, he would dance with her. She agreed, but Ryan was a horrible dancer. With her mouth hung open watching him hop around, again, she wished he would just stand still so she could teach him to move with the beat. Instead, she danced and laughed the night away. The dance floor was full of everyone of every age. Others enjoyed the refreshments and the special sweet treats that the cooks prepared. Chocolate was a rare treat, but tonight the sugar ran plenty.

Nobody was thinking about the sadness that would come when the students left the following morning. They lived in the festive moment and partied for hours. Shannon was the only one who walked around the hall admiring all the Christmas decorations. She especially loved the tree and all its handmade ornaments. Little did she know that Gabriel followed her in the same fashion. Lanterns were positioned in different places in the hall, some hanging from the ceiling, some were wall sconces, and some outlined the Christmas tree. Darcy, Brianna, and Lauren admitted they felt like princesses in a book. Wanda corrected the ladies and said she felt like a queen.

The fast dancing lasted for hours and it was almost midnight. This was one of the only nights of the year to have such a memorable and endless night. The band switched course and slowed it down. Ryan stopped hopping around and took Bianca by the hand and then held her close to slow dance. Wanda took one of the twins, she honestly didn't know which one, and spun him out to the floor for a turn around the room. Everyone grabbed a partner and the floor was crowded with romance or a friendly dance.

Ryan was getting nervous. He had Bianca where he wanted her, which was close to him. He danced her away from the crowd toward the entrance of the double doors where there was less of a crowd. This would be the only time he could do this, but he was getting panicky with sweat. His hands and armpits were getting uncomfortable. He didn't understand why it was so hard to get the job done. Looking into her eyes, he smiled and was ready to finally steal a kiss. Everything was aligned. She stared into his eyes and was expecting a little showmanship. He wanted to wait until almost the last note of the song to build up the moment. The notes were slowing down, like he anticipated, so he reached in to make his move. Then it happened. Right in front of them, the double doors to the town hall violently busted open and they made their way inside.

The warehouse owner and his son entered the room and made such a commotion, the band stopped, and everyone stared at the two men. It's not like anyone could turn on the lights because they only had the lanterns that were already lit, so the urgent conversation had to be had in their cozy, Christmas setting. But the warehouse owner's words harshened the event to come to an end. Mr. Boyce walked straight over to discuss the matter. The New York students also made sure they were nearby.

"Boyce, we have a problem," declared the warehouse owner looking serious. "I heard on the scanner that the National Guard are heading here first thing in the morning. Somehow this textile factory is on an old map and some of the officers think perhaps if the students got lost in the woods, they could've made their way here."

Mr. Boyce didn't want the National Guard exposing their village to the world. He needed the warehouse owner or his son to take them back to the city and drop them off at a hospital or a place where they could meet their families without asking too many questions.

"We need to go now," his son commanded. "They stopped the searches in the evening, but they will start everything back up in the morning."

"Don't worry," the warehouse owner stated. "We have a plan. You may not like it but we have a plan."

The warehouse owner and Mr. Boyce talked for a few minutes out of earshot confirming the plan and then he made the announcement.

"Students and Ms. Kim," began Mr. Boyce in a stately voice. "We will meet at the barn in ten minutes and depart."

Everyone was in panic mode to get moving. The sweet feeling of Christmas was replaced with tears, hugs, and goodbyes. Ten minutes would go by quickly, but it gave the students time to wrap up conversations and be on their way. Some students went back to their berthing areas to grab this or that. Some quickly wrote down emails or phone numbers for the residents in the event they ever left Ourstory. Many of the residents walked with the students, Mr. Boyce and Harvey scurried to the wagon. Gabriel couldn't make the walk to the barn, he was getting tired, but found Arcado before he left.

"I don't have a real brother, but if I did, I wish it were you," his little voice said sadly.

"I will always consider you my real brother," replied Arcado and gave him a brotherly hug. "I'll miss hanging with you."

"I love you, Arcado," said Gabriel innocently. "Nobody ever knows what tomorrow holds, but I do know that I cannot say that to you after tonight."

"Honestly, Gabriel," admitted Arcado, who knew that he would think of Gabriel for the rest of his life. "I love you too."

He gave him one more bear hug, smiled at him, and walked away not showing him the tears blurring his eyes.

As everyone walked toward the barn, Ryan held Bianca's hand. They were in the back of the pack lingering more than walking. Bianca stopped in place and looked at Ryan. The nervousness that filled Ryan earlier consumed her body now too. She didn't care, this was it. Looking up at him, she took the plunge and kissed him unforgivingly. When she released him from her lips, he instantly wanted more, and dove in for another. This would be their only kiss that would have to last a lifetime or until they saw each other on the Malloy Courts in years to come.

"Was it everything you thought it would be?" teased Ryan until the end.

"Meh, it was alright," Bianca said, downplaying it, but inside her heart was beating fast and she couldn't control her smile.

They arrived at the wagon and everyone was inside waiting for him.

"What are you thinking?" asked Ryan gazing into her eyes, absolutely dying to know.

"I was thinking," she wanted to say something profound but instead could only think of one thing. "That if I were a vampire, I would definitely bite you."

He smiled at her with a quizzical look.

"What are you thinking?" inquired Bianca back to Ryan.

"I was thinking that this was more than I ever dreamed of...meeting you I mean," admitted Ryan now looking into Bianca's glassy eyes as he hopped up into the back of the wagon. "I hope to see you again someday. Remember our plan."

Chapter 68 The Pre-Plan

They all stood up in the wagon and waved as they departed, but it was dark out and it was almost impossible to keep one's footing as the horses jerked their cart in motion down the trail. Ryan's eyes were glued to Bianca's, but soon they turned a corner and the residents were out of sight. Everyone felt uneasy about their departure. It would be different if they knew they could come back and visit, but that would never happen. The danger of anyone visiting on a normal basis would put the whole camp in jeopardy. The students also wanted the best outcome for the village and for the National Guard to avoid them, even though they were trying, in earnest, to save their lives. The warehouse owner and his son rode on horseback next to the wagon.

It was an hour before they reached the bridge. When they did, all of the students and Ms. Kim got out of the back of the wagon. Mr. Boyce and Harvey hopped down from the driver's perch. The students now would be apprised of the plan. This was as far as Boyce would be allowed to go.

He would now take the wagon back to Ourstory. From the bridge they would all walk to the warehouse. The crane was already in place to dismantle the bridge. It was necessary to take out the bridge, so the National Guard didn't have a way to get to Ourstory. After the students were returned safely back to New York City and nobody was searching for them, the owner's son would help the residents put the bridge back in place.

Looking up to the moon that shone down on all the students, Mr. Boyce was having a hard time saying goodbye. He had grown to care for each and every one of the kids and even Ms. Kim. He gave each a hug or a handshake and turned the wagon around to go back to the village, tears in his eyes. Harvey would accompany the students to the warehouse which made the students feel at ease. Time was too important to waste on long goodbyes.

Everyone crossed the bridge and the warehouse owner's son slid off his horse and handed the reins to Ms. Kim.

"If you know how to ride, go ahead and take her back to the house," he said kindly. "My work here will take a few hours."

Before the two rode into Ourstory, the son drove the crane to the bridge and his father rode on one horse with the other in tow. Now, he would dismantle the bridge as carefully as he could so that nobody could cross it. The plan was to keep it all intact and place it at the bottom of the ravine. The hope was that it would dissuade the guard troops to make the treacherous climb down the mountainside and back up the other in search of the students. Soon, the students would be declared found and that would be the end of any journey to the old textile factory.

While he worked on the bridge, everyone else would walk or ride back to the house which would take a few hours. After he would complete his task, he would drive the crane back to the warehouse and the two men and Harvey would take all six of the owner's horses to trot up and down the trail to hide the crane tracks. They had a plan to get the students and Ms. Kim back to the city. Timing was quintessential to the success of their plan.

Besides hiding Ourstory from the National Guard, the warehouse owner and his family also needed alibis not to have the finger pointed at them for abetting the missing children. Since their house and warehouse had been searched several times, if they were to notify the National Guard that they miraculously found them, there would be an inquiry for sure. Probing the warehouse owner and his wife would not be good for his business. Their warehouse was vital to the community and if the media thought they were suspected of hiding the students, they would be ruined. That would be the end of their support to not only Ourstory, but the Amish and nearby farmers who depended on their supplies. Getting them back to the city undetected would require delicacy and cooperation. The students walked with Harvey behind the horse riders.

The kids were amazed at how Ms. Kim put her foot in the stirrup and gracefully swung herself over its back as if she was born on a farm. Only Arcado seemed to know how handy she was with the farm animals. She never disclosed how she grew up in Seoul, Korea on a farm until her mother married a serviceman and moved to the states. This was in her comfort zone, but as she rode, all that she could think of was writing her memoirs of Ourstory. She couldn't help herself, when she was fixated on something, there was no letting go. Promises were made not to divulge Ourstory secrets, but she would write it anyway. At some point she would make loads of money on the book, she knew it in her heart. Opportunities like this were once in a lifetime and she would grab this one.

It was two thirty in the morning and they still had a distance to go to get back to the warehouse. They walked in silence. Even Wanda was quiet, surprising everyone. The only light they had was the moon above and the reflection on the snow. Nobody complained about the long trek, they all needed the plan, whatever it was, to go right.

The warehouse owner was the first to notice that the state road was ahead. Once they got to the road, they still had a few blocks to go. When he acknowledged the coast was clear, they all shuffled out of the woods until they reached his house. It was three thirty in the morning by the time the owner and everyone were safe inside his home. His wife was expecting them, so she was awake and greeted them. Doc Marta gave the owner a bag of the clothes they wore when they arrived at Ourstory. He handed the bag to his wife and she laundered the contents. The only remnants of Ourstory would be the shoes on their feet.

Harvey and the owner were getting ready to head back out to cover the crane tracks once his son completed the bridge demolition. Ms. Kim told them she would ride with them. Ryan, Arcado, and Vaughn also volunteered.

"It's too dangerous for you kids to be out and about," the owner said calmly. "We will be back in three or so hours."

"If we all go with you, we will get this done even faster," replied Vaughn. "I never rode a horse, but I am willing to learn so that we can make sure this is done in time."

Everyone knew Vaughn had a good point. It was getting close to morning and the guard would be up and about. The owner wanted to say no but knew that it would help to quicken their mission. The girls insisted that they help in some way, but the laundry was already in the washing machine. They sat in the cozy family room wanting to stay awake, but every one of them was asleep within minutes of sitting down.

It took an hour and then some to get the bridge pulled off its hinges. He worked one side at a time. When the bridge finally broke free, it was in one piece but bent. It didn't feel good to destroy something they had just built, but it needed to be done to protect the orphans. He placed it carefully at the bottom of the ravine. Next, he took the large tree that had originally ruined the bridge and laid it on top as if it were the purpose it fell. After he was satisfied that no sane person would try and cross the struts that were still standing, he left. He swiveled the machinery around and moved the large, heavy crane as fast as the motor could spend. Forty minutes later, he met up with his father and the crew on their horses. They would continue to the bridge site making hoof marks to cover up the crane's tracks and then head back home.

The boys were exhausted but adrenaline kept them upright and focused on leaving horse tracks everywhere. Ms. Kim was the best rider of the bunch and she masterfully made circles and backed up when needed. When they made it to the bridge, the three boys were afraid to get close to the edge. Ms. Kim rode her horse right up to the cliff and made all kinds of hoof marks here and there. Harvey stared at his destiny that was on the other side of the gap. He knew he would be back there in a few weeks' time, but the sight saddened him. They were running out of time, so the owner asked if they minded trotting into a small gallop to get home.

The tracks were made and they didn't need to cover anything else. The boys didn't know how to gallop. The three who did, charged their horses to go fast and the boys' horses followed. Arcado and Ryan didn't like galloping and found it painful, but they didn't know how to slow it down. In less than 45 minutes, they were all back at the owner's house. It was almost six o'clock in the morning. Everyone was beyond exhausted.

Soon the owner would head back into the woods on his horse before the guard got there. Part of the plan was to help lead the National Guard elsewhere. His hope would be that they would grill him about the students, the bridge, and the textile factory. He would feed them any false story they needed to hear to throw them off. It was imperative to protect all who mattered.

When they entered the house, the girls and Adam were sleeping, some in a reclined position, while others lay on the floor. The boys and Harvey followed suit and laid anywhere there was space. The owner's wife gave them pillows and blankets for comfort. Then, they slipped off to get a few hours of sleep. Earlier, while her husband and son went to Ourstory, the wife took the opportunity to set up the next part of the plan which would be tested in a few hours to come.

On Friday morning, Chauncy woke up early and went to
wake Tolbert to do some gaming, but then remembered he was
staying at his mother's. He grinned when he thought of
Tolbert's mom and her whiny New York accent taking care of
his best friend. Tolbert would stay at his mother's in
Manhattan for the next week, which would drive him to heal
faster. Chauncy daydreamed of Tolbert's mom's voice and then
another lady's voice popped into his head. They were starting
to blend. The voice kept saying "We haven't seen those kids in
over two years". First Tolbert's mom said it and then he
realized whose voice it really was, it was the warehouse
owner's wife the day he and Smith visited. What did she mean
by those words?

He started playing his video game to get the voices out of
his head, but it nagged him just like his theory of the bus going
down the side of the cliff. He played on for a few more minutes
until he put his console down. It didn't feel right, he thought.
Maybe she was confused with things and time. Maybe she had
a short-term memory. The speculation had Chauncy packing
up and out the door heading back to the warehouse to once
again play Sherlock Holmes.

The men working on Operation Tannenbaum knew that
the National Guard was checking the forestry off the state
roads, so they took a different approach. Their theory now was
that the bus went off the mountainside and crashed
somewhere. They each had a designated area to search down
the ravines. They were equipped with ropes, ice axes, gloves,
and all the necessary gear for rappelling down steep cliffs and
then climbing back up them. Some paths would be easier to
walk down, and some would need all their tools.

The youngest in their Ops group, all 26 years of age, was
finishing the last of the video tapes and then would grab his
gear. What came up on the screen was a bunch of kids in a
warehouse. When he saw this, he froze and got excited. He

motioned everyone over to check out the footage. But there were more than 11 students and they were of all ages. All five viewed the interesting tape, but the date stamp on the bottom of the footage was from two years ago. The leader pointed it out and told him to shut it off and get ready for the day. He was just about to turn it off when Dino approached him.

"I'll turn off the tape and secure it for you," he stated sternly. "I am already packed up and ready to go."

"Sure," the young man said and left.

Dino memorized each of those young faces from a mission he was sent to do two years ago. The client specifically mentioned that if he delivered the kids to him or their exact location, the $300,000 would be deposited the next day. He couldn't believe he found them. He would not let this opportunity slip through, but he had to be stealthy and smart. It was his team's job to ask questions and dig for answers, so he would need a good plan to leave his duties and seek out the man at the warehouse.

The scanner woke the homeowner and his wife. It was seven o'clock on Friday morning and they could hear the National Guard squawking that they were headed to scout the area to take them to the old textile mill next. Time was fleeting. The owner, with barely an hour of sleep, awoke to ride his horse into the wooded area and await the National Guard as planned. There was no need to wake the rest until a few hours later to prepare for the drive home. He loaded up pouches of his secret formula, grabbed a spray bottle, and headed out to the stables.

Chauncy drove his Ram up through the mountains alone filled with the excitement of solving the mystery. Reflecting on the woman's words, he thought she seemed hospitable and friendly. The words she spoke about the kids being there two years ago, gained a swift, stern look from her husband that day. It always bothered Chauncy the way he punished his wife with his eyes because she misspoke and today, he would find out why. Chauncy saw the thoughts of hiding or hurting the kids blaze across his eyes, and this enraged Chauncy. This had him already wanting vengeance because, in truth, he felt that he was still a kid, and nobody messes with kids.

The Operation Tannenbaum crew headed out in their SUVs. When they got to the state highway, some went left, and some went right. Dino's assigned cliff to search was to the left which would help in his endeavor to be closer to the warehouse. He traveled that direction with one other SUV to a site that was 11 miles down the road. They both got out, grabbed their gear, and went opposite ways to scale down their mountain paths. Dino went down his mountain path for a few minutes and then returned to his vehicle. His cohort was nowhere in sight. He radioed his coworker and told him that he sliced himself on a sharp rock and needed medical attention, advising him that it wasn't a critical wound and that he would return as soon as possible. He acknowledged Dino and carried on down his path. The other operation's team was out of radio range, but if anyone found something significant, they would get to a range to disclose their findings.

Four Humvees parked haphazardly on the side of the state road a block down from the warehouse owner's house. The National Guardsmen began their search down the trail that the crane had made to the bridge. There were eight soldiers and two hounds on the path walking at a good clip. Something strange happened to the hounds as they sniffed the snow here and there. They sneezed and whimpered. Their handlers had never witnessed such an odd reaction from the dogs. A few of the men admitted that they thought the dogs were overworked from endless hours and days of tracking. They pressed on and the dogs stopped sniffing the ground. The Master Sergeant in charge had the map and directed their team, including the miserable dogs, toward the bridge.

When they got to the bridge, they ran into the warehouse owner who was on his horse with his binoculars looking into the trees high above. He heard the hounds barking miserably before he saw the soldiers. The group looked down into the ravine where the bridge sat, half in a small stream and half on the snow-covered land.

"What are you doing out here and what happened to the bridge?" the Master Sergeant asked the warehouse owner in a suspicious manner.

"Shhh," the warehouse owner stared into the trees without flinching. "There was a Snow Bunting, but it's gone. I normally come out here with my son and we birdwatch for hours. I saw some Blue Jays just before you arrived.'"

"It looks like the bridge went out with the storm," remarked a corporal holding one of the dogs on a leash.

"Most likely," admitted the warehouse owner.

"Is that so?" asked a skeptical Master Sergeant. "Then why isn't it covered under snow?"

The warehouse owner panicked. He thought he was clever spraying different fruit scents on the trail to throw off the hounds from the picking up scents from the students. Dogs didn't care for grapefruit smells and it hurt their noses. His son did such a great job placing the tree onto the bridge and the horse tracks covered any signs of the crane. They thought of everything, but he could not come up with an answer for the bridge at the bottom with no snow build-up. He gave a deep sigh.

The owner's wife wanted to make a large breakfast to hold the kids over until they got back into the city. Everyone was still sleeping, despite some snoring. The lady of the house prepped an egg bake the night before while she waited for the students to arrive. She baked muffins, cut fruit, and squeezed fresh oranges. One by one, each of them woke to the sensational smell of the egg bake. It was filled with spices and sausage.

Everyone's clothing, including their coats, was laundered and pressed and awaited their fittings. Each of them changed back into the clothes that they wore the day they were on the bus. The rips and small holes were repaired back in Ourstory. The blood stains were gone too. Their clothes fit loosely on them since they had dropped weight in Ourstory. Ms. Kim lost the most weight and needed a belt for her pants. She hadn't ever remembered wearing a belt before. Her scarred leg was now just a little sensitive by the polyester pants hitting her skin.

While they ate the hearty breakfast, the students thought about their new family that they left behind and the anticipation of reuniting with their own families soon. Darcy nudged Adam and revealed a bag that had a pair of shoes in it. The cute little kitten heel was molded by Adam and attached by Darcy. The brown suede detracted from the femininity she was going for, but thought that the rugged, pretty look could start a new trend. Adam grinned and regretted not taking the last pair that he made. He would have loved to have shown his parents the skillset he acquired. He thought about it more and liked that it was a secret that he kept between him and Darcy.

Wanda talked to the twins almost the whole morning. She invited them to hang out at her house in the summer for their block fish fries. The stick that she stowed away from her last hunting trip now would be used for her fishing pole as she dangled it in front of the twins. Knowing that the boys were avid hunters, she invited them to fish with her and her grandparents. They smiled and agreed that it would be fun. Before the twins left, Travis handed Vlad a small bow and arrow set that the boys used to hunt rabbits. It was handcrafted in Ourstory, and he wanted to show them his gratitude. Travis half thought about giving Wanda the bolo but shuddered with terrible images and put it back in the weapon locker.

Harvey sat and marveled at their happy faces. He was friendly, quiet, and had an air of mystery that surrounded his wit. The students were glad he was there for their journey home. Even though Darcy and Adam knew him best cobbling shoes, Harvey had a connection to each one of them. He was known as Boyce's second in command. As much as Boyce would have rather been the one to escort the kids on this journey, Ourstory depended on him too much. If anything went awry, Harvey was needed but not as much as Boyce.

While the students chatted around the kitchen, Ms. Kim sat silently, mentally writing her book. She would soon have the conclusion to their story, in just a few hours. As she stared at the students, happy memories flooded back to when she was growing up on her grandfather's farm in Seoul, but it all was ripped away when her mother married an U.S. enlisted man full of promises. A few years after arriving in the states, they divorced and her mother lived by modest means. She thought that life was unfair, providing her no opportunities, until now.

She was no dummy and now the world would read her detailed book of recent events earning her a Pulitzer for her writing. She deserved this one opportunity to become famous and make millions.

As the soldiers stared down at the bridge on the bottom of the mountain, the warehouse owner's insides churned with anxiety. He didn't have an answer for the leader of the group and knew that they would investigate the bridge in full measure. The Master Sergeant eyed the climb down.

"I may have a theory of why the bridge has no snow or ice on it," spoke a female Private.

Until she spoke up, the warehouse owner thought there were only boys in the group, by the looks of everyone bundled in Army wear.

"Explain," commanded the Master Sergeant, staring at her in doubt.

The warehouse owner sat on the edge of his seat, with raised eyebrows. What could a pimply teenage girl possibly know about bridges? He was brainstorming other sound reasons before she began to talk.

"For my Industrial Polymers Course, I just finished a research paper on bridges," she continued. "To combat what they call ice accretion or ice shedding, they came up with a high-density polyurethane that has hydrophobic properties that make the snow and ice slide off easily. That way it can't build up and damage cars, people, and boats below."

The Master Sergeant looked at her and pondered if that was really a thing. She was brand new to the battalion, so he didn't know how to judge her one way or the other.

"Hmmm," declared the Master Sergeant. "Since there's no way to get to the textile mill without the bridge, it's likely the kids never got there either. We'll head back for further instruction. Let's move out!"

The warehouse owner breathed easier. He couldn't believe the youngest one in the bunch may have been the smartest. Inside his head, he thanked her over and over. He put his binoculars away, bid them a farewell, and trotted down the path until he was out of view and then galloped like a derby jockey back to his house. He could hear the dogs howling from the big pile of grapefruit juice he had emptied out of his pouch on the way back.

After the warehouse owner's wife served breakfast, she left the students and departed in their pickup truck to her son's house. She wanted to ensure the next steps of the plan were going smoothly. Before she left, she closed the blinds to the front and back of the house. In the case that any of the National Guard had another visit, the house would look vacant. But it wasn't the National Guard that came around.

Dino passed the driveway and saw that the warehouse owner's truck was gone. He drove down their street, turned around and parked his SUV on the opposite side of the road. His intention was to keep out of view from the surveillance system. There was a box of disguises in the back seat, so he put on a baseball cap that had long black hair attached. He had to get to the surveillance system in the warehouse to erase his SUV driving by. He wanted no evidence of his inquiry. Checking once more for onlookers, he made his way to the warehouse and jimmied the lock as he had done a few days back. The closet that held the surveillance tape was easy to access. He erased the last half an hour and then he stopped the taping altogether. Needing a good place to hide until the owner returned, he found a nice spot on the side of a large piece of machinery with a tarp placed over it.

Chauncy drove by the large warehouse. He saw the owner's truck missing. He drove down the street and turned around and parked behind a silver SUV at the neighbor's house. He walked up to the house to knock on the door and saw the warehouse door was ajar and wondered if the owner was in there. Creeping quietly through the door to spy on the owner, he slipped into the warehouse. There were the supply racks and machinery that he saw on his last visit, but he didn't see the owner. The thought occurred to him that this was a nice warm place to stay until he heard the owner's truck parked in the drive, so he did. There was a tarp over a large piece of machinery, so he slid down to the floor with his back resting on a large wheel.

Down the road, the mother and her son went over the next steps to get the students and Ms. Kim home. The son visited his fishing buddy, who was also the sheriff, daily for general conversations and observations. He started a journal days ago with the National Guard's patterns and noted the checkpoint locations and the times of the changing of the Guard.

On several occasions, he witnessed that when they switched shifts, the cars would not be flagged for inspection. The crew on duty needed time to brief the new crew and afterward, the car searches resumed. He also noticed that they wouldn't stop cars during an extensive truck search. The truckers complained because it took a good 15-30 minutes out of their already long day.

The warehouse owner put his horse back in the stable and entered the house through the back door. His house guests were cleaning up the dishes, just as they did back at Ourstory. His stomach was in a knot from dealing with the National Guard and momentarily they would put the plan in motion to take the group back to New York City.

The owner escorted everyone to the warehouse to await the van that would take them home. The students and Ms. Kim took seats at a table set up for them with folding chairs around it while Harvey and the owner confirmed the final details. There were blankets on the seats, so they snuggled up in them as they sat. They stared in amazement at all of the large machinery and shelves filled with farm supplies that surrounded them.

Chauncy stood behind the tarped machine. His jaw dropped when he saw the students and the bus driver sitting right before him. He remained silent and congratulated himself excitedly for not giving up on his instincts. There was always a motive, he thought. He would sit tight until the reveal came around and then catch them red-handed. As he looked around at the students, who seemed content and well taken care of, he was perplexed at who was culpable of foul play. The scenarios that played in his head earlier of the students being kidnapped or diverted to a hard labor work camp seemed to be weak in theory now. Each of their relaxed faces told him that they hadn't been through any traumatic experience. Whatever the reason, he wanted full credit for finding them, and he couldn't wait to rub this in Tolbert's face, better yet the Ice Queen's.

Chauncy was getting antsy with anticipation. He wasn't the only nervous hider in the place. Dino kept his hand on his gun and had to figure out what to do. These were the wrong kids, so he needed the owner to reveal where the orphans were hiding. The money he would get for the orphans would be his jackpot and these students now seemed irrelevant. Besides, he got paid his money no matter if they found these brats or not. The only person he needed was the owner but would remain quiet until the rest of the group departed, which he hoped would be soon. Everyone heard the owner's truck drive up and park. The owner's wife entered the warehouse and let her husband know that their son would be there soon.

The piece of machinery that the two were hiding under jutted out here and there but at any time could expose them if someone were to look at a certain angle. Chauncy decided he would move from a side niche to the back because he could still hear all the conversations. As he backed up, so did Dino with the same perception of being found. They both backed up until they smacked right into each other's backside. Dino turned first and pointed his gun at Chauncy. Chauncy wanted to be ever so quiet so Dino wouldn't get trigger happy, but if anyone were to be Wanda's soulmate in whispering, it would be him.

"What are you doing? Who are you?" Chauncy thought he whispered, but he did not. "And, most importantly, what's with the cheesy wig?"

Friday, December 18th
Chapter 70 Warehouse Surprise

Everyone in the garage heard the commotion behind the tarp and it startled them. Dino motioned for Chauncy to walk over to where the students were as he pointed the gun to his back. Everyone's faces indicated their confusion. The students just wanted to get back home and now they thought they were being robbed or, worse, murdered. The house owner didn't know what was happening but did recognize Chauncy.

"Take it easy," stated Harvey in a calm voice. "We don't have any money."

"I don't want your money," chastised Dino. "I want to know where the kids are."

"We are right here," said Wanda sensibly and then whispered. "He must be stupid or somethin'."

"Not these kids," replied Dino, staring at the warehouse owner and Harvey who had also been on the surveillance tapes from years past. "The orphans from a few years ago."

Everyone froze. If he was asking, he must not be a good guy, they all thought. The warehouse owner wondered how he knew about them and who else knew. Harvey was horrified. The jig was up for his family members back at Ourstory. The warehouse owner thought that playing dumb about the orphans may not be the best move.

"Tell me?" asked the warehouse owner. "How do you live with yourself trafficking children?"

Dino didn't want to know this. He wasn't supposed to know this. It was just a job for money, so he could pay his betting debts off and maybe have money left over to gamble just one more time. It was the money and the opportunity that only he had. As he held the gun to Chauncy's back, he concluded that he didn't care what the reason was, he was going to get the location of those orphans.

"I don't want those kids for trafficking," Dino justified and then he lied. "My employer just wants to make sure they're safe."

"Who employs you?" asked Harvey in a serious tone.

"I don't know," he said, not lying. "I just get instructions on finding people and things."

"How about if I pay you to be on your way and never look back?" said Harvey, desperate to come up with a plan.

He knew that no matter how much he paid the crook, he might come back for more or blackmail the warehouse owner.

"I am not sure you can pay me the half a million that my employer can give," he hyperbolized to see where this would go.

Harvey knew two things, one was that he could not come close to matching that sum, and the other was if anyone were paying him that much, it was not to check on the Ourstory children's safety. It was hopeless. He wasn't sure who the boy being held hostage was, but he would not sacrifice anyone's life.

The gears in Harvey's head were turning, trying to figure out how to get the Ourstory children and anyone else hiding from bad guys out of the village to safety after disclosing the location to this criminal. As he was contemplating his next words, he heard a scream.

"AAAHH, my hand," howled Dino, dropping the gun, falling to his knees, holding his hand in pain.

In one stealthy movement, Vlad took out his bow and arrow and nailed Dino's free hand with a shot. He dropped his revolver, which was held in the other hand, to care for his wounded one. Chauncy recovered it, handed it to Harvey, and then tended to Dino.

"First, you look stupid in this wig," said Chauncy unkindly as he pulled his hat off and threw it to the table revealing his bald head. "Second, you threatened me with a gun to my back. Third, you should learn to never mess with kids. We are your future, scumbag."

It wasn't as hardcore as Harvey would have reprimanded, but the New York students were all cheering for Chauncy. Wanda didn't forget about Vlad saving the day. She went right over and gave him a kiss on the cheek. This had him turning a little pink as he had never been kissed before. After the students cheered Chauncy, they turned and applauded Vlad for a job well done.

The warehouse owner's wife made her way over to tend to Dino's bloody and skewered hand. He cried out in pain. She picked up some tools from the bench nearby and clipped off the top and bottom of the arrow, leaving a jutted stick going through his hand. Then she instructed Chauncy to guide him to the washroom and hold his hand under the water while she went back into the house to get her medical instruments. She was once an ER nurse at the hospital down the road and luckily knew how to respond.

Dino was still in much pain and cursed like a sailor. Chauncy brought him back to the table where the students sat and put Dino in a chair like the nurse instructed him to. The owner's wife sat opposite Dino and injected his hand with a numbing agent. She looked around for something to use as a tourniquet and her eyes went right to Ms. Kim's valued belt that secured her waistline. Understanding the stare, Ms. Kim raised her eyebrows and whipped it off, and handed it to the nurse. Taking the belt from Ms. Kim, she tied it around his upper arm of the injured hand to prevent blood flow The next step was to dislodge the stick from his hand, which she did quickly, and then poured a disinfectant around the gushing wound and cleaned it. He yelped like a baby. Her needle was already threaded as she sewed the wound through the tiny amount of blood surfacing. In a matter of 10 minutes, his hand was sewed up and the blood drippings had ceased. She added iodine to the new sutures and wrapped a gauze bandage around several times and secured it with a metal clip. Next, she gave him a strong dose of Tylenol for when the local anesthetics wore off. She looked irritated all throughout the job, but now she was done and stood up to leave.

"Thank you, miss," said Dino, feeling ashamed of himself.

"You're welcome," she sat back down and stared at him with her honest eyes. "I believe every life matters, even yours."

He didn't say a word. He just sat there hanging his head low wondering what would happen to him now. The warehouse owner shackled Dino's leg to a nearby shelf, until he figured out what to do with him.

Harvey stood at the front of the table so that he faced everyone. He kept Boyce's promise to give them a good cover story for their return to New York City. Chauncy took a seat and listened. His thirst for curiosity would be quenched soon and he would know the whole story. Dino was already facing Harvey, awaiting his story, and sitting silently in misery.

"Does anyone know the time?" asked Harvey as he took out his shiny, golden pocket watch.

The students shook their heads "no". Nobody owned a watch that worked anymore. Harvey stood and played with his gold watch just letting it hang down to his side and it teetered, back and forth. Harvey slowed his breathing by taking deep cleansing breaths. It was contagious because everyone mimicked his moves. He encouraged them to relax and get comfortable listening to his story as he sat down and leaned forward in his chair dangling the watch back and forth. He invited them to close their eyes and envision the picture that he would paint for them regarding their story to tell their parents, teachers, classmates, friends, relatives, and the news reporters.

Soon they were all relaxed with their eyes closed and heads hung low as Harvey softly began his story. He talked about how their bus went off the road into a wooded area and was heavily damaged. He continued his story, detailing how a group of Amish people found the bus and took them in generously. They were treated fairly, met some nice kids, were fed, given comfortable clothing, and warm quarters and made to do chores to help the community. He explained how the Amish had no ways of communicating to the outside world once the snow let up and had issues with their carriages being frozen to transport the students safely. More vivid details about their accommodations and people were implanted in the story. The big issue between the students and the Amish community was the language barrier since no one spoke proper English. Then he taught them some simple Amish words to remember for verity. He imprinted in their minds to forget all about the specific people they met and the village of Ourstory now never existed.

Harvey finished delivering the details to fill any holes in the story that the kids could tell harmoniously. He implanted in their heads that they would soon see the Amish couple that took them in, and they would remember them as their heroes. Then he turned to Dino whose head was hung low listening to the account and told him that there were no orphan children that needed to be looked for and that he would quit his job searching for people and things and take up a job to help his community. He told Dino that he cut himself on a piece of sharp machinery searching for the missing students. He also recommended that Dino head to a hospital when he departed to get it checked out. He impressed upon everyone that once they left the warehouse, they would not remember ever being there, nor would they remember the owners. They would only remember the friendships that they built between themselves and Ms. Kim. The story wasn't too far off from the truth, so it was easy to believe in.

He counted backward from three and told them to open their eyes and stand up. They did as they were told, even Dino and Chauncy. He walked by each one of them with a smile, shaking their hands and letting them know that he would miss them. The students looked at Harvey as if they had never seen him before and were confused why he acted so friendly. It worked. In their deep relaxation, his hypnotism transformed their minds to meld with the story and now it was truly theirs to tell.

Ryan awoke and tried to remember why he had a pit still in his stomach, but it didn't quite come to him. He brushed it off as missing his family and teammates. Harvey did impart that Darcy and Adam were shoe cobblers and made such good shoes they would want to continue to do so and keep in touch. They remembered making good shoes but blocked out who had given them training. Wanda remembered that she did some hunting, but the great story of the bear in the woods would never be retold by her or the twins. She did, however, remember that she liked the boys and still wanted them to meet her family. Shannon didn't know how but remembered she wanted to be a different kind of student. She wondered if not being able to communicate with the Amish had any impact on the way she saw things. Brianna remembered sewing and despite what her mom and aunt might think, she wouldn't mind taking it up again once she was home.

Arcado remembered milking cows and Ms. Kim doing the same. He and Brianna did still feel a small attraction to each other but only knew it was because of the place that gave them a common experience. She did not remember how he saved her life on the bus filled with water. Vaughn never remembered how the choir elevated his music but yearned to get back to his dad and continue writing songs. The twins remembered that they too hunted and returned with small animals. They were happy to know they helped the Amish. There was one quiet girl left, who was too nervous to fall asleep in the hypnotic state. Lauren heard the story and would memorize it, but she was the only student to reciprocate Harvey's handshake with a slight smile.

Harvey knew she was the one. She knew it all, but if anyone were to keep the secret, he trusted her fully. Ms. Kim knew it all too. She almost cursed that the hypnotism didn't work because all the students would give one account and her book would give another. She told Harvey straight up that she remembered everything. If Boyce were here instead, he would have pleaded with her to keep quiet. Harvey didn't know her as well and wasn't sure what he could do about it but had faith that she would keep it to herself.

Chauncy introduced himself as a member of the National Guard and had felt it in his gut that they were safe all this time. He gloated that he was part of this happy occasion. He told them all about how he and Tolbert were the first ones to get to the armory in the blizzard and the first to search for them. The warehouse owner collaborated his story, somewhat remembering his visit. Chauncy was excited to know that the Amish took great care of the students, even though their group thought they had searched every homestead but must've missed that one.

The large warehouse door opened and a large, white, nine-passenger van drove in with the owner's son at the wheel. An elderly Amish couple stepped out of the parked van. The warehouse owner introduced the Amish couple to the students. There was an Amish village down the road that bartered with the warehouse owner routinely. They all exchanged nods with the 70-year-old man named Brutus and his wife of the same age, Lara, who gave a quick curtsy. They wore clothes that looked like they were from an 1800's period piece movie and spoke only the English words "Hello" and "Thank You". The students profusely thanked them for saving them in the storm.

The owner introduced his son who would drive them back to New York City, hopefully without a big fuss. The owner told everyone in the warehouse they had a plan. First, they needed to get past the National Guard checkpoints without being stopped. The second part was why they needed Brutus and Lara and that would be explained on the way back to the city. He expressly made sure that Chauncy and Dino would not disclose any information at the checkpoints they would come across.

Dino would not communicate anything to his team. For some reason, he felt an indebtedness to this group of people whom he'd never seen before. He looked down at his hand and thought how stupid he was to cut it so deeply and knew he needed to get to the hospital immediately. He thanked his newfound friends for taking good care of him and walked out to find his SUV to head straight to the hospital. Chauncy was thrilled to be a part of something special and knew he came here with the intention of finding out information. He was satisfied that he knew the answers and he would be silent at any checkpoint returning home. Besides, he wanted to make sure that neither the TACC nor any guard unit got the credit. He would hate to admit to Tolbert that he was so off base on all of his hunches. He thought to himself that he was certainly no Sherlock Holmes. After he was on the road, he remembered the story about the students and the Amish but couldn't remember which Amish camp he just came from. The warehouse that he just left was now forgotten.

Everyone loaded into the van. Ryan opened the front door for Ms. Kim while the Amish couple sat smiling on the bench behind the driver. Not everyone could fit in the four rows of seats, so some sat in the back storage area floor. The twins volunteered to sit on the storage floor, so of course, Wanda made an uncomfortable spot for herself right between them. Arcado pulled Brianna to sit on the third bench next to him along with Vaughn while Adam, Darcy, and Lauren took the fourth bench. Shannon sat next to the Amish couple and beamed in gratefulness. Ryan climbed in to sit next to Shannon. Ms. Kim sat comfortably in the front passenger seat but didn't close her door.

The driver was ready to go and everyone waited for Ms. Kim to close her door. She was writing something on a piece of paper and needed to finish.

"Is there something wrong?" the son asked her, impatiently.

"No," she answered and got out of the van. "Not anymore."

"Where are you going?" he asked, getting out of the van in concern.

Brianna and Ryan got out to make sure Ms. Kim was feeling alright. She stood straight up with her arms folded, looking for the first time, unsure of herself.

"I am staying," Ms. Kim looked like she'd just had a revelation. "I am happy here with the Ourst.... Amish. I like waking up and milking cows and havin' a community that surrounds me. You kids don't know me, but I grew up on this kinda' stuff and I miss it. Der's nuttin' for me back in New York and I can't drive a bus forever. Not to mention, they'll probably blame me for driving like a crazy lady, when Rooter...awe never mind. I am staying."

Everyone except for Lauren looked at her in confusion. Ms. Kim was known for her weird stories. Brianna gave her a hug goodbye as she clung to her like she was her mother. Ms. Kim folded a piece of paper and handed it to Brianna to read later. They all bid her farewell and loaded back up in the van. Ryan called shotgun and took the front seat. The driver buckled in and turned around to make sure he would not have any other issues. He chuckled when he saw Adam wearing the ball cap with the long black hair that he took from the table. The driver looked down at his clipboard with the National Guard map and times and then he checked his watch. He drove off slowly, knowing that the first checkpoint was 30 minutes down the road and shift change was 32 minutes away.

Ms. Kim had no thoughts in her head about staying in Ourstory until she met Dino just a bit ago. How dare he sell

330

those orphans out to make a buck, she thought, stewing quietly. If it wasn't for the gun he had in his hand, she would have pounded him to a pulp. If Vlad wouldn't have shot his arrow and injured him, she would have found a way. She realized she felt guilty and selfish about her own ambitions and her stomach dropped into queasiness. That was why she did not get hypnotized. She was so concentrated on the harm that she almost caused, that Harvey's words fell away. The only thing that made her feel better was the thought of going back to Ourstory and milking cows, reading mystery novels, playing cards, singing in the choir, talking to Boyce, and being part of a real community. She measured her happiness in the last few weeks compared to her happiness in the last few years and realized she couldn't even remember the last time she felt that kind of joy. Her life was about to change, for the better.

As the owner's son drove down the state highway, nobody spoke. Everyone was in silent thought about their return or the place they had just left. They remembered driving straight from the Amish farm that had saved them, although they couldn't recall exactly where that was located. Lauren was the only one who had the warm feeling from the place of Christmas she had just left and the beautiful music they made. The people there had become more than just residents to her, they were family. But she would never tell a soul.

The driver slowed his speed and pulled over at a gas station to make sure his timing was exact, just like the military shift change would be. A few minutes later, he eased back onto the road and was coming up to the first checkpoint. As predicted, the Humvee had just pulled up and both teams were in a huddle briefing and debriefing. The barrier arm was up and the driver went through without a stop. All went as planned with one more checkpoint to go. It was fifteen miles to the next one and he was behind a semi-truck going slower than he needed to go to make his precision timing. He decided to pass the truck, but once he did, he found a whole convoy of trucks in front of him. This was going to be tricky.

He was behind three trucks and the shift change was happening at the checkpoint 50 feet away. The barrier was up and the trucks started to go faster to roll on through without a stop. It was taking what seemed forever for the truck ahead of him to gain momentum to get through. Looking at his watch, there was less than a minute before the bar would drop and a checkpoint would once again start back up. The truck puttered at a slow speed and went through. As close as the driver stuck to the truck's back bumper, the bar dropped and a few guardsmen headed over.

The students dropped to the floor except for Ryan who was obviously sitting upright in the front seat. The Sergeant approached the driver at the window and asked him who his passengers were.

"I have, -er," the warehouse owner's son started to say and looked at Ryan who was wearing the ball cap with the long black hair under it.

"This is my neighbor Bob and we are taking my Amish neighbors to the hospital for emergency treatment."

The two elderly Amish in the second row waved with a grin as the guardsmen looked inside from the driver's window.

"He's in a lot of pain," said the driver contrarily to the old man's happy face.

"I don't believe you," said the Sergeant.

The driver's stomach dropped, and Ryan closed his eyes and sighed.

"You should've called for an ambulance," he said angrily. "Pain in the elderly can be serious."

"I agree," said the son convincingly. "They would never take an ambulance though - they have their pride. They would rather have taken the wagon, but I insisted."

"Well, good luck," the Sergeant said and then indicated to the corporal to lift the barrier bar up.

It was time to get the students home.

Friday, December 18th
Chapter 71 The Christmas Tree Lighting

Early in the evening, Cyril Haugen and his garden staff inspected the tree one last time, ensuring that any dead ends were chopped off and it was properly hydrated. His staff worked without speaking. This was a bittersweet production tonight. A large crowd of New Yorkers and out-of-towners, excited to see the tree lighting ceremony, started to arrive. The audience cheerfully wore their red Santa hats with white trim, brown reindeer antlers, or green and red elf hats along with their warm winter coats and scarves.

It was nearing eight o'clock and the spectators were getting restless with their cameras in place for the exact moment of amazement. News cameras were stationed at every angle around the chilly plaza, but most were near a platform area to the right of the tree. This was where the mayor, the students' families, the gardeners, and Mitch Jekel stood. A speech was prepared for the mayor and soon after the emcee of the event would do a countdown to the lighting.

The families gathered and greeted each other like old friends. There were hugs from the shared pain and comfort knowing that they had allies to go through the grief. There was a lot of crying and retelling of funny stories of their children growing up. Darcy's father quietly mentioned that the leader from the Project Tannenbaum texted him that so far there was no success in finding their kids. The struggle between hope and sorrow was heartbreaking.

The gardening team joined Jekel and the stressed families on the stage near the tree. The tree lighting never got old to any of the gardeners – the enjoyment of showing off their artistry. They looked around the plaza in excitement and waved to their family, friends, and neighbors who were all there supporting them in this prized moment. The gardeners tampered their enthusiasm to show respect to the relatives standing there.

Lauren's mother couldn't stop sobbing as she blurted out her regret. Every parent that initially thought the trip would be fun for their kids was now feeling guilty. Ryan's dad wanted his son to experience something cultural that wasn't sports related. Brianna's mom and aunt thought that this would be a refreshing experience for her, besides the usual protesting. Darcy's parents wanted to show that their daughter was part of an important decision that would look good on a college application. Aracado's parents thought he could truly persuade the others to not cut down the tree and let nature live.

Wanda's whole family came. Only her parents were on stage, but right below was the whole block of brothers, sisters, ti-ti's, uncles, and cousins. They all wanted a word in the microphone. Adam's mom wished she didn't fight with him about technology and just let him have whatever stupid gaming system he wanted. He was a good boy after all. Mrs. López was there with her husband and two daughters. She was silently sobbing making signs of the cross every time another family recounted a story. She lost the most. Two boys were gone. They were always the happiest boys that were helpful and dedicated to their families. She kept looking to the sky to ask God, why her boys? The families quieted down and stared at the tree nearby.

In Rockefeller Center, the mammoth tree was purposely dark with a few dim blue spotlights on each side at the base, searching back and forth and up and down the tree adding to the anticipation. Eagerness gleamed in every spectator's eyes as they checked their watches for the magic hour and minute the tree would light. The ice skaters in the rink below glided along in the exhilaration of having fun yet also carefully glancing at the tree to make sure they wouldn't miss that one moment. The crowd noise echoed throughout Rockefeller Center until the mayor's voice boomed into the microphone.

"I would like to dedicate the Christmas Lighting Ceremony to 11 New York students, who will never be forgotten," he said solemnly. "As this tree lights up, let us all hug our loved ones a little tighter tonight, because they are truly our best gifts."

He went on for a few more moments mentioning the names of the missing students. The families on the stage were linked hand in hand as the commemoration continued. They all bowed their heads as a sign of respect for their children.

The emcee took the mic after the mayor was finished and changed the somber mood back into an enthusiastic one.

"Five, four, three," the emcee counted loudly into the microphone and the crowd counted with her as she continued. "Two, one!"

The blue spotlights disappeared and in the blink of an eye, the splash of twinkling lights of every color imaginable flickered around and up to the heavens creating instant awe. The Swarovski Crystal Star atop the tree blazed white lights pointing in every direction like a beacon of hope for the world.

It was beautiful. There were 'oohs' and 'ahs' and flashes from cameras everywhere. The families of the students stood there speechless looking at the beautifully lit tree, their children's ornament pictures hanging, and thinking of everything it stood for.

Mrs. López was the first to notice and cried out loud in Spanish. Everyone thought she was losing it when she ran off the stage, even her husband wasn't sure of the reason. There were barriers but she crawled under them and ran to the tree.

Under the tree, like 11 Christmas presents wrapped, were the young, missing students and an older couple with silver hair wearing old garments like the old fashion Christmas carolers. They were all smiling.

When Mrs. López finally reached the tree, she exclaimed in Spanish, "Gracias a Dios."

Her boys ran to her and she embraced both of them kissing them all over their faces. The boys started to weep, having missed their mother too.

The camera crews that were filming the tree lighting production, no longer focused on the tree but rather on what was under it. Eleven children and an older couple. News reporters and crews rushed to move in, but before they could, the parents and relatives of the students hysterically ran to their kids. They pushed the cameramen and news reporters out of the way so they could reunite with their lost children.

Every hug and tear were recorded on film. The reuniting was overwhelming with parents, siblings, and students laughing and crying everywhere. Parents apologized to their children for making them go on this dangerous trek. When

Vaughn saw his dad, he anxiously hugged him and held on to him for dear life. When he pulled back, Vaughn noticed a feeble woman that stood behind Vegas barely having the strength to smile but smile she did. It was his mother. She looked tattered from the wear and tear on her body, but she needed to be there with all the grieving parents and now she was there to see her son's face smile back at her. It was a gift beyond Vaughn's imagination. He embraced her frail shell and felt the pain behind her eyes as she asked for forgiveness.

As Arcado noticed Vaughn's interaction, he recalled someone said there was a purpose for all of us and things happened for a reason. He couldn't remember who said it, but he witnessed all the families who became as close of friends as they all had to each other. The students calmed their worried parents' with hugs, kisses and smiles.

The slew of news reporters wanted answers from the students. None of the students were interested in answering any questions but appreciated the moment with their parents. The reporters moved over to the older Amish couple and bombarded them with questions.

Brutus and Lara just smiled at the reporters and nodded, knowing that they couldn't explain a thing. Back at the warehouse earlier, the owner convinced the Amish couple to help him 'for the good of the cause' – which could mean many things, but in Amish that meant they were serving someone with integrity without question to a request.

The owner knew this would be an odd request. His friends would oblige and do this favor for him and be exposed to bright lights and a busy city. The owner gave implicit instructions to his son, who also spoke a bit of Pennsylvania Dutch, the Amish language of Lara and Brutus, but was hidden out of sight wearing what looked like a chauffeur's outfit.

Their story would now be that the Amish took them in during the storm until it was safe enough to get them back home. There were so many different Amish communities in upstate New York that to pinpoint the single one that supposedly gave them shelter would be too difficult. Their memory of Ourstory did not exist any longer.

They nominated Shannon and Brianna to be their spokespersons to answer any questions from the press. Shannon explained from start to finish how their bus got stranded and broke down on a wintery road off the beaten path. And how Ms. Kim slid into a patch of ice and evacuated the bus. The Amish rescued the students and Ms. Kim and kept them safe and warm.

Brianna explained how Ms. Kim was a hero for driving the bus carefully and saving all of them from crashing. She enlightened everyone about Ms. Kim's obligation to stay with the Amish community and work alongside. The people in the crowd that knew Ms. Kim scratched their heads and thought this must be one of those Christmas miracles. Also, she surrendered a hand-written piece of paper that Ms. Kim wrote quickly as she said goodbye. It was a declaration of how she wanted her retirement check to go to the Bronx Orphanage at St. Stephens. She would check in online occasionally to ensure that things were in order. That would be sorted out in a legal way, but Brianna wanted the world to know what a generous person she was.

Mitch and Cyril kept their distance but smiled at the happy ending this would have for everyone including the mayor and governor. The children broke away from their families and approached the two gentlemen and stood before them silently. This was about the most painful thing that ever happened to Mitch and Cyril and now the kids stood before them quietly staring into both of their souls.

"Students, I would just like to say, we are so sorry, for the hell that you've been through," Mitch couldn't stand the hard stare from their eyes.

"Yes. I am most terribly sorry," admitted Cyril Haugen who knew this all started with his silly idea. "I...I."

"Mr. Haugen?" Lauren interrupted his next apology and spoke up confidently. "We all want to thank you for making this trip possible."

Lauren's parents were stunned. She never spoke in public. Her shyness had always been her curse and her parents, never in a million years, thought their daughter would be speaking to what would be counted later as a few million viewers on TV.

"We found within ourselves the possibilities that we could become," Darcy spoke this time.

"Yeah man, like the......Amish really taught us that we are resources," Vaughn added to the speech. He inserted Amish because that's how he remembered it.

"My parents will never believe this, but I am a hunter and provider," Wanda spoke up and then pointed and flirtingly smiled at the twins. "And so are my boys, Vlad and Sergei."

"I milked cows," Arcado said as he laughed.

"I, I mean, we cut down trees for firewood," Ryan added as he gave Vaughn a fist pump.

"And who knew, I am a shoe cobbler?" Adam declared and everyone in the crowd laughed.

"So, in the end, we are all healthy and safe," Shannon clarified. "We just wanted to thank you for selecting us for the Christmas tree project and if you ever need volunteers for this project again, call us."

Mitch and Cyril couldn't move for several moments contemplating the wonder that just happened. They were truly shocked at the kids coming back safe and sound and thanking them.

With all the commotion, no one took notice that Brutus and Lara slipped away back to the van. Then they were chauffeured around New York taking in the amazing sites of the big city at night. They had never seen so many people, so many buildings, and so many lights, especially in Time Square. They never had traveled outside the world of their farming community. Holding on to each other and gasping with joy throughout the whole experience, they wondered how they were so fortunate to witness such awesome wonders.

The students dispersed into the care of their parents and relatives and the crowd slowly disappeared. The news stations stuck around to the end taping the intensity of the night that would make national news. Before each student left, they spent a moment looking at the tall, glowing tree in silence. To some, a Christmas tree would be just a pretty decoration of lights and ornaments, but to each student, the tree would forever be a symbol of the kindness of strangers, a place in their mind where they found their inner strengths and the ability to connect to people of all walks of life. They all thought that they were truly saved by Christmas.

Epilogue

After the holidays, there were different news stories that appeared in the papers. First, the missing school bus kid's version of their astonishing rescue by the Amish. Next, the account of how the Mobile Maintenance Command National Guard unit saved lives during the storm. Not only were there comments from the hospital nurses and doctors, but from the patients whose lives were saved, not to mention the motorists who were stranded for days on the highway until they came along. Maxson's eyes lit up when the General called to congratulate his team on their remarkable heroism. An article in the New York Times highlighted the accounts of seventeen individuals who Chauncy and Tolbert picked up and took to the hospital. It was front page news with pictures of all sorts of patients, some holding their new babies, some with arms in casts, and some still in hospital beds. The story continued to page five where the news writer found social media pictures of Chauncy and Tolbert in full smiles from a monster truck event in which she cropped out the background. Maxson gave a smirk as he knew he needed to give full gratitude towards the two clowns of his unit that saved the city and gave credibility to the National Guard, especially his unit.

Six years had passed since that Christmas. Every year that the tree was lit in Rockefeller Center, all 11 students returned for a reunion to watch the lighting. Beforehand, the Venhill's would host a dinner for all the families as they had grown close over the years. By now Darcy had a brother aged four and a sister aged two running around the house. Wednesdays were the days all the Venhills served at the soup kitchen, but because tonight was a special event, Darby had the soup kitchen catered with the food he was catering to his own guests at his house. He came to know the people in his community and tried to help more than just serving food once a week.

It was the night of the Annual Tree Lighting Ceremony in Rockefeller Center and families started arriving at the Venhills.

This year was different because Ryan brought a date. As he introduced her to everyone, all 10 former students stared at her as if she was a famous actress that they just couldn't put a name to.

"Everyone, this is Rafferty," said Ryan as he introduced the tall, young lady with ebony skin and light brown eyes.

"Nice to meet all of you," she said with a smile, staring, trying to memorize their friendly faces.

"Rafferty goes to the University of Maryland," Ryan continued. "She's a freshman and the point guard for the women's basketball team."

After high school, Ryan was recruited to play basketball, but not at Syracuse, as he thought. The University of Michigan made him their starting center. As was expected, he grew to six-foot-nine inches and was considered to be the nicest guy on the team. He mentored younger players, but he had been doing that since he returned from that disastrous Christmas tree expedition years ago.

Darcy and Adam remained friends after the event as well. But after high school, Adam went to Columbia to study engineering and Darcy flew off to Paris to study clothing design. Coming back to New York annually, she would never miss this most important day to see all of her former "bus" friends. They both knew that they needed good jobs because they both were obsessed with great shoe ware. Not just anything would do, they could spot a cheaply made shoe a mile away. When Darcy flew home, they would go shoe shopping before Christmas every year and make a day out of it with lunch and dinner. There was no romance at all involved, only the best of friendships.

Vaughn's mom got the help she needed, thanks to Mrs. López and her treatment. His parents were with him at the dinner party and she looked as healthy as a 45-year-old woman could be. One night after Vegas closed the shop, he overheard Vaughn play the piano and sing one of his original songs. He secretly taped him and sent it to a music talent show. Vaughn reluctantly went and came in fifth place out of two thousand contestants, nationwide. It didn't win him a music contract, but the networking opportunity helped him sell a few of his originals that paid some bills. It allowed him to attend the famous Juilliard School for performing arts, in which he had one year left.

Shannon graduated early from high school and went to Rochester University to become a teacher. She took a job as a grade school teacher in one of the boroughs without a lot of funding. Her parents tried to talk her out of it, but her passion increased to help where it was most needed. She took charge of her classroom to have the highest standards and never let students have an excuse to do poorly. Every day was a challenge and every day she was ready for it.

Wanda was a big surprise. She worked, occasionally, at the Met's Citi Field with her dad, who did the narration of the baseball games up in the box. One day an older man walked in and told Wanda's dad, Ernest, if he ever wanted a job at a TV network to come to see him and handed him his card.

"If you ever want a job punching these buttons you can come to see me," whispered Wanda sarcastically to the man offering her dad a job.

The businessman in question was Lorne Michaels, the creator and producer of Saturday Night Live (SNL) and he heard every word Wanda whispered.

Not that what she said was funny, but the way she said it, gave Lorne Michaels an idea. He handed her his card to Wanda too.

"Miss uh?" he asked her name.

"It's Wanda," she said proudly. "Wanda Womack, queen of the Queens."

"Is that so?" he chuckled. "Have you ever thought about doing comedy?"

"Sir, when you grow up in a neighborhood that's nothing but family, you better have a good sense of humor," she answered. "I don't know if I'm that funny, but I could tell you some stories that will leave you in stitches."

And she did. Lorne Michaels had her come in, and with the help of a few celebrity comedians, they worked on her delivery and timing with her family stories, which were mostly true. Wanda had the comedians laughing hardily in no time. At first, she did improv at local places in New York and gathered quite the crowd. Then, she toured the country with her material and got raving reviews. Lorne promised her that after a few years, she could interview to be one of the prime-time players on SNL. This was the best job in the world, she thought, and it wasn't even hard. Her relatives gave her a hard time about using the family's business as her punch lines, but, in the end, they supported her. Her mother, Juanita, wanted something else for her daughter. She wanted her to go to college and marry one of those smart guys like she had done. Every time Wanda would return home for a week or two, Juanita reminded her it wasn't too late. As far as Wanda was concerned, it was.

The López twins went to work on their abuelas farm in El Salvador after high school for a few years. Recently, they turned 21, and got jobs working for the airlines as flight attendants. They tried to bid on flights so that they could work together and if they could not, at least meet at the hub for dinner and a good walk around the city. They kept in touch with Wanda and, with their jobs, it was easy to become her groupies. On their days off, they flew to Atlanta, Los Angeles, Seattle, or wherever to see her perform. Occasionally, she would point them out to the audience and tell a tall story of how she was dating them both. They were used to it by now. But in actuality, Wanda was dating another comedian on tour.

Arcado and Brianna dated in high school and he proposed to her five times before senior prom. Arcado found that she was beautiful inside and out. Her desire to fight for causes had him right by her side. Likewise, he showed her the culture of New York by taking her to art museums, music festivals, and poetry competitions. She loved him but wanted to live a little before she got married, so she turned down all his proposals. Brianna signed up and joined the Air Force to get out and see the world. Arcado was supposed to go to Yale but couldn't fathom being away from her, so he joined too. He signed up to be an Air Traffic Controller and Brianna was an Avionics Technician. She had always wanted to prove that this was not just a man's world. The best they could hope for was that they would be stationed together.

They attended Basic Military Training together but after that, they split off into different destinations to attend their specialized schools. They would email and call, but in the end, it was Arcado that found a girlfriend and stopped corresponding so much. Brianna knew this would be a possibility, but she wasn't without prospects. They considered themselves to still be the best of friends. They both showed up together in their Air Force Class A Uniform looking smart and sharp. Both of their families were ecstatic to see their arrival.

Lauren arrived with her parents and gave everyone hugs. She turned out to be the most shocking of all of them. The quiet, timid girl on the bus now started and established her own non-profit. She graduated with a degree in Psychology from the local university and would begin her master's in Business Management next semester. Her upright posture spoke volumes of her confidence.

Mostly the crowd gathered in the large, bright, white French kitchen that overflowed into the family room with softer lighting and a traditional, red brick fireplace ablaze. Also in the family room, an eight-foot Christmas tree stood in front of a bay window with white and blue lights sparkling all around and a glowing angel on the top. A sizable manger was lit up under the tree that held all the smaller children's attention. Everyone was off in their little corners talking and catching up on the year's event elevating the volume of the house. One could barely hear the gentle Christmas soundtrack playing through the sound system. Lauren noticed Ryan's girlfriend, Rafferty, and took the opportunity to say hello.

Ryan had excused himself to catch up with Vaughn and left Rafferty alone to fend for herself. Lauren picked up a glass of spiced apple cider and looked at Rafferty.

"How are you......Bianca?" asked Lauren, secretively.

"Wait, you know who I am?" asked Rafferty. "Harvey said that everyone was hypnotized to remember the Amish story so I would not exist to you guys."

"I was the only student not to fall for it," she said solemnly. "I know the truth and I am glad to remember everything that happened."

"You kept this secret to yourself for all of these years?" Rafferty inquired as she shook her head in amazement.

"It wasn't as hard as you think," said Lauren logically. "Everyone was so focused on the Amish story and the news reporters were content with a good ending, so it was impossible to ever speak otherwise. Also, I played the shy girl who didn't interview well and that was perfect too. So, does Ryan know?"

"No," said Rafferty as she smiled and remembered when he saw her for the first time after all of those years. "It's kind of a long story, but it's a great one."

They both stood near the large, white marbled countertop island in the kitchen where the hors d'oeuvres were spread out from end to end. There were conversations happening all around them, but nobody overheard any of theirs.

Rafferty, or rather Bianca, went on and told the story about how she turned 18 and could finally leave to find Ryan. That was always her game plan after Ryan left Ourstory that winter day many years ago. For years, scenarios ran through her head. Before she set off on her own out in the world, something dreadful happened. It was Gabriel. It was known that he had an auto-immune disease, but when he got so weak that Doc Marta was helpless, she took him to a hospital near Albany, New York. Her college friend was a surgeon there. Poor Gabriel had 4th stage non-Hodgkin's lymphoma. He received chemotherapy and other care that seemed at first to work. But a year later, it took his life. There was no way Bianca would leave Gabriel during his illness. He was her little brother, although she had felt more like his mother at times. It was his wish to be in Ourstory to live out his final days. Tears dropped from both girls' eyes.

"I can't believe he's not here anymore," said Bianca sadly. "For a boy, he had so much perspective and now it's gone. This world will never know what a remarkable person he was."

They both blew their noses into their cocktail napkins. This was a somber moment between them both. Bianca wasn't even sure why Lauren had tears in her eyes because she didn't know him for long.

"I think you're wrong," contested Lauren.

"About what?" asked Bianca, confused.

"You said the world will never know what a remarkable person he was," explained Lauren and she continued. "The little time that I spent with him impacted me in a powerful way. He said that we landed in Ourstory because we each had a purpose. He further explained that the purpose is different for everybody."

"Oh that sounds like Gabriel," laughed Bianca.

"Well, after I returned to school, I thought about those words so much that I was moved to do something about it," she enlightened. "I was never part of a sports team, band, Honor Society, student government, or anything else. I was a loner, always looking for a purpose, so I created one. I created a club for students to come and find their own purpose. I uniquely made it broad so that any student who felt outcasted, alone, or just wanted to do something could come. I made a charter with the high school but advertised it to all of the boroughs' high schools. At first, there were six of us and then it grew to thirteen and by the time I left high school, we had 78 members."

"But what was the purpose?" asked Bianca. "What did you do there?"

"Good question," affirmed Lauren. "We searched for things to do on the internet or make up our own fun. We attended free concerts in the park or made our own comedy improv games, and even helped each other with homework. It was a collage of ideas from anyone in our group. We would always try it out and then continue on to the next idea."

"It sounds like a fun group," commented Bianca.

"When I was graduating from high school and leaving the group behind, there were a few members that let me know privately how much this club meant," she continued. "They felt like they didn't belong anywhere and admitted that thoughts of suicide crossed their minds. I consider myself the lamest person I know, but I started a program that gave my peers a purpose. By the time I left high school, even athletes and band members who felt unfulfilled joined. I can still hear those words that Gabriel spoke to Arcado and me that silent night and they still inspire me to this day."

"He was amazing like that," sniffled Bianca, blowing her nose into a fresh napkin.

"So much so that the club was named after him," she said and smiled with more tears. "The club was called Gabriel's Purpose."

At that Bianca lost it. She laughed and sobbed into a few more cocktail napkins.

"After I graduated from college, I started a non-profit organization that has roots from Gabriel's Purpose," explained Lauren. "We have hotlines for people to reach out if they are lonely or having depression. There's a lot of training involved, but there's nothing I would rather do."

"I am so glad to call you a friend, Lauren," said Bianca with swollen eyes.

"Enough about me," remarked Lauren. "How did you get back into Ryan's life if he didn't know you?"

Bianca took a deep breath and told her the story. After Gabriel had passed, she left Ourstory and went to stay with the warehouse owner and his wife. Through the internet, she found stories of how Ryan had received several offers from colleges around the country and picked Ann Arbor, Michigan to go to school. By the time she was accepted into college, he was in his sophomore year and she would be a freshman at College Park, Maryland at the University of Maryland.

The warehouse owner and his friend from the FBI built Bianca a new identity. She picked her maternal grandfather's first name of Rafferty for her own. Her new name was Rafferty Roberts from a suburb of Atlanta, Georgia. She kept her date of birth but changed it by a year, making her younger. A social security card, a birth certificate, and a high school diploma were issued.

Rafferty arrived at the University of Maryland a month early to try out for the women's basketball program. The existing players were not nice to her whatsoever. They purposely teamed against her, which made her work harder than ever, but she proved that she could play better than any freshman that was recruited. That year she would be a second-string point guard. Eventually, the team embraced her and all of her talent.

During a weekend break after Thanksgiving the year prior, she remembered the Rockefeller Tree Lighting Ceremony. She purchased a train ticket to go to New York City and watch it. A youth hostel was suggested by a friend, so she dumped off her duffel bag and went in search of the spectacular event. When she got there, they were all there, front and center. Everyone in the Venhill house was a guest on a platform near the huge tree standing by the newscasters commenting on the ceremony. Rafferty was excited when she got a peek at Ryan. Of course, he stood out, because he towered over everyone but his dad and brother. Her heart flipped, but over the years she had come to realize that he was just a crush that would be remembered as young love, a nice flirting activity, but most of all, a pastime event. She had dated a few guys already that semester. She was sure that he moved on and most likely had the pick of any pretty student.

The tree lit up and everyone clapped and "oohed" and "ahhed". In the end, she had gotten everything she came for: the tree, the students, and a glimpse of a guy she really liked a few years past. Before she set home the next day and out of curiosity, she made a visit to the Malloy Courts in the Bronx to check out the place Ryan mentioned. There were a few young boys scrimmaging on one side and near them were extra basketballs sitting by the fence.

"Do you mind if I use one of your balls to shoot?" she asked kindly, dressed in her sweats and sneakers.

The boys noticed her tall stature and pretty face and agreed. She bounced the ball to an open court and stood at the free throw line. Making her comments about there being only three seconds left of the ball game and the team was down by one, she lofted the ball and it went in the net. She cheered herself on as a crowd would do and then used her mad dribbling to do some drills and then made another shot.

"Looking good," a voice from behind, surprised her.

He brought his own ball and shot from the three-point area and whooshed it in the net. She was going to be sick. It was Ryan and he just talked to her. Her heart was beating a million miles a minute and there was nothing but shock in her stare back at him.

"Whoa, I didn't mean to startle you. I am not here to jump you," he said, making another basket. "My name is Ryan, what's yours?"

"Rafferty," she almost said unsurely. "I was just passing through and thought I would get a little practice in."

She was rambling on but Ryan didn't mind. He looked into her deep, light brown eyes and felt something familiar stir. For years, he had a funny dream of meeting a pretty girl at the Malloy Courts, but thought she was beyond the most beautiful girl he'd ever seen. There was an immediate attraction and she picked up on it too. He stopped bouncing the ball and held it to his stomach with both hands, mesmerized by her beauty. Then, just like it had been years ago, she snatched the ball from his hands and took it to the net for two points. Ryan smirked deviously and peeled off his winter coat and threw it to the fence. His face looked serious and curious at the same time. There would be no mercy for Bianca once he had the ball in his hands. He made most of his three-point shots, but she made him work hard for every one of them. The intense stare, as she dribbled, from her brown eyes to his blues made the game electrifying. She could barely stand it because the feelings of years past were still burning inside her and he was staring back at her just like he had done years ago, still cocky, flirty and so handsome. They played one on one for an intense 30 minutes until they were both sweat-filled and exhausted.

"Hey, do you want to go for a coffee or something?" he asked in a friendly way.

"I thought you didn't like coffee?" she retorted and then realized she shouldn't have said it.

"How did you know?" he asked quizzically.

"Eh-most basketball players don't," she recovered.

"Hmmm," he continued. "Well, I also said or something, like tea or hot chocolate."

She agreed to join him. Handing back the ball to the young crew, she thanked them. They walked to an old run-down coffee shop a quarter mile away. The servers knew the regular patrons there and recognized Ryan. They sat in a booth and talked for hours. Rafferty had missed her train that day. Ryan felt so comfortable with a fellow basketball peer who was the

349

most stunning girl he had ever met. He knew they were at separate schools but thought they could make it work.

After Bianca's long story to Lauren, Ryan appeared behind his girlfriend and massaged her shoulders while greeting his former bus mate.

There was a loud noise from the front door and another guest arrived. It was Chauncy and Tolbert, who had their girlfriends with them. After the first year, the Venhill's decided to invite Chauncy, who for the past few years, just brought Tolbert as his plus one. By this year, they were all good friends. Chauncy escorted a young lady that was just about as tall as him. She had a delicate, pretty face, and her strawberry blond hair was affixed in a bun.

"Ladies and gentlemen, may I present my date, Mary Margaret Sheehan," announced Chauncy. "She's a Rockette."

They all greeted her kindly and loved having somewhat of a celebrity in the house. Everyone knew that the Music City Rockettes trained hard and the chance of making it into the famous dance company was near impossible. Recently, Tolbert had to attend physical therapy because the pain came back in his shoulder from jumping out of his truck years ago. The medical facility was always abuzz with patients. One day as Chauncy was waiting for Tolbert to finish, a young lady advised the receptionist that she was there for her shin splints. She announced herself as Mary Margaret Sheehan. Chauncy stood up, looked at her, and mumbled something inappropriate, not believing it was her. She recognized him right away, albeit he was a little taller and a lot more handsome. With a scowl on her face, she told him to leave her alone or she would have to hurt him again. They both laughed.

She was absolutely beautiful. After the eighth grade, Mary Margaret attended a private high school, so Chauncy and Tolbert never got to see the butterfly transformation from a big, beastie girl to a tall and lean dancer. Their reunion led to a dinner date and then a lunch date and so on. Tolbert reminded Chauncy, right in front of Mary Margaret, of all of the hypotheticals that they used to describe her. This did not phase Chauncy, nor Mary Margaret a bit. Thankfully, they both had a sense of humor.

The former students made it a tradition to stand by the Christmas tree while Mr. Venhill made his annual toast. Everybody raised a glass to celebrate another Christmas spent together. Then, a strange thing happened in the quietness before the toast. A familiar song to the students started playing on the Venhill's instrumental Christmas song track. Once they heard it, the words rushed back to them as if it were a repeated carol they had sung for years. It was "Born on Christmas Day". They all sang the song and were surprised by the notes and the harmonies that came through. It was this day, again, that they recalled they were *Saved by Christmas.*

Made in the USA
Middletown, DE
11 December 2022

18095208R00199